Crazy for the Countess

by

Jess Russell

Reluctant Hearts

Cover Art by *Teddi Black*

The Wild Rose Press, Inc.
PO Box 708
Adams Basin, NY 14410-0708
Visit us at www.thewildrosepress.com

Publishing History
First Edition, 2025
Trade Paperback ISBN 978-1-5092-6183-3
Digital ISBN 978-1-5092-6184-0

Reluctant Hearts
Published in the United States of America

Dedication

To my father, Colonel Russell R. Rausch, the real
Colonel in my life, and my first hero.

Acknowledgements

I would like to extend my heartfelt gratitude to the many people who helped bring this book to life. First, to my incredible friends and fellow writers: Fiona Davis, Hope C. Tarr, Addison Fox, and Wendy La Capra: you inspire me to reach higher and dig deeper, usually over a crafty cocktail or bottle of wine. To dear Jane Keiffer, who read this book in one sitting. To Anne Sansevero, for your thoughtful notes and for our much-needed golf outings with Tina, which provided a welcome, if alternate, source of frustration to balance the challenges of writing. To Cynthia Capley, for your steadfast belief in me and to Jordanna Brodsky for keeping my prose grounded and real.

Thank you to Ash, Veronique, Mary, and dear Lennie, for taking time to offer feedback, lend a comforting shoulder, or give me a much-needed kick in the pants.

And to the team at The Wild Rose Press, and most especially to my editor, Nicole D'Arienzo: thank you for believing in this story and providing me with the platform to share it with the world.

Much gratitude to all my readers (Kate M.) for hanging in there and waiting very patiently for another book from me! If you enjoyed Crazy for the Countess, please consider writing a brief review. Independent authors like me rely on your kind words to reach new readers.

Finally, to Bliss Bennett, Wendy La Capra, and Gail Eastwood: thank you for sticking with me through thick and thin. For believing in my talents when I couldn't see them myself. Your generosity of spirit and wisdom are truly priceless, and I honestly could not have written this book without you.

Prologue

January 1864
Mayfair, London

Nora St. James, Countess of Havermere, should not have attended the burial.

Gently bred women did not go to such events. They were deemed too frail, their emotions too uncertain to withstand the ritual of consigning a body to the earth.

An equally held belief was that women, being sisters of Eve, were sinful by nature, therefore not worthy to tread upon consecrated ground. The *ton*, no doubt, would ascribe the latter to Nora.

And last, but certainly not least, the good folk of London believed she had murdered the deceased.

She went anyway.

Men in black armbands slanted looks at her beneath their stovepipe hats. Some disapproving, but most slyly coveting. Their eyes slid over her veiled face and red hair to settle on her breasts, waist, and hips.

No matter. She was used to it.

Removing her glove with two quick tugs, she bent and dug her fingers into the dark earth. Musk and pungent decay filled her nostrils. She wanted the black beneath her perfectly manicured nails. She wanted it to seep into her body and somehow make this death real.

With a fistful she rose, squeezed, and then let it fall in a clump. It burst open, scattering over the pristinely polished ebony and rosewood casket.

Bile burned her throat at the memory of his white face turning yellow, the blood pooling in his lifeless body and the tang of urine as he finally released his brutal grip on life.

Nine years married. Just a raw, naïve girl when he'd claimed her.

Now he was gone.

Praise God.

An incredible lightness enveloped her as if she were suddenly within one of those hot-air balloons soaring over the top of the churchyard. She rose to her toes and lifted her chin higher. But she remained solidly on the frozen ground, imprisoned by mourners all huddled around the gaping hole and the black iron fence that surrounded St. Martin-in-the-Fields.

With the final benediction pronounced, she offered her own silent prayer—quite different from the Reverend Harmon's hope of eternal joy in heaven for the fifth Earl of Havermere—and then turned her back on death.

Penny press reporters, who had hung about like carrion on the edges of the churchyard, now swooped in to surround her. Their mouths formed questions, a barrage of words fired like so many shots, making her hot ears ring, their pencils poised to capture her answers, so eager to twist them into lies.

"Did you do it, Countess? Did you poison your husband, Lord Havermere?"

"No chance of the old earl sending you off to Ballencrieff Asylum now that he's conveniently dead is there, Countess?" another shouted.

"You must be relieved to have the inquest behind you. What will you do now? Perhaps find another rich husband?"

Havermere's plan to send her to Ballencrieff Hall, a madhouse in the Scottish Highlands, had been quashed by his apoplexy. No longer able to speak or write, he had lingered, lying in bed for nearly three months while servants wiped spittle and food from his twisted lips, faithfully turning his wasting body.

Once a day Nora had made herself enter his room to endure his accusatory glare. It could not touch her. *He* could no longer touch her. Hurt her. She'd breathed in the sour smell of death and stared back, her truth deflecting his vitriol.

That last day, she'd watched as he gummed down his favorite cake, delivered each morning from Downs Bakery. He smacked his papery lips, impatiently gesturing to his nurse for more.

Disgusted, Nora had turned away. Only a moment later, a panicked gasp had her whipping around. The old man lurched, and the cake flew, the plate clattering to the floor. Nearly knocking the nurse aside in his haste to haul his lordship into a sitting position, a footman thumped on the old man's back. White froth bubbled between his blue lips.

Heedless of his peril, he seemed to use all his remaining strength to raise his arm and point an accusing finger at Nora.

Try as she might, she could not move. That boney finger and glassy gaze pinned her to the wall as if she were already imprisoned in iron shackles.

In the ensuing pandemonium, the cake had been

thrown away. No evidence.

However, poison had been found in his body. Nora would not have put it past the old reprobate to do the deed himself if only to drag her down with him. But the brief inquisition ended with the ruling, "Death by persons unknown." Still, gossip had run rampant.

And now, with the old earl's funeral, it seemed the newly widowed Countess of Havermere was still a tasty morsel for a few voracious curs, yapping to tear over the last shred of scandal.

Nora ignored them, moving steadily toward the refuge of her waiting carriage. Her heavy black lace veil lent a curtain of protection, and her coachman's hand and gaze were sure and steady as he helped her inside.

She welcomed the dark interior and sat back into the squabs, pressing her fingertips against her dry eyes. "Drive on, Thomas."

Her voice surprised her. It sounded as if it belonged to someone else.

Someone with hope.

Chapter One

Two years later
May 1866
Skinner Street, London

"Are you sure there isn't a lady here that would suit your needs, Colonel?"

Farren Cavanaugh eased back in the rococo chair, an untouched ale in his hand, feigning a nonchalance he did not feel. Nearly all Madam Flora's "offerings" had been paraded by, some openly soliciting, others coy and subtle.

Not one fit.

He should move on. But as he started to rise, grief crawled over him, leaching into his body, into his muscles and bones, rendering him incapable of moving.

Battle weary.

Though this brothel was nothing like the blood-soaked fields of his United States' civil war, the soot-filled city of London town felt like death all over again. But this death had no face or body. Nothing to grieve over. Nothing to make it final. Only eight days in and already his hope was dimming as surely as closing a lantern.

Damn. He needed a victory.

Right. Time to get up.

He made a show of looking around again, and then

set his drink aside. "While no one could find fault with your ladies, Madam Flora, I am looking for a very particular sort of young woman—"

"A young blonde, so you've said." The madam snagged the nearest girl and whispered in her ear. The gal shrugged and headed for the beaded curtain separating the main room from an antechamber where it appeared the girls readied themselves. "Sally is nearly blonde and still quite young. I'm sure she will satisfy."

He hefted himself out of the chair. "I'm sorry to have wasted—" The curtain shifted. Through the beads, he glimpsed a woman. Just a sliver of a profile and yet...

In three strides, he crossed the room.

Madam Flora caught his sleeve. "Colonel, that chamber is closed to gentlemen. Why not come and finish your ale? I'm sure we will find someone who suits."

Shaking her off, he brushed the veil of beads aside.

The redhead wore a modest gown of a soft gray, but there was not one other thing about her that could be described as such. Her lush breasts, nipped-in waist and generous hips made the unremarkable frock seem decadent and deliciously indecent. Luxuriant, copper-colored curls haloed her heart-shaped face, the velvet ribbon mooring them affording a tantalizing view of her delicate nape. She was so lush, so ripe, he could almost swear she must be pulsing. As was he. Though the breadth of a room still stood between them, he felt himself stiffening.

"I am also partial to redheads."

Farren did not usually indulge in brothels. He stuck with willing widows and spinsters. But it had been a right long stretch since he had paid his cock any heed beyond his occasional, hasty self-ministrations.

A dozen or so beauties had already been paraded by him, but this woman was not merely beautiful. He sensed a depth within her, as if she had secrets—and many of them sad. Call it intuition, but she would be someone he would trust at his side on the battlefield. A kindred spirit?

Hell, he was being fanciful, projecting his own feelings onto a stranger. But still…

Standing at his side, Madam Flora followed his gaze. "Oh, I don't think so, Colonel. Perhaps Jenny will suit?" She directed his gaze back into the main salon toward a plump ginger-haired woman who looked to be forty if she were a day. The tart stretched on her chaise lounge and winked at him.

He shook his head. Ignoring the madam's scowl, he gave her his most winning smile. "The blonde I hanker for is—well, I have a picture in my mind and will know her when I see her. Until then, I reckon I can make do with that redhead." He nodded to the beauty beyond the curtain.

She was in conversation with another, younger tart, a girl; the latter, more interested in leading them in some sort of jig than in listening. The beauty shook her head and then laughed, the sound low and throaty. Giving in, she obliged performing a graceful pirouette.

"I assume she's available?" Parched, he swallowed, wishing he had drunk his ale.

"Colonel, I am not sure you understand—"

"I will give you twice what she usually goes for." The words were out of his mouth before his brain could register them.

A gleam came into the madam's eye. "Very well, as you wish. But you must pay up front." She held out her hand, and Farren peeled off one bill and then another. Satisfied, she waved her hand, and a young African boy scurried up to her side. "Algernon, see Colonel Cavanaugh to the Persian room."

The boy grinned, exposing a wide gap where his two front teeth had been. "Yes, Madam."

Farren glanced once more at the woman, now speaking in earnest to her friend. Copper head bent, hands held out to capture the younger girl's, her gaze intent and caring.

Like a shot out of nowhere, a swell of loneliness nearly felled him. How he longed to push through those beads and be the recipient of her kind ministrations. To feel her soft, white hands within his, their comforting pressure a balm against the rough calluses and scars that marked his own. To ease the ache of isolation that seemed to live at his very core.

"You comin', sir?" Algernon shifted from foot to foot.

Should he retreat and just leave? He took another look.

The beauty's gaze swung toward his. She could not see him, only a shadowed figure behind the curtain, but he would swear she saw right into him.

"Colonel, sir?" the boy's voice, like a chirping frog.

"Yes. Yes, I reckon I am." And before he changed his mind, he followed the youth up an elegant staircase and down a long hallway.

Each door they passed was painted a different color: Pale blue, deep green, a yellow, a pink, pitch-black. At the latter, he heard a snap and then a muffled squeal. They stopped at the scarlet red door.

His cock twitched, already priming for the satisfaction that lay ahead. It *had* been quite a while.

Algernon turned the knob and pushed the door open, stepping aside for Farren to enter.

What had been a middle-class bedchamber was transformed to a Persian bower fit for a Pasha. Intricately pierced shutters covered the casement windows, smudging the fading light into a soft lace-like pattern that dappled the walls and floor. Pillows, studded with winking mirrors, littered the patterned carpet like autumn's showiest leaves. The bed was round with an intricately carved bedframe. A crown of the same was affixed to the ceiling, where rich fabric of the deepest red hung in soft pleats. The silken panels were then caught up with golden tassels and affixed to several posts to form a kind of tent. A brazier sat in the far corner. A hint of spicy smoke still hung in the air.

"Shall I light it, sir?" Algernon indicated the burner.

Farren shook his head. "Naw, I'm hoping the lady and I will warm things up right enough." He dipped into his purse and flipped a farthing to the boy.

Algernon gawped at the silver. "Thank you, sir." He stuffed the piece into his pocket and bowed, then backed out of the room as if Farren were indeed royalty.

A fancy carved screen concealed—yes! A chamber pot.

Farren stepped behind the partition, unbuttoned his trouser flap and relieved himself.

Sweet release, not only from his bladder but from

his rapidly confining trousers. As the image of the red-haired beauty rose in his mind, so did his cock.

The door clicked and then shut.

"Good evening." Her voice matched her looks perfectly. She spoke like a lady. Must have quite the talent for mimicry to parrot the English upper crust so well.

"I see you have found the necessary." He heard her bustling about. "Good. Better to get that out of the way and have a good wash."

Odd way to begin a seduction. He was about to tell her so when she spoke again.

"You should remove all your clothing. Things tend to go more smoothly when we can see everything out in the open. I have done this many times before and seen all manner of physiology. You need not feel shy or nervous. It will be over in a trice."

In a trice? Not if he had any say. Perhaps these stiff English folk didn't put much stock in buttering the toast first. He preferred butter *and* jam.

"There is a sheet if you are modest. You need not be. I am quite skilled, and you mustn't worry. I will be gentle as you please."

Gentle? What kind of whorehouse was this? Surely Madam Flora did not think him a virgin? Well, in for a penny, in for a pound. Farren used the stool next to the chamber pot to yank off his boots, then stood, dropped his drawers, and pulled his shirt over his head. Like a divining rod, his penis pointed the way.

When he stepped out from the screen, the woman stood across the room, bent over a basin of water. Her elegant back rose from a tiny waist, the arch of her long, white neck beckoning him. Soft-footed as if he were once more on night patrol, he moved toward her. Coming up on her, he reached out with one finger and brushed aside a curl clinging to her nape.

She let out a scream to raise the dead and leapt back.

Water flew.

Even with her mouth hanging open like a beached fish, she was a stunner. Unfortunately, the not-so-warm water baptizing his nether parts put a bit of a damper on his ardor. But just a bit.

She took another step back, her bum now pressed against the washstand. "You—are not Gwendolyn Dawson."

Farren swiped droplets of water out of his eyes. He dipped in a small bow. His cock followed suit. "No, ma'am, I am not Miss Dawson. I suppose if I were I might have escaped a drenching?"

She stood with the basin perched on her hip, reminiscent of his ma when she was riled. But there the comparison ended.

"Flora Hollingwood, I will tear your hair out, damn you," she muttered to the ceiling, then met his gaze. "It would seem the proprietor has had a bit of sport with us." She glanced down the length of him and turned away to set the bowl down.

Farren eased back against one of the bed posts as she fumbled for a towel. "Sport? Well, sport is what I had in mind, but not the joking kind."

"Yes, well, I am afraid Mrs. Hollingwood has a bizarre sense of humor." She yanked a Turkish towel from a stack beneath the wash basin.

"You are not… available?"

She looked at him again, wet her lips and nearly

dropped the towel. The near loss of it seemed to snap her into action, much like a raw recruit being reviewed by General Sherman.

"No, not—*available*. I am here as a sort of...volunteer."

Whoring as a mission of mercy? Perhaps the evening wasn't a loss after all. Farren raised an eyebrow and smiled, hoping to make her change her mind about sporting.

She handed him the towel. "Take this and cover yourself, if you would? I find it is difficult holding a conversation with *both* of you."

Farren grinned outright now. Damned shame this gal wasn't one of Hollingwood's bevy of beauties. He liked her spirit as well as her looks. He pushed away from the bed post and accepted the towel. As he swathed himself, he wondered idly if, like covering the cage of a parrot, it might quell his livelier bits.

"You're a Yank," she said, as if that fact were the reason for his prolonged ardor.

"Born and bred. From around Baltimore—that's in Maryland. Colonel Farren Cavanaugh of the Seventh Regiment Volunteers at your service, ma'am." He gave her a rakish salute. "And who might you be?"

"I am—Mrs. St. James. I sometimes help with instructing the girls—" She stopped abruptly. "On how to ... take proper care of themselves. An unwanted child is a terrible thing to inflict upon the world, both for the mother and the child."

"Ah, so you instruct them as to how they might prevent that."

She raised her chin. "Among other things."

"Like how to avoid the pox?"

She flushed, but her gaze didn't waver. "Yes, if you must know."

"I applaud you, ma'am. The pox is hideous for men and women alike. Believe me, I saw enough of it in the war to support anyone who takes on the task of easing such a mighty misery."

She must have been doing just that when he'd spied her through the curtain. When he'd felt so forlorn and empty. God, he wanted to hold someone—to hold this woman. To lay down with her and press her against the curve of his body, bury his face in her feathery hair. To sleep. Just sleep.

"Well then," she said, turning toward the window.

Dang. He'd been staring. More like devouring her.

In the silence, he adjusted the towel more firmly around him. She wiped her hands on her apron. "I assume you require no instruction on donning a 'French Letter'?"

The image of her helping to sheath his—he shook his head. "We call them 'English Overcoats' in America."

She snorted. "Well, you would, wouldn't you? The Americans and French have always been in bed together." She found and then fiddled with a loose thread on the pocket of her apron.

"I reckon I should get dressed, since you don't appear to be interested in improving relations with the Americas?"

"Not in the bedchamber or the political arena, thank you," she said definitively. Perhaps a might *too* definitively?

The flush on her cheeks and neck lent credence to his theory, but he would not press her.

"Shall I send up another companion, Colonel?"

Another companion? The idea of another woman made him nearly wince. "No, thank you. Though some ale would be appreciated. I'm right parched." He smiled.

She gave him a tightlipped smile. "I will have the ale sent up, Colonel. I bid you good day, sir."

"Ma'am."

Crinoline swaying, she made her way to the door. Not until her skirts licked the closing door did he sink to the bed and cover his face with his shaking hands.

Somehow the loss of her made him want to weep...

Hell, he was just tired. So. Dang. Tired.

But he had at least three more houses to get to this evening.

Right. No time for indulging in wishful fantasies.

Chapter Two

Greene Street
Cheapside, London
Spruce Lawn House

Small estate near Corsham. Seven bedchambers, large attics. Five acres, several dependencies including a barn, storehouse and dairy; walled garden suitable for flowers or vegetables.

Nora ran the pad of her finger over the well-worn advertisement, pausing at the listed price.

Sixteen hundred pounds.

Stupidly, she'd taken the train out to see the property. Now the place was imprinted on her brain—no, her very heart. It was perfect.

A spacious home to house at least twenty girls and gardens where they might run free.

She looked around the rather dreary parlor of the Greene Street house, her home for the last two years. Her husband had willed her the place, not out of any largesse, but simply to scuttle any hope she might have of claiming her dower rights. The added insult, this was the very house where she had come to meet her lover, Lord Devlin. Likely Havermere had thought the shame would break her, but he was wrong. From her worst devastation rose an unshakable sense of purpose, planting even deeper the seeds of her convictions. Life was not over. She could still be of use. In fact, this house had become a real home, even a haven, for her little family.

"Thomas is out back with the carriage."

Nora quickly closed the ledger on the bit of newsprint and the columns of red numbers cataloging their debts. "Opal, when will you learn to knock?"

The girl could slink into a room quick as fog over the Thames. Opal's only reply was a derisive sniff. "Thomas says the new earl of Havermere has finally arrived from some place called Alberta. Says he's a widower with four daughters and looks like a nervous ferret with spectacles. Used to be a clerk or some such. Thomas says he doesn't know his head from 'is arse."

"Opal, would you please refrain from using the language of a dock worker?"

Mr. Bartholomew, her solicitor, had already written to Nora with the news. Her dead husband's fifth cousin twice removed, Mr. Orville St. James, had finally been found.

"I'm only repeatin' what Thomas said." The girl flopped onto the settee.

Linden House, the earl's London home, would be occupied again. No going back there, even if she could stomach entering the place again.

Nora had personally removed the knocker from the front door directly after the Earl's funeral and moved into the Greene Street house. She had taken her full two years of mourning. All too happy to disappear. After all, she was only following their good Queen Victoria's example. Indeed, her majesty, indulging in her sober black, her veils, and extreme rustication, had elevated the act to almost a lifestyle.

If she were sensible, she could have lived for years on the little stipend Mr. Bartholomew had carefully budgeted for her. But how could she be sensible when so many needed so much? And so, in these last two years, she had winnowed her meager funds away.

First Opal came, and then Agnes and now Mari. And there would be more. There must be more. Because she could not simply walk by as if these poor girls did not exist.

With the coffers bare, and her mourning over, there was no more hiding away. Past time to reenter society and see if she could gain some charitable support for her Corsham dream.

"Thomas says some nobs have begun callin' at that Linden place asking for you. You won't be able to hide out in this dump much longer playing the crow. I expect you'll soon be getting leg shackled again in no time." Her lower lip jutted out along with her chin, making the white corded scar that ran down her neck more prominent.

As many times as Nora had reassured the girl that she would never desert her, Opal remained unconvinced. Too much heartache packed into her short life to let down her guard for long.

Nora had encountered the girl in a brothel. Not spreading her legs but dressed as a young gent, fleecing swells of their allowances. The girl could count cards. A dangerous game when pride mixed with too much drink. One chap took exception to her winning and flayed open her neck, slicing off half her ear in the process. She had been with Nora ever since.

She ignored Opal's question, having told her girls thousands of times she would never remarry. "Is that something in your pocket?" The gilt edge of a card and what looked to be several letters were tucked into the girl's apron. Perhaps an invitation?

The girl snorted and plucked out a square of heavy-looking vellum as if it were a dead rodent. "A calling card from that Milton fellow and another from that Finchley fop." She dropped the cards onto the small side table.

Sweet Lord Finchley. Now nearing his mid-forties, Benton Finchley had been on the hunt for a bride for as long as Nora had known him. Indeed, he had been in the running for her hand in marriage all those years ago, but once the Earl of Havermere entered the bidding, well, Nora's mother had had the settlements drawn up immediately.

Lord Finchley was one of those men who liked women a great deal and particularly admired their beauty but could not love them. She knew such men existed and sympathized with their plight. Oh, how she wished she had married him …

Nora shook her head seeking to rid herself of terrible memories.

Lord Milton had been a friend of the old earl and had visited Linden House often. He had always been kind and very respectful to Nora. Never once displaying any salacious interest in her—something that could not be said of Havermere's other male guests.

"And that last letter? I don't suppose it is addressed to you?"

"Cor, it's from the good Queen herself. Invitin' me to tea, she is!"

"Hand it over." Nora extended her hand.

Opal dipped into a deep and elegant curtsy,

proffering the letter. "My lady."

No wonder Opal had held the letter back. It was from Mr. Bartholomew. Nora squeezed her eyes shut. She knew what the letter contained: a plea for her to come to her senses and remarry.

The image of that American colonel flooded her brain. She slid the note into her ledger book. There it would keep company with all her debts.

No invitations. And so, no opportunity to convince a kind benefactor of her worthy cause.

"Mum, look what's come!" Marigold called out as she ran into the room, followed closely by Agnes.

The little girl held out a posy of red roses. Agnes held a card.

Nora's little family.

Sweet Agnes had nearly been trampled by a barrow man when she had not moved quickly enough. Her flowers had been crushed into the mud and her fellow sellers had taken advantage and stole the few coins she had. Nora had immediately asked if Agnes would like to come home with her. After touching Nora's face and "breathing her," as Agnes had called it, the girl had nodded. And so, she became part of their odd little family.

Mari had joined the group only four months ago. Nora had found her standing in line to work at a match factory. Far too young to be taken on. Nora had seen the effects of phossy jaw, the child's lower jaw eaten away by the toxic phosphorous used in the matchmaking process. By God, she would spare at least one child from that terrible fate. But there were so many. So many to save...

The image of a white-blonde halo of hair, a fixed

frown, lips pressed into a firm line as if she were holding a world of secrets and pain.

Lily.

Nora jerked herself out of the memory.

"Mum! Look!" Mari repeated, thrusting the roses up for her to take.

Nora had not received a gift of flowers since early in her marriage. Such an offering should fill her with breathless anticipation, but instead a wary feeling stole over her. Men, seeking her out, wanting something from her. The old earl had often given her flowers after he had been particularly cruel.

"Ah, they are lovely," she lied, touching the edge of one lush petal. "And do they smell sweet, Agnes?"

"Yes, Mum. Roses have petals of velvet, but you must be mindful of their thorns," Agnes said, a small, worried frown between her sightless eyes.

"Who are they from?" Mari chirped, hopping around Agnes who held the card against her, guarding it from the younger girl's grasping hands.

Opal rescued the flowers from Mari. "As usual, Marigold, you have not wiped your feet. Go on and shuck off your shoes. Then it's time for history."

Mari turned to Nora. "But, Mum, I—"

"History first." Nora smoothed a blonde curl from the child's forehead, tucking it behind her ear. "I must go out soon anyway."

Agnes dutifully offered up the card to Opal.

Reluctantly, the girls left the room, one set of muddy tracks now marring the old carpet.

Opal gave a brief sniff to the roses and set them on a nearby table. "Whoever sent these weeds will turn tail when 'e gets a gander at the baggage that comes with you—particularly my mug. 'E ain't gonna stand for it, you mark my words."

"Opal, I will not have this conversation again. And, I will not have you slinking out again to gamble." Two weeks ago, she had found the girl dressed in her "young gent" togs about to sneak out the back garden gate and into the mews. Surprisingly, Opal had not put up much of a fight when curtailed. It must have taken a boat load of courage to step back into that old life. "We have Mari and Agnes to think of now," Nora replied in a gentler tone. "I need you alive, with all your parts attached. Please."

"And I will not have *you* throwing your happiness away on some fop," the girl mimicked in tones a duchess would be lucky to emulate. "Best get a move on. Thomas is waitin' in the carriage," Opal called out before quitting the room.

Nora started for her veiled bonnet, but instead, she picked up the vellum card beside the roses. She slid a fingernail under the plain seal and withdrew the note inside.

Accept this posey, tribute to your splendor,
Although too soon it fades, a mere pretender.
Unlike your wondrous beauty, a constant sun
Fair rivals, moon and stars—rendered to dun!
Cast off, at last, are barren widow's weeds
That fertile black now used to sow new seeds.
This ardent gardener, keen, expectant, waits,
To pluck the bloom of his belovéd mate.

No signature.

The cloying smell of roses wafted up, not from the flowers, but from the card.

Good heavens! Who could have sent this odd

offering? She wanted to laugh at this flowery language, but there was something about the poem that made her unsettled. Likely the thought of some man having power over her again.

She threw the note into the firebox. An ember came to life, glowing red as it fed on the paper. An edge blackened until it finally bore a flame. The note shuddered and then writhed as it was consumed. Good riddance.

A knock sounded at the front door. Nora ignored it. Another followed only a moment later. "I will get it," she called out to Opal. She opened the door primed to send whoever it was on their way.

The man had turned, ready to depart. He wheeled like a startled bird. "Ah, I—that is—I did not think anyone at home." Then his jaw dropped.

Nora waited, used to the male sex gawping over her beauty. Just a hurdle to get past before they found their way back to sense.

He smelled of some overwrought cologne, and his thin, pomaded brown hair lay plastered to his scalp, while his side whiskers stood out from his cheeks like two squirrel tails. He shifted from foot to foot.

Only then did it dawn on her. A bespeckled ferret with whiskers. Heavens, Thomas did have it just right. This man was the new Earl of Havermere.

"Good afternoon, ma'am. I am seeking Lady Havermere, but I fear I have the wrong address."

Blast! Naïve to think she could put him off with the note she'd penned last week. Very well, best to get this over and done.

"I am Lady Havermere." She stood up straighter. She would not be ashamed of her home.

"Lady Havermere, that is, Countess. I—forgive me. I did not expect you to be—so—young. I am Orville St. James, that is Lord Havermere. I mean—if I may be so bold—your cousin," he chirped, making a hopping-like bow with each appellation.

"Welcome to England, Lord Havermere. Please do come in."

"Thank you." He nodded to his coachman and then stepped into the hall.

"Who was at the—" Opal stood in the doorway of the "schoolroom." Agnes and Mari's faces flanking her. "Get back you two."

Oh, dear, what must his lordship think of this peculiar group? Nora gestured him into the rather shabby little parlor.

"I am afraid you have caught us in the middle of lessons and errands, your lordship."

"Cousin Orville, please."

She nodded. "Cousin Orville."

"I was unaware you had children, dear cousin."

"Oh, they are not—well, they are not of my blood but are very dear to me."

"Ah, yes, children are a great comfort," he murmured almost to himself rather dubiously.

"Please, won't you be seated? I will ring for some tea." Nora indicated an armed chair covered in faded chintz.

"Oh, thank you, but no tea. I will only take a moment of your time." He waited for her to settle herself and then took his seat.

"I am sorry for your loss, Cousin Nora." He bowed his head and touched his breast. "I, too, was widowed in my prime. My dear wife, Edith, perished almost five years ago to this day, and I still feel the sting." He pulled out a rather yellowed handkerchief, lowered his spectacles, and dabbed his eyes.

"Genuine grief calls for no apology, sir." Nora was truly touched by this odd little man's devotion to his departed wife.

"Do not regard me, dear lady. It seems I have turned into a watering pot when I called to bring you comfort. I wish to see to your every need, just as your dear husband would have done were he still in this realm."

Dear God, had he been the one to send her the roses and that horrid poem?

The earl suddenly jerked upright. "That is—I mean to say—Charlotte and myself—that is, all of my daughters and myself, will be exceedingly pleased were you to make your home with us. *We* would see you comfortable and happy."

Happy? Nora had not known one moment of happiness within the walls of Linden House. "I thank you, Lord Havermere—Cousin. You are very generous, but I have no wish to intrude upon your family."

"Bah! No intrusion, m' dear." He leaned forward as if about to impart some dire secret. "Truth to tell, you'd be doing me a great favor. I confess I am but a minnow seeking to navigate the waters of London society." He swiped the back of his hand over his glistening forehead. "You see my eldest, Charlotte, is set on making her come out *this* season. Must get her settled properly, I'm told, so as to make the way easier for her sisters."

Nora smiled. Poor man. Despite the chilly room, sweat beaded his upper lip and rolled down his temples into his side whiskers and cravat. This man was no hopeful suitor, more like a cuckoo in a jay's nest.

"Cousin Orville, I thank you, but I must decline your generous offer."

The earl glanced to Nora as if perhaps he had made another faux pas. "Are you quite certain?" He wiped his hands over his canary silk breeches. "My Edith would have known how to set Charlotte on the right foot, but me—well, I confess I am more comfortable with tallying accounts than escorting young ladies." He gave Nora a shy smile which was sweetly charming, a flicker of the man on whom his Edith must have doted. "I'm sure when you meet my girls you will soon care for them as I do. Charlotte is particularly worthy."

"I have no doubt Lady Charlotte is very dear, but I am only in the last stages of my mourning." A slight falsehood. Clearly, being new to town, Orville St. James had not heard any of the rumors that still clung to Nora. Besides, she had no time to shepherd a young girl who was entirely ignorant of London *ton* society through her first season.

"Oh, of course, your grief. I would not interfere with your bereavement, not for the world." He found his handkerchief again, sniffed, and applied it to his nose. "I will simply tell Charlotte she must wait another year or so to make her curtsy."

It was difficult to tell behind his thick spectacles, but Nora thought she detected relief in the earl's eyes.

"I am certain there are any number of matrons who would be delighted to sponsor Lady Charlotte. I could give you a few names if you'd like?"

"Oh, I think we'd best put it off for now. I will tell Charlotte she must bide her time."

"Well, you know your daughter best, cousin."

He frowned, looking slightly worried. "Yes, yes I do."

"Pardon, your ladyship. Should I unharness the horses?" Thomas stood in the doorway.

"Oh, Thomas, I am sorry to have kept you waiting." She rose and turned to the earl. "Cousin Orville, I have neglected an appointment."

The earl hopped to his feet. "Oh, certainly, my dear. Perhaps I might drop you somewhere?"

Nora nearly burst into laughter. "No, I thank you. Thomas has the carriage ready in the mews."

What would the dear man think of his offer if she had told him the truth?

Oh, that would be just ducky, cuz! I am headed to a notorious bawd's house where I give out counsel and condoms.

Chapter Three

Sixteen hundred pounds.

As the carriage rattled over the uneven cobblestones it seemed to chant the impossible number.

Sixteen hundred pounds. Sixteen hundred pounds.

It might as well have been ten thousand.

Greene Street house was mortgaged to the hilt. And Nora's only other commodity, tarnished as it was, her title of countess. The *ton* had very long memories when they wished. Certainly, a gamble to see if the good ladies of society would welcome her into their fold, much less contribute to her charity home. But to reenter society she needed to look the part. A few new gowns—ones that had not been dyed black or sold for bread, or made over into dresses for the girls.

She pinched the bridge of her nose and squeezed her eyes shut.

There was one other option for funds. She had been praying not to have to take this step. But desperate times…

The portraits. She would write Devlin before she thought better of it.

The carriage slowed nearly to a crawl. A sudden roar of applause momentarily drowned out the incessant hawks of street vendors. Always a slow go through Covent Garden Square.

Needing air, she cracked open the carriage window.

A white-blonde head bobbed through the crowd. Nora's heart caught in her throat. She pressed to the glass. That loping gait.

Lily!

"Stop! Now!" Nora fumbled for the latch. The door banged back against the carriage. Not waiting for Thomas to pull to the curb, she jumped down, stumbling as her thin soles smacked the cobblestones.

"My lady!" Thomas called out, juggling the horses.

Unwilling to waste precious seconds, she ran past him.

It couldn't be. Lily is dead ... yet ...

Weaving through the foot traffic, Nora flung her veil over her bonnet, straining to keep the girl in sight, bracing herself for disappointment, yet hoping for a miracle.

"Where's the fire, luv?" a barrow man jeered.

Nearly jerked off her feet, Nora staggered, clutching the wheel of a cart so as not to fall on her backside. Breath coming fast, she pressed her fingers into the stitch in her side, ignoring the barrow man.

Blast! She spared a precious second glancing behind her to see where she was caught.

Infernal skirt. Snagged on a hook projecting from the cart.

Before she could wrest it free, the man had the heavy bombazine fabric between his grubby fingers.

"'Ere, little bird, I've snared you well and good."

Nora twisted away, scouring the street for that silver cap of hair. *Where did she go?*

A sea of humanity eddied around stalls and carts,

all jockeying for the best deal.

Nora put her foot on the hub of the cart's wheel, heedless of the picture she presented, and hoisted herself up.

Nothing. Vanished. The girl was gone.

That nearly-white halo of hair, the tilt of her head, the slightly olive complexion, the coltish stride, had sucked Nora in. Again. This was the fourth time she had seen this phantom and each time her heart was wrung out just a bit more.

Thomas's six-foot-three-and-three-quarter inches bore down on the fishmonger.

"You can call off yer goliath." The barrow man released her skirt and then held up his hands. "'Twas only a bit of a lark, is all."

Thomas took her elbow and guided her to safer terrain.

"Did you see her?" Nora rose on her toes.

"Who, your ladyship?"

"Lil—" she broke off, leaden depression settling in her gut. "Nothing. It is nothing."

Lily is dead. You watched her die in the bedroom at Greene Street over three years ago.

A short time later Thomas pulled up to a neat terrace house with its iron fence and perfectly pruned hedges. A solidly middle-class home, yet inside lived a goodly number of former milkmaids and young soldiers' widows who had fallen on hard times.

Nora entered through the servant's door and then stepped inside the small side parlor the madam used as an office. With a sigh, she flipped back her heavy veil.

A man occupied Franny's best chair, his back to Nora. She caught Hackett's small shake of the head and began to back out of the room.

Too late. The man turned.

"We meet again, Mrs. St. James."

Hell's bells.

Colonel Farren Cavanaugh.

The man rose from his chair. He seemed even larger now she met him fully clothed.

His face was still the same, though.

Nora supposed some would call him handsome if one tended toward wild, windswept cliffs instead of calm, rolling hills. This man was no tame gent. Oh, he could play the part right enough, she had no doubt. She guessed he did most things well … But only a fool would believe the role of gentleman to be his true nature.

He eschewed the fashion for extravagant whiskers. He had no need to disguise a weak jaw line or chin. Indeed, the light glanced off his freshly shaven cheeks as if to highlight that very fact. A shock of wheat-colored hair, shot with silver blond any woman would kill for, lapped over his collar and swept his forehead.

She preferred dark-haired men, she reminded herself.

Rather than the pale slimness currently in vogue for gentlemen, he was broad and muscled. Too tanned. Too … wild looking.

No slave to fashion, he wore fine, though well-worn, riding boots. His coat was of the best broadcloth but not in the first stare of fashion and rather plain compared to the plaids and checks many gentlemen favored. His only nod to excess was an elaborately worked timepiece with a ruby fob any man would have envied. She supposed he must be in his mid-thirties, to have achieved the rank of colonel, though he might be younger. A winking dimple, a strong cleft chin, and one of the most beguiling smiles that ever crossed a male face, made him nearly irresistible.

No, he was not handsome—or dark-haired—but she could say with definitive certainty that he was the most attractive man she had ever beheld.

This conclusion did not give her the least bit of pleasure. The opposite, in fact. Her stomach felt as if she were in an ill-sprung carriage.

"I see you're acquainted with Colonel Cavanaugh, Mrs. St. James." Madam Frances rose from her chair, shaking out her navy serge skirts. The ring of keys on her chatelaine bounced with her effort. Frances took pains to look the part of the respectable matron.

Nora felt herself flushing. "Once."

Franny Hackett turned away from Nora as she hooked her arm through the colonel's. "Colonel Cavanaugh was about to select a companion for the evening." She slanted a look to the doorway. "I have a new crop of beauties on offer, all perfect English roses fresh from the country."

Why should this fact bother her so? Cavanaugh was a man, after all. And men had their vices. Apparently, he had an outright addiction. "Do not let me keep you." She started to back out of the room when a half dozen young girls filed in.

"What is this, Frances?" Nora demanded, an edge to her voice. None of the girls looked older than fourteen.

The madam's smile slipped, and her gaze hardened. "You promised you would not interfere again, Mrs. St. James. You may peddle your French

Letters and pessaries to my ladies to your heart's content, but you are not to interfere with my trade."

The colonel turned to Nora. "You misunderstand, Mrs. St. James. I—"

"I do not think there is much here to misconstrue." Nora could not bear to hear his explanation.

He rubbed his hand over his eyes. "Send them away."

Frances stared. Her hand on the colonel's bicep slid off. "*All* of them?"

He sent Nora a sideways glance. "Yes, all of them."

Franny Hackett clutched her skirts as if preparing to leap atop Nora and pummel her.

The colonel stepped between them.

Hackett took a breath and smoothed the fabric of her gown. "Surely, colonel, one of these young beauties appeals to you? Jasmine has just come to us from Shropshire." She prodded a mousey blonde-haired girl forward. "And Chastity is only twelve, aren't you my dear?"

Chastity? Even the colonel nearly smirked at the out-and-out lie.

The girl tried to make her eyes wide and doe-like. The poor thing only succeeded in looking half-witted.

"You must not heed Mrs. St. James. She is just leaving, aren't you?" The woman gave Nora another lethal glare.

"Ladies." He nodded to the girls, and they simpered appropriately. "Thank you. Would you leave us now?" He gestured toward the door. The girls filed out, the last casting one final look at the colonel while tittering behind her hand.

Colonel Cavanaugh pulled out his purse.

The madam brightened. "Ah, you have made your selection then? I assure you won't be disappointed." Madam Frances rubbed her hands together. "Who shall it be, then?"

He peeled off several bills and passed them to Frances.

Frances counted the money twice. Her eyes widened. "I—Colonel—that is—you want them all?" Even jaded Franny Hackett had trouble not gawping at such excess.

"God, no." His gaze remained on the closed door. "My payment is for your trouble, ma'am."

Was he addled? Perhaps he was unused to English money?

Franny frowned. "I don't understand," she said, looking as if she were trying to work out some complicated mathematical equation.

"Pretty as they are, none of these gals is right. I have a ... particular picture—"

Nora's stomach heaved up to knock against her heart. Disappointment mixed with anger. His gaze settled on her, but she would not allow herself to look away. She gave him the full measure of her repulsion.

"I—that is—" Then he shook his head. He suddenly seemed weary almost as if he was playing a part that was not quite to his liking.

"Yes, well." Frances coughed. "As Mrs. St. James will attest, I do not go in for the ... exotic. However, if you change your mind, my girls are all clean and willing to accommodate *natural* needs." She clutched the bills as if he might try taking them back. "I trust you can see yourself out?"

"I can, and thank you again for your hospitality." He favored her with his wicked smile but this time it didn't reach his eyes.

"Mrs. St. James, I will have a word with you later," Hackett said to Nora before closing the door.

"I reckon I owe you an apology, ma'am." He stood in the very center of the room. To reach the door Nora would have to walk through him.

"An apology? Why? You have contributed mightily to this house, sir. Good heavens, the girls might get meat twice a month due to your largesse."

"I'm speaking of the other day, Mrs. St. James."

She'd known that. But she did not want to think about his large naked body, much less discuss it.

"I have already put the matter behind me." She turned away, and bent to riffle in her satchel so he did not see the blush flooding her neck and cheeks.

"Behind you …. really?" he said, his tone silky as twice-churned butter.

She could feel his gaze on her bum and jerked upright. Oh, what a rogue. *Sorry, my arse!*

She wheeled on him. "Colonel, you must not *regard it* a moment longer. I know I do not. It was such a trifling thing." She dipped her eyes to the fall of his trousers and then back. "A joke, really. One I have taken Flora Hollingwood to task for. Let us forget the matter at once and speak of it no more."

He knew damned well there was nothing the least trifling about him. For all her bravado, she felt like a mouse whose tail was pinned by a very large cat's paw.

"Trifling?" He took a step toward her. "I don't recollect you thinking so at the time. But mayhap we don't share the same sense of humor?"

"I dare say we don't. Now if you would be so kind as to move aside, I should like to get on with my work."

He bowed and stepped to one side. "Far be it from me to stand in the way of your good works, Mrs. St. James. I'm sure we will meet again."

He smiled wider and her foolish heart did a neat flip within her tightly laced corset.

"I doubt it, sir. As Mrs. Hackett said, if the exotic is indeed what you seek, you will be venturing into environs I dare not tread." She quickly brushed past him. "Goodbye, colonel."

"Not goodbye, Mrs. St. James. Until we meet again."

Cocksure of himself. And depraved. A reminder why she would never again subject herself to any man.

She stepped out into the hall, pulling the door closed behind her with more force than she'd meant to. No doubt he was grinning behind it. The image infuriated her. *Bloody Yank!*

Unfortunately, that wicked grin of his stoked something as hot as fury but a good deal baser. And decidedly more dangerous.

A feeling she had not known in … well … ever.

Chapter Four

The Gilded Angel

The bar looked as if it were built as an afterthought, wedged between four-storied tenements, hunkered down like a starving beggar. No wonder he'd missed the spot in his searches through the Seven Dials of London.

Parched, Farren pushed through the door. Weak afternoon light filtered through threadbare curtains as a haze of smoke and dust motes wafted above the motley assortment of patrons. A heavy smell of fish and unwashed bodies hung in the stilted air.

He elbowed his way up to the bar. The tapster, however, seemed more interested in eating a plate of oysters than serving any ale. He was about to call out to the fellow when an odd feeling settled over him. He turned to his right. A man was staring at him, a look of disbelief on his face. Then, as if he were caught, the man ducked his head and shuffled off his bar stool, disappearing in the miasma.

"Excuse me," Farren called after him. The man turned back but then pushed farther into the crowd.

Farren tracked the fellow easily as he was taller than most of the other drinkers. He caught the man's arm. "Do I know you?"

The man stopped. "Ah, no, I don't believe so.

Thought you looked familiar."

He was about Farren's own age, spoke like a fancy gentleman, and dressed like one as well. But there was an air of desperation and dissipation about him. Still, what was he doing in a place like this?

"My name is Cavanaugh, Farren Cavanaugh."

Again, the man looked as if he'd seen a ghost.

A shiver pricked the hairs on Farren's arms. His foray into The Gilded Angel might not be a total waste. "You might have seen my brother, Brendan."

"Your brother? But he—" The man shook his head.

Great God, this man obviously knew Bren. "Came to town about fifteen years ago? Summer of fifty-one? But he could be here now, in England."

The man's face shifted and reordered itself as he decided on a story. Finally, he relaxed and smiled. "By God, yes. It was fifty-one! Hottest August on record. Nearly threw myself in the stinking Thames. Had to stay foxed just to get through the day." He looked about, slightly uncomfortable. "You say he might be in London?"

"I don't know. I'm here to look for him. I don't suppose you've seen him recently? Say, in the last year?"

The man smiled and leaned against a post, but Farren sensed a nervousness that belied his easy pose. The man was clearly a drinker. Maybe hadn't hit that sweet spot yet and was jittery. Or maybe he knew more than he was saying.

"Naw. And unless your brother's changed his stripes, I would have bumped up against him. He and I had the same tastes when it came to entertainment. You and he appear to share the same likes as well as looks."

A bawd with enormous tits sidled between them. The man gave her a smart slap on her ample rear. "Move on, Sally, this lad's new to town, and I'll warrant he ain't ready for the pox yet."

"Sod yourself, Guppy." Sally jerked her corset up, making her breasts ripple like sludge on a disturbed pond. She waddled off into a haze of cigar smoke.

"If you share his tastes, maybe you're acquainted with an Iris Darvan? I believe my brother kept company with her," Farren probed.

The man took a long look at a pitcher of ale on a nearby table and wet his lips.

"You, there," Farren called out, stopping a barmaid. "A bumper for—?"

The man hesitated. "Gillingham. Oscar Gillingham."

"Ale for my friend, Gillingham, here and me."

The gal turned her back on Gillingham to take Farren's measure. "Is you paying?"

Farren flipped her a coin. "Yes, and keep them coming."

Gillingham held out his hand. "Ah, if you don't mind, I prefer gin."

"Gin it is then. Bring us a bottle, ma'am."

"Very well then, luv. I'll be right back."

"Thanks, Cavanaugh. I'm just a bit short today. End of the quarter and all."

"Understood." Farren knew the needs of a drunk and waited until the gin arrived and Gillingham took a long pull. "So, Iris Darvan?"

"Oh, yes. The Butterfly. Most blokes know of ol' Iris. Named the Butterfly on account she'd light on one gent after another. Very uppity was Iris. She took a shine to your brother though. Liked his accent as well as his looks. Silly cow." Gillingham finished off his gin in one toss.

"Do you know where I might find her?"

"Why such interest?"

Farren shrugged, feigning nonchalance. "I'm interested in my brother. If she was connected with him, then I'd like to talk with her."

"Haven't seen her in years. Wouldn't be surprised if she died of the pox, or maybe had her throat slit by some jealous cove." He licked his lips. Farren gestured for his glass and refilled it.

"I have been to see a Mrs. Eunice Lockhart on Cuddle Lane. That was the address Miss Darvan last wrote my brother. I got some information. But Lockhart wasn't all that inclined to talk with me."

"Bawds never are."

"But I didn't say she was a bawd." Farren took a sip of gin. Raw and minerally with a slight taste of oil.

"You didn't have to. If she was connected in any way with 'Madam Butterfly,' then she was in the game somehow." Gillingham drank deep and swiped his lip.

"Gents, take your seats, the show is about to commence," the barmaid with the enormous tits barked.

"Shite!" Gillingham fumbled at the pocket of his waistcoat. "Shite!" he said again. "Look here, Cavanaugh, do you have the time? I seem to have misplaced my watch."

"Just half past five."

"Blast." He threw back the rest of his gin and then slammed the glass on a table. "Hate to ask, but can you spare a few bob for a cab?"

"Why not take me along? I'm new to town, and,

like you, I'm always game for a pretty lady and the chance to fill my pockets. Besides, I could use someone to show me around."

Gillingham laughed and shook his head.

Oscar Gillingham was the first real lead Farren had. It might be advantageous to follow him. "If it's a quarrel you face, I'm right good with my fists. Just as good as my brother." Farren offered.

The man seemed to look at Farren with new eyes.

Farren jingled the coins in his pocket and then raised the half-full bottle. "I have money for a cab and more."

Still Gillingham hesitated, as if the fate of his old granny was at stake.

"Why not face the music with a friend at your side? I'm sure my brother would have done the same."

Gillingham perked up, and, just like that, the scales tipped in Farren's favor. "Right you are! Best face the music! No fists needed, my fine fellow."

A voluptuous bawd with outrageously red hair took the stage, followed by a fiddle player.

Gillingham jerked his chin toward the stage. "My dear Cavanaugh, we go from the ridiculous to the sublime! Follow me, and I'll promise you not only stellar music, but a gander at a beauty like none other. Ten bob and dinner says your jaw will hit the floor."

"And who is this paramour?"

"Why, none other than the infamous Countess of Havermere."

Farren had no idea what lay ahead, but the man had known Brendan, and it was worth a shot to follow. He tipped the last of his gin back and set the glass down. "Lead on. But if you are wrong about this famous beauty, you'll be buying me dinner."

****

An invitation had finally come.

As Nora stood on the threshold of Lord Milton's home, she smoothed the gray taffeta of her thrice-made-over gown, vainly wishing she still had her lavender silk. But it had been sold only a fortnight ago. Sacrificed to pay the coal man.

Opal had nearly cut the gray dress up for rags, as the hem looked, "like it had been attacked by a herd of vicious, muddy cats." But Nora had stopped her just in the nick of time.

"It is for a musical afternoon with the famed Mrs. Carden," she had explained to the girl hoping for some enthusiasm. None had been forthcoming. "Surely there will be one or two matrons among the guests who will be sympathetic to our cause?"

Opal had muttered that she didn't know about sympathetic ol' biddies, but she reckoned there would be a few "slick society gents dandling pots of money to lure hopeful young widows into their snare."

But being the stickler she was, the girl couldn't tolerate Nora wearing rags. So, she'd duly slaved away, expertly hacking up an old shell-pink petticoat in order to cover the worst parts of the gray. A wide band of pink now covered the shredded hem line, as well as the soiled sleeves and tattered neck. Black velvet soutache, meticulously picked off an old riding habit, trimmed the whole ensemble.

Nora had no jewels, but when she'd looked in the mirror, she could honestly say, while not in the first stare of fashion, she would do quite well.

But, oh, how she longed to be tucked up safe in her

drafty, dark house wearing her old, faded kerseymere instead of facing Lord Milton's phalanx of footmen.

Perhaps Thomas and her carriage were still out front?

"Nora St. James, Countess of Havermere," the butler intoned.

Right. No going back now.

Every pair of eyes looked up. All astonishment, then falling into one of three equally unwelcome expressions: curiosity, derision, or pure lust.

Seven steps down. She counted each one as she descended into his lordship's grand hall.

Lord Milton waited for her at the bottom of the staircase. At least there was one welcoming face in the crowd.

"Lady Havermere, I am delighted you could join us this afternoon." His silver eyes looked deeply into hers. He seemed loathe to break from her gaze but finally bent to perform the courtesy of a bow.

"Thank you for your kind invitation, Lord Milton. I was very happy to receive it. I remember hearing Mrs. Carden years ago."

"May tenth of fifty-five. At Somerset House." Milton smiled.

"Good heavens! You've quite a memory, Lord Milton."

"Actually, yes I do, but that particular evening was especially memorable." He did not elaborate, but she had been married in April of that same year. Could his strong recollection be linked with the first time she and her host had met?

"What a lovely home you have, Lord Milton," Nora said, changing the subject. "This hall seems particularly suited for a concert. And the floral arrangements are stunning." All manner of flowers in a riot of color festooned the hall's huge pillars and spilled from its tables creating a kind of indoor garden.

"Horticulture and music are a few of my passions. What good is being a peer of the realm if one cannot indulge them? I had the room renovated to be acoustically perfect—or as near to perfection as possible."

"Ah, well, mankind will strive to mimic God."

"I could not agree more, Lady Havermere."

"I believe another passion is your dedication to the less fortunate, especially needy children. I understand you support several charity houses," she said, hoping to steer the conversation around to her girls. "There are so many in need of help."

"Yes, I agree, Lady Havermere. Far too many." He smiled. "But you are here for pleasure. Let us leave the unfortunates for a few hours and enjoy the talents of Mrs. Carden."

Nora took her cue from her host that the discussion was over. At least for now. "Yes, of course."

"I was glad to see Linden House opened once again. I called several times but was told you were not at home."

Bless those loyal servants, like Thomas, who had remained at the house and who kept her secrets. The *ton* would eventually root her out at Greene Street, but she was not yet ready to reveal her modest address. "Well, I am here now." She laughed a little too brightly.

He seemed to want to say more but only responded with, "Yes, yes you are." He smiled. "I have fond memories of my past visits to Linden House. Especially seeing you."

She should smile and say something kind back to him. But she could not.

"But perhaps you do not even recall my being there?" His smile, rueful. "Lord Havermere and I were usually hashing out the latest political mess. I imagine it must have been dreadfully dull for you."

Havermere had insisted she be present whenever he received callers. For that was what he loved above all, to flaunt her in front of men who could not have her. She had always felt dirty and used afterward. "I remember," was all she said.

Milton frowned. "Well, perhaps fond is too strong a word. I learnt much from your late husband," he amended. "As one who did not anticipate coming into a title and then did, I thought it wise to glean what I could from the earl. He became a sort of mentor. In some ways."

Her husband had always had his thumb on the tail of Parliament. Lord Shaftsbury, head of the Commission on Lunacy, had been the old earl's puppet. His debts to her late husband had nearly sent Nora to Ballencrieff Asylum, the place where Havermere had got rid of his third barren wife, who had developed a taste for laudanum and drink. The poor wretch had jumped from the minstrel gallery at Ballencrieff, conveniently making way for the earl's fourth and final wife, Nora.

The asylum had also witnessed the death of the earl's less than suitable heir, Major Randolph Cummings St. James. The young man had come back from the Crimean war blind and missing an arm. Her husband had taken one look at his fey nephew and promptly deposited him at Ballencrieff where he, obligingly, hanged himself.

And finally, Havermere had enjoined Shaftsbury, this time with the help of Lord Devlin's own father, to imprison Devlin in the madhouse. His punishment for daring to dally with Nora.

What a price to pay for their brief affair. A little over two months respite before the guilt of betraying her marriage vows began to spread between them like a dark stain. Only the arrival of Lily prolonged the affair, reviving Nora's will to live—the chance to be needed by someone.

But it could not last. Lily had died. And Devlin had been sent away to that hellish place where he, in fact, nearly went mad with abuse.

Her punishment. For daring to want.

Even from the grave, her late husband had continued to turn the screws. In his last will and testament, Nora might have enjoyed a fortune of ten thousand pounds—if she agreed to commit herself to the asylum for the term of ten years. If not, she would remain destitute, save for the Greene Street house.

But the joke was on him. The old man would turn in his grave if he knew that the cramped, dark little house was not the prison he'd imagined but the first real home she had ever truly enjoyed. Where she felt useful and free. Well, as free as a near penniless woman could.

And Devlin had found love within the walls of Ballencrieff. He fell head over ears for Anne Winton, the young woman who had been his savior at the asylum.

Certainly, they deserved a bit of happiness after paying so dearly for their transgressions?

"But, come, Lady Havermere." Lord Milton proffered his arm. "As you say, you are here now. Allow me to reintroduce you to my guests."

Though she had been among society for nine years as Lady Havermere, Nora did not really know these people. She had gone from the schoolroom to the prison of her marriage. Only in that last year, when her husband's health was failing, had she enjoyed a modicum of freedom. And even then, Havermere had employed his henchman, Ned Macready, to dog her every step.

Luckily the man had not been familiar with London. Nora's one friend, Lady Bentley, lived nearby in a monstrosity of an old house that boasted a number of secret passageways. One tunnel started at her ladyship's withdrawing room and ended in the mews behind the house.

Nora had "visited" Lady Bentley and used that tunnel to escape to Greene Street. And when Devlin rescued Lily from the streets, Nora had thrown caution to the wind and come nearly every day so that she might tend to the girl. Not that Lily wanted Nora's tending …

But she reminded herself, there were so many girls who did. Could one of these guests be her potential patron?

As Lord Milton squired her about the room, it did not appear likely.

When Nora ventured to introduce her idea for her charity home, Lady Harper ignored her instead, asking rather snidely for the name of Nora's modiste. Lords Radford and Edgemont dared not approach but salivated from behind the skirts of their respective wives, who cut scathing looks at Nora, hissing, "*Murderess*," behind their fluttering fans.

And so it was with Mrs. Worthington, and Lady Adderly, and on and on. Apparently, the *ton* had a very keen memory for salacious gossip.

"I do not see Lord Finchley?" Nora had received another note that he had planned to attend this event and hoped to see her there.

"No, he is indisposed, I believe."

"Ah, I do hope it is nothing serious?"

Milton smiled. "Is anything ever serious with Lord Finchley?" His lordship's quip was tossed off lightly, but Nora sensed an undertone of real derision.

"Ah! Lady Gadwick is one of your guests." Nora spied the marchioness at the foot of the stairs with her daughter. Her ladyship was well-known not only for her love of music, but also for her largesse. "Her ladyship was very kind to me when I first entered society as a married lady." The marquess, her husband, had run off with an opera singer and left his new wife and baby daughter to fend for themselves. Nora fancied the lady had felt a kind of kinship with her. Would that still hold true all these years later?

"Allow me take you to the good lady," Lord Milton said, extending his arm. "We will begin soon."

Her ladyship greeted Nora with some warmth. Well, with as much warmth as her stoic bearing would allow. She then introduced her daughter, Caroline, who, now grown, would be making her curtsy this season. Lord Milton excused himself rather abruptly.

"I do hope nothing's amiss." The lady frowned, lifting her quizzing glass to follow Milton. "I am looking forward to hearing Mrs. Carden play."

"I am sure it is nothing. Only some late arrivals, it seems." Anxious to make an impression, Nora hastened on. "I trust we will see each other at various entertainments over the coming season? As you can see, I am out of mourning and am looking forward to strengthening friendships. I hope yours will be one of those, Lady Gadwick."

The woman looked as if her corset was suddenly several inches too tight. *Oh, blast, not another poisoned against her.*

"Yes, I am glad to see you out of your widow's weeds. To my view, you have done quite enough penance for such a man as old Havermere."

Dear heavens, a real ally. Do not gush, or worse, fall at this lady's feet. Millicent Gadwick would never approve of such an emotional display.

"I am sure you will be quite busy chaperoning Lady Caroline." Nora smiled at the rather shy-looking girl. "But I hope you will still have time to consider new charities?"

"I will never be too busy to ignore the less fortunate of this world, Lady Havermere."

When Nora settled herself next to the now dear Lady Gadwick, she felt as if maybe the world could be a kind place. Maybe, just maybe, she and her girls would have their dream.

****

Farren stood with Gillingham at the top of the stairs to behold the fanciest parlor he'd ever seen.

A huge chandelier glittered above an even grander piano, that if he hadn't known was black, he might have sworn the instrument was made of mirror. And it seemed as if every flower within five miles had been plucked and stuck in some fancy pot. They even hung from the walls and pillars.

Of course, since coming to London he'd only visited brothels and his own modest digs at the Wellington Arms, but he was quite sure had he been in twenty or more homes of the *haute ton*, this place would still eclipse them all.

The guests were assembling themselves into rows of chairs. His gaze snagged on a tall man who looked daggers at the new arrivals. Gillingham had assured Farren he would be welcome, but this man seemed right put out. He had the bearing of a general and appeared very fit despite his being an older gent. A fellow soldier? A shot of silver ran through his dark hair. His eyes matched the silver, appearing almost colorless before he turned away and took his seat.

"Come," Gillingham urged, "We are late. Milton runs a tight ship."

They found seats in the back. A large woman entered the room by a side door and, after curtsying, took her seat before the huge piano. Farren settled in, idly scanning the backs of heads for Gillingham's famed beauty.

Jumpin' Jasper?

Farren knew several women with red hair, but he could not recall one with such a perfect combination of shade, texture, and softness as the woman who sat two rows ahead to his right.

She turned to her companion, an older woman, and smiled.

By God, Mrs. St. James.

One look at Gillingham's smile confirmed Mrs. St. James of the brothel was none other than the famed beauty, the Countess of Havermere.

Seems he owed Gillingham dinner.

The rest of the concert was lost in a haze of Farren's fantasies, beautifully accompanied by Mozart. He was only brought back to the here and now when the guests rose to applaud.

She wore a pale silver-gray gown trimmed in pink, and in the candlelight it shone luminously. A pure diamond among paste.

Yet diamonds were hard and multifaceted—tricky in their shiny splendor. How many sides were there to Mrs. St. James?

Shock froze over her face as her wandering gaze caught on his. Then, quick to recover, her mouth turned upwards in a tepid approximation of a smile, but her eyes looked haunted.

He gave her high marks for staying put as he navigated the sea of chairs between them.

"I believe the saying is, 'the third time's a charm'?" He made his bow to her.

She quickly dipped into a curtsy but not before he'd seen a blush flush her cheeks.

"Ah, Lady Havermere." Gillingham, who had followed, bent to buss her hand. "Such a pleasure to see you out in company once again. Mourning seems to have agreed with you." He looked between Farren and the lady. "I promised Colonel Cavanaugh a treat. But perhaps I do not need to make introductions? Perhaps, you have already met the colonel?"

"No," she said hastily before he could answer.

Their gazes tangled as if negotiating a standoff. He backed off first.

"I thought so, but I was mistaken. The lady is

correct, Mr. Gillingham, I have never met the *countess*."

"Well, well, Cavanaugh, seems there is a story here." Gillingham narrowed his eyes and looked him up and down. "I look forward to hearing all about it, Colonel. But for now, I will leave you both so you might get your tale straight." Gillingham bowed and left.

"I wonder where we will meet next and what name you will be using." His voice pulled her attention back to him.

"Under the circumstances—that is, when we first met—I never use my title. I'm sure you understand," she said in a freezing tone.

"No, I'm not sure I do. But I hope to." He smiled again, undaunted by her cold demeanor. The flush of heat still stained her bosom. "A fellow can sure get tangled up in all these English titles. So many rules to follow."

"You do not strike me as the type of man who adheres to rules."

"Ha! You should meet my older brother, Brendan. Contrary as they come. But, to answer you, depends on the stakes."

She looked around her as if the room might provide her with a safe topic. Her gaze lighted on the piano. "You are fond of music?"

"I generally am, but today I was a might distracted. You see, Gillingham promised me a gander at an unparalleled English Rose. '*A diamond of the first water*,' he said." Farren rubbed his chin with the pad of his thumb. "I challenged him that my United States of America had the most beautiful women and that no gal could rival Miss Gloria Sutton of Howard County, Maryland. Gillingham only laughed. Said he had not a shred of doubt I would soon call Miss Sutton an out-and-out hag."

"He did, did he?" She stood up straighter as if standing in an inspection line. "And what have you concluded?"

He clasped his hands behind his back. "Seems I owe Mr. Gillingham a wad of cash. And dinner."

A pure delight to witness the battle she had trying to squelch the smile that eventually bloomed on her lips. She immediately bit the top one.

Lordy, she was a stunner.

"I believe Mr. Gillingham delights in testing society's strict boundaries. You should not let him take you in."

"Oh, but I don't reckon I was taken in a' tall. In fact, I count myself as getting a bargain." Seeing her eyes widen, he did not need to elaborate. "Besides, isn't this a case of the pot calling the kettle?" When she did not respond he continued. "Testing boundaries and all?"

She blushed all over again. She looked down at her reticule and then back up to him. "I would ask that you not mention—our previous meetings, Colonel. It would do my cause no good."

"Of course, Countess. It will be our secret." He laid his hand over his heart. "You have my word as a soldier."

She seemed to weigh his words and then nodded. "And how did you meet Mr. Gillingham?" she asked, clearly wanting to change the subject.

"I met him at a—"

"At a brothel," she finished. Disappointment flared

in her eyes and her lush lips firmed into a tight line. "You've a bad habit, Colonel."

Now was no time to tell her his sad tale. He scanned the room looking for a topic suitable for benign conversation. Men cast covetous looks their way, but one pair of silver eyes met his dead on and then settled on Nora St. James as if he owned her.

"Who is that man?" Farren asked just as the tall man reluctantly shifted his gaze from the countess to Gillingham, who had just arrived at his side.

"Why that is none other than our host, Lord Milton," she answered, finally smiling. "Or, at least he is *my* host."

Too handsome. Too cock sure of himself.

Gillingham was now leading the man over to them.

"Lord Milton, allow me to introduce you to Colonel Cavanaugh, from the United States of America. Colonel, may I present Lord Milton."

Now face to face, Farren nodded as if they were adversaries preparing for a duel instead of a guest and his host at a party in Mayfair. Why did this man make him feel like a hayseed?

"Have we met?" Farren asked. Perhaps Milton, like Gillingham, had known Brendan.

"No, I am sure we have not." Milton sniffed as if the very idea were an impossibility.

"I didn't think so. But I couldn't help but notice you staring. I suppose I deserve that, arriving without an invitation."

His lordship's reply was only to raise an imperious eyebrow.

Farren did not begrudge him his ire. After all, he had pushed into the man's home, drunk his champagne, and ogled the same woman Milton seemed to have a hankering for. He reckoned he'd be riled too.

"Are you in town long, Colonel?"

Farren had no wish to tell this man his business. "I'm not rightly sure. Depends." He smiled at the countess.

"Well, I'm sure Gillingham here will endeavor to show you some of London's hidden treasures before you depart."

"Oh, right you are, your lordship. Right you are," Gillingham repeated. A soldier receiving his orders did not stand to as neatly as Gillingham just had.

"You!" An ancient woman dressed entirely in black stood at the top of the stairs. Milton's butler hung at her side, clearly uncomfortable. The old woman raised her arm and pointed.

All eyes followed her direction to—

The countess?

"You dare to show your face in good society? You hussy, you!" The old crone spat out the words as if they burned her mouth.

Lord Milton stepped forward as if to shield the countess from the vitriol. "Who is this woman?" he barked at his butler who was now trying to curtail her as she haltingly made her way down the steps.

"I am Augusta St. James," the old lady shouted over the butler.

St. James? Was the ancient crow somehow related to Lady Havermere?

A hiss of whispers rose from the assembly. The middle-aged lady who had been seated next to the countess visibly stiffened.

Lord Milton crossed to the woman. "Lady Augusta,

we are all friends here. I would ask that you join us in good will or depart."

"I have no wish to stay. I only came to proclaim the truth!"

"Then Ridgley will see you out, your ladyship." Milton signaled to the butler.

"The truth! I spread truth! My brother was an evil man, but she—" Again, the old lady pointed at the countess, "—she wanted him dead. She poisoned him!"

"Lady Augusta," Lord Milton interrupted. "As you well know there was an investigation, and the matter was put to rest."

"Aye, to rest. Just as my brother was put to rest." She wheeled on Milton. "And you, you are a degenerate! An evil man! And the Queen is a traitor with that German husband of hers. Thank the good Lord he is dead and gone before he could do more harm!" the lady continued to spew even as Milton gestured to his butler and now two footmen who then ushered her out a side door.

A burble rose from the assembly but hushed when Lord Milton turned to address the company. "Well, it is clear that poor Lady Augusta is quite infirm. I trust no one here will repeat her bitter falsehoods?"

His guests nodded, some rather grudgingly.

So, the old gal had quite a bone to pick with her sister-in-law. Lies, he was sure ... or nearly sure.

"As for Lady Havermere, who has recently come out of two years of mourning for the late earl, I welcome her into our midst. And again, I am sure you all," he said, looking pointedly at the assembled, "will extend your felicity as well."

The Countess of Havermere, Mrs. St. James, the

most beautiful woman he had ever beheld, managed to paste on a smile.

What other secrets lay behind that façade? Well, he could never resist a mystery.

Chapter Five

Nora pulled her skirts up from the sucking mud as she picked her way from the mews into the back garden of Greene Street. No matter, soon they would have a proper garden.

Opal appeared in the kitchen doorway, her arms crossed. "Before you ask, no package has been delivered."

Should she write to Devlin again about sending the portraits? Perhaps she would not even need them now.

"So?"

"Lady Gadwick says she will be glad to contribute to our Corsham house."

"How much?" Leave it to Opal to get to the bone of the thing.

"She didn't go so far as to say, and I did not press, but she is known to be very generous."

Nora had just attended a lecture with Lady Gadwick given by Thomas Barnardo who was soliciting funds for his Ragged School for boys.

"And do girls not deserve an education and chance at happiness?" Nora had asked the good lady. Encouraged, she told her all about the property and her plans to start a small school. Her ladyship was most intrigued and vowed she would contribute.

Lord Milton, who was also in attendance, listened very attentively as well. Though he did not commit in any formal way, Nora was fairly certain he would also contribute to Nora's dream, but she was equally sure he would want her along with his donation. As solicitous as he appeared, she had the feeling he could not be managed.

The memory of that American officer, Colonel Cavanaugh, flooded her brain and body, drowning out any other man. She took a deep breath. No, she would not go down that road again. Her affair with Devlin had been a terrible mistake, costing them both much suffering. Lord Finchley was more to her taste these days.

"I think all in all, the afternoon went well." She would not mention the snubs and flirtations which were more like veiled seductions.

"Humph."

"This is good news, Opal."

Still, the girl frowned. Flossy, who was circling Nora's exposed ankles, decided to attack. Opal charged into the mud and chased the poor bird up into the boughs of a dead poplar.

"What has you in such a tizzy?"

"You've a guest. I told her you weren't 'ere, but she wouldn't leave." Whereupon Opal turned and squished back through the mud and then through the kitchen doorway.

"Who?" Nora called out. She quickly followed, removing her muddy slippers and then stepping into others set by the door. In the hall she shucked off her bonnet and cloak and draped them over the banister, catching the eyes of a maid huddled in the foyer who clutched her cloak as if she feared someone might make off with it.

Opal had stopped just inside the door to the parlor. "Lady Havermere." She flung her hand in Nora's general direction. "Lady Charlotte." Likewise, she tipped her chin toward a girl.

Cousin Orville's oldest.

Charlotte St. James, in her lemon-yellow gown, shone like a beacon of light in Nora's dim parlor.

"Lady Charlotte, this is a surprise."

"She showed up with her maid," Opal hissed, jerking her head toward the hallway. "The carriage is still waitin' out front, if you've a mind to send 'um packing, Mum." Opal flung out the statement like last week's scraps, but their visitor looked as unaffected as a potted sunflower.

"Opal, I believe we will need some tea. And some of the good bread with a little butter. Would you fetch those, please?"

The girl took a moment to consider the request, sniffed, and then swept out of the room as if she were the Queen herself.

Charlotte St. James must have drawn the long straw when it came to looks. Or perhaps she favored her mother? Not one ounce of ferret did Nora perceive in the girl's face. She would undoubtably fare well, at least among the young blades of the *ton*. However, the matchmaking mamas would be apoplectic with this stunning and entirely new offering being let loose among the few eligible bachelors of the season.

The newly-minted earl may not possess much town bronze, but his coffers were full, and his daughter fair. If the chit had some sense, she would do quite well. Perhaps even better if she didn't. Many gentlemen were just as happy to have a wife with the intellect of a sheep.

"I decided to take the bull by the horns, Aunt Nora."

Aunt Nora? Apparently, Lady Charlotte St. James was no sheep.

"Does your father know you are here?"

The girl looked Nora straight in the eye. "No, I came on my own. Papa insists that I must stay at home until a proper chaperone is found. Only he is too preoccupied with—well, honestly, I am not sure what occupies him these days. He runs around like a hen in the rain muttering unintelligible orders to various pieces of furniture. Or pouring over Debrett's Ranks and Privilege of Peerage."

"Well, at least you had the good sense to bring your maid."

"I will not pretend I have been raised with much decorum. I never dreamt—well, to be in this situation. My father was a clerk and my mother the daughter of a pig farmer," the girl admitted with no sense of shame. "I am hoping to convince you to take me on." Charlotte smiled and, in an instant, turned from a merely very pretty girl into a shining beauty.

"You are extremely forthright for one so young." Nora flung the words up like a shield against this girl's charms.

"I suppose that is a fault?" She beamed. Seems the girl already knew how to use her charms to her advantage.

"While I admire frankness, I am afraid the *ton* will not countenance such, shall we say, pluck."

"My family don't admire it much either." Her winning smile invited Nora to share in the little joke.

"Here's tea, madam." Opal entered with a tray. "Shall I put it on the table here?"

Opal flounced over to the small table by the couch, the only table large enough for the tea tray. Opal was putting on airs. The girl could appear the most top-lofty lady, her speech perfect, her bearing straight and lithe as a willow branch, or turn into a cockney gutter snipe. She laid it on particularly thick when threatened. If she were a peacock, she would be showing all her feathers.

They must be nearly of an age, Lady Charlotte and Opal. Both beauties, but as different as could be in coloring and circumstances. One recently raised by chance to an earl's daughter, and one—well, who knew where Opal had begun life or where it would take her. Most people would say Opal's beauty was ruined by her scarred neck and mangled ear, the best she could hope for was to secure employment as a governess or lady's companion. But with her hair styled over her ear, and a high-necked gown, one could barely perceive Opal's disfigurement.

But there was no hiding for Opal. Hair scraped back, she wore her scars like a banner emblazoned with the words: *Do not approach!*

Instead of giving the girl a reassuring smile Opal would only resent, Nora nodded curtly and said, "Thank you, Opal. That will be all."

Opal jerked her chin up and sniffed, giving Lady Charlotte full view of her "bad side" before she marched out of the room.

"Shall we sit?"

"Yes, thank you." Charlotte looked thoughtfully at the now closed door. "What happened to Opal? Her ear—and the scar on her neck."

Nora raised an eyebrow.

"I am sorry, another fault of mine, too curious by half."

"I know I should not say this, but I would like to think there are some worthy folk out there who value a curious woman who speaks her mind. But, as to your question, I cannot answer."

"Ah, I am too presumptive."

"You are." Nora could not help but smile. "But honestly, I do not know much about my Opal's history. To be fair, I have never asked about her past. She is very proud. But as for her disfigurement, I will leave her to tell you that tale if she has a mind to."

Charlotte sat on the very edge of her seat, eager as a pup, as she pondered Nora's explanation. "She does not seem to consider it as a disfigurement. I applaud that. Indeed, I see her as very beautiful and mysterious."

Easily said from a girl who now held a silver spoon, but Nora could not help but admire Charlotte St. James just the same.

The girl, whether conscious or no, mimicked Nora's posture even to the way she folded her gloved hands together. "I know you do not want me, Auntie. My father has said as much, and to leave you to your grief. But I could not. Yet another fault. You see, if I let matters rest with Papa, well, they would rest there until I was an ancient crone without a hair on my head or tooth in my mouth."

Nora raised an eyebrow. "I might add a penchant for the dramatic to your list of faults."

The girl laughed but sobered quickly. "I am already one and twenty and, other than coming to England, I have been nowhere and done nothing. I want to live a little. And I want to choose my own husband." She raised her chin. "I cannot do so sitting at home, or worse, having Papa arrange something for me."

If the girl had been given a script, she could not have plucked at Nora's conscience, or heartstrings, any harder.

"I see you are wearing gray now. Your mourning must be nearly over. With no mama, I am the vanguard for my younger sisters. I must make a good marriage, and I want to make one with a man I can love. My mama would have delighted to see me through this miraculous change. I know she is looking down and adding her spiritual supplications to my own." Charlotte's eyes misted and she sniffed and looked away. "Ah! You see how the lamp flickered just then?"

Nora turned her gaze to follow the girl's. Indeed, the lamp seemed to brighten for a moment. But believing in spirits was ridiculous. "My, you *are* fanciful, Lady Charlotte."

"I grant you I may be, but I have always felt her by my side. Especially in times when I need her most.

Not once had Nora felt her own mother's benevolence. After her father's death, and the discovery of his debts—well, more of his debts—Nora had become nothing more than a commodity to her surviving parent, her only worth her beauty, which her mother guarded with a strict vengeance. *If you remove your corset again in the night, I will take away your doll. You must wear your straightening rod at all times. Did you practice your French today? Your dancing? Your harp? Do not think of going out in the sun, Nora Elizabeth!* The list of improvements and admonitions went on and on.

"You are new to town. I must tell you that there were—are—rumors surrounding my husband's death."

"Rumors?"

"Many believe I poisoned the earl. There was an inquiry."

"I see. And you are not sorry he's dead?"

"No. No, I'm not."

The girl looked at her for a very long time. "I am sorry you've had such troubles."

It seemed that within this one sentence this young girl had divined the whole of Nora's past. "You still have not answered my question, will you take me on?"

"I am not sure you understand—"

"Actually, I believe I do understand, if only just a bit. And, if I am not too presumptive, you might need me as much as I need you."

"You are very insightful for one so young."

The girl only smiled, but oh, what a smile.

Oh, to have the chance to do it all over again. To be young and in love ….

The lamp flickered.

Nora looked back at this stunning girl full of hope and promise wanting a chance at romance.

And, as Charlotte had divined, her entrée into the season could open some doors for Nora …

"Will you pour the tea, Lady Charlotte?"

The young lady looked as if she were ready to launch herself from her chair and into yet another argument but stopped herself and instead resumed her seat. She bit her lip and picked up the tea strainer.

"No, you must warm the cups first, my dear."

The cup clattered against its saucer.

"Have a care. That is Sèvres China, the Louvre pattern which is no longer made."

Suddenly the girl sat up and beamed. "We are beginning, aren't we, Auntie?"

Nora's silly heart fluttered in the sweetness of this girl's sudden devotion.

Nora firmed her lips. "I take milk only, just a splash."

Water sloshed, and Nora was enveloped in a warm embrace. "Thank you, Auntie! Thank you so much for taking me on." A heated cheek pressed against hers.

My God, she had never been embraced by a woman before. A child, yes, but never a young woman. One who needed her.

"Very well, Charlotte." Nora pulled away. "I see we will have to work on your decorum."

Charlotte sprang away and then sat demurely in her chair. "I will be the best student ever. You will see, Auntie."

"*Hmmm.* For the time being, until you have the right of it, I believe it is best you nod and smile. Yes, I would say smile a lot, my dear."

In answer the girl gave Nora a brilliant grin.

"Hell and damnation," Opal's voice rang out.

Bang!

"Excuse me, my dear." Nora set her precious Louvre-pattern teacup down carefully and rose. "There seems to be a—disturbance in the hall." She opened the door.

Opal knelt on the floor in front of a long narrow crate. Marigold scampered about, asking all manner of questions and offering various theories as to what it could possibly contain, whilst Agnes's fingers flew over the rough wooden boards as if she might divine the contents by touch. Charlotte's maid pressed herself up against the door.

"Sorry, Mum," Opal groused. "I thought I had it, but this one—" She jabbed a finger at Mari. "Got in the way, as usual, and it was either the box or 'er."

"You chose wisely, Opal."

"Is it a pianoforte, Mum?" Agnes asked, as if they might be before the Holy Grail.

"It is fortunate it is not a pianoforte, Agnes, else it would be ruined, I expect."

"Oh, I would dearly love to hear a pianoforte!" Agnes clasped her fingers together at her breast.

Charlotte appeared in the doorway. "Might I be of assistance?"

Opal snorted.

"Oh, what sweet children!" Charlotte crouched to speak with Marigold. "What a little doll you are."

"I am not a doll. I am a Marigold. Mari for short."

When Nora had first encountered the little girl and had asked her name, the poor mite had looked confused and then said, "Girl."

"I am five," Marigold said with pride. "Well, we think I am. What's your name?"

"Pleased to meet you, Mari. I am Charlotte. You know you are just my sister Diana's age." She turned then to Agnes who had cocked her ear to this new voice. "And you I would guess to be at least eight or perhaps nine?"

"I am nine and three quarters. My birthday is in July, on the seventh, then I will be ten." Agnes shuffled closer to Charlotte and sniffed. "You smell like flowers and … porridge. Oatmeal, I think. With a beautiful spice …"

"Cinnamon. Heavens, you are correct, Miss …?"

"Agnes. My name is Agnes Jayne Burleigh." She bobbed a curtsy. Agnes was always one for remembering niceties. She licked her lips as if she could taste the heady spice.

"And *my* birthday is *next* month, ain't it, Mum?" Mari stood on her tiptoes, making her teeter as her clubfoot was not much use.

"*Isn't* it, Marigold." Nora took her hand just as she was about to careen into the crate. "And yes, we will celebrate on the twenty-fifth."

Nora was just as happy to have the attention diverted from the crate and its contents. And the memories associated with what lay inside.

She closed her eyes. *Devlin's portraits of her.*

She had not thought it would come to this. No, that was a lie. Even with a contribution from Lady Gadwick, finances would always be tight. Either the paintings would have to be sold, or she would have to sell herself.

Marriage.

She winced as if a bandage was being ripped off an old wound. No. Never. Not unless all other avenues failed.

Very well, if these paintings must go under the hammer so she and her girls might live unfettered, then Nora was prepared to let them go.

"Lady Charlotte, I am afraid we will have to cut your visit short. I must deal with—with this business."

"Of course, Aunt Nora."

Opal stared daggers at poor Charlotte.

"I am looking forward to our time together and

learning everything there is to know about society," the beauty said, totally unperturbed by Opal's less than charitable attitude.

"You may change your tune when you are wrestling with, does Lady Titmouse go in to dinner with Lord Pompous? Or does Lord Longbottom take precedence?"

Charlotte laughed. "Come, Hattie."

The little maid, who had finally had the presence of mind to close her mouth, stepped forward.

"We must get home before we are missed." Charlotte smiled at the group while skirting the crate.

Opal followed and then shut the door rather too firmly. "Mari, Agnes, time to feed the chickens. Go on."

"Will we have cows and horses at the country house, Mum?" Mari asked, her face awash in hope.

"And a pianoforte?" Agnes asked as her fingers keyed the air.

Oh, why had she ever mentioned the possibility of a new home in the country?

Nora shooed them down the hall. "We will just have to see, but first you must learn to tend chickens before we can take on a cow." That got the younger girls moving right enough. "Opal, will you help me get this up to my bedchamber?"

"Of course, your ladyship."

Oh dear, when Opal felt the need to resort to *your ladyship*, things were bad. Nora usually confided all her schemes to the girl. Opal's curiosity would be ratcheted up to the nth degree with the arrival of this crate, yet she said nothing.

Together they carried the box upstairs. "Thank you,

Opal. You are my rock, do you know that?" She took the girl's hand. "My gem."

Opal froze.

"What is the matter?"

Opal only minutely shook her head.

Oh, why wouldn't this damaged girl let Nora in, just a bit?

"It's nothing. Just someone else used to call me that. That's all."

Perhaps her mother? Or someone who loved her before all her troubles? Nora dared not pry.

Opal sniffed but gave Nora's hand a small squeeze before pulling away. "I will go see what those two scamps are up to. With their particular 'tending,' it's no wonder we've got no eggs. Agnes keeps disturbing every nest wanting to touch everything, and Mari delights in trying to catch the birds."

"Best go then. And thank you again, Opal."

The door latch clicked and Nora turned to the wooden box.

The lid pried off after slipping her brass shoehorn between the rough boards.

Among the packing straw was a note.

Malvern Grange

March, 29th

Nor,

I'm sorry it has come to this. But they are only paint and canvas, not you. Not really. You have moved beyond this woman. Use her as you will.

Anne and I wish you only the best for your future. You are due a bit of happiness. Real happiness.

Please come for a visit. Ellie is walking now and chattering non-stop. She has begun to hammer at the pianoforte, and actually shows some talent. I am not sure where she comes from. Her mother and I are constantly dumbfounded. She is wanting a brother. So, we are obliging her as indulgent parents do. September will come soon enough, but the duke is ever impatient to have a grandson.

Take care, dear friend,
Devlin

She'd been all but a virgin when she'd finally succumbed to Lord Devlin's considerable charms. Her husband had tried to bed her, humiliating and painful encounters for them both. He'd even made Nora pleasure him in other ways as prelude. But he'd never been able to complete the act, and later, had not even been able to begin it. That was when he turned cruel, berating her for the deceptive snare of her beauty, then physically punishing her, but still his flaccid penis refused to rise.

There would be no child to love, no sweet babe to lessen her despair. She had nearly thrown herself out the window of her prison-like room.

Desperate, she finally yielded to Devlin's wish to paint her portrait, knowing full well what would follow.

He had been so patient with her ineptness. *Lud*, he must have been well and truly smitten, for James Drake, Marquess of Devlin, was one of the least patient men of her acquaintance. But when she had finally climaxed, her release had confounded her. She'd had no idea her body could do such a wondrous thing. And yet, miraculously, it had done it over and over again.

Would she ever know passion again? Love?

But Devlin had never really loved her. A small curl of jealousy unfurled in Nora's breast as she thought of his Anne. She tamped it down. Devlin had endured his own hell. He deserved happiness.

Two dozen or so canvases lay coiled within the straw packing.

She slid one out, took a deep breath, inhaling the sweet musk of straw and a slight scent of vanilla. Dev had always used vanilla to rid his fingers of turpentine.

She pulled it open like a scroll.

The top of a rococo full-length mirror appeared. She'd forgotten, Dev had the behemoth hauled in one day. It nearly hadn't made the turn in the stairs.

She unrolled more of the canvas. A bed, its quilt bought from a gypsy woman who swore love was woven into the very fabric. Nora had traced those patterns of tiny stitches, imagining a husband who loved her, a child cradled within her arms.

Now for the last bit.

The woman lay upon the bed, her white body stark against the deep jewel tones of the quilt. A river of red curls hung over the edge to pool on the floor. Her limbs were open, languidly sated as she gazed at a figure just outside the frame.

This was a woman who believed in love.

Nora tossed it aside and unrolled the next. And then the next, as if she would find some truth hidden within these canvases. As if they might provide some clue as to her life back then. Those few months of bliss.

But no. These pictures were only an illusion. This woman was an illusion. If one looked deeply, one would see beyond the beauty into the ugly despair.

This woman was a sham.

Good riddance.

For with the death of the old earl, a new woman

had risen out of that bitter unhappiness. From the child who had idolized her profligate father and could not understand her mother's terrible jealousy and bitterness. To the young woman who submitted to marriage in the naive hope it might provide a kindly home, only to be made into a frightened prisoner. And finally, this woman in the painting who sought love outside of her marriage only to find it was not love at all. Only desperation.

No, the person she was now was not so trusting, far from innocent, but stronger, wiser.

The remaining paintings were easier to go through. Another nude. She tossed it into the not-for-sale pile. A modest one of just her face. She added it to the for sale lot. The next, a rather prim pose of her wearing her emerald-green riding habit buttoned to the throat. But the skirt was hiked up to expose one long white leg. A crop dangled casually from her fingers to graze her inner thigh.

If she could burn them all, she would. But she must harbor these beauties for a while longer and then she could be shut of them. And this stranger, with her mysterious smile, full of innuendo, and false confidence, might be her ticket to freedom.

She rolled it back up. Another not-for-sale.

Delving into the crate, she searched for any more that might be lost in the straw.

"Mum!"

Marigold clumped into the room gesticulating wildly.

"What? What has happened?" Nora crouched before the child, her hands skating over the girl, searching for an injury.

"Mum!" Mari twitched, flinging off Nora's ministrations and then caught and pulled at her hand. "You must come!"

"Who is hurt? Is it Agnes again? How many times must I tell her she must learn to use her cane."

"Not Aggy, Mum. We got an egg! Miss Fox-tail hatched an egg!"

A bloody egg.

Nora's heart still hammered in her breast. One paltry egg, but what a gift. So much more precious than all these paintings.

"Ah, and I had my money on Flossy. Well, lead on, Miss Marigold, and let us see this miracle."

Chapter Six

Ryeland Park, Wiltshire

Farren's hired mount Claudius flicked his ears and threw his head. A nervous man made a nervous beast.

But it was time to face his grandfather. Past time. Once this nasty business was over, he could get back to his search.

Still, it was good to be out of the city with its choking soot and cramped streets. And its damned bawdyhouses.

Since putting in at Southampton almost two weeks ago, he'd visited thirty-eight brothels in search of his brother and an elusive blonde, green-eyed girl, aged fifteen, who fit the description of his missing niece. All a waste. Well, except for meeting Oscar Gillingham, whom, Farren suspected, knew more than he was saying.

And Nora St. James, Countess of Havermere. That was a right fine memory—he shifted in his saddle—but he'd had no luck there either.

Crested wrought iron gates came into view. As he approached, they swung open. A liveried servant pulled his forelock in deference. Farren was expected. He took in a lungful of brisk country air as if it might fortify him against what lay ahead.

Claudius lifted his head as his hooves left the

muddy road to crunch over pea stone. The drive stretched into a pink horizon and then disappeared among a bank of live oaks. The sky looked as if God had taken a hay rake through the clouds, sorting them into neat furrows of blue and white. Farren took another deep breath. They must be scything the lawn somewhere upwind. The smells of fresh grass and newly turned earth put him in mind of home. The prospect of life just waiting to burst forth but for a little effort and a bit of good weather.

He shook his head. He no longer had a home. Or land. Hayland Farm was gone, sold to his neighbor whose five sons had all miraculously returned alive and intact from the godforsaken war.

Nothing left to tie him to America.

For good or for bad, it was done. England would be his new home.

Surely if Brendan was still alive, he had to be here in England. Farren touched the letter tucked against his breast as if it might conjure his brother to appear, a devilish smile on his face, a dare in his eyes.

Mayhap the only family Farren had left lay at the end of this drive. A grandfather and uncle whom he had never met—hell, his pa had barely even mentioned his English family from across the pond. Ma had hinted at a terrible rift, but whenever Farren had probed, she only shook her head and looked away. What secrets lay buried here? Secrets that would drive a young man to leave everything behind for America. Secrets that would poison his heart so no love could ever take root there again.

The house came into view, emerging steadily from behind the hills, which fell away to reveal a façade of silver-white stone curtained in purple-green ivy. The fading sun's light caught the windows, and they flashed as if to wink at him and Claude.

The horse's ears twitched, perking up, and his gait became livelier. How did these livery animals know a pail of oats lay only a few minutes away?

If only Farren were as eager to arrive.

By Saint Crispin, what a place. Nothing like the fantastic tales he had spun as a child of a dark, haunted castle surrounded by a moat. In his child's mind, his grandfather was a gruesome, humpbacked old troll, and his uncle an eye-patch-wearing henchman who wielded a magical sword. They had held his ma captive while Pa battled the dragons who protected the castle.

Instead, Ryeland Park, stood gleaming white, its wide portico, and soaring pillars, reminding him of the home where President Grant and his family lived. Farren had been invited to the mansion to accept the Medal of Honor. He'd got as far as the drive and then turned right around, knowing he wasn't any more a hero than any other man who had stood on the battlefield. Instead, he'd found a tavern across the river in Alexandria and drunk himself under the table with several soldiers from the Iron Brigade.

His pa had called their place on the banks of the Chesapeake Hayland Farm, the name clearly a nod to his boyhood home of Ryeland. But that was where the similarity ended. The old clapboard house with its smoking fires and leaking roof would be only good for kindling on this spread. And instead of acres of corn and dairy cows, sheep dotted the surrounding hills, looking more like ornaments than income-producing livestock.

"Come on then, Claude. We may be only poor common folk, but we must make our bow to these highfalutin' gentlemen, and hopefully get some answers, for good or bad." He squeezed his knees, urging the horse forward. Hell, he was so hungry to belong somewhere he might just embrace the devil himself if Old Scratch held out a welcoming hand.

They approached the house, a huge fountain stood within a manicured circle of box hedges. Poseidon, commanding a phalanx of verdigris dolphins and mermaids, directed the water upward, shooting it up as high as the third story of the manse. Farren's ogling was interrupted by a liveried groom who had jogged up to take hold of Claude's bridle.

"Good afternoon." Farren dismounted and then ruffled the horse's coarse mane. "This fella's name is Claudius, Claude to his intimates." The horse bobbed his head as if in agreement. "He has worked mighty hard. Could you see he gets a full measure of oats?"

"Certainly, sir." The young ostler bowed and then led Claude away to the stables and his dinner. If only Farren could join the horse in the barn with a strong ale and a steaming bowl of stew.

Before he could knock, the huge door opened. An elderly man with the bearing of a military officer bowed. All this bowing had Farren on edge, as if he was supposed to be someone he was not.

"Welcome to Ryeland Park, Colonel Cavanaugh. I am Pratt. Shall I show you to your rooms? No doubt you'll wish to refresh yourself before you meet the viscount?"

"Thank you, Mr. Pratt. I'd be right glad of a wash."

A huge marble staircase wound up to a gallery that

stretched near forty feet. He followed the butler up three flights and down a long hallway into a bedchamber with a view of the front lawns and fountain.

With hands and face cleansed of the dust of the road and some bread and cheese in his belly, his body felt substantially better. His mind and heart were another matter.

Farren tugged the bell pull. A footman arrived a moment later and led Farren past statues and huge paintings, past countless doors and staircases. Finally, they stopped by a heavily carved door, which the servant opened.

"Colonel Farren Cavanaugh, your lordship," the servant intoned as if Farren had arrived before St. Peter at the Pearly Gates.

He stepped into the room and the footman retreated, closing the door behind him.

An old man sat before a small table stacked with books, playing cards, a large magnifying glass, and several glass cases filled with what looked to be huge black bugs.

Apparently, the Cavanaugh blood ran strong. The viscount had not risen to greet him, but Farren could see that his legs were long. They also shared the same cheekbones, strong jaw line, and cleft chin. His grandfather's hair was white but full with a slight curl. Farren could well imagine it once being wheat-colored as his own, as his father's, and Brendan's. His eyebrows, however, were still heavy and dark. Another Cavanaugh trait. But what was most shocking was the warmth in his smiling green eyes. As if he loved Farren in spite of never having met his youngest grandson before.

"My boy, you have come. At last."

Farren had prepared himself for a cold, stony face with bristling eyebrows over steely eyes. This man was none of those things.

"Sir." Taking refuge in niceties, he bowed and then took the indicated seat.

The old man pushed the table aside. On casters, it rolled easily. "You must pardon my staring, but the resemblance is shocking." The viscount narrowed his eyes and shook his head. "I see my son in you, of course, and something of myself as well. But your brother, Brendan—" He broke off in a fit of coughing.

Farren rose, but the viscount waved him away. He took a small sip from a medicinal cup, grimaced, and then set it down next to one of his large black beetles. Then he took a deep breath and seemed to steel himself as if he were lining up to face a firing squad. "How is Duncan—your father?"

Farren stiffened. "You did not receive my second letter?"

"None beyond the one informing me of your coming."

There was no softening this news. "He is dead, your lordship."

His grandfather's lips tightened and then he slowly nodded. "I suppose it would not have mattered … still, it is hard to give up a dream." His gaze slid to the open window, and he blinked several times.

"In his last days, Pa was adamant I see you, sir. After his stroke, it was difficult to understand him, but I believe he spoke of mending fences. Of forgiveness."

"Ah," was all the old man said.

Not knowing his grandfather, Farren had no idea if the viscount often suffered such lapses or if the man were truly overcome with grief. He waited.

The clock on the mantel sounded like the battered snare drum Donnie Bartlet constantly carried and tapped on when he was nervous. The chair springs groaned as Farren adjusted his position. A mourning dove called out to its mate as the splash of the fountain played softly under it all. An ambient quiet so poignant it compelled one to whisper so as not to disturb even the air of the place. It put Farren in mind of the great basilica on Cathedral Street in Baltimore where he often went to feel a bit of peace when memories of the war threatened to overwhelm him.

"You must forgive me. Your news has caught me up." His grandfather reached for the bell on his table but did not ring it. "Did he ever speak of … England?"

Farren shook his head. "He never spoke of what happened—what drove him away."

His grandfather frowned, and his lips drew together as if holding back words.

"But I reckon he forgave you in the end." Farren wanted to bring the old man some peace. "He looked so desperate in his last moments. It was very important to him that I come to you, that I offer an olive branch."

He looked up sharply. "An olive branch?"

"Well, that's my interpretation, your lordship. He wanted me to have family. In the end he wanted us to mend, I believe."

"To mend? Yes, well, Duncan had a knack for getting people to do his bidding."

Farren had no wish to dwell on his grandfather's grief. He did feel sorry for the old man, but he'd had ample opportunity to reach out to his son but hadn't. "Sir, I am sorry to bring you such sad news, but I was hoping to speak of my brother, Brendan. I know he came to visit you briefly all those years ago. Did you have any hint as to where he might have been living? Know of any friends or connections?"

The old man shook his head. "He came to me for money over sixteen years ago, the scamp. Couldn't, or wouldn't, stay. Had to be on his way posthaste. Reminded me of your father." The viscount rubbed a swollen knuckle, lost in thought again. After a moment, he regained his composure. "I was hurt by your brother's cold manner, and I am afraid I reacted badly. Told him he was not to come looking for a handout and then thinking to be on his way with not so much as a by-your-leave."

"Well, with all due respect, sir, can you blame him?"

The old man gave him an odd look. "You say your father never spoke of me? Or of his brother, Geoff?"

"No, sir. I believe those memories were quite painful for him."

"And his life in America, was he happy?"

Farren hesitated but he owed the viscount no fairytale ending. "No. No, he was not happy. My mother tried. Tried to love him, but after my sister, Sara, died it seemed any love he might have had died with her. Ma finally gave up. Pa seemed relieved."

The old man looked down at his hands. Admittedly, it was hard to reconcile this kindly man with the one whose cruelty had forged a damaged man incapable of love. Farren had stupidly tried over and again to win his pa's regard. Unlike Brendan, who seemed to be able to exist without it.

His grandfather finally looked up. "It is time you met your uncle." His hand shook slightly as he rang a bell at his elbow. The butler appeared in the next moment. "Bring my son to me, Pratt."

"Very good, milord." The servant bowed and left the room.

Silence yawned. Farren rose and paced to the window. A fine-looking stable stood in the vale. Claudius would be getting his oats by now.

He turned back to his grandfather. "There is only you and my uncle now, sir?"

"Yes," the old man answered with a weary nod. "Unless, of course, Brendan can be found. After your letter, I made inquiries but thus far I have not made any progress in uncovering his whereabouts here in England. If indeed he is here. I find it remarkable nothing has been discovered in America."

"You mean recovering Brendan's body? You were not there. Thousands died. In the summer months, there was no way to sort through the bodies. Disease ran rampant, and the dead were shoved into mass graves."

The viscount shook his head. "Damned war. Brother against brother. Senseless."

"Well, I believe our African brothers would disagree with you, sir. But, yes, I believe war is generally to be avoided if at all possible."

"You were not together?"

"No. Brendan was in a different unit." No sense in telling the old man Brendan had come home in the middle of the war from his escapades out west only to fight on the opposite side, for the South. And not out of any conviction. He had done it solely to spite their father.

He'd tried to find out news of him, but it was near impossible. And Bren was no writer. His brother could shoot a spinning nickel at ten paces but ask him to clean and oil his pistol … well, that was beyond him.

"Might he have deserted?"

Farren hesitated. Plenty had. As a commanding officer, he was supposed to hang the wretches. He had.

Once.

Justin Carpenter. A boy, just off the farm, with no real stake in this civil war. His wife, with a young son and an infant, left unprotected, their crops rotting in the fields. Her letter, begging him to come home, still clutched in his hand when the sergeant slipped the blindfold over his eyes.

Farren stopped playing by the rules after that.

"So, he could have deserted his post," his grandfather's voice penetrated the horrible memory. "I must admit he did not strike me as someone who'd remain constant."

"Maybe." Sweet Jesus, he dearly hoped Bren wouldn't have left his battalion in the middle of a skirmish—not unless the circumstances were extraordinary. "He was seen in the conflict near Richmond on March 26th. I tracked down one of the corporals in his company after the war. The boy said Brendan was among the lines one minute and gone the next. Said they combed the field for him but found no trace. But it was unseasonably hot, and the dead were buried with great haste."

"But you do not believe that?"

"He would have been recognized. Someone would have seen him go down." Farren shook his head, dispelling the images of his brother heaped with other bodies in some unmarked grave. "If he was dead, I would feel it."

When Farren had returned home in July, he'd found the old strong box they'd buried out in the back garden under the sun dial had been pillaged. Farren prayed Bren had taken it. If he had, that meant he was likely alive.

"On his deathbed my pa ranted about finding flowers in London rookeries. At first, I thought he must be delirious. But later, when he could no longer speak, he kept pointing at the wall. Finally, to humor him, I went to where he was pointing. A portrait my ma had painted of the three of us children. He got very agitated.

"Wedged in the back was this letter I wrote you about." He withdrew the well-worn paper from his breast pocket. "Not sure how Pa got it, or if Brendan even read it. It's posted from London, England, from an Iris Darvan, and dated fourteen years ago."

Before he could elaborate, the door opened and Pratt pushed a man in a bath chair into the room.

"Ah, here he is." The old man's face lit up. "Farren, meet your Uncle Geoffrey."

Farren stood. And nearly sat down again.

The man before him was a twisted imbecile.

He looked to his grandfather, but the old man only smiled.

Farren had seen plenty of misery in the war but never expected to encounter it on a viscount's country estate.

His uncle's hands were clasped together but jerked in spasms. His shoulders were wide and looked muscled, but his legs, silhouetted beneath a thin shawl, were skeletal. Though his hair was cropped rather short, Farren could tell it was the same blond as his own. And the eyes ... He might have been staring into his brother Brendan's.

He stepped forward and then back again. Finally, at a loss as to what to do, he bowed.

"I am pleased to make your acquaintance, Uncle." Could this man even comprehend?

His uncle's mouth worked and his neck craned while his gnarled hands flexed and twitched.

Farren stepped closer as if his proximity could help this poor wretch.

"Daaaa! Dunnnn!" The man grinned as if he had accomplished the most witty and eloquent speech. The Cavanaugh dimple appeared in his left cheek.

"Yes, Geoff, he does look a good deal like Duncan."

How his grandfather made a rejoinder from that garbled gibberish Farren would never know. "I am Farren, sir. Duncan's youngest son. I am—so pleased to finally meet you, Uncle," he repeated, not knowing what the heck to say.

This man would have been shockingly handsome—more beautiful than even Farren's father— if he had not been so damaged. His green eyes crinkled into crescent moons as his smile nearly split his face in two. He waved his hands at Farren.

Farren stuck out his own and his uncle captured it and took it between his.

Criminy! He caught his grandfather's grin as Farren's hand was nearly crushed in his uncle's grasp.

"Geoff!" his uncle said, continuing to pump Farren's arm.

Pratt stepped forward and deftly dabbed a bit of spittle from his charge's mouth. He must do this dozens of times a day, but the servant seemed oblivious, as if everyone needed mopping up every now and again.

Farren clasped both of his hands around his uncle's, hoping to extract the trapped one before its bones shattered. "Geoff, I am Farren. Remind me not to challenge you to arm wrestle."

"Dunn?" Geoff looked about the room.

"Duncan could not travel, Geoff," his grandsire answered giving Farren a speaking look. "He sends his love and hopes to come sometime soon."

Geoff's face crumpled and his hand went limp and slid out of Farren's.

"I expect you will get a letter within the week." The old man smiled at his son and then turned to Farren. "Duncan is a faithful writer."

Farren's throat closed painfully. The love between these two damaged people was palpable. He couldn't recall his father ever looking at him with such blind devotion.

"Now, Pratt will take you for your evening exercises, and then Cook has prepared a ham. And for a sweet there is your favorite, syllabub."

Geoff grinned once again, the order of his world seemingly restored. Dear God, to appreciate such simple pleasures. He had a great deal to learn from his uncle.

"I'll say my farewell then, Uncle Geoff. I am very happy to have met you."

Geoff's mouth worked, but he could not make the words come. At last, he simply bobbed his head and smiled. Pratt wheeled him out of the room.

"It is better not to tell him of Duncan's death. It would be too cruel. He does not deserve any more cruelty in his life."

Farren nodded, still reeling from this interview. "You write the letters?"

"Yes. Another deception. But harmless. I hope."

How could this be? His grandfather was supposed to be a monster. The man who had made his father incapable of love and so destroyed Farren's family. But this man seemed concerned and caring. He certainly loved his son.

"I am sorry, sir—I—it is rude, but what happened to Geoff?"

The man smiled sadly. "There is a decanter of brandy there on the sideboard. Would you pour a glass for me and one for yourself, if you've a mind?"

Brandy sounded just fine. He poured two glasses and brought one to his grandfather.

The old man took the glass between his hands as if it might warm them. He stuck his nose in the bowl and inhaled deeply and then took a small sip. His eyes closed in a kind of bliss. Then he set the glass aside.

"A father is not meant to have a favorite, but I did. Bright as a penny, he was, my Geoff. Everyone said so. He came late in my life. I did not think the viscountess and I would have a child, but God was good. And then four years later, miraculously, Duncan was born. We thought we could not have been more blessed. But, the Lord giveth and He taketh away. Martha, your grandmother, took her duties among the tenants very seriously. She brought baskets faithfully to those in need. We didn't know smallpox had found its way to Ryeland until it was too late." He touched the edge of the brandy glass but did not drink.

"Geoff doted on his younger brother, but as they grew the difference in their temperaments became more and more obvious. Geoff's steady and true, and your father's, changeable as a girl in her first season. I tried to hide my preference. I was even harder on Geoff because of it, but the feelings were there. I think somehow Duncan knew.

"After Duncan came of age and received his portion, I lost all control of him. Geoff was the only one who had any influence over him. The only person your father listened to."

The viscount closed his eyes. Tipping his head back, he took a long breath in. "There was a young girl, Sarafina Thomanson."

"Sarafina?"

His grandsire nodded.

Good, God, his pa had insisted they name his little sister Sarafina.

Unaware that he had just revealed a crucial piece of the Cavanaugh puzzle, his grandpa continued. "She was the daughter of the local vicar. Sarafina was quite a beauty and betrothed to a Mr. Dashal. But it did not matter. In fact, Duncan saw it as a challenge and would not give her up. They ran away one night."

Like a cannon primed, the fuse only waiting to be lit, Farren steeled his body, preparing himself for the terrible tale.

"Geoff found out and tried to stop them."

Farren's mind clicked to battle mode. *Cannoners post!*

"As near as I could find out, shots were fired."

Rammers sponge, his hands twitched.

"The carriage horses shied."

Solid shot! Load! He squeezed his hands into fists.

"Geoff tried to catch the runaway team, but he was hit."

Fire!

"Tangled in his stirrup, he fell beneath his horse and was dragged some yards. His head must have hit a rock. The young girl...she was thrown. Neck snapped."

Neck snapped. A hiss of pent-up air escaped his lips.

"All I know for certain was that the poor girl was dead. And my sons were brought back to me utterly broken—one in body, the other in spirit."

By God. Sarafina. It all made sense. Neck snapped. No wonder his pa had never recovered from Sara's death.

His grandfather looked out the window, his eyes glassy. He sniffed and raised his chin. "We paid the family off. Disgusting business. The fiancé was ready to call Duncan out.

"Duncan, he stayed with Geoff, his constant nurse, making himself sick. Geoff would not wake, you see. Duncan could not look at me, much less talk to me. He spoke only to Geoff, to ask him to please awaken. Geoff did, finally. After nearly two months. We were called immediately. Duncan rushed into the room, such a smile on his face. He even took my hand and smiled at me."

The old man shook his head. "But the Geoff we knew was gone. His brain too damaged. Both body and mind broken. Broken beyond repair."

His grandfather fell silent, and his body slumped, as if all the life had drained out of him. Farren sat forward, ready to summon Pratt. But the old man rallied, taking a deep breath which pulled his body up straighter. "Duncan could not stand it. He took the first ship for America and married your mother straight away, I believe. I wrote many times, but I never received a reply."

Where was the monster Farren had hated? The villain who had sent his father from his home and had made him into a brittle and bitter man, incapable of love? No, that story had been all wrong. Old history warped and shifted with his grandfather's new tale.

Years and years of telling himself if Pa had only had love, he might have had love to give. Hell, anything was better than the alternative: that Farren himself was unlovable.

Hatred leached from Farren's body. He dropped onto the nearest chair, feeling as if his limbs had been rearranged and he did not know how they worked anymore.

Deep silence filled the room, the kind that happened after a battle, when despair swamped the combatants.

"You should know I am not well."

At his grandfather's declaration Farren's head snapped up. "Not well?" he echoed stupidly, knowing the old man was ill. Hell, even a child could work that out. Still, just having found family, the prospect of losing it wrenched his heart.

His grandpa looked longingly at the brandy but again did not take any. "My heart, they say. You are ostensibly the heir apparent."

"Uncle Geoff—?" But it was all too clear his uncle would not be capable of holding the title or producing a son to carry on.

"Until Brendan is found, we must proceed as if you are next in line after Geoff. You will be the conservator while Geoff is alive."

He had come vowing to expose the truth and to chastise his grandfather for his cruelty. Farren would not be the mortar to mend his crumbling family. But with this new history his entire world shifted. His grandfather was not a fiend, only a dying man who had suffered the loss of both his children.

His grandfather thrust out his lower lip, a look of pain crossing his face. He touched the sleek shell of the beetle next to him and smiled ruefully. "Your grandmother has much to answer for, leaving such a great hole in my life when she decided to quit this world in such an untimely manner." He looked into the fire. "I should have remarried, but did not have the heart to replace perfection. I had the heir and the spare." He shook his head and made his hands into fists. "Maybe Duncan would have listened to a mother."

Farren had lost his own mother at the age of sixteen. She had always been a shadowy figure. Always holed up in her room, her romantic dreams dashed by a man who could not love her.

When he was a boy, before his mother had given in to despair, she had played the fiddle. He loved watching her head nod and bob over the instrument. Eyes closed, brows alternately raised or furrowed, so intent on coaxing the purest sound from this oddly-shaped wooden box. Every part of her body telling the story of her music. Her passion. Her love.

His ma had tried to woo his pa with her music. But he remained numb. Even slamming out of the house when she began to play. Then she stopped altogether. Farren would stick her fiddle under her nose and say, "Play, Ma! Play that jiggy song." *For me*, he had wanted to add but could not risk so much. She had only looked at him oddly and then went back to her mending. He'd even learned a ditty on the thing—more like a screeching cat in heat—but she paid him no mind, only saying he'd better get to his chores.

"Now you have come, I am hoping you will remain. I am hoping you will take an interest in the estate and in your uncle. I will not be here forever."

"I thank you for your hospitality, sir, but I can't stay."

The old man's lips firmed, and he raised his chin. "Ah, your brother was not interested in the estate, either. Farming is not to your taste? I am sorry to hear it."

"Sir, you misunderstand. If I were free, I would love to stop a spell. Get to know you and my uncle. See your holdings. But I can't. You may have given up on Brendan and your granddaughter, but I haven't. Your true heir is out there, and in England, if my instincts are correct. I need to get back to London tomorrow and continue the search."

"That speaks well of you to be so tenacious. Very well, I do not discount gut feelings, lad. Then I suppose we shall go to town as well."

"We?"

"Geoff and myself. He has not been to town in an age. Loves going to Tattersalls to see the horses. It will do him good. It may even do me good. Doctor Unger has been hounding me to try this new man in town." His hands fluttered in his lap, and then he closed his eyes.

Thinking his grandfather had slipped into sleep, Farren rose to take his leave.

"I would like you to get to know Geoff." Startled, Farren turned back to the old man. "To love him as I do." He coughed and then rubbed his eyes. "We will leave the estates for the present and work on the town end of things. Have you thought of taking a bride?"

Whoa! He reckoned Grandpa was tenacious as well.

Well, he was nearing his thirty-fifth birthday. He did want a family of his own. A wife and children who loved him. He was ready. So tired of war in his country, and in his family. Perhaps by marrying an English girl he could begin to mend this heartbroken family.

A flawless, ivory complexion framed by a cloud of copper hair and studded with ruby lips and amethyst eyes suddenly swamped his brain. Nora St. James.

A painful flare of hope leapt in his breast. "Yes. Yes, sir, I would like to marry.

Chapter Seven

What!?

This must be the wrong address. Once again Nora lifted her veil in order to read the direction still clutched in her hand. Number 14 Hart Street. She retraced her steps back to the front door. Yes, that was the number above the doorway. Thomas had been correct.

But it couldn't be. Hancock had said he had a buyer—a single buyer for the portrait. A full-blown auction was in process. Rows of chairs filled with gentlemen, and a few ladies, their paddles raised, shouting out bids.

A podium stood on a dais at the front. Various paintings—not hers—were displayed in a semicircle, flanking one central painting which stood on an ornate brass easel, shrouded beneath a damask drape. A burly bruiser hovered just to its right, putting the kibosh on any buyer wanting a preview. The *pièce de résistance.*

Her?

The auctioneer turned from examining the next painting up for bids to take his place behind the podium.

Bloody Hell.

Lucius Hancock.

Hancock had come by way of Mr. Bartholomew. The old solicitor had a client, an avid art collector, and he had recommended Mr. Hancock as a reputable art dealer.

"I know of the marquess' landscapes," Hancock had said when she met with him to discuss the sale. "They are quite sought after. But his earlier portraits, while less innovative, are still highly prized. And, a beautiful woman, if you do not mind my saying, will always fetch a ripe sum." Hancock smiled a wolfish grin. "However, they must be marketed with an air of mystery."

She had wanted to sell them all at once, get it over and done with. But the dealer derailed her idea. "We must build up expectation, my dear Lady Havermere. Give the art world but a taste, and they will clamor for more. Flood their palates and they will be sick with too much richness."

"Well, I leave that to your discretion, sir. But the less notoriety, the better. I am assuming you know how this is best accomplished."

"Of course, discretion will be my watchword, dear lady."

Discretion, my eye.

She waved, trying to get Hancock's attention, but there was no hope of him seeing her with every other fellow raising their hand. Besides, the art dealer was in the throes of power. The power men often felt when they were the center of attention. He wielded his gavel like a scepter, reveling in his tiny kingdom.

Hancock had told her to meet him here as he had a prospective buyer. If the man approved of the painting, he would write out a check then and there. But he did want to meet the subject of the portrait first.

Hancock was directing his assistant to bring

forward the next painting, a landscape featuring a band of gypsies. The women appeared to be bare-chested, dancing around a fire. In short order, the work went to a sober-looking man with a monocle. His lady, in an over-decorated gown, draped herself over his arm as if, given the chance, he might escape.

Perhaps she could pass Hancock a note. She would simply ask Thomas to leave the carriage and deliver it for her.

Drat it; she had no pen. She spied a door to her left and slipped into the room hoping it might be some sort of office.

Strange primitive looking masks, erotic sculptures, paintings with garish colors depicting—she was not sure what—crowded the narrow room. A holding room. However, one that did not seem to have one inkwell or pen.

By the time she got back into the main room, the still-shrouded painting was front and center.

Hancock's gaze locked on her.

Oh, dear God. She crushed the paper in her hand.

He could not be gesturing for her to come forward? She shook her head minutely. This was all wrong. But it was too late, all eyes turned to her. Never was she so glad of the protection of her heavy veil.

Settle. Perhaps she was being a ninny. After all, this painting was simply one of the five modest portraits she had selected—merely of her face, nothing salacious. Plenty of ladies had sold their likenesses for a good cause.

Hancock signaled to the hulk guarding the painting to step closer and then left the dais, weaving his way steadily toward her.

"What is going on here?" she hissed in his ear.

"Why, the auction, my dear lady." He smiled benignly.

"Auction? I don't understand. We were to have a private meeting."

Hancock at least had the decency to look slightly contrite, but only slightly. "Once I saw the painting, my lady, well, I thought it advantageous to expand our original plan."

"But is all this really necessary?" She cast her gaze over the patrons.

"It is if you want the best price for your charity girls, Lady Havermere." The young man had the cheek to look almost affronted.

And so, it had come to this. Being on display for all the world to see. The private life she had shared with Devlin, her one bit of happiness, soon to be flaunted before anyone who wished a gander. And some old reprobate would go home with a piece of her to hang on the wall of his hunting lodge. Just another trophy, betwixt a stag's head and a wild boar.

The image of Colonel Cavanaugh rose to fill her brain.

Heat swept over her chest and neck. She shook herself as if by doing so she might rid her body of the hot shame.

Devlin had offered her an outright loan many times, but, even in dire straits, she could not take his money. At least the portraits were something she had partially earned.

Earned. Nora winced at the word and resisted the urge to dig her fingers into her aching scalp. Oh, how she longed to be back in the muddy yard chasing churlish chickens instead of pimping herself for these gawkers.

As Hancock retraced his steps back to the dais, he stopped to whisper to a man on the end of a row and then laughed just a bit too loud. Vulgar and overreaching. But there was no going back.

Which one had he chosen? It was of no consequence, really. Eventually all five would have to go.

Besides, this painting was not her. Not anymore. It was only oil and pigment and a bit of varnish.

Not me. She retreated to the back of the room ready to depart. *Not me.*

A burble of voices ratcheted up several degrees and then hushed as the hammer cracked against the top of the podium.

"And now, we come to the final piece." Hancock's fingers teased the bottom edge of the drape covering the painting. "A never-before-seen work of one of London's most celebrated beauties by James Drake, a man famous for his appreciation of the feminine form."

Her teeth met and ground, making her head pound all the more.

"I'll give you two hundred pounds sight unseen!" A stout man in a checked suit called out.

"Two fifty!" Another man stood up, hand in the air.

Hancock grinned. Unsettled, Nora retreated into the doorway of the storeroom. No holding back the tide now.

Most everyone was on their feet, shouting bids. Hancock's assistant furiously scratched down the numbers on paddles. The painting still lay shrouded behind its drape.

At every increment Nora's heart raced faster. Overjoyed for her girls and the dream home she now might afford, but horrified for herself, that her person could provoke such a tawdry bidding war.

"I have six hundred and seventy-five guineas from Sir Dumfry here."

"Seven hundred and seventy-five." A new voice, surprisingly calm, cut through the tense room.

Nora looked up. Sir Dumfry, turned to confront the man who would dare to enter the bidding just when he could smell victory. Nora's gaze followed.

The crowd peeled back to reveal a small, rather nondescript balding man who seemed to have just entered the room. He moved toward the dais, as if he had all the time in the world and faced his adversary.

Sir Dumfry puffed out his huge chest and jabbed his paddle in the air like a knight wielding his broadsword. "Seven hundred and eighty!"

Hancock mopped his brow, his eyes darting between the men.

"One thousand." The new bidder did not even deign to raise his paddle.

Nora's gasp echoed through the crowd.

"One thou—? Why, that ain't fair!" The beet-faced man sputtered and looked about him for support. "He don't even have a number!"

"Sir," Hancock chimed in. "Do you have a paddle?"

The throng buzzed, wanting a showdown.

A man standing next to the bidder shrugged and laughed and then handed his paddle over. The bald man merely nodded and seemed to accept it as a matter of course.

Hancock's fingers tapped the podium as his lips silently moved, no doubt tallying up his commission.

"Hey, now Gillingham, you can't just hand over your paddle! That ain't fair!" Sir Dumfry roared.

Oscar Gillingham? What was he doing here? The man didn't have a pot to piss in, much less blunt to buy a painting. Just like Gillingham to add fuel to the fire.

"Going once. Going twice." Hancock gestured with his gavel to the knight, who shook his huge head in fury. Throwing his paddle down, he pushed patrons and chairs aside and quit the room.

"Gone!" Hancock's voice rang out.

Gone. Such a sum for one painting? At this rate, she might not even have to sell another.

The winner of the painting, in contrast to the bullish Sir Dumfry, carefully moved aside a chair to make his way up to the easel.

"No, no, Mr. Hancock." He stopped the agent from removing the cover. "I have no need to see the work. It will be revealed in good time."

The onlookers surged toward the front of the room.

"But sir, surely—" Hancock obviously saw the makings of a riot.

"You cannot mean to take it away without allowing us a view?" An irate Frenchman rapped his cane on the floor.

"Yes, it is only fair to let us see what we missed!" another man shouted.

But the winning bidder held fast. He passed a bag of coins to the bruiser who hefted the purse and then nodded, stepping in front of the painting, his beefy arms spread wide. There would be a brawl soon. Something she could not afford. If she could only make it to the storage room ….

"Gentlemen!" Hancock said, over the roar. "We are fortunate to have the original in our midst. Let us hear from the countess herself."

Nora froze.

The men's gazes seemed to pin her to the wall and then settle on her as if they were groping hands.

Hancock had made his way to the back of the room where he snagged her arm.

The urge to jerk out of his grasp and slap his face had her twitching, but she would not give this rabble the satisfaction of seeing such a display. The patrons parted as she allowed Hancock to usher her up onto the dais. Those closest to the painting pulled back but only enough so as to be able to take all of her into view. The possibility of seeing the Countess of Havermere in person as well as on canvas kept them like vultures over a bit of flesh.

Nora wanted to sink into the floor. But instead, she lifted her veil, smiled and stood straighter. "Thank you all for coming."

Hancock preened. Damn his hide.

Nora turned to the bald man. "Sir, congratulations. I thank you for your contribution to my charity. I hope you will not be disappointed."

"Oh, I am certain the painting will give my employer hours of pleasure."

Hancock stepped between them and addressed the crowd in general. "This work is one of many. Mark your calendars, the next will go up for bids a week from today."

Dear God, she wanted a bath; these men made her feel so dirty. She gave Hancock a freezing look and then calmly waited for the crowd to part. When they did so, she made her way toward her escape. Let them look or no. She would no longer be a part of his side show.

A collective gasp stopped her dead. Some over-eager puppy must have penetrated the henchman's parameter. It took everything in her not to turn back. It would only feed the frenzy. *Damn Hancock.*

Thomas would be waiting with the carriage. And Hancock could be dealt with later. Just as escape was within reach, she felt a prickling in her shoulders.

"Countess?"

Blistering Hell and Hades! She turned toward the direction of an American accent. Colonel Farren Cavanaugh stood before her.

"We meet again." She caught the flash of his dimple just before he made his bow to her.

"Ah, Lady Havermere. A pleasure." Oscar Gillingham joined them. He bent over her hand. "You must forgive us for pushing in. I heard of the auction today. The colonel and I were set to go to Tattersalls, but I lured him here instead." Gillingham bowed. "Ah, excuse me. I see a—friend." He made his way toward Leticia Denby, who was certainly not here to buy a painting. More likely trolling for a new protector.

Bloody Hell! If Hancock were nearby, she would wring his skinny neck.

"Who told you of this event?" she asked without preamble.

"A note came for Gillingham, and he seemed in a tear to get over here, so I tagged along. He didn't say who sent it."

She had not paid much attention to who was bidding, just focusing on getting through this debacle, but now she found herself asking, "And did you bid?"

He shook his head.

"Ah, perhaps Mr. Gillingham has fleeced you of all your funds?" she probed when she should have let it go.

He quirked his mouth. Even an American knew it was not polite to talk of money or the lack of it.

"If you'll excuse me, Colonel Cavanaugh, I believe I must sign some papers—"

"Lady Havermere!"

Dear God, that rolling baritone could only belong to the Marchioness of Gadwick.

Nora's teeth met and ground.

Dressed in stiff bombazine, the lady lifted the edge of a heavy veil. "I am seriously displeased," the marchioness hissed, and then produced a quizzing glass.

"Lady Gadwick, may I make introductions?" Nora said, trying to defray some of the hideousness of the encounter.

The lady raised her glass as if it were a weapon and gave the colonel a thorough going over. "Is this man a gentleman?"

Nora pressed on, ignoring the glowering lady. "Lady Gadwick, may I present Colonel Cavanaugh, lately from America."

The Colonel bowed over her ladyship's hand.

"A colonel?" She raised her glass once again. "I collect you were involved in your country's Civil War?"

"I was, your ladyship."

Nora could not see this thread of conversation going well. Millicent Gadwick disapproved of any sort of rebellion. "Lady Gadwick is considering supporting my charity work. I cannot tell you what a difference your contribution would make to these young women." *How in heaven's name had she found out about this auction?*

"It is well I came when I did. I cannot countenance these—shows, Lady Havermere."

"Shows?"

"This circus." She adjusted her veil while gesturing to the men still jousting to see the painting. "I will not have my good name associated with debauchery."

"I am sorry you feel that way. As you know James Drake is an accomplished artist who has contributed his paintings to the Queen's pet charities. I only thought to do the same."

"My dear Lady Havermere, have you actually seen this painting?" Her ladyship waved her quizzing glass in the general direction of the dais.

To placate the woman, Nora glanced toward the dais. A narrow window in the curtain of men allowed her to glimpse a bunch of grapes.

Grapes? What? Noooo! She took a step, holding out her hands as if she could possibly reach the thirty feet it would take to rip it off the easel.

Grapes?

Her mind frantically shuffled through the canvases. *No grapes.*

Dear Lucifer, there must have been another painting hidden in the straw. Marigold had run in with news of her precious egg and Nora had hastened to see. Later she had simply rolled the *for sale* canvases together and tossed them back in the box. Thomas had then delivered them to Hancock.

The window of men closed, and Nora was spared

seeing any more of herself.

How bad was it?

Her heart hammered against her constricted throat. "A mistake," she rasped. Her scalp tingled as blood surged to flood her entire head. "That particular work was never meant to be sold."

"I should say not. To my mind it should never have been painted." The marchioness sniffed derisively. "I realize it was *my* mistake to think to ally myself with your ... good works." Lady Gadwick puffed out her chest like an irate hen.

"But, Lady Gadwick—"

"It is well I heeded the missive I received just this morning, else I would have been caught unawares. Our connection has ended, Lady Havermere. I bid you good day."

"Lady Gadwick, I trust we can resolve any—"

"Pardon, Colonel Cavanaugh." Her ladyship turned her back to him and faced Nora square on. "There will be no further discussion of the matter," she whispered. "I cannot take the chance of a potential scandal. As you are well aware, Caroline has already weathered a considerable tempest. She cannot sustain another. I must withdraw my support." Her ladyship snapped her quizzing glass closed and turned away but stopped and addressed Nora once again. "I sympathize. You are between a rock and a hard place, Lady Havermere. You can either go by the straight and narrow, towing the line of the *ton,* or you can be lost to society and live on its fringes." She gestured to Leticia Denby who lurked on the edge of a group of men, like some runt looking for scraps. The marchioness shook her head. "I have a daughter to think of and therefore no choice in the matter. Good day."

Nora could not blame Lady Gadwick. Had Nora a daughter to launch, she might very well do the same. But she had no offspring. No husband. No family. Was she prepared to give up the only world she had known? To perhaps sell all the paintings and dive in the murky waters outside good society? Would the money last? Or would she end up like Lady Denby, who was now smiling thinly at a stout man with a huge set of whiskers?

No, Nora was not that brave, or foolish. Lady Gadwick was right. Her title was her anchor. Without it she would drift who knows where. A woman would need a huge amount of money to cut all ties with society while supporting a large house full of needy girls. Only last season Libbet Foster had flung caution to the wind and was now some merchant's mistress, utterly dependent on him for everything. And, by the looks of it, Leticia Denby would soon follow in Libbet's footsteps.

Charlotte. How would this affect the girl and her presentation? Oh, what a terrible tangle. Would nothing go right?

"Colonel, I am sorry you were privy to this conversation." Nora fiddled with a loose bit of lace at her sleeve.

"Is her support so crucial to your plan?"

Remembering the painting's winning bid, she shook her head. "No, I suppose not."

But at what cost? What had she forfeited?

The crowd of men was dispersing now. Hancock had managed to re-cover the portrait. Her lips felt dry as chalk. "I must ask, did you see the painting?"

"I did."

"And was I…"

"You were. Well, near enough. An artfully draped shawl—"

The painting assembled painfully in her mind. "And well-placed bowl of fruit?"

He nodded. "A pineapple surrounded by purple and red—grapes, plums, strawberries and such. And one lone exotic banana—very strategically placed."

"Ah." The picture now fully formed in her mind. Dev setting up the fruits and admonishing her for eating them. As a finishing touch, he'd painted her with a plump strawberry between her lips.

The room seemed infinitely smaller. She couldn't get a proper breath. "I should have taken care in choosing a more discreet dealer. Lucius Hancock is only interested in making a sensation. I see that now."

"This fellow's employer." He nodded to the bald man. "Seems to want to keep the painting private. And it was re-covered right quick. I would guess only a few got a real eyeful."

It might as well have been a thousand.

"Are you all right?" He touched her arm.

She sifted through his words and the cast of his features to ferret out any shred of pity. That she could not stand. But she found none in his eyes or tone. She shifted her gaze away.

"May I at least escort you to your carriage?" He held out his arm to her.

Only then did she realize how shaken she was. She took it gratefully. His muscles strained and bunched beneath her gloved hand. So strong. His arms could hold her up with no effort should she choose to become a watering pot.

"You wondered why I didn't bid," he said as he guided her to the entry.

She shrugged and fussed with the lace of her veil, wishing only to have his arms surrounding her, cocooned within his strength, his warmth.

"I didn't bid because I am holding out for the original."

She jerked her gaze to meet his, all thoughts of him providing comfort gone. "The original? I assure you, sir, that painting is certainly an original. I would not hock a forgery."

"I was not referring to the painting, Countess." He said *Countess* softly as if he were somehow testing it, as if it were a made-up name and didn't really belong to her.

Every other man would have slid his gaze over her body, but he kept his beautiful green eyes focused on her own, as if he could see through her veil into her very soul.

Her carriage stood at the curb, Thomas looking rather pugilistic as he waited to assist her. But one look at the colonel seemed to make him stand down.

Farren Cavanaugh opened the door, set the step, and handed her up into safety.

"I reckon fate has something in store for us. Until we meet again, Nora St. James."

Chapter Eight

Number Twenty-eight.

Farren read the house number.

A very run-of-the–mill, middle class house, steps neatly swept, windows sparkling, a tattered-looking ivy creeping up the brick façade. Nothing that might indicate a young girl had been butchered here four years ago. At least that was what old Jeb at the Fig and Clove told Farren in the wee hours of this morning.

Farren knocked. The door opened. A tiny sprite of a girl, about five years old he'd guess, stood before him.

"Hullo," she said, exposing missing front teeth. "Are you my prince?"

He'd just bent down to her level when an older girl swept in and pulled the youngster behind her skirts.

"Marigold, you've been told a hundred times you are not to answer the door. Go. Now." When the older girl turned to shoo the youngster away Farren saw her ear was nearly gone. A twisted, heavy scar ran from her ear hole into the neck of her gown.

Young Marigold raised her pert nose and walked away regal as a queen, or would have, if she didn't have a club foot. The older girl—her sister?—turned back to him with the precision of a hard-trained infantry soldier, exposing the other side of her face, perfect peaches and cream.

"May I help you, sir?" The gal looked him up and down. If he didn't know better, he'd have thought he'd forgotten to put on his trousers. He stood straighter in his boots.

"I would like to speak with your … er … father, Miss."

She thrust her chin up even higher in order to look down her nose at him. "Humph, I'd like to have a word or two with him as well, but that ain't likely to happen." She turned and gave him her scarred side.

Not a daughter. A sassy maid, perhaps? "Then the master of the house?"

She shook her head. Now a game for the girl, she awaited his next guess. When he didn't ante up, she rolled her eyes and started to close the door.

He shoved his foot into the doorway. "Then the marquess? Does Lord Devlin still own the house?"

Finally, he struck gold. The pressure of the door eased against his boot. She frowned and seemed unsure of her next move. "No, Lord Devlin ain't here. Just the mistress."

"May I speak with her, then?" He gave the girl his best smile.

She looked him over again. Thank goodness he had polished his boots and run a comb through his hair.

"Who should I say is calling?"

"Colonel Cavanaugh. She will not know me, but I am here to inquire about a former resident of this house."

He must have passed muster because she stepped aside and gestured for him to enter.

"Wait in here." She opened a door to a small

parlor. "I won't bother with a fire. You won't be staying long, and the mistress don't like to waste good coal."

Warm and fuzzy she was not. If this little soldier was any indication of her general, he should prepare himself for a skirmish.

Baskets of needlework were stacked neatly in one corner. Another corner held a box of slates and chalk. The only real ornament in the room was a huge bowl full of flowers—peonies? His ma had banks of them outside in the back garden at Hayland Farm. *They don't like to be moved,* he remembered her saying. *But once they take hold, they are there for life.*

"I suppose it was too much to hope there are two American colonels with the surname Cavanaugh."

He whirled around.

He'd taken a ball in a little skirmish in Tullahoma, Tennessee. Saw it coming. The rebel raising his rifle, sighting, and pulling the trigger. Farren, caught flat-footed, his boots mired in thick mud, had managed to turn and take the ball in his right shoulder. The Countess of Havermere felt like that ball, though he never saw her coming.

She was rather plainly dressed today, her hair scraped into a bun, a shawl wrapped around her shoulders. It made no difference. She might as well have been in a frothy negligee.

"Opal, you may go now. See to some tea for our guest."

He recovered himself. "No, don't bother yourself, Miss Opal. I haven't acquired a taste for tea. I thank you all the same."

Opal snorted.

"I am afraid we do not keep coffee or ale."

"Should I seal up the letter to that Hancock fellow?" Opal asked.

"Yes, send Thomas with it. Thank you, Opal. That will be all."

The girl closed the door behind her.

The image of her portrait once again crowded his mind as it had over and over since the auction. The painting had shocked him. Not her body—though it had been exquisite. It was her face, no, her eyes that had seared into his brain. He didn't know a damn thing about art, but the painter, this James Drake, had captured her so essentially. Looking into those eyes, only for those brief moments, he felt as if he knew this woman. Drake had exposed some tender inner part of her.

Jealousy flared hot and heavy in his breast, leaching into his belly and then his groin, pulling his balls taut with a kind of rage. Drake had known her that well, seen her that clearly.

He shook his head minutely. Ridiculous to be so enraged over a portrait of a woman he barely knew.

"I'm sorry, Countess. You have me at a loss. First, I meet you in a bawdy house, then a mansion in Mayfair, next a private auction, and now what seems to be a charity home? What is this place? And why are you here?"

"I might ask the same of you, Colonel. Why are *you* here?"

"Pardon, I reckon I did not expect—"

"No, I imagine you didn't." She pulled her shawl more tightly about her. "What can I do for you, Colonel?"

"Well, I suppose I am here on a wild goose chase. I was hoping to find out about the former owner of this house, a marquess, Lord Devlin."

The countess remained mute.

He pressed on. "There was a murder here a little over four years ago—September of sixty-two a young girl. Her name was Lily."

Her ladyship turned and then seemed to find something of interest on the ceiling. She took several steps. He thought she might actually leave the room. Instead, she moved to a bookshelf. She took down a rather ugly pot and removed a bottle from inside. "I believe I will indulge. Colonel, will you join me?"

He'd struck a nerve. "Yes, I reckon I will."

She found glasses and poured out a neat two fingers. Her hand shook ever so slightly as she handed him his drink.

By God, not a wild goose chase. Mrs. St. James, Countess of Havermere, Charity Benefactress, knew something of Lily's death.

"Before I begin—if I begin—I need to know why you are interested in this girl, Lily. Who is she to you?"

"I have reason to believe she is—was—my brother's daughter."

The countess tipped her brandy back, finishing it in one toss, and then fingered the bottle. "I see."

"I don't reckon you do. It's complicated. My brother, Brendan, came to England a little more than fifteen years ago. He was here to meet our paternal grandfather and to make amends with the family here. He was not successful. However, he did meet one Iris Darvan and apparently created his own little family."

"Why is your brother not here to enquire after

Lily?"

"He is missing." The words came out in a rush. "Some believe him to be dead. He never returned from our American Civil War."

"Oh, I am sorry." Her hands hung by her sides, a frown fixed on her face, looking as if she had dropped some treasure and was at a loss as to where it might be.

"Well, it's not conclusive. The war was brutal." He did not wish to elaborate. "We never recovered his body. It was odd no one saw him fall."

"And what leads you to believe the Lily who died in this house was your brother's daughter?"

"Her mother, Iris Darvan, wrote very specifically about events and even described the babe's coloring— blonde with green eyes and one dimple. Cavanaugh coloring. I believe she wanted to prove my brother was the father. And the age is right as well. When Brendan came back from England, he mentioned he had a fairly long dalliance with a woman he'd met there. I have been making inquiries. The address on the letter was Miss Darvan's last address, a house in the Seven Dials on Cuddle Lane."

Four years of his nation's Civil War had not prepared him for the kind of degradation he'd found in London's underbelly. This was a different kind of war. Filthy children, their bare feet running with sores, their shriveled bodies huddled in alleyways, tearing at each other over a scrap of bread. But far worse were the poor mites who had given up. Their dead eyes glazed over with hopelessness, empty bottles of gin cradled to their shrunken bellies.

"Miss Darvan wrote my brother when she discovered she was with child and on several other occasions after she delivered. The last letter begged Brendan to come and take them away from London."

"Poor woman."

"There were no more letters after that. Mrs. Eunice Lockhart at 13 Cuddle Lane told me Iris Darvan disappeared eight years ago. And is likely dead. And that her daughter, Lily, had supposedly been murdered at the hands of the Mad Marquess."

The countess winced at the name. She seemed on the point of tossing him out but then sighed and closed her eyes. "Devlin found Lily on the streets, very near Cuddle Lane."

"Lord Devlin? The Marquess of Devlin?"

The countess nodded. "Lily never solicited him, but he always gave her a coin and sent her off. Then it became impossible to ignore her, so he brought her here."

"How did you become involved?"

Nora St. James turned away, took a deep breath and faced him again. "Lord Devlin was my lover. I used to come here to this house to be with him."

Another piece of the puzzle slid into place. Devlin and the painter James Drake must be one and the same. He shouldn't have been surprised. Women had affairs all the time. Still, his gut twisted to think of her in another man's arms. Downright crazy to be possessive of a woman he hardly knew.

"Lily said she was fourteen when she came to us. But she was lying. Even with malnutrition there was no way she could be more than twelve." She smiled a frozen smile. "I had—have—no children of my own."

"I'm sure she was right lucky to have you."

Nora St. James looked at him as if suddenly

realizing he was still in the room. "Lucky? No, it was far too late for Lily to be lucky. But I would have given much to have had the time to mend her, just a little."

Brandy felt sharp and biting on his tongue as he took a fortifying sip. "I am sorry to probe into such sad memories, but I must know for my peace of mind—for my family's peace, what happened to Lily." *And why you are living here now.*

"She stayed with us for almost three months. She would disappear now and again. The first time I nearly went to pieces. But it was useless to lock her in. Slippery as an eel, my Lily. She always came back, though. Never said where she had been or what she had done. I never asked. Too frightened of what she might say, I suppose." She laughed ruefully. "Then she stopped leaving. And I began to hope."

He waited, wanting her to go on.

A far-off look came into her eyes. "But she had just given up. Whatever she was seeking out there was gone, and with it went her will to live. Then ..." She squeezed her hands together, gripping her fingers and slowly shook her head as if she wanted to rid herself of her thoughts. "It was too soon, you see. I couldn't stop it. She was so very small ..." Her mouth opened as if in a silent scream.

Farren set his brandy down and stepped toward her, but the countess seemed unaware of him.

"I didn't know what to do." Her chin trembled, and she clamped her teeth shut.

"Lady Havermere ... Countess ...?" He took another step unsure how to ease her pain.

But she shook her head and drifted away. She sank into a chair as if she were one of those hot-air balloons whose fire had gone out. "Lily was perfectly well in the morning. We had just finished Mr. Dickens' last installment of *Our Mutual Friend*. Smart as a whip she was. Took to reading and writing like a cat to his cream."

She took a deep breath. "Lily came to me—I'll never forget her face—so grave, so resigned." She looked up at him then, her eyes pained. "Her gown was soaked with blood. So much blood. I thought she must have cut herself somehow. 'What have you done?' I asked. But I knew."

Farren knelt at her feet and took her cold and shaking hands between his. *Please God, don't let it be what I am thinking. Please, no.* Yet he knew as sure as Nora St. James had known. Lily had been with child.

"I carried her upstairs. She never cried out, bless her. So brave, my Lily." The countess's fingers gripped his—her tale its own kind of birth.

"Hot water, towels, brandy. This I knew, but the rest—God, I was so utterly useless." She sniffed and blinked. "Then the screams. Mine. I screamed for her because she did not. I screamed for her not to give up.

"Devlin finally came. He was foxed, damn him, but he did everything he could. He took over and gave me my orders. Salt, silk thread, his razor, more brandy."

"The marquess?"

She nodded. "Dev could have been a surgeon. Studied anatomy for years, even assisted in surgeries."

She shook her head again, her teeth grinding, her knuckles white with strain. "But he couldn't save her.

"I saw her go. I swear she almost smiled—I'd never seen her smile, not once since she had been with us. She looked at me with … forgiveness. In her death, she forgave me."

Now her hands lay limp and slightly curled in his, like two white seashells against dusky sand. She sighed.

"The babe was a little girl. So impossibly tiny. And like her mother, she never cried. She breathed for only a moment—a fragile little bird all wet and bloody, but so perfect, so incredibly, perfectly, beautiful ..."

A clock somewhere in the house bonged, and her hands fluttered in his. He did not know how long they had been there, her, perched on her chair, and him, at her feet, their hands cradled together, bonded over their mutual grief. So much death and pain. He craved comfort. Her comfort. And to comfort her. To ease some of the terrible pain in this world.

"You must forgive me. I am sure you did not imagine you would be subjected to such drama when you knocked upon my door this afternoon."

He handed her his handkerchief, though he realized she was not crying. Still, he wanted to give her something. She ducked her head, likely for some privacy to collect herself. She did not like displaying her emotions. He rocked back on his heels. After testing his cramped legs, he stood and then drifted to the window, welcoming the cold that seeped through.

Obviously, he had known Lily was dead, but hearing the way she had died—and her child, yet another loss—made him want to howl.

By God, if Brendan was alive, he had much to answer for.

He studied her reflection in the window glass. Finally, she stood, her face rigid with restrained grief. He turned to her as she folded his handkerchief and put it in her pocket. "I see now why you have been haunting the brothels seeking a young, blonde girl. Well, I am sorry your search has to end this way."

He had met the do-gooder, Mrs. St. James, and then the Countess of Havermere, and now Nora, just Nora, in a modest house in Cheapside. Never had she looked more beautiful.

Never had he wanted a woman more. To give her some comfort, to give her some joy.

He turned to face her. "But my search isn't over. Lily had a sister.

"A sister?"

"Her twin, Rose."

Chapter Nine

A twin?

Nora shook her head as if the word would shuffle into sense.

Lily had a sister? Was Rose the reason Lily kept leaving the house? To find her twin?

Oh, why had she never asked for their help? Why had she not trusted them? But Nora would never know now. It was all too late.

But no—!

"My God, I have seen her!" The girl in Covent Garden with the white-blonde hair. The girl that had haunted Nora ever since she'd spied her months ago.

"What? Seen her? Where?" The colonel stepped toward her, his hands fisted by his sides.

"Covent Garden. I thought I was losing my mind. That Lily had not died. But it was Rose. It has to be Rose!"

They were out the door and found a hired carriage in a matter of minutes. But that was the only thing that went smoothly. Traffic was a quagmire. They might as well have walked from Cheapside.

Inside the confines of the carriage, neither spoke. He must have a million questions, but he seemed to know she could not answer him now. Not when hope hung so palpable within the small space. It fairly buzzed between them.

Finally, nearing Wellington Street, she could no longer stand the inertia as an overloaded omnibus pulled out, blocking the entire intersection. The inept driver could not back up or go forward.

"Blast it! Let us walk the rest of the way," she said, already knocking on the cab's roof.

As they approached the market square, barrow men and flower sellers clogged the alleyway. The colonel, who was quite large, acted like a battering ram while Nora huddled behind his wide shoulders. They finally gained the open square, but the crowds did not dissipate.

He reached back to take her hand. His enveloped hers so thoroughly, making her feel small and protected. Silly to let a touch, given solely out of necessity, stir her so. She would have pulled out of his grasp if she could be certain she would not lose him in the masses pressing in on them.

"Let's make for the arcade. I can step up on one of the pillars to get a better view."

Nora simply nodded and held his hand more tightly.

Costermongers called out, "Two for a pence." Flower sellers waved watercress and violets at the colonel, hoping he might buy a bunch. Children darted between them and scampered under carts to escape irate barrow men, stolen apples in hand. None had white-blonde hair. But four years had passed. Years during which a girl would develop into a woman. What would Lily—no, Rose—look like now? The girl Nora had seen must be about fifteen or sixteen? Or younger, perhaps? Lily had frozen in Nora's mind at the age of twelve. Doubt crept over her heart, squeezing out fragile hope.

"Sod off, ya pecker!" A boy crashed into them and the colonel's hand slipped out of hers.

Like a piece of flotsam in a swift moving stream, she was carried away from him, her huge crinoline skirt whipping one way and then another with each brush of humanity. Just as she thought she would drown, she was bodily swept off her feet.

"Oh!"

"Confound it, woman, do you want to be trampled?"

His mouth loomed just over hers. He had very white teeth and his lashes, thick, stubby, and dark, spiked into neat points. She had the sudden urge to brush her finger over them, wondering if they would feel as marvelous as they looked. Her body pressed against his, he smelled of wool and leather and … mint.

A path opened for them as the crowd seemed to sense this man's urgency and downright dominance. Indeed, he strode through the crowd as if he were a king. Too soon, he set her down against a wall near the fancy fruit. Strawberries perfumed the air, drifting over the heavier smells of boiled cabbage and fish.

"Of course I do not wish to be trampled." She could not seem to get enough air in her lungs. "I am not a nincompoop, Colonel."

"No, I'm sorry."

Good heavens, did he need to stare at her that way? She batted at her infernal skirt as if it were some pest.

"It's not you, Countess, just this dad burned crowd. Can't see a dam—dang thing."

Likely he couldn't because the *dratted* man was

still staring at her. "If you help me up on this barrel, I can get a good view," she said, wanting to be away from his heat.

"Can you manage up there?"

She did not deign to answer. As a girl she'd had to balance three books on her head whilst walking on a two-inch beam. She lifted her skirts, but his hands had already spanned her waist and he hoisted her up. Between his carrying her and now this, she'd not been so man handled—well, not since Devlin.

"What do you see?"

Heavens, she was not here to imagine Farren Cavanaugh's hands upon her but to look for Lily—

Rose. A fifteen or sixteen-year-old Rose.

The masses swirled and eddied around wagons and carts, but Nora saw no bright blonde head among them. She shifted on the barrel and felt the colonel's hand brush her waist. Only seeking to steady her, she reminded herself.

"Anything?" He looked up at her, hope reflected in his eyes.

"Many of the women are wearing caps, but the girl I have seen never wears one. Perhaps she is a little vain." Or perhaps she knows her lovely hair is an asset for trade …

Nora did not want to imagine Rose being used like her poor sister.

Drovers whistled to each other as hawkers called out their wares. "Hot pies, oh boy!" "Fresh peas, lovely as you please!"

Kerchiefs, bowler and stovepipe hats, newsboy caps, dark hair, ginger heads, an occasional lady's hat lilting with feathers all bobbed and weaved below her, but no bright blonde girl.

"Come on down. It is getting late and by the looks of some of these fellows they'd like to be on you like rust on a pump handle," the colonel said, giving a stevedore lingering nearby a stare that would have curdled milk. Once again, his hands wrapped around her waist as he pulled her down.

An explosion sounded in her ear. Her cheek felt hot and stinging. Screams rent the air as the crowd surged away. A barrow cart toppled, its produce scattering over the cobble stones.

Then all she felt was the wall behind her and the colonel's chest pressed up against her face.

Her smashed crinoline twisted and flipped, protesting such nearness.

"Hell and damnation," he ground out.

She felt his hands beneath her skirt. "What the devil—!"

His fingers found the tape of her crinoline and jerked it. The cage of whale bone and netting dropped to the stones.

"Come on." He scooped it up while taking her hand and then pulled her along the wall toward the nearest exit.

Hoisting her skirt, she felt the freedom of not having to contend with the huge bell shape.

He hailed a cab and thrust her inside. Only when they were moving did he take her face in his hands.

Dear heavens, was he going to kiss her?

She felt herself lean in, her eyes closing. *Yes! She would take this kiss.*

Only when she felt the dab of soft cloth against her cheeks did she open her eyes.

Hot shame flooded her stinging cheeks. *Not a kiss.* Only him tending to her. She hissed out of pain as well as embarrassment. The cloth came away dotted with blood.

"Shards from the wall behind you. I think that's all." His hands skated over her arms. "Do you feel any other hurt?"

She shook her head.

"Do you have any enemies, Countess?"

"Enemies?"

"Someone just took a shot at you. Or me. I'm not entirely sure."

"I don't understand. There is no one I know who wants me dead." Surely Augusta St. James could not be that vindictive.

"Well, mayhap it was just a shot gone wild." He did not look convinced.

Gloom, not hope, now permeated the cab. Foolish to think they would find one girl in all of London so easily.

"We will find them, Countess."

"Them?" But Lily was dead. "Oh, yes, of course, your brother."

Outside their cab, the world went by as any Tuesday would. Yet, Nora's world had undergone a sea change. Yes, Lily was gone, but Rose, her sister, might still be found.

"I will hire a room on the square and set a man to watch for a towheaded blonde girl aged about fifteen."

Nora nodded and then turned to him. "Please, you will let me know if you—when you find her?"

"Yes, when we find her." He helped her down from the carriage.

She stood there awkwardly, not wanting to leave him. Only because he had given her new hope, she told herself. And because he was not a degenerate. He had visited those brothels out of necessity, trying to find his niece and his brother. But her body said otherwise. What had been an inexplicable attraction, now bloomed into something deeper. And far more dangerous.

The door to the house opened and Opal stood, waiting like an impatient spinster aunt.

"Well, thank you, Colonel." Nora turned to leave. "Oh, where might I find you if … well, if something important occurs to me?"

"I'm at the Wellington Arms, for now." He tipped his hat. "Good day, Countess."

He swung himself back into the carriage. So light and graceful for such a big man. There was a readiness in his bearing as if his body was primed for any eventuality. A loose and malleable quality as if he might spring into action like a cat.

She brushed her waist, remembering the feel of his hands there, warm and firm. His wide mouth and the cleft in his chin … The smell of him … His beautiful lashes …

"Are you going to stand out there gawking, or are you going to come in for your tea?" Opal said with her hands on her hips. "And what have you done with your crinoline?"

As Nora brushed by the girl, she thought she detected a slight smile on the girl's face.

Chapter Ten

"What are you doing here?"

Nora St. James stood outside the door of his room at the Wellington Arms, a mere fourteen hours after they'd parted.

A few hours earlier, she had visited his dreams.

How did she get past old Harrison? As modest as his digs were, the porter was as stuffy as they come.

Harebrained question. One look at the Countess of Havermere and a man had trouble breathing. One bat of her eyelashes and his brain turned to mush.

This morning, she was dressed in a deep purple gown in the military style. Perched on her head was a jaunty cap, a white ostrich feather curling over her left shoulder. Somehow the severity of her dress only made her all the more arousing.

"I'm coming with you." The feather danced around her ear, flirting with her cheek which still bore the traces of the scratches from the day before. "You need me. I know what Lil—Rose looks like."

He was torn between getting her inside his room and out of the way of possible prying eyes or keeping her outside and at a safe distance. "Countess, while I appreciate your fervor, I am going into some right seedy neighborhoods, and I am not taking you."

"Very well. I will simply follow you. Or better yet,

I will go on my own. After all, I know London better than you. I believe you said Cuddle Lane?" She turned to leave.

Best to just let her go. She wouldn't follow through, would she? "You are enough to make a preacher cuss, do you know that?" he called after her.

She stopped. "I have been told that on an occasion or two. Though I have never heard it put quite that way before." She took the few steps back to him. "I suppose you also have no interest in seeing a drawing of Rose?"

The countess looked very much like a dog robber after nabbing a fine pair of boots.

"A drawing?"

"Well, technically it is of Lily, but they are—were—identical, no?" She dug in her reticule and then held up a scroll of paper.

He reached for it.

"Not so fast, Colonel." She held the paper away while she slipped past him into his rooms. Her clean scent filled his nose. He imagined she would wear something exotic, but she smelled like powder and a vague hint of lavender. She wheeled in the middle of the room, her skirts belling out. "Do we have a deal?"

He caught sight of her ankle encased in a trim-looking boot. Which led him to remember the feel of her stockings and garters, the plush softness of her thigh, as his fingers sought to release her from her hampering crinoline just yesterday in Covent Garden.

He found himself with his boot tips just beneath her skirts. He leaned in. She raised her chin to meet his gaze. Brain to mush. *Jumping Jasper,* she smelled good enough to eat. The nicks on her cheek already healing, but a reminder of danger.

He should not take her.

But he could not deny her. She had valuable information.

He covered her hand with his and took the drawing from her. "A deal," he whispered against the lilting feather. "But first you best get rid of the dress."

"Ah, that kind of deal. Just when I had begun to think better of you."

Oh, how he wished. "I only meant that dressed in that rig should we need to hightail it out—well, that there cage you're wearing is apt to slow us up a mite. Not to mention having to pay out a small fortune in bribes to every Tom, Dick, and Harry within at least six of the Seven Dials for information when they get a gander at you in all your finery."

"Oh," she said, smoothing the front of her gown. This woman did not like being found wanting in any way. "You are right, of course. I did not think." Ridiculous disappointment shot through him now that she would not be going with him.

He was about to usher her out when she brushed past him and then disappeared into his bedchamber.

What the—?

Like some dumb animal, he followed her only to have the door firmly closed in his face. A dozen or so delicious scenarios flooded his brain, most involving the large unmade bed that dominated the room.

Dang. He'd nearly crushed the rolled-up drawing in his hand. Best put some distance between that doorknob just begging to be turned.

He moved to the window where the air was cooler and the light better.

Brendan.

This scroll of paper bore the image of Brendan's daughter—a part of him.

His last meeting with his brother had nearly ended in a brawl. He and Bren had always had a sort of feast or famine relationship. Thick as thieves one moment, at each other's throats the next. Choosing to fight for the South, and not even out of principle, but out of spite, Brendan had caused a rift in the Cavanaugh family so deep it had been impossible to bridge. Their very own civil war...

Fingers shaking, Farren unrolled the drawing.

Dear God. His heart suddenly felt too big in his chest.

He ran his finger over the white-blond hair, then her straight dark brows, high cheekbones, and too-wide lips.

Sara.

By God, this gal, Lily, and his sister could have been twins.

Farren squeezed his eyes shut, willing away those painful memories of their beloved Sprout's death. Fishing one moment and then the next—

Farren shook his head. He opened his eyes and focused once more on the paper.

Not so alike now that he looked closer. Their Sprout had always been singing and smiling, the utter joy of the Cavanaugh clan. This little gal, Lily, her mouth was tightly compressed as if she were irritated by the waste of time it took to sit for her portrait. His gaze slipped lower as his thumb traced her hands, idly pleating a fold in her skirt which lay over her belly. Looking at this drawing one could miss the slight swell. No one would guess at the terrible pain this poor girl had endured in her short life.

The artist, Lord Devlin, was very skilled. The drawing was only in pen and ink, but the coloring was all there, even to her sea-green eyes. Farren knew if she smiled a dimple would appear in her cheek. Probably the left. His was on the left, as was Bren's, and Sara's—

A *thunk* came from within his bedchamber, then a rustling and finally an "oof!"

He stood, happy to concentrate on the here and now. What *was* she doing in there? "Mayhap you need a spare hand?"

"Stay where you are!"

Farren re-rolled the picture. Two cups of coffee and three scones later she reappeared.

"Shall we go?"

The Countess of Havermere had gone into his bedchamber, but a rather too-beautiful, chubby boy had emerged. Yet another persona to add to her ever-growing number.

He rose, forgetting the crumb-laden napkin on his lap. "Well, I'll be blessed. You've missed your calling, Countess. Should have gone on the stage."

She performed an elegant bow showing a leg like a courtier of old.

Everything was huge on her. He stood six foot three and a smidge in his stockings. But somehow, she had managed to shove the extra yards of fabric—and perhaps a small pillow—into trousers which she held up with braces. Her neck swathed in a cravat, which she'd wound at least three times 'round, disguised its delicate beauty. His old slouch hat completely covered her hair, settling down over her perfect ears. As a final touch, she must have taken a lump of coal from the fireplace to stipple on a bit of a beard.

The look on the porter's face as Farren and this "lad" left the Wellington Arms was one Farren would not soon forget.

"Stay close to me." He threw his arm over her.

"I don't believe I could get away if my life depended on it. Must you drape yourself all over me? Norman is not a ponce."

"Norman?"

"Yes, gov, me name's Norman. You twig?" She sucked on her teeth and then spit.

By God, she—or he—had turned into a cheeky cockney.

"Well, Nor-*man*, you smell like a Nancy right enough. What is that perfume you're wearing?"

Farren smiled at his companion's ferocious look.

"Never you mind. It's ripe enough 'round 'ere. I'll soon blend in like a flea on a cur. Like a rat in a granary. Like pox on a—"

"Listen, Dumpling, do me a favor, don't speak. Let me do the talking."

"Right you are, guv. Mum's the word." She gave him a saucy wink. His dick twitched in response.

Eunice Lockhart's house lay at the end of a narrow alleyway. Farren had to drop behind Norman to fit through. The stench of rot and waste was thicker here, having nowhere else to go as the buildings canted over the alley with only a sliver of slate sky visible. The countess momentarily abandoned Norman's bravado to step delicately over a pile of—something.

Mrs. Lockhart was none too happy to see the likes of Farren again.

"I told you everything I know before, when you came the last time. Them girls are long gone. One was butchered up by that Devil Marquess. The papers made a big ta do over it. Of course, being a duke's son, the bloke didn't swing for it. Got carted off to a madhouse for a spell and then reemerged a few months later right as rain. Damn toffs. The other 'un, Rose, I ain't seen in over four years."

"How long did you have the girls after Iris Darvan left?" Farren asked, wanting to get a firm timeline.

"I took good care a them chits, I did. No one will tell ya different. Iris always 'ad 'er nose stuck in the air saying she were going to go to America as soon as her beau come for 'er. Daft cow believed it."

"Did you ever see her American gent?" Farren hastened to ask seeing that Norman was primed to speak.

"Naw. She wouldn't bring 'im 'round 'ere. Like her shit didn't stink." Eunice spit something viscous and brown into a pot near her feet.

"The money ran out, see. I ain't no charity. She gave me some baubles and a few dresses, enough for a year at most. I held on to them girls another seven or so months, but they drew too much attention. Too unusual they were, especially 'round 'ere. The 'Twin Angels' they were called. Blokes kept coming by to offer for 'um. Twin Angels my arse. They was different as chalk and cheese on the inside. One sweet as jam and butter on toast, the other like the dregs of this 'ere spittoon." Another shot of brown liquid hit the center of the bowl and Lockhart gave a satisfied snort. "I could a made my fortune on them if I wasn't the God-fearin' woman I am." She leaned in and lowered her voice. "The devil one, Lily, she were sharp as a knife. She got the lay of the land right enough when Lord Fancy Pants suddenly appeared. And that was it. The next day they just disappeared. Poof! Good riddance. I did my part. Ain't nothing more I could do."

"Did you know this man?"

"Naw. He looked them over and asked their age. Wanted to take them right then and there. But I'm a soft 'un, I couldn't do it. Besides, I knew he'd be back for 'em."

Likely she'd just wanted to make him squirm a bit first before she upped the price. "And did he come back?"

"Oh, yes, but they was gone. Took my silver snuff box wif um, the ungrateful brats. Shaped like a four-leaf clover it were. That's what I get for my trouble."

"Silver snuff box?" Brendan and he had been given the trinkets when they were thirteen. Bren had said he'd lost his, so he convinced Farren to risk his in a poker game. Of course, Bren had won.

"Don't you go getting yourself in a twist. Ol' Iris, she give it to me for my troubles." The woman shifted the wad of tobacco to her other cheek. "Mister Fancy Pants was fit to be tied."

"The man was a gentleman?"

She nodded. "High in the instep as they come. Wouldn't deign to sit 'is precious arse in me best chair."

Farren, who was currently sitting in said "best chair," could see, and worse smell, why the man had been so reluctant.

"Could you describe 'im?" Norman piped up, thumbs hitched in her braces rocking forward on her toes.

Lockhart narrowed her eyes, giving Norman a look that would sear bristles off a boar.

Farren jumped in, wielding his best smile. "Was he about my age?"

"Naw, he were older, with black hair and a long nose. Handsome, some would say. Me, I like 'um big and blond." She twitched her hips at him and grinned, showing a few stained teeth.

Norman snorted and spit in the pot near Lockhart's feet.

Holy hounds. If he didn't know better, he'd say Norman was jealous.

"Did you ever see the girls again when you were out and about?" Farren asked to divert Lockhart's attention back to him.

"Hard to miss one towheaded girl, but two of 'um together alike as my two eyes? Naw, word was they got snatched for one of the fancier houses. That Lily got her just desserts, if you ask me. But Rosie, she might have ended up as some Toff's doxy. Didn't you try Madam Flora's?"

Farren nodded. "And Mrs. Fletcher's establishment, and thirty or so others." He was getting a bit of a reputation even among the most jaded rakes as having an insatiable appetite. These visits, and the gossip that was beginning to flow, wouldn't help him attract a reasonable wife. And hacking around with Norman would only add fuel to the fire. Well, he would smooth that road when he came to it.

"Hmm, I would have thought with their looks, and their ma's history, they would have naturally leaned toward the life of a doxy. Possible they ended at the workhouse or one of them charity orphanages."

"Do you have a guess as to a specific establishment where we might start looking?"

The old woman looked at him narrowly. "That snuff box a mine was right dear. I reckon it were worth five quid or more. And then all my care and frettin' over them chicks …"

"Yes, of course." He peeled off a fiver. "And if your information is good, there will be more."

She snatched the bill and then stuffed it into the gaping neckline of her gown. "You might try Cripplegate. Or, Camberwell."

"If you think of anything else—if you remember the gentleman's name or any more particulars about him."

"Sure, I'll let you know. Only next time, leave yer boy at home." Eunice winked at him.

He stood. They were done here. Greed had a way of loosening lips, but once money was introduced, it often tainted the information. He'd learned that early in the army.

"Remember, we'll pay for good information, nothing else. You can find me at the Wellington Arms."

"Wellington Arms. Oooh, well, it ain't the Albany, but not so bad. You could do better than 'angin wif the likes a this cove." She jerked her head toward Norman. And then she spat again, swiped her lips with her sleeve and stuck the card between her sagging breasts. "But I never judge what gives a man his ease and pleasure."

Farren bowed and Norman snorted as they left the room.

"As if Norman would ever be interested in the likes of you," the lad muttered in cockney tones, but it was the *countess* that flounced down the stairway and into the alley, all luscious feminine ire on display.

"You'd be darned lucky to have my attentions, you half-baked pie." Farren grinned.

"*Psh*! I told ya, I like girls. Pretty girls." Norman punctuated his statement by hiking up his sagging trousers. "Not large bacon-faced oafs."

"Bacon-faced?"

They left the alleyway and entered onto the street. The air might have been marginally better out in the open but the light was just as non-existent. A storm was coming. Fast.

"Lockhart's hiding something. Didn't perk up near so much when I flashed money this time."

"Really? Her frock looked new too. Gaudy, and stained but the silk was as fine as it comes. Should we go back? Shake her down some?"

"Shake her down?"

"Very well, we'll leave her for another day. Come on, Prince Charming, let's get a move on. Cripplegate is this way, I believe. We'll go there first and then on to Camberwell." Norman ambled toward Blackjohn Lane.

"No, it's late and if I'm not wrong, we're in for a toad strangler." This infernal country dumped water down at the most inconvenient times and with great regularity. "I don't want you in these neighborhoods at night."

"But I'm invisible. I'm Norman now."

"What you are is naïve if you think your little disguise will go far."

"What will you bet I can get that girl to make eyes at me?"

Farren followed her gaze to a young red-headed

girl with a huge basket of laundry perched on her hip. "Never look at you twice. Now me, I am used to such attention from the fair sex."

"First one to get her to smile gets a pint at the next pub." Norman threw back his shoulders.

But the heavens decided to open, and the young laundress ducked into the nearest house.

Farren yanked Norman into another doorway just as lightning hit. A whap of thunder followed right on its heels.

Norman was fast turning back into Nora. Her soot beard ran as rain blew into their doorway, making her cheeks and lips glisten. Her hair escaped in curling tendrils from under her slouch hat.

"I'm thinking of one girl I wouldn't mind getting a smile from. At the very least." His arms bracketed her as protection from the elements, he told himself. "But then I am a bacon-faced oaf, and the girl I fancy might just be a lad." He leaned closer. "Which are you?" Cold rain pelted his back while his front regions were warm as toast. Some warmer than others.

Mist gathered on her lashes. His thumb, now hovering next to her ear, reached out to swipe the last bit of coal from her cheek.

"Am I addressing Norman? Or Nora?"

Thunder snapped.

She put her hands against his chest. It was uncertain if she meant to push him off or draw him nearer. He didn't want to give her an option. He captured her hands in his and pressed them to his beating heart. "My heart seems to be in a tizzy. I hope to God it's not for a snot-nosed cockney with an exaggerated opinion of himself."

Her answer was to take one of his hands and almost shyly press it against her own heart. Her eyes did not meet his. Dear God, she must have left her corset behind when she had turned into a boy. All thoughts of Norman fled as he imagined his fingers sliding over, encountering a soft, full breast.

"I reckon that answers my question. But are you Nora, Countess of Havermere, or do-gooder, Nora St. James? Or is this a woman I have yet to meet?"

Her eyelashes now fanned her glistening cheeks. He thought she would not answer. "I honestly do not know who I am with you," she finally said.

The symphony of rain hitting windows, canvas awnings, and cobblestones lent a curtain of privacy to their nook. The wet took the stench out of the air and the light perfume of her filled the narrow doorway.

He tipped the brim of her hat back until it made a kind of pillow against the rough wood of the door. His fingers curled through her hair. The perfume was stronger now. She must use something when she washed her hair. He stepped closer. Her breasts and the pillow she had stuffed into her trousers pressed fully against his chest and belly.

"Whoever it is, I am right sure I'm going to like her."

Thunder cracked again and, being somewhat of a dramatic soul, he took it as his cue to move in. No tentative brush of shy lips, he embarked on a full-on siege. Ready to lay her to waste.

He was not prepared for what met him. Not the countess with her perfect speech and elegant manners. Not Prim Mrs. St James. Certainly not Norman. This lady was someone altogether different. All woman. She opened her mouth to him, tasting of rain and heat and something decadent.

He pressed his tongue inside, wanting to savor all of her. She opened to him, meeting his tongue with her own, enveloping it. Sucking.

God, this woman fit him. She slipped into all his nooks and crannies, finding the empty spaces, filling them with her softness. He pulled her even tighter, and she inched forward, her long legs now cradled by his. His hands dropped to skim her arms and then dipped to pull her bum snug up to his cock. She groaned into his mouth, her buttocks tightening, and he bit her lip in response. He was vaguely aware of a dog barking somewhere. She must have heard it too. She was pulling away. Her soft bits extricating themselves from him, leaving him raw and exposed.

God, she was stunning. Breath coming hot and fast between swollen lips, her hair a riot of escaping curls, her cheeks flushed, and every feature dusted in glistening dew.

"I will manage a better costume tomorrow," she said, swiping at the wet on her lips. She looked toward the still barking dog and hoisted her false belly back into position, once more disguising the swell of her breasts. The pillow must have migrated into the leg of her trouser with the force of their ardor.

The storm had moved off.

Apparently, the clearing weather had brought sanity, at least to her. He still felt at sea.

Rain dripped from his hair into his collar. He bent to rescue his old hat from a puddle, shook it off, and then clamped it back on her head. It helped, a little. But grubby Norman could not be resurrected. Not after that kiss. Nora St. James was the most mysterious woman he'd ever met. Mysterious and mercurial.

Why was she so intent on finding his niece? And why did she want to save cripples? What had her marriage been like? And what had driven her to seek a lover?

Well, one thing was dead certain. He would find out.

Chapter Eleven

Stepping out of the carriage, wet and bedraggled in her Norman costume, Nora looked left and right, hoping no one was about. A man was just disappearing around the corner of number forty-five. Good, he had not turned back to see her.

Safe.

She ducked inside.

Opal, ever at the ready, raised her eyebrow and quirked her mouth.

"W'as 'is name?"

Nora lifted her chin. "Norman."

Opal nodded slowly. "A good name. Not so good a getup."

Unsurprising that Opal, who could turn herself into a young gent and gamble all night long without her mark so much as raising an eyebrow, found poor Norman coming up short.

"Well." Nora hoisted her belly up again. "I was forced to improvise. Next time, I will come to you for some of your old togs." She did not want to stand before Opal, who seemed to always be able to see through her. Her lips still stung, and her nipples peaked hard against the soft lawn of the colonel's shirt. "I will just wash and change."

"A note came from that money gent, Mr.

Bartholomew," Opal called out.

"Oh, good. I expect he has gotten the funds from the sale of the painting. I will look at it after I change."

As if fire nipped at her heels, she dashed up the stairs. Pulling the door shut, she flung the old slouch hat on her bed and wrenched off Farren Cavanaugh's coat and then yanked the pillow out and peeled the trousers off. Lastly, she pulled his shirt over her head.

But it did no good. She had rid her body of his clothes but still felt swaddled in him—in his kiss. The damp wool and linen still held a breath of him. Starch, a hint of tobacco, and male.

Stop.

She sloshed water on her face, welcoming the sting as she scrubbed over the tiny cuts. The mirror still showed flushed cheeks and bruised lips. She threw on her peach-colored wrapper.

"Lady Charlotte! What have you brought me this time?" Mari's cry heralding Charlotte's arrival wafted up the stairway.

Drat. In her excitement at the prospect of finding Rose, Nora had forgotten Charlotte was coming today.

"That girl, she's here. Again." An irate Opal stood in the doorway.

"Good heavens, Opal. When will you learn to knock? You will never be a proper lady if you don't adhere to the rules." She cinched her robe more tightly about her, well aware she was acting like an utter prude, not to mention a total hypocrite. If the girl had spied the same wanton Nora had just seen reflected in the mirror—well, it just would not do.

"Lady? Rules?" The scarred side of her face flared pink. "Don't confuse me with that chit down there waiting for you. I'm not a lady, and I never will be."

Opal flounced over to fetch Nora's corset and crinoline. Nora submitted to being trussed up as *The Countess* again. She twisted her hair into a tight bun and then followed Opal downstairs.

"Greetings, all!" Charlotte's lovely soprano rang through the room as Opal and Nora entered.

"Now, Lady Charlotte! They are finally here." Mari pulled them farther into the room.

"Yes, Mari, thank you for being patient. I do have something for you and Agnes." Like a magician, Charlotte whipped two ribbons from the gusset of her pagoda sleeve and bestowed one on Mari, the other on Agnes.

"I am sorry to be so late." *Ooo*'s and *ahh*'s from the little girls punctuated Charlotte's apology. "I nearly did not come at all. Papa was worried about taking the carriage out in the wet. But I told him if we were to never stir out of doors because of rain, we should never go anywhere." She laughed at her little joke. "And, as you see, Hattie and I survived." The perpetually sullen maid bobbed a curtsey and then reclaimed her seat against the far wall.

The younger girls trailed after their beloved Lady Charlotte as if she were the Pied Piper, both clutching their bright ribbons.

"Mine is so very soft," Agnes piped. "Is it velvet?"

"Yes, silk velvet, mind you. And the prettiest apple green you have ever seen!"

"'Cept Agnes has never *seen* any color, 'Apple Green' or otherwise," Opal opined, flinging herself into a nearby chair.

"But I can *smell* an apple, and imagine a color to

144

match," Agnes said judiciously. Meanwhile Mari twirled around, whipping her primrose ribbon like a baton until she got tangled up, her damaged foot not quite catching up with her good one.

"How clever you are, Agnes." Nora touched the top of her dark head. "Shall I tie it in your hair?"

"No, Mum, thank you. I just want to hold it."

"And here is your gift, Opal." Charlotte held out a slim book.

Opal bit her lip and sat forward.

"I took a chance, knowing you act as teacher to Agnes and Mari."

Indeed, Opal loved books and Charlotte St. James was clever to have divined that fact. When Opal did not take it immediately, Charlotte set it on the nearby table.

"And my gift to you, Auntie, is a new gown for my come-out ball."

"But you have already ordered a gown for the presentation."

"I am selfish and want my family to be the most handsome in the entire room. So, you must indulge me. How else am I to repay your generosity?"

"I have been soaking your old rose silk," Opal interjected. "Most of the black dye has come out."

"Well, I dare say Auntie will find many occasions to wear the rose, Opal," Charlotte said, ever the diplomat.

A cough came from Charlotte's maid. She held up another package.

"Oh, thank you, Hattie. I had almost forgot." Charlotte rose to meet the girl and took the box from her. "We found this on the front stoop as we were arriving."

Bouchard's telltale packaging of lilies, violets and roses decorated the paper.

Perfume.

Years ago, her husband had paraded her into the shop, purchased a heavy scent of jasmine and tuberose, and insisted she wear it. She'd eventually gone nose blind to the smell, but Nora still regarded a gift of perfume a man's way of marking his territory.

Four pairs of eyes, even blind Agnes's, were on the box. The girls' faces were cast in various expressions. Opal, suspicious; Agnes, slightly wistful; Mari expectant; and Charlotte, merely curious.

"Is it from the colonel?" Mari trilled, working her hands as if she might tear off the wrapping herself.

Nora wished she didn't have an audience. Her name, meticulously written across the front, looked to be the same hand, and the paper the same expensive vellum, as the last unwelcome gift of roses.

She handed the box to Mari. "Here, will you open it while I read the card?" Hopefully, the girls would be distracted by the perfume.

Charlotte immediately became an arbiter between Mari and Agnes. Only Opal's gaze remained fixed on Nora.

She broke open the seal of red wax.

Your bud cannot withstand foul poisonous paint.
Anoint your velvet petals without such taint
To stay pure, we must kill the parasite.
For only unblemished Red mingles with White.
Then will we meld, making the perfect Blush,
A scent from heaven, binding the three of us!
Poisonous paint?

The paintings. Whoever sent this gift and note must

have either been at the auction or at least known of it.

Binding the three of us?

Could Farren Cavanaugh be behind this note? These gifts? At the auction, he had chided her for hawking herself, saying he would wait for the original. And perhaps it had been his idea, not Mr. Gillingham's, to attend the auction? The first gift of roses had arrived just after they had met. Of course, he had thought her someone else at the time, but perhaps he had followed her home?

The idea seemed far-fetched. The colonel had been genuinely shocked to find Nora living here when he had come to call enquiring about Lily's death.

And that bald man who had bought the painting. Who was he? An agent for someone, so Hancock had said. But who? He had not wanted the painting uncovered, wanted to keep the portrait private and unexposed. Hancock had said the buyer wished to remain anonymous.

Hancock had told the patrons that the second auction would be later this week.

Not a bloody chance in Hell.

For some reason luck had been on her side and there had been no mention of the auction in any of the papers. Opal had scoured them all. Nora would count her blessings, collect her money, and inform Hancock he must return the other portraits. Besides, the first painting had brought her a small fortune.

But at what price? Lady Gadwick had withdrawn her support, and now some man was admonishing her with gifts and bad poetry.

Someone intimately acquainted with Nora's comings and goings.

"Oooh! It's roses! It smells of roses, Mum." Mari had found Nora's skirt and was tugging at it and holding out her wrist. "Smell!"

Nora had no need to bend down to Mari. The scent wafted up to flood her nose as bile filled her throat.

Agnes brushed the velvet ribbon against her nose. "I always preferred selling violets, with their nimble stems and fuzzy leaves."

"Were you a flower seller then, Agnes?" Charlotte asked.

"I was, but then Mum rescued me." Agnes's hand found its way into Nora's.

She gave it a reassuring squeeze and the girl's frown released just a fraction.

"I believe she has come to my rescue as well." Charlotte smiled. "Here, Opal. Let us have a poem now." Charlotte thrust the book at Opal. "Go on, it won't bite you. Though many would rather encounter a snake than listen to poetry." She laughed.

Yes, snakes disguised as poetry.

For only unblemished Red mingles with White.

Was she the red—red hair? And the white? White-blonde…

A feeling of dread filled her body as overwhelming as the heavy perfume.

Rose.

"Who is it from, Mum? Is it your prince? Will you marry him now?" Mari tugged on Nora's skirt. "And will he take us all away to live in his castle?"

Both the gifts were roses.

Dear God, could this mystery man be connected to Rose?

Chapter Twelve

The knocker sounded. That would be him.

Nora took a final look in the small mirror set between two wall sconces. Lips and cheeks too red despite the powder she had applied. She stood straighter and adjusted her collar and then turned to face him.

A burble of banter erupted as Opal admitted Farren Cavanaugh.

"'Ere's that colonel, Mum." The perfect side of Opal's face was slightly pink. And had she styled her hair to cover more of her missing ear? The girl ducked her head lest anyone see even a hint of a smile and then left the room.

The colonel held out a posy of red roses.

"Don't look so startled, Countess. They are in lieu of an olive branch. I'm hoping you'll forgive me for taking advantage of the English weather?"

The bouquet looked so very like the one she had received two weeks ago with the first poem. But he was alluding to their kiss in the rain. She shook her head to clear her thoughts.

His extended hand with the flowers drooped. "You don't like roses. Dag nabbit, I tried to get peonies, but they weren't to be had."

Should she mention the gifts to Farren Cavanaugh? And her suspicion that the giver was somehow connected to Rose?

"Do you write poetry, Colonel?" The words came out before she could check them.

His mouth quirked in a cockeyed smile, his dimple appearing. "Why, should I have included a poem?"

"No. No, of course not. They are lovely. Thank you." She took the posy. She would hold her peace for now. She did not know this man, not really. Could he be teasing her with these gifts?

"Then I am forgiven?"

Did he regret their kiss? "There is nothing to forgive." She flung out the words like emptying a chamber pot.

He raised an eyebrow. "Good—I think." The colonel looked her up and down. "So, who do I have the honor of sleuthing with today? Not the Countess. Certainly not Nor-man. But I am intrigued. Mighty."

Opal had unearthed a very sober-looking gown and had fashioned a white bib-like collar to it along with matching cuffs. The large old-fashioned poke bonnet, lying on the nearby table, would complete the ensemble. "Norma Pledgeheart, at your service." She dipped into a curtsey.

"Pledgeheart? Hell's bells. Where do you come up with these names?"

"In the middle of the night when I can't sleep."

"You can't sleep?"

Best not to mention that he was the cause of her latest nocturnal ramblings. "No." She put the roses into a vase and then added some water from a nearby pitcher. "I wish I liked to read. I end up wandering around the house or playing cards. Sometimes Opal will play with me."

"Opal?"

Nora nodded. "Hers is quite a story, and I am privy to only a fraction of it. Suffice to say, she almost always wins. And she cheats."

"Best not introduce her to Gillingham, then." He gestured toward the door. "Shall we get going?"

"In a moment. Opal has one other prop to complete my ensemble."

"I thought we'd start with St. Augustine's in Chelsea."

She nodded. "I have copied the likeness by tracing over it so that we might have several copies."

He took it from her, looked it over and nodded curtly like she was some over-reaching infantry pup. He tucked it into his breast pocket and proceeded to take over the room like a cur marking his territory—nosing into corners, touching her personal things—Lily's needlepoint so carefully displayed in a gold-leafed frame.

He moved to the window. "You have a love for dead plants?"

The sill of her window held a potpourri of various pots filled with cuttings.

"I beg to differ, Colonel Cavanaugh, they are most certainly not dead. They are simply waiting to take root."

"Ah, I didn't see that distinction, Countess. I will revise my statement. You have a love of lost causes."

She elbowed him out of the way, very cognizant of the fact she looked like a wet hen protecting her chicks.

"Ow!" He rubbed his ribs.

Another dead leaf on the geranium. She tenderly pinched it off. Too much water? No, the soil was only slightly moist.

Why did this man stir her so? What a bother, this heightened sense of being—this aliveness. Why must he upset her plans? Why must he make her think of other things besides her girls and holding on to her freedom?

He had crossed and now leaned against the mantel, a strange look on his face. She ducked her head, putting the dead leaf in her pocket.

This dratted man kept slipping the confines of the niche in which she had placed him, that of being useful. One moment he was the rogue, the next, as solicitous as dear Mr. Bartholomew. Now, the word *sweet* came to mind.

"What's this?" He held up the bottle of perfume.

Oh, she'd forgotten she had tucked it behind a book on the mantel. Very well, she would see what he had to say about it.

He frowned at the bottle then turned to her. "May I?"

She nodded.

He took out the stopper and sniffed. "Woo!" He staggered back and clutched his heart as if the bottle contained poison instead of perfume. "Is this a gift from a lover?" he said with an edge.

She only raised an eyebrow.

"If so, I'd throw him back. He doesn't know you at all." He shoved the stopper back into the bottle.

"So, you did not send it?"

He looked genuinely shocked. "Me? Never." He set it back on the shelf.

He seemed satisfied that at least he had no known rival. And she in turn, was happy to know he clearly hadn't sent the perfume.

"No Mrs. Cavanaugh pining for your … return?" Nora would never dally within the bonds of marriage again, not after she and Devlin had paid so dearly for her brief indiscretion.

Heavens, why was she even thinking of dallying?

"No, there is nothing left for me in Maryland. My pa died last September. I sold everything." He swallowed and his jaw line twitched. "So." He slapped his hands against his thighs as if he might banish his sadness. "I'm free as a bird."

He pushed off the mantel and settled into her shoddy chair. His long limbs splayed and draped over the worn tapestry of *mille* fields dotted with courtiers lolling at the feet of their ladies.

"That is another prong in my plan. I want to start a family." One huge hand stroked the scuffed woodwork. His booted foot, the one nearest the fire, flexed against the heat. A big cat he was. Looking very domesticated, but she was not fooled. Cats could spring into action in a moment, their paws pinning a wriggling mouse.

Her skin prickled. His eyes spoke of the predator within. He was daring her to test him—to make him strike.

Oh, why must he look at her so? As if she were a delicious secret he wanted to know.

And why must she continue torturing herself reliving that kiss? It was only one kiss in the soaking rain, mind you. Her best boots had been nearly ruined with the damp and mud.

"I feel like a rascal relaxing while you wear a hole in your carpet. Won't you come sit down, Countess?"

Said the spider to the fly. His voice trailed off to silky nothing, a snare wielded with the lightest, softest tease. Seemingly so innocent, yet the offer swamped her nearly as much as his kiss in the rain.

Hell's bells, she nearly found herself in his lap.

"Ah, here is Opal." And just in time.

Nora took the Bible. "Thank you, Opal. I knew I had one somewhere." She turned to the colonel. "Shall we start out?" she asked, tugging on her gloves.

"Your ladyship, don't forget Mr. Bartholomew. He said it was most urgent," Opal cautioned, holding out a drab cloak for her to slip into.

"Yes." The old gent took his job very seriously. His careful devotion felt a bit like the grandfather she had never known. "I will see him tomorrow."

Opal stepped forward and situated the huge poke bonnet on Nora's head.

"Best take my arm, Miss Pledgehart. Our dray horses did not wear such blinkers as that bonnet of yours."

Norma Pledgehart pursed her lips and clutched her Bible tightly to her breast. Whereas Nora St. James was mightily tempted to thwack him with the Good Book. Thank goodness Miss Pledgehart was of a more placid temperament.

****

Nothing at Saint Augustin's, or Our Lady of Mercy in Notting Hill, nor St. Humphries in Bishop's Gate.

Mrs. Lottie Beecham at Aldgate's Workhouse took one look at the drawing of Lily and declared they were looking in the wrong place. "Such a beauty will have seen where her bread was best buttered. She'll have ended up in a bawdy house." She *tsked*. "Too much a temptation to be hired on as a maid. We always find ladies prefer to employ our plainer girls."

"Might we have a look all the same?" the colonel asked, pressing a coin into her hand. Mrs. Beecham stepped aside and gestured for them to pass.

The children were all at various tasks, mostly weaving baskets or sewing caps. As she and the colonel passed, each looked up expectantly and one little girl, no more than Mari's age, stood and dropped her sewing reaching her arms up to them. "Please, take me, mum. I'll work hard."

"Back to work, you insolent girl," Mrs. Beecham barked.

Nora had to rely on Colonel Cavanaugh's eyes after that. Her own were glazed with useless tears. She stared straight ahead, chin up. She could not save them all, she reminded herself firmly. Indeed, she would be lucky to house but a handful. Her heart felt heavy and full to bursting with sorrow.

They had no more luck at number five and six on her list; number seven had been closed due to "unsanitary conditions." Dear God, what must it have been like if these other places had passed muster?

"Tomorrow, we will go to the hospitals."

But the next day bore no luck. Not at St. Bart's, Bethlehem, or even Martin's Home for the Infirm, a hospital specifically for wayward girls who were in trouble.

Now dressed as "Norbert," who was a bit of a dandy and far more fashionable than poor Norman, Nora was just putting one of the colonel's roses into her lapel before going to meet the colonel at The Bull Inn when Opal called her to the front door. An ancient carriage stood in the street, and Mr. Bartholomew was alighting with the help of his coachman.

Drat, she had meant to go by his office yesterday but had been so caught up in the search for Rose she had forgotten.

Norbert could not meet Mr. Bartholomew. She would just duck out into the mews and leave Opal to deal with him.

But the old man had already seen her, his bushy eyebrows raised in surprise.

"Lady Havermere?" Bartholomew said, his old hound-face now sunk back into its worried lines.

"Yes, I am sorry you have caught me trying on a costume for Lady Alderly's masked ball," the lie rolled off her tongue far too easily. Best to get this done and hear what he had to say. "Please come in, Mr. Bartholomew."

The old gent nodded and shuffled in.

"I won't stay but a minute, my lady. I see you are busy, but if Mohamed won't come to the mountain, then ..." he trailed off.

"Please, won't you sit?"

He looked up from the carpet. "Yes, I believe I must."

Once settled, he looked up with such sadness. She had the urge to take his old, papery hands within hers.

"There is no good way to say this, your ladyship. I have failed you."

Nora sat forward. "Failed? How?"

"The funds—the funds from the sale of the painting—they have not been deposited."

A terrible feeling hit her gut. "But it has only been a week. Surely Mr. Hancock is simply a bit lackadaisical."

The old man shook his head, his loose jowls like

sails in the wind. "Hancock cannot be found. He has decamped and taken the money and the other paintings."

"But he came highly recommended—"

"Yes, I thought so. But Sir Charles steered me wrong."

"Sir Charles? Sir Charles Brocket?"

The old man closed his eyes and merely nodded.

Oh, dear God. Devlin had made a fast enemy of Brocket when the man's wife had solicited Dev to paint her likeness, declaring she must have a true "master." But Devlin had sent her packing with nary a peck on the cheek. Unfortunately, Brocket could not let it go. Someone must be punished, and it had been Dev. His offering for the Queen's exhibition had been dubbed, "Tits with Tiara." Brocket, who was the exhibition's director, had "skyed" the painting, hanging it up near the rafters making the perspective all askew. And then the next year, he had been in cahoots with Nora's husband to steal Devlin's portrait of his wife, Anne.

Poor Mr. Bartholomew looked so utterly dejected. "I immediately called on Sir Charles hoping he'd know where Hancock might be found, but he said that he had never even met the man. The recommendation had come from another source, one he would not name. You may be assured, I will do everything in my power to locate this—cur, and bring the full extent of the law on his head."

Unreal, the whole scenario was unreal. No one could be as unlucky as she.

The front bell sounded, and she nearly jumped out of her skin.

Opal entered. "Excuse me, your ladyship A runner

just brought this." She handed over the missive. "Said it was most urgent, and there's a carriage waiting."

She covered her mouth as a bark of laughter erupted. Oh, the absurdity of it all. Taking the risk to sell a painting to remain free, and then, in the end, being back at square one, destitute once again. Surely if Hancock tried to sell any of the other paintings, he would be caught.

"Mum, the note," Opal reminded her.

"Oh, yes, if you will excuse me, Mr. Bartholomew—"

"Certainly, dear lady. I am only sorry to bring you such dire news. I don't suppose you have anything else of value to part with?"

Selling the nude portraits would send her beyond redemption. And Charlotte would, by association, be tainted as well. But she would not add more angst to the old man's suffering. "I will think of something, Mr. Bartholomew." Thank heavens she had not moved forward with the house in Corsham.

The old man rose, his movements like a magic lantern show, all jerky frames. "I suppose it is fruitless to ask you to consider marriage?"

"As I said, sir, I will think of something. Thank you for coming all this way."

He only shook his head again. "I can see myself out, Lady Havermere." He stopped and turned to her. "Please know that I will not rest until this is resolved."

"Yes, I know you will. Thank you."

The old man nodded once and then shuffled out of the room. Nora cracked open the note.

Dear God, when one window closed, another opened.

Chapter Thirteen

"My man said the gal looked very like the drawing, as best as he could tell from his vantage point on the third floor," the colonel said as he dragged Norbert along. "But when he got to the spot where he had seen her, of course she was gone."

"But he thought it could be her? It could be our Rose?"

"He did." The colonel grinned.

"Well, I'll take the south end, you take the north—"

"No, we stick together, Norbert." Nora could not help but notice the bulge in his coat pocket. A pistol. "We'll show the drawing around and stay here till the cows come home if need be."

"Very well, then you might buy me a bun. I ran out without eating."

Hours went by. The binding on her breasts chafed, and she needed the necessary. Being a "lad," she should just avail herself of a nearby wall, but obviously Nora could not do so.

"There she is!" Her cone of roasted corn tumbled to the cobble stones.

A bright blonde head bobbed among the drab browns and faded caps of the general population.

The colonel, much taller, had a better view and a

longer stride. Nora waded through the sudden onslaught of pigeons fighting over the dropped corn.

"You, Miss!" The colonel called out.

Nora followed in his wake.

The girl disappeared behind a milk wagon.

Colonel Cavanaugh leapt ahead.

"Hey! Watch yerself, ya great lummox!"

Norbert elbowed aside the tinker whose pole of pots rattled in concert with their irate owner.

Where was he? She scanned the crowd.

There! Keeping the Colonel's fair head in her sights, she leapt over a young match girl, who sat crossed legged against the wheel of a cart.

Near the alley, the crowds were thinner. Colonel Cavanaugh reached out for the girl and caught her.

She spun around.

Nora gasped.

Disappointment slammed into her with a force that knocked her back like a blow to the chest.

Wrong.

The eyes were wrong. Blue. Not the color of the sea. And the chin, too pointed. Still …

"Rose?" she asked. Like forcing a piece of puzzle into a place that nearly fit, but clearly did not.

The girl dismissed Norbert with a toss of her head, giving the colonel the full measure of her charms. "Sure, I'll be yer English Rose if ya want me ta be, luv. In fact, for you, I'll be any flower in the garden you've a hankering for."

Nora closed her eyes, her hands pressing into her still heaving ribs, willing herself to slow her breath.

Wrong, she had been wrong all along. This was the girl she had seen so many times.

She had been chasing a shadow.

"Come on then, handsome," the girl said to Farren. "Ditch your boy here, and I'll give ya a toss right yonder in the alleyway. Three bob."

Nora turned away, the roasted corn she had recently eaten churning in her belly. An arm came around her, shoring her up.

"Cost ya four to 'ave 'im watch." The girl sniffed, tossing her head at Norbert.

He stepped in front of the girl and took Nora by the shoulders, making her meet his eyes. "If she is alive, Countess, we will find her. You can take that to the bank."

"Cor," the girl snorted, "if you prefer your boy to me, I'll 'ave none of ya. Damn shame though, to waste that bonnie face and biscuit on a poncy pup."

Nora stared into Farren Cavanaugh's eyes. Eyes so like Lily's—like Rose's.

She nodded like a good soldier, but tears pricked her nose and filled her throat, making it tight and raw.

What now?

She should go home. But where was home? Certainly not Linden House. And not Greene Street, not really, though she had tried to make it feel like one, filling the rooms with things she loved. Rescuing girls who needed her. But in truth, they were rescuing her, filling her empty house and heart.

But now, with Hancock running off with her money, she would likely be moving anyway.

She turned to the man at her side. Dear God, she did not want to leave him. This American colonel who was becoming her hope.

As if he read her mind, "Come on."

"Where are you taking me?"

"I have a—friend—who has a house not far from here."

"But I am dressed as Norbert. What will your 'friend' say?" Was this the home of his mistress?

"Nothing. He is not in town yet and won't be until later this week."

Nora only focused on the word "he." Not a mistress.

Their cabbie stopped, and the colonel jumped out of the equipage. He held his arms up for her. Norbert would have snorted and pushed them away, but Nora could not reject that waiting embrace. Strong hands circled her waist, and she longed to simply sink into his body. So bloody tempting. Once her feet hit the all too solid ground, she pulled her hat lower against his gaze and turned to slam the carriage door. Heavy fog had settled over the city. For once she welcomed the thick blanket as if it might cocoon her from the real world.

But the press of a hand at her back sent her up the steps and then inside a large, old-fashioned manse. A rather pugilistic-looking butler, still in the midst of tugging on his coat, was heading their way.

"Good evening, Wellfleet."

"Good evening, sir," he said with a deep frown. "I did not expect you this evening. I understood you would be away until his lordship arrived on Sunday of this week."

"Yes, I am sorry. I had planned it that way, but I am hoping you will throw me a bone, and let me camp out tonight."

The butler's gaze narrowed as he looked Norbert up and down, clearly displeased with his evening being disrupted. "I'm afraid the cook is off, and there is only myself at home to attend you and your—guest."

"Young Norbert and I can see to ourselves."

Nora jerked her hat down lower and muttered a gruff reply of "Lay off," to the servant when he attempted to take it.

Wellfleet struggled to resume his nonplussed butler-look but failed. His lip twitched in an odd sort of grimace. "I have not opened the reception rooms, sir."

"Oh, that won't bother us."

"I will just light the fire—"

"No need. I can see to that."

"There are the makings of a cold supper in the larder, sir. I will be but a moment."

"Thank you, Wellfleet, but I can rustle up something. Please, take the rest of the evening off. I believe his lordship mentioned your father has been ill?"

The butler gave him a surprised look before resuming his poker face. "As you wish, sir. Thank you, sir." He bowed and then retreated.

The Colonel crossed to a set of huge double doors. "I will never get used to all this bowing and scraping. I reckon I got used to doing for myself, especially since the war." He opened the left door and gestured to her to enter.

The drawing room was spacious with full-length windows facing the street, but the furniture stood draped in Holland covers.

He went to the firebox, adjusted the wood to his liking, and then set a match to the kindling. A flame sprang to life and the wood popped. He stood back and they both watched as the fire took hold, its light drawing her closer. "I think there is some French brandy about. Will you take a drop?"

"Yes. You may pour me a healthy glass, please." She hovered behind a ghostly winged-back chair as if it might protect her from him.

He went to the sideboard and poured several fingers of Camus Frères into two glasses.

"Now, this," he said, swirling the thick amber liquid, "is something I have come to appreciate. The blockade runner's stores had an occasional bottle or two of wine or whiskey but if my men had to go without, well, I couldn't rightly indulge and leave them high and dry. When I came home, I guess I stuck with what I was used to. Ale." He was trying to put her at ease with his stories.

She could well imagine the young men he would have commanded. They would have looked up to him with such admiration. Yes, she would have followed him to the ends of the earth. There was such a confidence about his bearing, as if he could solve all the problems in the world.

But that was a fantasy. He could not. He could not make a Coventry whore into the twin of Lily. He could not bring Lily back from the dead. He could not save her from her financial woes.

He held out a glass to her. The barricade of the chair now seemed silly. She crossed to him, feeling his eyes on her, but she would not meet his gaze. Instead, she concentrated on cupping the bottom of the heavy crystal-like chalice so as not to touch his fingers. Again, ridiculous. She took a fortifying drink. The brandy felt thick and smooth in her mouth. The familiarity of better days long past.

She took off her hat, suddenly wanting to shed Norbert. Her fingers found the pins digging into her scalp and flicked them out, sliding them into her pocket. The jacket she pulled off and flung onto a nearby chair. If only she could release the binding that held her breasts flat. Several spirals of hair had escaped, snaking down her back, a few wisps tickled her cheeks. Why did she suddenly feel so aware of every blasted part of her body?

He'd been staring at her. Likely that is why her body felt so primed. He took a healthy swig of brandy. His Adam's apple dipped and bobbed back up. When had he removed his cravat? A shadow of dusky blond hair teased the opening of his shirt.

"So, his *lordship* doesn't mind you using his home?" she probed.

"Naw, he is very generous and has a soft spot for a Yank," he said, grinning.

She took another sip of brandy. Liquid courage. A flame of heat ran up through her.

"I will fetch that supper now." He tossed back the rest of his spirits and then left the room.

His lordship. Not the house of his lover.

But what was she doing here?

The Covent Garden girl's image rose again, filling Nora's vision. So alike, and yet so different. The memory of her lewd solicitation made Nora wince. All hope gone. Washed away with the turn of her head, blue eyes and a too sharp chin sizing up Nora and the colonel as potential marks.

She cradled the brandy against her breasts. Why had she allowed Farren Cavanaugh to bring her here? Her head might not know, but her body surely did.

She needed something. Something only he could give.

Dear God, how maudlin.

The air in the room held a hint of must. The lively fire, now leaping merrily in its box, cast huge shadows of the shrouded furniture over the papered walls.

Two miniatures sat side by side on a low table, as if the house's owner could not bear to have them covered. She picked up the nearest. A young man—boy really—with wheat-colored hair and sea-green eyes. This boy, with his slightly wicked smile and plump cheeks, had felt no sting in his tender years.

The other portrait was of a somewhat older boy. He was almost too beautiful. If he had been wearing a frock and had longer hair, he could have passed for a girl. They were clearly related. Likely brothers.

"A veritable feast," the Colonel said, using his hip to close the door.

She hadn't heard him enter. He carried a tray laden with all manner of meats, cheeses, bread, fruit and some pies. Also, a bottle of wine, which he had tucked under his arm. "Wellfleet may think me an American rube—and now, since bringing you here, quite possibly a nancy as well—but I will have to thank the cook for keeping such a well-stocked larder. A soldier always knows who to make friends with first."

He placed the tray on a small, low table and began shifting plates and cutlery.

"So, you are leaving the Wellington Arms?" Nora said, setting the miniature down next to the other.

"Why not? Beats paying for rooms. And the food is better." He spoke quickly as if he might not be telling the full story.

"His lordship. Is this man someone I might know?"

"Not likely. And I will have to be careful if I introduce you to him. He'll be besotted, I have no doubt." He pulled at the holland cover to reveal a dark brocade couch. He tossed the muslin onto a nearby chaise.

"Besotted?" She sat down wanting something to do and then shook out the napkins. "You will swell my head." She laid his on the far side of the tray. Why did his words please her so? She who was used to lavish compliments.

"I reckon there's not a man standing who wouldn't fall under your spell."

"Only because of the outer package," she said with what she hoped was finality, but his intense gaze did not waver. Even dressed in her Norbert togs, this man made her feel more desirable than were she decked out in duchess satin.

"And what of the woman inside?"

She plunged the knife into a ripe camembert and slathered pungent cream on a wedge of bread and then handed it to him. She made one for herself, sculpting the cheese as if her life depended on it, not knowing how to answer. "I was married very young. Then have been in mourning." She made herself shrug. "A woman is schooled to fulfill the expectations of others—to be obliging. I think I have done that most of my life."

Except for Devlin.

"And you no longer wish to do that?"

She shook her head. "I wish to be free. Well, as free as a woman may be."

"No wish to remarry?"

"Heavens, no." She shuddered, thinking of her

narrow future. She did not add that she would likely have to marry now. Unless she found a patron for her girls. Any man who might contribute, would want other things. She thought of Lord Milton and his piles of money.

Lord Finchley also had money, or would when he married, and he would surely leave her be. All she would have to do was be his hostess now and again to keep up appearances.

"Your marriage was not a happy one."

Was it a question? Images flashed through her mind, being locked for weeks on end in a dark room, bruises where they wouldn't show, but the mental abuse had been the worst.

The colonel waited. Apparently, he did want an answer.

"No," she finally said.

"And so, you have given up on the institution?"

"Given the option, why would I ever choose to subject myself to a man again?"

"To experience what has eluded you." He took another sip of brandy. "Love."

"Love?" The word pricked her as surely as if the knife in her hand had slipped to pierce her skin. "I do not believe in love anymore. At least not love between a man and a woman. And even if I did, why would I have to marry to have it?"

"To have a family. A lover who is kind and worthy, and a father for your children."

She turned away. *Blast him.* How did he know these things about her? Her Achilles heel.

"That may be your dream, Colonel, but do not assume it is mine." She spat out the words hoping her vehemence might make them ring true.

No matter how impulsive their ardor, she and Devlin had always been very careful. All the months of research, speaking with midwives, using her own funds to purchase sponges, vinegar, herbs, and French letters, and then instructing women in how to use them. She had simply applied the preventatives to herself. Never would she bring a bastard into the world. Not when there were so many children in need of care.

"Aw, Countess, I didn't mean to make you weep."

She pulled farther away from him. "I never cry." She dared him to refute her. "The fire is smoking from a cold flue." She stood and then took up the poker. As she jabbed at the logs, flames shot up, giving the lie to her pronouncement. "I'm not sure why I came here."

"Aren't you?" He had stood. His voice nearer.

She shrugged, still holding the damn poker.

"Maybe this will remind you." She felt him take the poker and set it carefully against the tiled fireplace façade. Giving her plenty of time to fly away if she chose.

She licked her lips.

The pad of his thumb brushed her bottom lip. "I believe you liked this the last time. I know I did."

Last time.

In the alley. Cold rain had pelted her eyelids from his hat brim, the rasp of brick behind her as he had pressed her to the wall, his hot mouth on hers, as if he might devour some hidden part of her which seemed to rise painfully near her hammering heart.

This time she would not be surprised. She knew the angle her chin must reach to accommodate his height. Knew the texture of whiskers that would graze her cheeks. Knew his lips would be plush velvet. And hot. She closed her eyes and raised her mouth to him.

Nothing. Had she got it wrong? She turned away, but his hands caught her arms.

"Nora …"

Her name, whispered in her ear, echoing his whispering hands on her arms as they traced circles though the fine cambric of her shirt.

She shivered.

She knew nothing. There was nothing predictable about this man. He didn't like rules. He would trip her up every time, keeping her off balance. She'd expected him to take what she was offering. But he wasn't taking. His breath caressed her ear. He was waiting. Asking her for something beyond a mere kiss. This would be no hasty embrace stolen in the midst of a rainstorm. She did not need to open her eyes to know his lips still hovered near her ear, ready to ask again.

Because this time he wanted more.

She could push him away and laugh and then search out her half-drunk brandy, take one last sip before braving the fog, and then huddle in her cold bed at Greene Street with only the memory of his touch and the empty heartache of a lost Rose.

Or not.

A simple choice. So simple.

She could open herself to physical love again. To be with this man who worked upon her like no other— not even Devlin.

Silly to be so nervous. She had done this hundreds of times. Sometimes as much as five times in one day. But not in over three years.

When Lily had come into her life, Nora had stifled

that part of herself. By then Devlin had been drunk or high much of the time and Nora had not much cared. Lily had consumed her.

But Lily was gone. Rose was likely gone, too. The past.

And the future … Well, she would not think of that now.

Now, life was here, right before her.

He was pulling away. "It is late," he said, flexing his hands.

"Yes, it is. Too late."

"Then I'll see you home."

"No. I think not."

He stopped in the middle of finishing his brandy and stood frozen. Finally, he set the glass down. "Countess, don't mistake me for an adoring fop who will fawn and grovel at your feet, staying precisely where you put him."

"I would hope not. That is not very appealing in a lover."

He raised an eyebrow but stood his ground.

Oh, what did this man want? Didn't he see how hard this was for her?

"You are unhappy with your casting?" she continued, hoping to hide behind a light flirtation of words. "Would you prefer the Fool? I must caution you that role has already been claimed by too many. Besides, I do not believe you could play it with any real conviction."

She ducked below his penetrating gaze, fumbling with napkins and sweeping up the breadcrumbs from their dinner. *Henwit.*

She found her brandy and drank deep. The liquor

warmed her belly and her breast and cheeks. She should stop. She took another mouthful. "Sadly, I have not been so lucky with the men I've cast in the role of Lover. My first—the earl—was the Villain disguised as a Lover. No, that's wrong. Never a lover, more a grandfatherly sort." A bark of harsh laughter escaped her mouth. "Let us just say, he was a villain from the prologue to his final curtain call, which lasted nearly nine years."

"And Lord Devlin?" he prompted.

"Ah, he was unfortunately miscast. Though it took a while to find that out. And since then—well ..." *Lord, why had she gone down this bumpy road?*

He gently took her hand, then her glass and set it on the table. He straightened, his fingers still holding hers. "Are there no other roles available?"

His eyes blazed green with life, with a world of possibilities.

"None that you could fill." The sadness in her voice shocked her. She pulled her hand from his and retreated to the window.

She watched his reflection as he swiped his fingers through his hair. "Well, Countess, I must warn you." She thought she saw his smile in the darkened glass but was too cowardly to actually turn to face him. He was crossing toward her. "I am not an accomplished actor. I've never memorized lines or taken direction."

"Ah," was all she could say as he moved closer still.

"But I'm a quick study." He stood right behind her now. "Maybe you could start me off? Give me my first line?"

She swallowed.

"Not the director you thought to be?" His finger brushed a stray curl from her shoulder. "How about, 'take down your hair'? I think that is a fine opening line. It holds a lot of promise. What do you think?"

In answer, she reached up, her hands trembling, and fumbled to remove a comb from her chignon. He stepped back to give her room. She took a breath. Heavens, this was not going as she'd imagined. She was to be in charge. A handful of pins followed the combs and then her hair floated over her shoulders and down her back.

His jaw line twitched as his hands fisted against his legs. "My next line, Countess?"

His jaw twitched again. She was learning when he was off balance. She pushed him a bit further. "Your line is: Might I remove my coat?"

In answer, he did just that.

"Next?" he asked, unbuttoning his shirt.

Now it was her turn to feel off balance. This man had been a soldier. His chest muscles bunched as his hands flicked open buttons.

"How 'bout I give you another line?" He smiled, knowing she was caught but good.

She nodded, wishing she had finished her brandy.

"Let's see … I am much more comfortable—at least my upper half is, down below, well, I'm feeling a might cramped." He shifted his feet. "Let's see … your line is: I think you should pull the drapes now."

"Pull the drapes." The words came out in a hissed whisper.

He smiled. So tender. So kind. Surely, he could not know how starved she was for simple kindness. He moved leisurely to the windows. As he slid the heavy velvet closed, the light from the streetlamp extinguished itself, enclosing them in a deepening cocoon of darkness.

"What now, Countess?"

Her body hummed in anticipation. She stepped toward him. "Now," she prayed her voice would be strong. "I think we might try a bit of improvisation."

Chapter Fourteen

"I am all too happy to go off book."

Farren knew she was hurting. The twin-like girl not being Rose had sapped her of hope. Hell, it had shaken his optimism as well. But he would not think of that now. Not when they were quite alone and she within arm's reach. Not when he had the chance to give to her. To fill her with something sweet and real.

He should talk to her of strategies and options. He should convince her that hope must not die. That just because this girl was not Rose did not mean she was dead. Just as it did not mean Bren was dead. But right now, he didn't want to talk, didn't want to think. He only wanted to love.

Long legs encased in top boots, a belt cinching her tiny waist, the fine linen of her shirt billowing to disguise the lush breasts he knew lay beneath. Her hair, now a riot of cascading curls, licked her shoulders and breasts, teasing the rounded swell of her sweet bottom. His hands would fit over those swells right well.

Ladies' bums and legs, and the sweetest parts, were buried beneath yards of petticoats and a crinoline cage. If a lad were lucky, he might get a peek at an ankle.

Despite having been to nearly every brothel in this blasted city, he had not indulged once. Nearly five months since he'd had a woman. His last, Mrs. Gwen

Harwell. Half overseas with drink at The Horse Tavern in Fells Point he'd been, and she'd been more than willing. But their lovemaking had ended with her sobbing on his shoulder, weeping for her dead husband and son.

He knew damned well his fierce reaction to Nora Havermere had not one thing to do with his monkish state. If sweet Gwen Harwell was a slingshot, this woman was a three-hundred-pound Parrott Rifle primed and ready. And she was saying yes. Yes, she would have him. Still …

He dared not move. This was no alleyway where they took shelter from the rain. This was no spontaneous kiss, hot, wet and frantic. No, this time he would wait for her. Here in his grandfather's home. Now Farren's home. This time he would give her time—this frozen moment where she could withdraw or tip him into bliss.

"Are you sure?" He wanted to hear the words.

She let out a sigh, almost a huff. "Yes, I want you."

His last shred of principle dimmed like the slow closing of a lantern until the blackness hid his honor completely. He could have this woman. She was not married. And she wanted him. No possibility of retreat now. Life was all too short. Four long years of war had hammered that lesson into him until he fairly rang with it.

Besides, it would not end here.

"Then come to my bed."

She stiffened just a fraction.

"There's no one here. Just us. And tomorrow I happen to know Wellfleet and Mrs. Horton have a half day. I want to do this properly. As delightful as having you on any, or all, of these various pieces of furniture would be, I reckon that can be saved for another day. Come." He extended his hand. *Please God, let her take it.*

Her fingers found and worried a button on the fall of her trousers. She glanced at her coat still hung on the back of a chair.

He clenched his other hand and waited for the final verdict.

Her slightly chilled hand filled his. And he released the breath he had not known he was holding.

As they ascended the stairs, she just ahead of him, he nearly lost his resolve to reach the bedchamber. After all, the long curving banister would be a fine place to bend her over and push into her hot—

He made himself turn to the frozen faces that hung on the walls. A plump old biddy with a soft double chin. Good. Next, a self-important looking gent surrounded by hounds. The dogs looked underfed. After that, another young man in a ruff and feathered hat, the beginnings of a stringy beard, who could have been his brother. Then a lush peach of an arse encased in cranberry flannel trousers—*Damn it*. His eyes had strayed again.

He'd better get a hold of himself if he was going to last even two minutes with this woman.

With Nora.

Good, no more stairs. He took the lead and strode down the hallway to the room where he slept.

Wellfleet had laid a fire. Farren struck a match, and the tinder caught in a *whoosh*. He shoved his fingers through his hair.

Nora stood in the middle of the room, like a child

waiting for instruction. Waiting for him to make magic with his body and hers.

Problem was he wanted her too damn much. This humming within his body awed and frightened him. What if it scared her as well?

He'd never had patience for arrogant gentlemen, who feinted and parried with their true feelings, always needing the upper hand. Such men made him shake his head. He called a spade a spade. And he called love, love. He was falling in love with this woman. With Norman/Norbert/Miss Pledgehart. With Nora.

Instinct told him if he let her know one whiff of his true feelings, she would turn tail and run.

What to do? When he wanted something, he generally went full tilt. Did he have the ballocks to call this off?

She flicked open a button on her shirt and his doubts ceased to plague him.

He stood, feet planted wide, hands dangling useless.

She turned her back to him and pulled the shirt up nearly over her head. A tiny waist appeared, one he could span with his hands.

"I'd like to do that. If I may?" He stepped toward her.

She turned, dropping the shirt back over her body like a dutiful child, her gaze fixed on his chest. Nerves. This beautiful woman was nervous as a virgin—or how he imagined a virgin might feel, never having bedded one.

Inch by inch, he ruched the linen upward. Heated silken flesh grazed his knuckles. She shivered, her eyes still not meeting his. Instead of sweet heavy breasts, he found a binding. Of course. How else could bounteous Nora become boyish Norbert?

She raised her arms, and the shirt slipped over her head. He dropped it to the floor.

He touched the cloth. "Opal's idea?" he asked, not so much because he wanted to know, but to lighten the atmosphere.

She only nodded, her hands fumbling to seek the end of the linen tucked midway around her back.

"No." Her hands froze as his covered hers. "May I?" He stepped closer and dipped his head to whisper in her ear. "I never could resist a wrapped package. My ma despaired of me at Christmas. No hiding place was safe from me."

She dropped her chin, submitting to his wishes.

He pulled her closer still, exploring her delicate shoulder blades and the long slope of her back before his hands spanned the sweet nip of her waist. Now up over her ribs, he teased the end of the binding free.

She began to turn around, to unwrap herself.

"Stay still. Please." Her eyes met his. "Will you humor me?"

Her gaze dropped once again, but she stood quiet as a trembling fawn.

As he circled her, he pulled the linen through his hands until it spilled upon the floor. Now a third time around, and she was breathing heavier and worrying the pink flesh of her upper lip.

Soon, perhaps only once more around. The fire was at his back, her fire at his front. Now.

She gasped as the last wisp of the binding pulled free.

Shy. Nora St. James, Countess of Havermere, was

shy. She who had posed unabashedly for her lover, she who was touted as one of the most beautiful women in the British Isles, she who strutted around in breeches thumbing her nose at all manner of unsavory humanity, was unsure of herself here in his bedchamber. A smile tugged at his lips. He would reassure her. But then he looked down.

Blistering Hades. If one did not believe in God, the sight of her perfection would prove the poor sinner dead wrong. Pure creamy breasts, so full and round. Their tips kissed with two luscious, pebbled raspberries.

His hands twitched at his sides, aching to touch. He pressed his palms against his thighs, feeling the taut muscles bunch and strain beneath.

"I'd like you to remove those britches now." How he got the words out, he didn't know, but she now looked at him with more assurance. As well she should. In over his ears and he hadn't even laid a hand on her. If he touched her now, he'd be done.

Her hands fluttered over the front fall. Too much to take in. He wanted to watch her unbutton but could not relinquish the sight of her breasts. The scale tipped, however, when she bent to slide the flannel over her hips and down her thighs. They dropped to pool at her feet, and she kicked free of them. She wore no drawers.

"I tried them," Nora said as if she read his mind. She flicked a mass of unruly curls back over her shoulder. "Norbert is a bit of a dandy, and underthings would have spoiled the line of his trousers."

He nodded, well aware he looked like some punch-drunk clod.

"Now you." She nodded at his clothing.

He jerked his shirt out of his waistband and then

wrenched it over his head. When he emerged, she had moved to the bed. She sat primly on its very edge, ankles crossed, her hands folded in her lap so close to her—

"Now the trousers."

He tossed his shirt aside and scrabbled to find the buttons on his fall.

"Slower," she admonished, shifting to cross her ankles the other way.

He turned his back to her. Easier to concentrate without her gaze raking over his too primed body. And besides, he didn't want to scare her off. Get her used to the tamer bits before he turned around. His was not a gentleman's physique, but women cooed over his bulk just the same. Besides, she'd seen it all before at Flora Hollingwood's brothel. His lips pulled into a grin. Well, to be fair, Mrs. Nora St. James had tried mightily to *not* look at his nether parts.

He hooked his thumbs into the waistband and— slowly—eased the buckskin over his bum.

The sound of her expelled breath almost had him turning around, but by sheer will he held his position. Was she repulsed or admiring?

Time to turn around and see.

Chapter Fifteen

He was huge. All over.

His penis bobbed against his sculpted belly, its glistening head flirting with his navel, the hair at its root a dusky blond—so different from Devlin, who was nearly the same height as she, with pale skin and slim darkness. The only other man she had seen, her husband, had been withered as an old carrot. And though tall, the earl's gray skin had hung in loose folds like wet papier-mâché on a skeleton. As if all the life had run out of him

This man made her feel petite, even dainty.

Her body seemed to recognize a worthy lover even before her mind caught up. Her breasts swelled and her nipples drew up into tight buds. And below—she closed her thighs more tightly, pressing her ankles together.

He kicked his trousers aside and stood arms akimbo, as if waiting for her to give some signal that he might approach.

A flare of panic cinched her belly and leapt into her throat. Over three years since she had lain with a man. Would she be enough?

"So, Countess. Will I do?"

There was something so vulnerable, yet so assured in his tone that her heart squeezed along with her legs, belly, and throat. *He* was slightly nervous as well.

In answer, she stood and took a step, and then

another, closing the gap between them.

He raised his hands to frame her face and tilted her head up. Clearly, he wanted her to meet his gaze. A matter of a slight shift on her part, but it terrified her even as it thrilled her.

Courage. She could weather his tenderness and not lose her head over him. *Or heart.*

Done.

If eyes could smile, his did so. He brushed the pads of his thumbs over her cheeks and then over her eyebrows. He wove his fingers into her hair and gently pulled her to his lips.

At the last moment she closed her eyes.

Their lips met softly, almost as if they were testing the way they might fit together—hers plush and full against his firmer flesh. She felt the slight rasp of his whiskers above his top lip. Her hands found his cheeks. Wide, high bones and a broad nose that crooked ever-so-slightly to one side. Thick lashes and wiry eyebrows. Lush hair with a hint of wave—like a lion's mane.

Yes, a lion. This man was a golden lion.

As if he could hear her thoughts, he made a deep growl and dipped his head to kiss the place where her neck and shoulder met. His teeth grazed the sensitive flesh, and she pulled his head tighter against her, wanting him to somehow mark her. Claim her, if only for this night.

To belong to someone. To share a bed and fold her body within his. To take him inside her and hold him there. To not have to be strong for just a few hours.

His hands skimmed her shoulders, over her arms, nipping in at her waist, and then down over her hips and buttocks. He pulled her closer. The hot length of him pressed into her belly. Her breasts, now crushed against the fine hairs of his massive chest, burned for more.

"I want you so much, Nora St. James." Then he set her away from him.

He could not be saying no, not now.

He moved to the bed and pulled the coverlet back.

Not no.

He put another log on the fire and lit two lamps. Details emerged, a washstand, framed portraits, the now rumpled counterpane embroidered with passionflowers and thistles. No more deep shadows where she could hide. With the lightening of the room, the glare of reality shone out as the day's events intruded, Hancock's deception, the hopeless search for Rose.

"Don't," he whispered from just behind her. "Don't leave me now." He gently turned her, using a thumb under her chin so she might meet his gaze. Need and hope co-mingled within his leaf-green eyes. His vulnerability enveloped her. Oh, he had his cares and disappointments, yet what he offered was a respite from the world. A balm they could share. If only for this moment.

He dipped his head, and his lips brushed hers. He pulled back slightly and then assaulted her again with his tender caress. The third time she opened to him. Yes, yes, she would give herself this joy.

His thigh pressed next to hers as he knelt on the bed, guiding her to lie beneath him. The linen sheet felt fine and cool against her skin, a contrast to his heat. She stretched, trying to lengthen her body to feel all of him as she pulled him against her, wanting his weight to engulf her, to make her be one with his strength.

Again, he pulled back, not allowing her to hide

within him. The stubborn man. He wanted all of her.

His gaze bore into hers with a tender insistence as his hands cradled her cheeks.

"You are so beautiful."

His words tore into her. Desperate to believe he did not just mean her face or body, but perhaps he saw something beautiful and worthy deep within her. Something she could not see.

She closed her eyes. Too much. Like jumping off a cliff. And she was afraid of heights.

She reached for his cock.

He hissed as her fingers surrounded him. She bit her lip and arched, pressing her breasts into his chest, squeezing her hand. He bucked and then groaned.

Eyes still closed, she sensed his resignation as his body took over.

Yes, she would allow herself this beautiful release, but it would be utter folly to fall too far under his spell.

Though his gentle kisses against her eyelids nearly did her in. Another squeeze of his cock and then grabbing his buttock had him exhaling a soft curse and positioning himself at her very center. Still, he hesitated. She squeezed her eyes shut and pushed onto him.

"Ahh!"

She did not know who cried out, so lost in the fullness of him filling her so completely. Her fingernails raked at the huge expanse of his back, feeling the muscles bunch and ripple as he pushed into her. His hands cradled her bottom as he adjusted to fit her more tightly against him. Wrapping her legs high on his back, she pulled him even closer. His breath came hot and panting in her ear, his hips pumping to this primal music.

More. Oh, more. She raised her arms overhead to push against the headboard.

He seemed to hear her silent plea and increased his tempo.

Her body gathered itself, so tight, so tense with need. Dear God, she would not survive.

Her hands let go of the bed, the world rushed and spun, rising within her body.

"Ahhh!"

Bursts of light danced before her as her body jerked and shuddered. A long while later, when loose-limbed euphoria stole over her body and her mind could fix on sense, the word that came to mind was, miraculous.

Chapter Sixteen

Once.

It was over and she would not indulge again.

But her body did not seem to be in accord with her mind. Before it could betray her, she slid out of his bed, praying he would not awaken, yet hoping he would. Hoping to hear him call her back to him, to make love once more. But he slept the sleep of death.

Such a fool! They had not used any preventative.

Quick calculation of her cycle gave her a bit of peace. Too early. She hoped.

She slipped back into her Norbert togs. Lastly, balling up the linen binding and stuffing it in the pocket of her coat. Poor Norbert was looking a bit worse for wear in the wee hours of the morning.

Early morning fog still clung to the streets, obscuring nearly everything. She looked back at the house where Farren lay sleeping, wondering which window might be his room. She made herself turn away.

A half hour later she slipped into the mews behind Greene Street, entering the townhome by the front door. Avoiding the fifth creaky stair, she padded down the short hall and peeped into the girls' room. All tucked up asleep.

She crept into her bed, the oddly familiar ache

between her legs, her breasts tender and still so sensitive. Sleep seemed impossible.

****

Light touches rained down her arm. She turned toward the caress, but instead of a bass rumble, a soft child's voice piped.

Agnes.

The girl stood before Nora. Weak sun filtered through the window, gilding her eager face.

"There was a man lurking about the house, Mum."

Nora jerked to a sitting position. "A man?"

"I could hear him—heavy footfalls, a wheeze, had a habit of jingling something. And I could smell him. He likes spirits. My old mum used to like her gin. He smelled like her."

"Did he come to the front door?" She swiped at her eyes and fumbled for her wrapper as if the girl could see her shame.

"No, not that I know of. I couldn't sleep. You know how sometimes I confuse day with night. It was late. The clock had struck two. I went out to see to the chickens. I startled him. He ran to the garden gate but then he stopped when I didn't scream. See, I pretended I didn't know he was there and just went about my business."

"Why, Agnes? He could have hurt you."

"He didn't want me. I think he wanted to get into the house. I thought it better, safer, to let him think himself invisible. But he didn't know I see in other ways."

Yes, Agnes perceived more than most people.

"He did not come near you?"

"Oh, he did. He thought it was funny to see how

close he could get to the poor blind girl." Agnes smiled.

She took the girl by her thin arms. "Did he touch you?"

The girl flinched but shook her head.

Nora eased her frantic grip and pulled Agnes to her breast. Silken hair brushed her chin, and she inhaled the girl's powdery smell. "Did he try to enter the house?"

Agnes's fingers skated over the worn cotton of Nora's wrapper, finding the frayed ribbon at the neckline. "Oh, he tried, but I was too clever for him. I stood before the door as if I didn't know he was there at all. Scared him, I did. He didn't know what to make of me. Then I lit a lamp and sat in the kitchen most of the night." She grinned. "Silly man should have known a blind girl would never need to light a lamp."

"You must take care, poppet." Guilt burned like a hot coal in Nora's breast. She had been in Farren Cavanaugh's bed while some stranger bent on who knew what had prowled about. She pushed the thought aside.

Devlin's portraits were stored under the bed. She bent to look. No, all still there.

Were they the reason for the prowler? And those gifts, could they be connected with someone wanting to get into the house?

"When I went out this morning to feed the chickens, I nearly tripped over this." Agnes held out a thin, flat package.

The paper was damp with dew. Agnes sat on the bed waiting to find out what was inside.

The wrapping fell open with a pull of the string. The scent of roses filled her nose.

She dropped the box. Pale cream tissue paper

parted to reveal…

Gloves.

A pair of gloves of the finest cream-colored lamb skin. Tiny rows of pearl buttons at the wrist, minute embroidery decorating the sleeve.

Roses. White rose buds twined with full-blown ruby roses.

The note lay next to the box. The same paper. The same hand.

Behold these two, a perfect matchéd pair,
So should it be, for fair must go with fair.
Take care, lose not one precious lovely lamb.
And n'er will you bide in fair Corsham!
For e'en the slightest slip portends downfall,
Condemned e'remore to a barren world of gall.
What use a glove without its matchéd mate?
You must prove worthy to embrace your fate!

Corsham?

The impossible dream of her charity home for her girls. Who had she spoken to about the house? Lady Gadwick, but was there anyone else?

"Mum?" Agnes's fingers touched Nora's face, light as the wings of butterflies. "You do not like them?"

"Oh, they are a surprise is all." She took the girl's hands. "I think it is time we took the earl and Charlotte up on their invitation to stay at Linden House. Would you like that?"

The girl frowned. "Would you? Would you like to move?"

Nothing got past Agnes Jane Bromley.

Nora's heart squeezed. Nora had never really talked to the little girls about the old earl or her previous life, yet Agnes instinctively knew Nora was unsettled. "Well, I will certainly miss our little home, but I do recall Linden House has a beautiful pianoforte."

That bit of information tipped the scales, and Agnes smiled.

Nora could no longer afford her pride, or this house.

****

"Where are the other notes?" Farren held the newest poem in one hand, while the other slapped the gloves against his thigh.

He'd arrived as she and the girls were packing. All she wanted to do was to climb into this man's lap and feel him deep within her. "I burned them. They were vile and I wanted to rid myself of their taint."

"Damn it, woman. Why won't you learn to trust me?"

"I did not think—"

"When did the first arrive?"

Let's see … she had been set to go out. To Franny Hacket's. "The roses came the day after I met you."

The sound of leather slapping stopped. "And the next?"

"Sometime after the auction. He wrote about 'polluted paint.'"

Farren spun around, shaking his head.

"I remember! The perfume arrived just after we kiss—we visited Eunice Lockhart."

"And these came." He held the gloves out. "Early this morning?"

A damned blush flooded her cheeks. Why did he have to look at her that way? "Yes, I assume it was the prowler, but it could be someone else I suppose. I did not see the box, as I entered through the front door." Hell, she could have tripped over the package and not paid any mind, so caught up in her own world.

"Promise you will tell me when the next comes."

"You are so sure there will be a next?"

"As sure as the rent comes due."

A curl of fear stirred in her belly.

"We will be safe at Linden House. There are servants galore." She did not add that she could no longer afford this house, that it was mortgaged to the hilt. Or that the thought of stepping a foot back inside Linden House made her want to retch.

"It's not the girls this man has got his sights on. It's you."

Yes, that made sense. Agnes would have been an easy prey if the man had truly wanted her. The thought gave her some comfort. She could look out for herself.

"I will go to Corsham," he said, "and visit the property you had in mind. Might be a clue there."

"Take me with you."

He was already shaking his head. "Not a chance."

"You said yourself this person is fixated on me. If I am out of town then everyone will be safer. Myself included."

He ran the gloves through his fingers, his thumb finding the pearl buttons. She could see the very moment the idea of spending a full day and perhaps night with her bloomed in his mind.

"I know the property and have been in contact with the agent," she added. "I'm sure he will remember me."

"That might be a problem."

"Then I can dress as Norman."

"I like Norbert better."

Was he thinking of last evening?

"We'll take the early train on Friday."

Chapter Seventeen

"Aggie, it does not look like a linen house at all. It is as big as the match factory, only beautiful!"

Opal grabbed the ankle of Mari, whose little body hung almost entirely out of the carriage window. For the entire ride from Greene Street to Linden House, Mari had been reporting everything she saw to Agnes, Agnes asking question after question, and Opal pretending to be nonplussed, but Nora knew how this move affected her.

Nora pressed herself back into the squabs. The old equipage groaned and shifted as Thomas pulled to a stop and then jumped down from the box.

A sick headache pressed at her temples.

"Me first, Thomas!" Mari cried as she launched herself into the coachman's arms.

Thomas set Mari safely on the brick drive and then assisted Agnes. He held out his hand to Opal, but she only pushed it aside, admonishing Mari with a sharp, "Desist, Marigold, or I will whack your bottom!"

Charlotte's sisters could be heard calling out to their guests. Opal ignored them, still hovering by the carriage door.

"You go on. I will be along in a moment," Nora said, giving the girl a smile of encouragement.

Opal looked as if she were going to the gallows

instead of a mansion in Mayfair. But being Opal, she lifted her chin and mounted the stairs.

"My lady?" Thomas, now having deposited Agnes with one of the sisters, stood waiting to assist Nora.

"In a moment. See to the horses."

"Very good, m'lady." He touched his forehead and left.

Stop being so bloody dramatic.

But her stomach was not cooperating with her reason.

Don't be a henwit. Get out. Now.

She pushed off the bench and ducked her head as she exited the carriage, then stepped to the pavers below. A horse neighed. That would be Valentine. Thomas shushed her, seeming to sense his mistress's mood.

Nora looked up.

Well, it would not be forever.

Please God, it couldn't be.

She nodded and managed to smile as children and servants whirled around her. Thank heavens for all the hoopla of excited little girls. Cousin Orville was not at home, but Charlotte conveyed his welcome. Three lovely blonde girls bobbed their curtsies to her, their names a mishmash as she acknowledged them, and then they scampered off with Mari and Agnes to the nurseries.

Nora found herself farther down the hallway. The door to the front parlor was open. Black scorch marks still marred the marble mantlepiece. It would have to be replaced, she thought, vainly seeking to put aside the memory of that terrible day when her husband had nearly set her on fire. But in the end, he'd only managed to burn himself. The hideous carpet of cabbage roses still covered the floor. The servants must have been able to remove the blood. Or perhaps the garish pattern simply disguised the stains?

"Auntie?" Charlotte and Opal stood behind her in the doorway. She must have crossed into the room without thinking.

"Would you like to get settled?" Charlotte smiled, a sharp contrast to Opal's grim face.

"Oh, yes. Thank you."

As they ascended the stairway Charlotte chattered on about fittings, and invitations, and the dinner hour …

Nora touched the brass railing, the same one she had tried to grab when he had pushed her down these very steps in a fit of temper. The servants had rushed in, drawn by the clamor, but when they saw the old earl at the top of the stairs, they had backed away. Only Thomas, ignoring the others, had reached down to help her, but she'd waved him off. He would only be punished. She'd tested her legs and then used the brass railing to heave herself to her feet.

She squeezed her eyes shut, her temples throbbing in concert with her pounding heart.

It is only for a little while.

Thank God Cousin Orville was occupying the earl and countess's suite of bedchambers. She would never go back there. Ever.

The nude paintings of her had been moved just yesterday and were now packed away in a chest in the attics, where someone decades from now might stumble upon them and wonder at the sort of life the sitter had lived. And the chickens, which they could not leave behind, were, for the time being, inhabiting the little greenhouse next to the mews.

The girls had been given rooms in the nursery. Nora had worried how they would be greeted, where they would fit into this household, but if their welcome was any indication, the family seemed thrilled to have them. Perhaps Canadians were not such sticklers for the rules of society. Or, more likely, they were just dear, sweet children, and their father merely happy to have someone to lean on.

In the next few days, Mari had slipped right in with her new family, and Agnes, though still unfamiliar with the house and its layout, was becoming fast friends with Cynthia, Charlotte's second youngest sister who happened to play the pianoforte.

But poor Opal was miserable. Used to being second in command, the girl clearly felt *de trop*. Mrs. Gowan now had the charge of Agnes and Mari, and Charlotte's overtures of friendship were met with stiff disdain.

"But you have only just arrived." Cousin Orville's side whiskers twitched like a cat in the rain when Nora informed him she would be leaving for a few days. "The season is nearly upon us! What of the presentation at court?"

"Never fear, the dress is well along and thankfully Charlotte is a quick study and a good mimic. She will do well." The matter-of-fact words flowed from her mouth to soothe a fretful father. "You must trust me, and, more importantly, trust your daughter."

"You will be gone a day or two at most?"

The room was sweltering. She had to get away. "I will be back in time to chaperone Charlotte on Tuesday for the Constables' rout. She should wear the salmon batiste with the ivory lace overlay. It should be ready by then. I have written a note to Madame Broussard. The final fitting for the court presentation gown is Wednesday afternoon. It is all noted on the calendar."

The earl moved his mouth with hers as if by echoing her words their incantation would make all roads smooth.

Poor soul, so in over his head with four daughters and his beloved wife gone. Nora teetered in her resolve to leave.

"Good night, cousin," she said before she could change her mind.

She'd not slept a wink. The old case clock in the hallway marking the hours, a painful reminder of the boredom and misery she'd experienced when she'd last inhabited this house. Thank God she would get a reprieve from it for the next two days.

"Please be careful." Nora said to the three faces she loved so well.

"Charlotte has promised to take us to the menagerie and Sanger's circus!" Mari said, performing a graceful *port de bras*.

"*I* will see to these two, Mum." Opal gave Mari a sour look. "You must not give us a thought."

As an extra precaution, Farren's man, the same person he had hired to watch for Rose in Covent Garden, would now be stationed in the mews behind Linden House.

"Very well, Opal."

The girl's only acknowledgment, a derisive sniff.

"That means no going out in the middle of the night. Mari and Agnes need you." She gave Opal a speaking look.

"I know my duty, mum." The girl stood straighter, her scar accentuated as her neck pinked with ire.

"Yes, I know, my dear one." She squeezed Opal's hand and hugged the two little girls.

Late June air hit Nora's flushed cheeks providing little relief to her overheated body or her overwrought wits. Despite the seriousness of their visit to Corsham, her heart jumped at the thought of being alone with Farren Cavanaugh once again.

Widows had their dalliances. And the colonel was unmarried. But Nora must guard her reputation with a vengeance. Rumors had swirled about her and Devlin, and again after the old earl's death. And just recently, Lady Augusta's harangue in front of Lord Milton's guests, and then the near nude portrait of herself … She could not afford another bout of scandal.

Oh, to let all her worries go for just a few precious days. To let Rose go and those terrible gifts, to let Charlotte go, and her brilliant smile and incessant questions, to let her girls and the lack of money go, and the thought of marriage. To slough it all off and escape into decadence with this irresistible man.

She hated her weakness. The *once* of her resolve rang over her like an admonishing refrain. Now she had slipped further, giving herself a precious day of indulgence. Then she would be done with him.

Besides, what could happen in a few days?

****

"I'll be gone only a few days," Farren had explained to his grandpa and Uncle Geoff who had arrived earlier than expected. "I may have a lead on—a man in Corsham who might have been in contact with

Bren." A falsehood, but he did not want to worry them unnecessarily.

"You'll watch yourself, lad?" The old man took his hand and squeezed it.

Farren squeezed back, blinking away the threat of sudden tears. His family. One he was anxious to know better.

"I'll be back by Sunday latest. And then we'll go to Tattersalls."

Geoff grinned and made a neighing sound Farren would swear was near to an honest-to-goodness horse.

He arrived in a hired carriage at Linden House and Nora slipped in next to him without waiting for him to descend and assist her. And at the train station when he tried again, Norbert let Farren know that *he* would be having none of that.

Farren spent a while stowing their bags, hoping when he returned Norbert would be more friendly. He/she had not spoken beyond a rather terse greeting when Farren had met her in the mews behind Linden House.

Could he keep her safe? At the time, he'd thought that the bullet smashing into the wall next to them in Covent Garden a coincidence, but now he was right certain it was meant for her. Or him. Or … Brendan?

His pistol weighed heavy in his drab overcoat, and he adjusted his old slouch hat over his eyes, feigning sleep.

"I want to stretch my legs at this next station," Norbert said, pulling on his fancy-tied neckcloth.

He could do with some air himself. He shucked off his coat, transferring the pistol, and dropped his hat over their bags.

"Swindon!" the conductor called out.

Several other passengers were taking the air as well, a man with a child who seemed a touch green about the gills, and an older woman dressed in black.

The sun still hung lazy overhead. They would have just about enough daylight to make it to the cottage and perhaps have a swim. His cock twitched at the thought of Nora swimming naked …

"All aboard!"

They shuffled back onto the train and it rolled out of the station.

"Stop! Thief!"

The woman in black screeched even as the man with a small child called out, "I've been robbed!"

Farren pushed his way to Nora and their baggage. Sure enough, his hat and coat were gone along with their bags. Only his rucksack of food remained.

"You there," someone called out. Farren turned.

The train screeched to a halt, creating even more chaos.

A man in a beaver hat charged up to him and then stopped.

"Is this the man, sir?" Two conductors stood behind the irate man.

"I'm not sure now. Same build. Same color hair."

Could the thief be Bren?

"These two gents." An older man in a cap pointed at Farren and Norbert with his pipe. "Were out on the platform the whole time. They got off and back on at the same time as me. It weren't him that stole from you."

"Our stuff was nicked as well," Norbert piped up rising to his toes. "Got my best wescoat, he did."

Farren sent Norbert a look. "Took our bags and my coat and hat. Likely to disguise himself, I reckon."

"You a Yank?" The conductor asked as if being an American somehow made him suspicious.

"That's right. Why, was the thief an American?"

"Naw, Cornish I would say," the man with the pipe offered. "Definitely weren't no Yank."

In the end, and several hours later, the train departed with nothing being recovered, but Farren had been thoroughly exonerated.

When they departed the train at Chippingham, and hired their horses for the ride to Ryeland, the sun was dipping into the trees. No time for a swim. Hopefully, they would find the cottage before dark.

Weeks ago, when he had toured Ryeland with his grandpa's steward, Mr. Kincaid, Farren had spied the charming cottage situated near a pond nestled deep in the woods. Darned near perfect. The home farm's fallow fields surrounded by forest.

Farren held the lamp high. *Yes!* There was the opening. And just beyond, the cottage.

Put it down to the impending darkness, or nerves, but they had not spoken the nearly two-mile ride. Likely she was bone tired. He jumped down, happy to be busy instead of thinking. He reached up to help her off her mount prepared to have her wave him off but as their gazes met, she placed her trembling hand in his. Her body slid down his. Thinking to whisper some inane platitude about keeping her chin up, his lips brushed her ear.

She turned her mouth to his. Her lips opened, her tongue seeking, while her fingers dug into his hair, fixing his mouth to hers. Like a broken dam, all the passion held in check came pouring out.

Not tired.

He swept her up in his arms, somehow keeping his lips locked to hers.

The horses could stand another half hour. Dear Lord, that was all he would last.

If that.

He fumbled for the door latch. Locked. Still holding her and wedging his knee under her bum and against the door frame, he felt above the door sill. She bit his neck as his fingers found the key. He nearly dropped it. Now to fit the key into the lock—ah! She found his nipple.

Dad burnit! The key almost dropped again as she trailed her hand lower, heading straight for his cock.

"Hummm," she breathed softly into his ear.

"Confound it woman, a man can only take so much," he said through gritted teeth. "Now, you have a choice, I can either take you right up against this door in front of the horses, or we can be civilized and get inside."

In answer, she pulled back and bit her lip as her hands stilled.

"Right. We will be civilized. For the moment," he said with a shade of disappointment.

He nearly dropped the key a third time at the music of her laugh. The key slid home and the lock clicked.

The door banged loudly against the wall as the key dropped from his hand, a solid *thunk* on the floor.

****

"Civilized, Colonel?" Nora now had a greater appreciation for his military rank. He had besieged her body, going at her with all guns fully loaded and taking no prisoners. She lay utterly spent. "You promised civility. I hardly think taking me on the rug with the door hanging open and my britches about my ankles to be polite."

"My dear, Countess," he said, making a mocking bow, "I expect you'll soon change your definition of civility. This little encounter"—he gestured to the rag-rug where she lay— "was mighty tame. I've nearly four weeks of pent-up fantasies to enact with you. I confess this was one of them, but by no means the least civilized."

"Oh, you and your promises," she said in her most top lofty tone, adjusting the lacy garter that held up her stocking.

He looked out the open door at the poor beasts snuffling in the leaves for some tender shoots of grass and then back at her and once more out the door. "Ah, the sacrifices a man must make. You'll pardon me while I see to the horses."

He skirted around her as if she were a snare that might trap him.

Unable to let him out of her sight, she rose to peer through the window, spying on him like a green girl.

He spoke softly to the horses, soothing them. She imagined his murmured apologies for keeping them standing so long. He ran his beautiful hands down their loins and over their bellies.

One beast's huge head bobbed by the colonel's buttocks to nibble at his trousers. Buttocks she'd had a hold of only moments ago. Hard and round as she squeezed, feeling the muscles gather to push into her.

He laughed and said something to the curious gelding. She would swear the horse understood and laughed back. She pressed into the glass but only heard the rumble of his words and an answering *nicker*.

Satisfied, he solicitously led them toward a small shed where he must be promising sweet oats.

One could tell much about a man according to how he handled his cattle.

She dropped her head into her hands. Oh, dear God, how would she survive one night with this man, much less an entire day?

Chapter Eighteen

The fire popped and sparks flew. The remains of their dinner, cheese and bread, lay on a small table between them. She sat across from him in the twin chair flanking the fire. She could barely look at him sprawled out, thinking of how he had offered her a wedge of cheese and she had ended up with her legs wrapped around his waist, gripping the wings of his chair to push harder against him.

Yet, now they sat sedately, like an old married couple. He held the bowl of a chipped goblet lightly between his long fingers. Rolling his wrist, he sent the golden liquid twirling, seemingly fascinated as its legs ran back down to pool in the bottom of the glass. He looked up, catching her lick her lips.

"I suppose this cottage is part of an estate?" she asked mostly to distract herself.

He only nodded.

"And does it belong to your friend who is partial to Yanks?"

He took a moment to consider and then nodded. They lapsed into silence again. "Tell me about your life."

The question surprised her. By the look of him, she had supposed—hoped—he'd had another fantasy to tick off.

"What do you want to know?" She did not mean to sound so suspicious, but no man had ever been interested in her life.

"Everything." His long leg reached toward her dangling foot and his toes flexed against hers. "You could start with your childhood? I reckon you'd be in charge, commanding all your playfellows. The General."

Playfellows? She hadn't any. One doll named Rainbow, who had lost an eye and a hand, and the old hound, Wally, from the neighboring estate, who placidly submitted to her tea parties. A worn-out doll and a decrepit dog were the extent of Nora's entourage. But she had loved Rainbow and Wally fiercely. Perhaps that was why she loved the Opals and Maris and Agnesses of this world.

"Yes, I was the General," was all she said.

He raised an eyebrow but wisely changed his tack. "Do you want to talk about Rose? About Lily?"

She tucked her foot under her and sat up straighter.

"Would you mind?" He leaned forward drawing his legs under him. "I would love to hear about Lily."

The fire's embers pulsed as if alive. A flame leapt from the glowing coals. How much to let him in? Another flame shot up. Or perhaps it was not so much letting him in as letting Lily out.

She set her brandy aside and then folded her hands together. "Lily did not want me as a mother." The words came out clipped without any of the emotion that seethed just beneath. Perhaps she could do this. "She did not have much choice. I was so determined." All her motherly efforts—or how she had imagined a loving mother might behave—had been met with disdain. "Then I tried to manage her. Silly idiot that I was. Lily was not one to be managed. She resented me. Didn't want to take anything I had to give. And she needed so much." Her nails bit into the flesh of her palm. She flexed her hand and then reached for her brandy.

"I swear I would have locked her in the house those first weeks if I'd dared. Every time I set the key into the lock at Greene Street, I was sure she would be gone, along with anything of value. But when I called out, there she'd be, rag or broom in hand." The fire swelled as a gust of wind rushed down the flue and rattled the windows.

Farren now had his elbows on his knees, his gaze intense.

"I had the odd notion that if we could make her smile, just once, all would be well. But she never did."

He sat up, transferring his glass to the table. "We? You and Lord Devlin?"

She nodded. "Though, by then, he was gone more frequently than with us. I suspect he'd begun to tire of me … or of life. I am not entirely sure which." She pasted on a smile. "Poor Dev. I turned from eager mistress into mother hen protecting her chick. Hardly an image to inspire love."

He did not come back with a witty rejoinder as she expected but instead seemed to give her words deep consideration. "Hmm, not sure I'd agree," he finally said, his eyes too penetrating.

Nora stood to escape his gaze. "She liked being useful, washing things, sewing. I suggested making a layette for the baby, but she only shook her head."

Brandy burned her nose as she inhaled the peaty smell.

"Mostly, she loved tending to my plants. Particularly a miniature rose bush that grew—or rather, didn't grow—in the window box outside of my bedchamber window." Warm liquor rolled over her tongue, bathing her mouth.

His gaze too intense, she found herself at the window overlooking the cottage's neglected vegetable patch. Wind whipped the old stalks, ruffling the few remaining leaves. "Lily never talked much, but I would hear her murmuring to that bush." Nora had known better than to approach the girl and had stayed behind the door, ear pressed to the crack, only hearing a sweet singsong cadence. "Then one day a miracle happened. I remember it like yesterday. I was writing a letter to my solicitor when Lily grabbed my hand. I thought she was ill she was in such a state. But she took me to the window ledge and pointed to a tiny pink bud."

Nora dropped the edge of the lace curtain. "She never got to see it bloom."

Her brandy was being taken from her. She turned to find the colonel next to her. He scooped her up in his arms and held her against his breast.

She was not a petite woman, but he made her feel so. She should protest, demand to be set down. Instead, she burrowed into his chest, the knocking of his heart so steady and assured against her ear. The fine linen of his shirt smelled of musky smoke and pine. After a long moment, he sat down in her chair and cradled her on his lap.

Time to sit up and remove herself. Perhaps she'd call for the cat—Farren had dubbed the stray tabby Trigger when he'd darted into the cottage looking for scraps. But she didn't. She was weak against the power of his kindness. For she'd never been held thus. Not by Devlin. Or even her nursemaid. Certainly not by her mother.

You will crease my dress. Get up this instant. Her mother nearly pushed Nora onto the floor. *Nurse Batten, come and take her away!*

The old memory lashed at her.

Get up, toss off your brandy and go to bed.

Leaving his warm lap was like hacking that tiny rose bud off its branch.

He said nothing as she made her way up the stairs alone.

****

Orion had slipped sideways in the Western sky, making room for Hercules.

She had opened the tiny window in the bedchamber. Stars now dappled the night sky. Her papa had taught her the star signs. Rousting her out of bed in the dead of night to take her up to the widow's walk at the very top of the house. She remembered being frightened by the height but exhilarated at the same moment. Looking as much at her beloved papa as at the stars he was pointing out. The Pleiades, Andromeda, Cassiopeia, and so forth. She did not know then he was a drunk and a gambler. To her, he was only her jolly papa whom she only saw a few times a year, but who always had a smile for her.

The stairs creaked and groaned. Unhurried, steady footfalls.

She scurried into bed. Hugging herself tight, she pulled the linen sheet to her chin and squeezed her eyes shut. As if she had a hope of arming herself against this man.

The door opened and then clicked shut. Water splashed and trickled into the basin. Simple intimacies that set her heart racing. She let out a tiny snore—

The sounds of water stopped.

Good gad, not as tiny as she had hoped.

She imagined him turning from his ablutions, that wicked smile upon his lips.

She had never spent an entire night with a man. Certainly, never with her husband. She and Devlin had made frantic love only to doze before making love again. Or more often she'd hurried back into her clothes and dashed off before she was missed at Linden House.

To sleep all night next to Farren Cavanaugh seemed more intimate than even the act of lovemaking. Terror flooded her as she gripped the mattress.

Surely, he would let her sleep?

The bed sighed and dipped as he climbed in beside her. She held on to the edge lest she roll into the snare of his body.

It didn't matter. She couldn't have resisted him if she had been in a bloody tower.

Oh-so-gently, he slid one arm around her and pulled her right up against the warm curve of his body. Spoons in a drawer. A perfect match.

Dear God, it felt like home.

Chapter Nineteen

He'd overslept. The bed was empty. Had he really expected her to stay? Still, he reached out to touch her pillow, as if he were missing a vital part of himself.

He had simply held her for a long while, but then she had stirred and pressed back into him. Hell, he needed no other invitation. She turned and mounted him. Eyes closed, she'd driven herself down on him. Almost as if in anger. As if somehow the act might purge her wanton desires.

He didn't want her to wish to be rid of him. He longed for her to see him, to embrace him completely. But, dang, he was only human and so he took her anger as well as her loving. Hell, he would take anything she'd give.

Afterward, in the dawn's light, she had touched his scars, put her fingers into a deep gash on his side where a Bowie knife had flayed him open after venturing too deep into the Wind River Canyon, looking for an escape route for his men. Once each had been thoroughly examined, she had hovered over him as if wanting to do something for him.

He had been ready to talk, to reveal some of his horror, but she'd remained silent. Disappointment pricked, but he was being feather-headed. Why would he ever want to expose her to such a dark time in his life?

This woman was like a drug. His nightmares staying deep within his brain, he hadn't woken in a terror-soaked sweat ready to kill someone. The only other time he'd found such peace was the last time she had laid next to him.

He found her in the small kitchen tucked like an afterthought into the side of the cottage. "What's for breakfast, woman?" He grinned.

She looked about the room as if just discovering where she was. "Colonel, I am a lady."

"You could have fooled me." He waggled his eyebrows, thinking of her on top of him, pinning his wrists over his head, teasing his mouth with her breasts, sweet dangling fruit.

Like some irate jaybird, she flicked her tail feathers at him then turned to the window. So different from the siren who had occupied their bed only an hour ago.

"Ladies do not cook," she said to the curtains.

He moved farther into the tiny kitchen, sending her fluttering from her perch to fly about the room.

"What exactly do ladies do?" He pulled out a chair, laying claim to more territory.

She frowned.

"Come on, Countess, give an American rube a few pointers."

She stopped her fluttering and stood with her hands on her hips, her nose in the air. "We drink chocolate, we bathe, we change our clothes, make calls—staying precisely fifteen minutes. We change our clothes again, drink tea, change clothes yet again, and then go to evening entertainments."

"Hmm, now that does sound like a full day's work. Certainly no time for cooking."

She sniffed, giving him that high-fallutin' look he was beginning to love.

"But I reckon allowances must be made. After all, you provide a home for future cooks, and seamstresses, and teachers."

"Yes, well, it is most unladylike of me to do so. A lady may dabble and bring an occasional basket to the needy, but to actually take them under her roof and then to peddle French Letters to bawdy houses—well, that is unpardonable."

"Yet you continue."

She gave him a shrug.

"Why? Why put yourself in that difficult position?"

"Because I must."

It took all his will not to scoop her up and crush her in his arms. Sure as an ornery bear she would not appreciate his ardor. "As it turns out, you are in luck, my lady. Happens I am an excellent cook."

****

A hundred questions tumbled in her mind as she rode behind him on their way to Corsham. Did he like liver? Could he sing, or perhaps play an instrument? How did he get the tiny scar near his left temple? Or that horrible one just under his left ribs? Did he know how the feel of his large, square hand on her breast made her want to weep?

She would never know, for she would never ask.

Already she was finding out too much about him. Tidying up, she'd moved his boots from the side of the bed only to find them back precisely where they had been. Only then did it occur to her that they were there for a reason. She hadn't asked, but she had heard stories of soldiers sometimes killing for a good pair of boots.

214

And boots must be at the ready to jump into at a moment's notice. No, their day together could not end soon enough for her poor heart.

Only a short ride from the village, the estate was just around the bend in the road. There! There it was, the house with its four chimneys and walled side garden.

Her heart squeezed. So perfect.

Caught up in her fantasy, she nearly rode into Farren. He'd abruptly stopped, holding out his hand to stay her, his body primed, like a snake ready to strike.

She reined her horse next to his. Then she saw it. The entire back of her dream house was a pile of charred, black, rubble.

****

"A drinker was old Gordy. Likely had too much and were careless." The tapster at the *Hounds Rib* said when Farren and Norbert stopped in.

"May we speak with Mr. Gordy?" Nora, as Norbert, asked the man.

The man's gaze narrowed as he took in Norbert. "Naw, he were burned in the fire. Held on two days but then, poor soul, he went to his maker."

"Careless?" Farren tried to make his question sound idle.

"Aye, they found him there in what was left of the kitchen, bottle and pipe still clutched in his hands."

Could it be true? Just a tragic coincidence?

The barman moved off to serve a man who had just come in. A local. The tapster asked after his wife. Something about a missing ring?

"Should we speak to the police?" Nora whispered.

Farren shook his head and then held his finger to

his lips.

"Never such doings as this past week." The new customer took a swig of his ale. "A fire, then that train theft, and now a shooting."

"Aye, we'll have the London papers here sniffing about wanting to make a tempest in a teapot." He shook his head at his mug of ale.

"Excuse me." Farren said to the local man. "You say someone was shot?"

"And what's it to you, Yank?"

"I was on the train. Took my coat and hat and a bag of clothing. Nothing much. I reckon he snagged it to disguise himself."

The local nodded, warming to Farren. "He got my wife's wedding ring. Found it in the man's pocket when they were going over the body."

"Body?"

"Some trigger-happy fool shot the bastard in Chippingham this morning."

"I'll be darned. Who was the fellow?" Though the conductor had said the man was Cornish, Farren still had to be sure it was not Brendan.

"The thief? Name of Davey Hornsby. Happens he'd been thieving from trains for a few weeks now. Big man, like yourself. His description matched complaints from other robberies."

"The shooter run off when he realized the man was dead," the tapster added. "Haven't been able to track him. My guess is the police ain't bending over backwards."

The men went on to talk of the weather and Silas Wigman's new thresher.

Before leaving, Farren asked the barman for some

food from his larder. They would take the train back to London in the morning. Only a few precious hours left together before the world intruded.

The fire and shooting—a man who looked like Farren and wearing his coat and hat—could be just a terrible coincidence, or not …

Chapter Twenty

Only the odd call of a bird broke the silence as she and Farren rode from the village back to the little cottage.

When he helped her down from her horse, she only wanted to be held tightly against his muscled body. To feel safe.

But he seemed preoccupied as he set her away from him. He handed her the package of food before seeing to the horses.

When she was nearly at the door, he called out to her.

"There is a small pond not far through the trees there." He indicated a narrow path off to the left of the cottage. "Let's have a picnic."

She loved the idea, but Farren still seemed distant, as if he took no real pleasure in the plan.

A short while later, after gathering together a basket of food and blanket, they came to a charming pond surrounded by trees. An outcropping of rock sheltered a sandy bank.

No sooner had Farren laid the blanket down did he take her in his arms, his mouth on hers, his hands everywhere. His lovemaking almost desperate.

"Yes," she gasped against his mouth.

He mounted her, hands beneath her bottom, urging her to meet him. The musky smell of wool filled her nose as she dug her heels into the blanket, arching away from the rough fabric to grind her center to his silken heat, making a frantic rhythm with their breath, their bodies, and *yes*, she thought, even their minds.

After, they lay panting next to each other, their only connection his smallest finger entwined with hers.

Too hot. Too close. She heaved herself up and shucked off her chemise. Cool air like cream coated her body, but she wanted freezing. Running, she plunged into the pond. Icy water stole her breath and made her feet ache. But this frigid reality was just what she needed.

She headed for the far side of the pond, where a weeping willow's long branches kissed the water. And then started back. Too cold.

He'd been watching her swim, sitting up, his hand shading his eyes, primed as if he might spring into action at any moment.

Self-conscious, she pushed through the water, revealing more and more of her body, part of her wanting to duck beneath the murky green and part reveling in his appreciation of her. Everything about him might as well have said, *You're mine. You know it, and I know it. But I will play your way. For the time being.*

"Did you love him?"

His question and the sharpness of his tone made her falter near the water's edge.

"Who?"

He only looked at her. He couldn't mean her late husband. She'd hated him and he her. She crossed to the blanket and used her chemise to dry herself—cover herself. "Devlin?"

He nodded, his jaw line twitched.

What to say? Dev had been her savior. For months she had resisted the beautiful and talented Marquess of Devlin, but he'd worn her down. In her desperation for something that would keep her from despair, she took him. The lover part had certainly been eye-opening and delightful, but what she'd really craved was tenderness and companionship.

"No, I did not love him."

Still, Farren Cavanaugh waited.

"I suppose ours was more of a bargain." She ducked her head through the neck of her chemise and pulled it down over her still-damp body. "He got to paint me and bed me, and I got—an escape."

She reached for Farren's discarded jacket, needing to be more covered. Then wished she hadn't. His smell surrounded her. "I am not sure I am capable of that kind of love. Or, if I was, I am not anymore."

He had been propped on his elbows, but now he sat up fully. "And what is 'that kind of love'?"

She shrugged, hoping the action might give the lie to how close he was getting to her most vulnerable spot. "Love for a man, a husband. I think that is why I loved Lily so. And why I love my girls. My love has to go somewhere—I am not a monster who is totally empty, thank God."

He frowned. "Why would you ever think that?"

"Colonel, I will not be so callous as to equate my situation with what you must have endured in war." Scars puckered his magnificent body, telling a brutal tale, but somehow they made him even more beautiful—more real and worthy. He had fought for a cause, for freedom and unity. Her scars only spoke of an old man's rage. "I can't begin to imagine the horror you must have endured during your Civil War, but I experienced my own prison and cruelty. It damaged me. Part of me is dead like a rotten limb. Better to saw it off than kill the whole tree."

"And will you be content with your girls and your charity home?"

This man was clearly out to push her. She dug in. "Yes, content."

"She said, as if facing a dose of castor oil." His words were light in tone, but his eyes said something quite different.

She shrugged, as if the action might end this conversation. *But had she really said it that way?* "It is my ambition," she said, hopefully putting a final period on this subject.

"Only that? Surely as a young girl you had some romantic dreams."

Damn him. She would not let him see how cruel he was with his not-so-innocent questions. "Of course, I had silly dreams. A handsome, charming young swain who fell madly in love with me, and I with him, but only after leading him in a merry chase. After all, one does not want to be caught too soon." She laughed, hoping it did not sound as forced to his ears as it had in her own.

"But you were caught. And far too soon."

Ah, he knew how to jab with surgical precision. She sat on the very edge of the blanket, her toes flexed against the felt of grass, as she stared out over the water. The willow waved its long fingers over the placid pond, teasing its surface. In response, the water seemed to wink up at the tree. Nature in conversation.

Such harmony. Such beauty …

"I was just seventeen. No Season. No come-out ball. No fireworks over the Thames, no routs, no Venetian breakfasts. Not one carriage ride in Hyde Park, or waltz in a glittering ballroom. And certainly no clandestine meetings. No heart knocking against my ribs, no …" She dug her toes more deeply into the grass and hugged her knees. *Silly. And stupid to feel so exposed.*

She made herself sit up straight. "I met my husband-to-be only once before we were married, when he came to look me over. I say this not to seek pity, only to give you a clear picture. Now I think on it, I'm surprised he did not require me to open my mouth wide to check my teeth. Isn't that what you gentlemen do when you look over a horse you wish to buy?"

"I didn't mean to ruffle your feathers. I am sorry." He shoved his hand through his hair. A gesture, she was learning, when he felt particularly frustrated.

Damn the man. She turned on him. "Sorry? Why should you be sorry?" A snort of derision escaped. "This is a woman's lot. My husband wanted a trophy and a breeder. When I did not increase—well, he was most displeased. The earl was seventy-four when we married and had gone through three wives already. He was desperate."

The Christmas of fifty-nine, he'd demanded her presence. Her lady's maid cowered in the corner. The earl held out a gorgeous inlayed box. When she opened it, it contained her bloody menses rags. "You are useless! Get out of my sight," he had cried.

He'd banished her to his estate on the coast in Norfolk.

It was there that she realized her husband wanted her to sleep with someone else. They both knew he could not—perform, yet he needed an heir, and so he expected her to find a man to provide one. She had failed at that as well. And then when she did take a lover—Devlin—she had made very sure there would be no child of that union. Perhaps her resolve was to thwart her husband, but also because it was just too deceitful.

From her window, high above the coastline, with its southern view, she'd craned her neck to see a sliver of sea. An old chest, dragged under that window, had been her perch for hours on end. She'd inhaled the brine, marked how the clouds scuttled across the deepening sky, counted the waves into the thousands. But she never got to dig her toes into the soft sand, or to rush into the foamy water and then run full tilt as the cresting wave threatened to overcome her. Three months and thirteen days in that room without even a candle and then she had been summoned back to London in order to play hostess.

She squeezed her eyes shut as if that could stop the feelings. "It is an old tale."

She felt the barest brush of his fingers against her cheek.

She jerked away. Pity was the last thing she ever wanted. Especially from this man.

By God, she would not dissolve over the past just to be mopped up by some prying Yankee.

She was *not* his. She belonged to no one. Her tree would grow without the fruit of a loving husband and her own children.

But what of her core? Perhaps she would die deep

inside, as rot took hold and beetles bore into her. How could she support limbs if she had nothing at her center?

****

The threat of rain lay heavy and pulsing, the surface of the pond reflecting the darkening clouds above.

They should pack up and avoid the deluge.

Yet he did not.

One moment sunshine, the next, black, churning clouds.

Life was too uncertain. Too damned short.

Now.

The word broke over his heart.

Now.

Like crashing waves, the insistent hammer of time pounding away. Each passing hour dragging pieces away, eroding life with every minute, every second.

Now.

So many of his men alive one moment and then gone in the next. His grandpa's illness. Finding Rose. Finding Brendan. Threatening gifts and poetry. Misfired shots. Robberies. A man dead—

And finally, Nora.

She lived within his body now. She had seeped into him and claimed every fiber. He could not lose her.

The sun was buried once again. Thunder rolled in the distance.

Now.

"Marry me."

****

Her papa had performed a trick once—a parlor stunt—where he jerked a fine damask tablecloth from beneath her mother's gorgeously set table. Not one thing had been disturbed, yet the china and crystal looked entirely different upon the bare wood.

Marry me.

Two words and Nora's world turned upside down.

She jumped up from their shared blanket.

He stood as well, hands ready by his sides as if he might draw a pistol.

He took a step toward her. She shook her head, backing away.

No way to get that tablecloth back under all that shining silver and crystal. No way to un-say those two words. But she must try.

"No. No." She pulled away from him. "Don't. Please don't."

"Don't?" His gaze so terrible in its sweet tenderness. "But I must." He looked up at the black sky as if it might lend him support. "You wouldn't know this, but the war nearly finished me. I—well, I decided to live. So many didn't have a choice."

He swiped his hand over his face. "Lord, I am making a hash of this." He took her trembling hand, his thumb absently drawing little circles over her knuckle. "What I mean to say is, I don't want to wait anymore. I am ready for life. For love. For you."

If only she could look away. But his eyes burned into hers, his words seared her heart, his stroking finger so warm and sure against her hand.

"You make me hopeful, you give me joy. My heart thumps like a wild bronco just at the thought of you."

He brought her hand to his chest, and she felt the truth of his words. He bent to one knee. "Mrs. Norma Pledgeheart, Norman and Norbert, Mrs. Nora St. James,

Countess of Havermere, and finally, my love, will you marry me?"

Stupid tears threatened. She hadn't cried since her wedding night— Blast it all, she would not turn into a watering pot.

"I know, it requires you changing your name yet again—and I hope for the last time—but I think Mrs. Nora Cavanaugh sounds right fine."

The expectation in his eyes had her heart squeezing within her breast, clogging any words she might have uttered.

She swallowed and looked up at the leaves above, willing her eyes to stop swimming.

Why? Why must he ruin this fantasy? They were due to go back tomorrow. Too soon and yet an eternity. One moment she longed to disappear here with him forever, and the next, desperate to flee back to the real world where she knew the rules and what her future would be.

He smiled then. The bright and unaffected one he wielded with utter assurance and ease, as if it rose from a warm and golden place deep within him to kindle her own flame.

She would have run if she wouldn't look the utter fool. Instead, she pushed him away with words.

"I want you. Does that make you happy? Does that fact stroke your male ego? I burn for you as I never have for any other. You. Only you. Since I was five and ten, men have been salivating to lead me astray, but I have not been the least bit tempted." She took a breath. "Until you. But I cannot give you more than this admission, and my body for these few precious hours. If it were only myself, I might very well cast myself at your feet and tell them all to go to the devil, but I am not alone now. I have my girls to think about. And now my niece, Charlotte. I would jeopardize not only my world but theirs as well. I am their rock, and I will not let them drift."

"Nora—dag nabbit, woman, we are not at war. Do you baulk at the idea of marrying a plain Mr.? Or is it the notion of having any husband at all?"

She shook her head, not as an answer but as if the action might make his words stop. Her heart hammered in her breast, a caged bird desperate to fly free.

Here was this beautiful man. A man who said he wanted her, who knew of her dreams—or at least some of them. A man for whom her body sang. A man she could love—

A husband.

The word pricked her, but she did not know if it were out of want or fear. He stood there with his easy smile, in his unaffected American brashness, so confident and so … ultimately unknown.

In this idyllic spot, where they could pretend the world did not intrude, he was perfect. The perfect, solicitous, charming lover.

Too perfect. It could not last.

The rules of the world would worm their way into this beautiful cocoon they had created. A wife had no say, not with finances, not with children, not even over her own person.

The men in her life had all betrayed her trust. The father she'd idolized, so charming and effervescent, had been nothing but a wastrel, bankrupting his family. And then the old earl, solicitous and grandfatherly at first, but turning cunning and cruel. And finally, Devlin. She had thought to find love with him, but they had both deceived themselves.

Did Farren Cavanaugh imagine life was some storybook romance? He may have been a hero in his Civil War, but outside this parkland he was only a man, and one she had known only a few brief weeks. Did he imagine after so short a time she would throw herself headlong into another alliance? One that might well break her?

And what of his family? He seemed to have no ties left in America, and the family he had here he was reticent to speak of. Were they so crude? He mentioned his grandfather and uncle were farmers somewhere, but perhaps they were so horrible that he chose to forget them?

Oh, she was so angry. Why did he look at her this way? Why did he have to ruin this one moment of perfect bliss by wanting more?

Old Wally, her childhood companion, flashed over her mind's eye.

Filthy, flea-bitten cur! Her mother had said when she'd found Nora entertaining the dog and her doll for tea. *If I catch that mangy mongrel on this estate once more, I will have him shot.* Her mother never made an idle threat.

In young Nora's haste to rise from her little tea table, her doll Rainbow fell to the floor. Ever valiant, Wally hobbled forward to retrieve her. *Get him out, now!* Her mother screeched. Nora had grabbed the first thing she could, her favorite teacup, the one with only a small chip from its fingernail-thin rim. She hurled it at Wally, screaming at him to go home and never come back.

Poor thing could not understand. He looked at her with such loyalty even as she picked up her second favorite teacup, the one that had been his. Her arm cocked back. Wally only looked at her with sadness in his soulful brown eyes as if he could see how pitiful she was.

She never saw sweet Wally again.

Nora squeezed her eyes shut against the image. Life had been infinitely sadder without her dear Wally, and her two best teacups, but she had survived. And she would do so again.

She pushed through this gauntlet of emotions, finally grasping at anger—pulling it like a shield around her. Now fortified, she opened her eyes.

"No." She let the word go like the whoosh. A single, deadly arrow. One that would kill her dreams.

He frowned slightly and then smiled. "No, plain Mrs. Cavanaugh will suit you fine?"

"No, I will not be Mrs. Cavanaugh. I will not marry you."

****

Farren waited, sure this was just another one of his nightmares. Surely if he breathed deep and focused on something mundane, like that leaf that seemed at one moment silver and then a shocking green …

She turned away from him.

The nightmare continued. "That's all you have to say?" he asked, desperate to rewind this moment.

"I have answered. Please do not press me further."

He tried to take her hand again. She pulled away as if his touch burned.

"Why? Is it because I am an American? Because I have no title?"

She only snorted.

Wind blew the branches above them, making the leaves shudder. The entire sky seemed to darken, as if a giant, suddenly tired of day, finally snuffed out the sun.

"But we have made love."

"And?" She tossed her head like a high-strung thoroughbred, knowing he was grasping at straws.

Yet he continued all the same. "We must marry."

Her laugh was raw and ugly. "Why? Why must we?"

"Because … because—" He broke off, knowing full well his argument was hogwash.

"Because that is the rule? And I thought you didn't like rules, Colonel."

He did not know how the world worked any longer. It had been so long since his yearning heart was filled with something other than desperate hope. So long since he'd felt love.

Because I love you. The words hammered in his heart. He clamped down on them. Still, fear pushed out from his breast, leaching into his entire body. He who had faced General Kirby-Smith at Bull Run, he who had surged forward to certain death when the front line had broken, and his men would have been trapped. A slew of dire situations crowded his mind. But each seemed suddenly nothing compared to this red-haired beauty who held his heart in her white hands.

"Why isn't this enough for you?" She spat the words out. "Why must you ask more of me than I can give?"

Thunder rolled in the distance. She turned toward it, as if it were her accomplice, summoning Mother Nature to beat against him with its wrath. To drown this flame.

"It is not fair," she shouted at him like some avenging fury when he remained silent.

"I'm not asking for more than you can give," he said quietly, hoping to check her madness.

But his calm only fueled her anger. "And how do you presume to know what I can give?"

Thunder rolled in the distance.

Damnation! This was all wrong. He took a steadying breath. "Nora, listen to me. Someone's been sending you threatening notes, shooting at you in Covent Garden, burning down the house you wanted to buy—who is going to keep you safe?"

She froze and then slowly took a step toward him and then another until she was right under his nose.

"Safe?" she said through gritted teeth. "Is that what this is about, you wanting to keep me safe? By God, you are a good little soldier after all, Colonel."

"You may be with child."

She blinked and her mouth opened as if she could not breathe.

Worse and worse. Knowing her, now she would feel his proposal was yet another obligation. *He could not get this right.*

Yet he waited. He would take her under any circumstances.

When she said nothing, he pressed. "We have not been careful."

The world around them seemed suddenly airless as if the storm had hushed, waiting along with him for her response.

She looked at him with a kind of surprised awe, but then turned away. "No, we have not."

He hated the thought of tying her to him through a babe, but if that is what it took, then so be it. Besides, he would never allow a child of his to be raised as a bastard. He could make her love him.

"We will wait and see. And from now on we will be careful," she said as if pronouncing a death sentence.

"So, you will have my body, but not me?"

She shook her head. "You put it too simply."

"To my mind, it is simple. I am in love with you."

There, it was out now. Not so difficult jumping off a cliff.

"Love?" She tossed the word out as if it was the dregs of a spittoon. "You'll pardon me if I question your sentiment." She whirled away from him only to turn back. "How can you possibly love me? You do not know me. Not really."

The world tilted. His heart bobbed in his breast. He took a deep breath, trying valiantly to stay steady. He made himself say the words. "You do not love me? Even a little?"

Rather than drawing her nearer to him, his words had her turning in circles as if she might screw herself into the ground. She stopped suddenly. "I—I love this." She spread her arms wide to encompass their picnic blanket, the cottage, the pond, and him. "But this is not real. This is a dream and dreams do not last."

"Why? Why can't they?"

God, she looked like a trapped animal. As if his proposal was the biting teeth of a gin trap.

"All right." He held out his hands in a staying motion, as if confronting a wounded animal. "I reckon the world will intrude from time to time, but that is life. That is living. I have no hankering to exist in a fantasy.

I want to live in the world with you. With you as my wife and be a father to your girls and any others we might be blessed to have."

She twisted away from his words but then wheeled back to him. "The mother of your children? Is that what you really want? A ready-made family of women who will dote on you? Is your life so empty that my family must replace the one you have lost?"

Her words hit him like cannon shot. Their ruined picnic a battlefield. His left boot in the middle of a slice of bread, the strawberries scattered and trampled, their red juice-like blood, soaking into the woolen blanket.

Instead of retreating he stood to, primed to face the death of his dream. "So, you will not have me?"

"I wish to be free."

Birds called out to each other, preparing for the storm.

"Free. Funny, free is what I was hoping to be by marrying you."

She opened her mouth to refute him but, like the darkest cloud, a hardness stole over her face, her chin rose, her mouth firmed to an implacable line and finally her eyes glazed over. He would swear she was not even seeing him.

Still, he would have to hear it from her lips. "You do not love me?"

She flinched as if he had struck her. A flash of pure anguish crossed her face, then nothing.

"No." Very deliberately, she turned away.

Damnation. Pain lanced through his chest, and he stepped back, wanting to sink to his knees.

He had not pegged her for a coward. But by God, she could not even face him.

He had only been a distraction for her. She had never meant to give herself to him, not in truth. Likely, she had only used him to find Rose. The chance to heal the terrible wound Lily had left in Nora's heart. Rose is what she really wanted.

Thunder snapped and then rolled.

"Farren—" she'd turned back to him.

"Pack your things, Countess. We leave at first light."

"But—"

"You will write to me when you are certain."

"Certain?"

The leaden sky bulged as if trying to kiss the earth.

"That you are not with child."

"But, surely—"

"This affair is over."

Lightning forked, splitting the bruised sky. Thunder cracked the heavens wider and a moment later the snap of rain hit the trees.

Chapter Twenty-One

Where Farren slept that terrible night, Nora did not know. The rain continued incessantly even after the drama of the storm passed. Water ran down the windowpane, obscuring everything beyond. The bed beckoned as the hours ticked by, but she could not lie down in it. Would not have her last memory of it be one of desperate isolation.

The ride back to Chippingham and then the train to London had been just as hideous. Not one word spoken beyond his terse 'goodbye' in response to her thanking him for seeing her safely to the back gate of Linden House. She touched the hired carriage's door not wanting to part like this, but he'd turned away.

"Drive on," he said, knocking on the roof.

Opal stood at the open door, hands-on hips, a frown on her face as she watched the carriage disappear.

The girl turned on Nora. "Didn't expect you back until this evening." Making it abundantly clear she assumed their early return had been all Nora's fault. "Ya didn't hightail it back on account of us, did ya? I told you I would manage everything."

Again, leave it to Opal to take everything as a personal affront. The girl shook her head and turned back to the house. Dear God, why did she feel as if she might burst into dreadful tears?

"I assume all is well? No incidents?" Nora called out.

"Quiet as a brothel on Sunday." Opal threw her answer over her shoulder.

"And where are Agnes and Mari?" Nora only wanted to hug their little bodies, stick her nose in their hair, and hear their sweet voices.

"With Lady Charlotte at the menagerie."

"You did not go?" she said, mostly to cover her disappointment.

Opal did not even deign to answer. Of course.

Nora fled up to her room and shut the door as if it might barricade her against the world. Against her heart.

He'd said he loved her.

He also wanted to keep her safe. Wanted a family, a child. Her hand drifted to her belly. Was there a miracle inside her?

Dark, velvet drapes hung over the windows. Flocked wallpaper in a puce color covered the walls. The heavy black walnut furnishings seemed to crowd in on her.

Suffocating.

She had to get out.

A change of clothes and a splash of water on her face, and she headed toward the mews.

Linden House was not her home. Where was home now? And would she ever feel at peace?

She had Thomas drive to Greene Street.

The house seemed so small. And rather forlorn, despite the fairly fresh coat of Wedgewood blue paint on the door and the struggling plants she'd hoped would grow but hadn't. This old brick building had first been Devlin's retreat. Then their trysting place. And finally, a place of respite.

Her gaze traveled to the easternmost window box where the meager sun was the strongest. Lily's dead rose bush canted out, as if unable to relinquish its grip on life.

Nora squeezed her eyes shut, raising her arms as if she might fend off the deluge of memories.

She could turn back and never go through that front door. Tell Mr. Bartholomew to sell the house and be done with it.

Nora set the key in the lock and opened the door.

A plain, dim hallway, yet crammed with memories. Devlin falling-down drunk, laughing as he tried to snag her skirt. Lily, appearing on the stairway like a ghostly fairy, the bulge of her belly so incongruous with her childish frame. Agnes counting the steps to the kitchen and various doorways. Mari attempting to slide down the banister only to nearly break her head while Opal shouted from below.

So many memories.

Nora tugged off her gloves and laid them with her reticule on the small hall table along with the key.

In the main parlor, a film of dust, like rime on a frozen lake, already coated the mantelpiece. Above it, the wallpaper showed the ghostly shadow of a painting long taken down. Devlin had filled the space with a portrait he had painted of her. He had propped it there, its impermanence a harbinger of the brevity of their affair.

She had never liked having to look at herself. But he had only laughed, calling her his "Shy Venus".

She moved on to the kitchen, hoping for a lingering whiff of baking bread or bacon.

Nothing.

She lifted the latch and peered out into the back garden. So quiet now without the squawk of chickens and the screeches of Mari. Still a quagmire of mud.

Making her way back to the foyer, she touched the plain oak banister. It felt cold and powdery against her fingers. Ten steps to a short landing—the fifth creaked as it always had—and then another seven to the floor above. Fingers on the latch, one tug down, the *snick* of the keeper lifting, and the door swung open.

Just a room. Four walls, a shallow coal fire box, two large windows overlooking the street. Quite commonplace. Harmless.

Except for the memories that crowded every corner.

Time to move on.

She forced open the old cockeyed window and inspected Lily's rosebush. Still dead. No miraculous shoots of tender, new-green growth.

Right. It suddenly seemed important for her to remove it, to make room for something that might actually live.

She eased the brittle stalk out of the soil, being careful of the tiny thorns. It came out all too easily. Nothing had taken root. She dug her fingers into the ragged hole.

Something hard. Not a rock.

Lily must have buried something here in the window box. Nora remembered the soft crooning she had heard when she had listened outside the door. Lily loved to come up here to talk to her rosebush.

Nora carefully lifted out a tin box no larger than a penny loaf of bread and brushed the top layer of dirt away.

Two angels, arms entwined, golden heads bent toward each other, hovered among dappled clouds.

She took the box over to her bed, wiped her fingers on the old counterpane, and then flicked the tiny clasp, prying the lid open.

A folded piece of rough muslin lay inside. Lily's serious face seemed to float before her as Nora carefully unfolded the parcel of fabric.

Soft batiste linen. An infant's dress embroidered with the most beautiful roses in various shades of pink. A white needle-worked lily lay over the left breast of the gown; the palest pink rose lay over the right. Their stems entwined in the middle to form a heart.

Lily had shown no interest in making a layette for her child, yet this exquisite gown had clearly taken many days to make and embroider.

"Oh, my sweet Lily."

Some brown stains marred the fabric. Moisture must have seeped inside the box from Nora's frequent watering.

She laid the tiny dress out and smoothed its creases as best she could.

Something else was in the bottom of the tin. A silver box. Oh God, a snuff box shaped like a four-leafed clover. The one Eunice Lockhart had said the girls had taken from her. Nora flicked it open. A piece of paper was wedged inside.

With trembling hands, Nora unfolded the paper, smoothing it. The ink had run in some places, but it was clearly Lily's careful hand.

My dearest Rose,

You are gone. I failed you. I could not keep you safe. But we will not be separated for long. This baby I am carrying will die, and I with it. We will all be together again, my sweet Rose. And then, if the promise of Heaven is real, we will have no need to keep each other safe ever again.

Your loving sister,

Lily

She had known. Known her sister was dead. That is why she stopped going out. That is why she was so resigned to her own death. She wanted to join her sister.

As if a mightily fortified dam broke, tears flooded onto Nora's cheeks. She didn't wipe them away. It was time they came. Long past time.

Wrenching sounds she did not recognize as human escaped from her mouth. Shocked, she buried her face in the pillow and howled louder as if she might rid herself of this desperate sadness. For Lily and her child, for Rose. And, finally, even for herself.

A long while later, she gathered the gown, silver box, note and tin.

The fifth step groaned one last time. She picked up her gloves and reticule. Took the key and closed the door on this chapter of her life.

Chapter Twenty-Two

Eight days now and nothing from her.

Nothing about receiving another gift, and nothing about a child—or not.

She had accused him of wanting a ready-made family. Was it true? He had his grandpa and uncle, but to have a wife and children—Nora and her girls ...

Stop it. She did not want him.

Farren had been back to Corsham. Twice.

Speaking with the police, they also admitted the thief from the train had looked much like him, tall and with the same blond hair. He'd been wearing Farren's jacket and hat at the time he'd been shot and killed.

Could that bullet have been meant for him? And the incident in Covent Garden—had he been the target, not Nora? Or maybe the shots had been meant for Brendan? Mayhap someone who thought Farren was Bren?

The man who sent those gifts and poetry was obsessed with Nora. He would not want her dead. But he would want a potential rival out of the way.

The rest of his time he spent helping to settle his grandpa and uncle into the town house. Doctor McKay had been several times to see to his grandpa, but did not seem to be the savior Doctor Unger had hoped for. Worried and restless, Farren made trips to the villages surrounding Swindon and Chippingham, He'd met up with Gillingham a few times but had no luck with divining any other clues.

The one clear thing in his mind: staying away from Nora St. James.

****

Pen poised, Nora slashed through another day.

The calendar was her bible, ordering all of Charlotte's social events. The girl had made a conquest of the Queen. Victoria had been charmed by Charlotte's open and unaffected manner. The floodgates opened and invitations streamed into Linden House.

This past week, the Constables' rout, and the Douglas' tea, the Neelands' Venetian breakfast and just last evening, Lord and Lady Loften's musical. The days to come crammed with more and more events— obligations.

No new gifts had arrived. No visits from Farren.

Good, she told herself.

Nora traced the tiny question mark she had written in the very top corner of tomorrow, Wednesday. Then she made herself close the book and go find the housekeeper, Mrs. Fullernoy, to discuss the menu for Charlotte's ball.

Wednesday came and went. Nothing.

She transferred the question mark to Thursday.

Thursday. Nothing. Now a mark on Friday.

Friday, also nothing. She did not mark Saturday.

Hope and dread ricocheted 'round her brain.

Saturday dawned.

She rose from her bed and felt a wet drip down her inner thigh.

Numbly, she observed how dark the blood looked against her white thigh.

No child.

Good.

Heedless of ruining her night rail, she scrubbed at the mess. Her skin now stained pink, wet tears dropped onto her leg making clean rivers.

Such a *mess*.

Such a *fool*.

Her skin, now free of blood, burned from rubbing.

At least she would sleep now.

But she knew in her heart the onset of her menses would not quash her fitful dreams. Dreams of blonde, green-eyed children scampering around a tall hulk of a man. The sun shone so brightly on his hair she could not see his face.

But then she didn't need to see it.

She yanked her night rail over her head and then fumbled in a drawer for padding.

So stupid flirting with disaster. She knew her cycle. She knew those days at the cottage had been her best chance of increasing. Good God, she'd peddled French letters and instructed women on how to prevent conception.

Thank heavens, she whispered to herself over and over as she tied the cotton pad around her waist.

Life would go on.

But no life within her.

She must write him.

But unlike the blank sheet of paper before her, her mind felt crammed and muddled. No child. No Rose. No love …

God, she did not want to make it real. This ending.

She had been cruel, rejecting him so thoroughly. But surely, he now realized his mistake, realized how broken she was. How she had spared him. She could not love him as he deserved to be loved. He must see that now. That is why she had not seen hide nor hair of him despite her crammed calendar.

Besides, he'd only offered for her to keep her safe, and in case of a child. She could manage herself. And there was no child.

Still, in the wee hours of the morning when dreams tantalized her fitful slumber, she imagined life with him. A love that would hold true and never ebb away, or turn cruel, or even worse, indifferent. Fantasies where it did not matter that he had no money and no title. Dreams where she would be enough for him— whole, and able to love him. A world where she would be proud to be Mrs. Farren Cavanaugh …

No consequences.

N

Two words, severing any further connection between them. She sealed the note before she could tear it up.

Taking another sheet of paper, she wrote a second letter.

To Lord Finchley.

Chapter Twenty-Three

Only a few hours later Nora held Lord Finchley's unopened reply. The gold seal with its stag's head crest caught the flicker of light. She covered it with her thumb.

Mr. Bartholomew had made no progress in recovering the missing funds or Lucius Hancock. Nora had even gone so far as to visit Charles Brocket, the man who had recommended Hancock. Sir Charles had declared he had 'no idea Hancock could be so nefarious.' And then offered her a small fortune for the other nude paintings. Lecherous sot.

Nothing else of any worth left to sell except the mortgaged Greene Street house. Then she would sell herself.

She cracked open the seal.

My dearest Nora,

I was so pleased to receive your proposition.

I accept!

I think we will do very nicely together. As you wish, we shall keep our betrothal quite secret until the end of the season when we will wed. Secondly, you shall have your home in the country, and four thousand per annum to support your efforts. These funds will be yours until you pass from this earthy realm. And then a trust for beyond. I will have the settlements drawn up immediately for your approval.

I should be very glad of your company now and again, when you can spare the time to come to town. Otherwise, we shall live quite separately.

As for children, I have four nephews and two nieces. I fully expect the eldest, William, will take up the reins of the title. So, you need not have any fear of me importuning you in the bedchamber.

I shall look forward to seeing you at Lady Hemphill's salon where I shall compose an ode to your beauty.

Until then, I remain devotedly yours,
Finchley

"You've a caller." Opal stood in the doorway.

Nora shoved the letter under the clutter on her desk. "When will you learn to knock?"

"How am I to spy if I knock?" She turned tail and departed.

Was it Farren? No, Opal surely would have said. The girl was now half in love with the colonel.

Surely not Lord Finchley?

Nora glanced in the mirror, reset a comb more firmly into her hair, and smoothed the placket on her bodice.

A liveried footman shifted and pawed the carpet like a pent-up racehorse. He bowed and handed her a note.

Viscount Clifford? The name meant nothing. What could the viscount want? The missive gave no hints. Perhaps he had heard of her cause and wanted to pledge something? Could he be the answer to her prayer?

"Yes. Tell him, yes, I will come."

****

The carriage arrived just at three o'clock the next

day, an older equipage, but elegant and well-cared for.

She had debated whether to take Opal.

"I can't be traipsing off with you to lend a decorous polish to your pandering. I've got to make a silk purse out of a sow's ear," Opal groused. "How I am to get twelve yards out of seven is beyond me."

Dratted fashions these days, where it took a dozen yards of fabric just to make up the skirt of a gown. Oh, for the days of her great-grandmother in her light Empire dresses, with only a wisp of cloth for stays.

Nora's hand brushed her nineteen-inch waist. Was that why his seed had not taken root?

Ridiculous. Plenty of young ladies conceived with waists smaller than hers.

"Whoa!" The driver's cry brought her back to the here and now.

The carriage door opened, and the footman handed her out.

The house looked vaguely familiar.

Nora's breath ceased in an unladylike gulp. "There is some mistake. I am to go to Lord Clifford's home."

"Yes, my lady, this is the viscount's town residence."

Though the weather had been foggy that day, she was fairly certain she was standing directly in front of the home where she had made love not three weeks ago.

Wanting to flee, she turned back to the carriage. What could this man possibly want with her? And, more importantly, was Farren within?

The footman stood patiently, as good servants did, waiting to help her up the steps. "The carriage, your ladyship, will be at your disposal when you wish to leave."

"Thank you. I will not be long, I think." *I hope.*

If the butler, Wellfleet, recognized her, he did her the great courtesy of not showing it as he took her shawl. "This way, my lady." He led her down a short hall and into—blast—the very same room where they had—

"Ah, Countess!"

A kindly-looking old man smiled at her from his armchair.

"Lord Clifford?" She had expected to meet a man of about the colonel's years, a rake like Gillingham, but with money and a title. She curtsied to be polite, but mostly to cover her surprise. "Thank you for your kind invitation." A quick scan of the room revealed no large, blond gentlemen.

"Not to worry, the lad is out and about," the older man said, as if reading her thoughts. "Investigating and doing whatever young men do these days." The viscount smiled. A hint of recognition twitched in her brain. "Please, sit down."

She sat on the very same couch—*oh, heavens.* Her blush swept over her cheeks, having no effect on quelling the myriad of questions crowding her brain. She swallowed and gave him her most placid smile.

Lord Clifford sat in a large armchair, his hands steepled under his chin. "Forgive me, Lady Havermere. I have, of course, heard of your famed beauty but seeing you in the flesh—well, it is slightly overwhelming. My grandson did not provide a clear enough picture. He is usually so spot on in his descriptions."

"I beg your pardon, I do not follow. Your

grandson?" She continued to smile despite her confusion. "I fear this has all been a mistake, Lord Clifford. I am not acquainted with your grandson."

"Really? That is odd. Farren said he had spent a good deal of time with you of late."

"Farren?" Her heart suddenly fluttered too close to her throat making her gulp. "Did you say your grandson's name is Farren?"

"Ha!" *That smile.* "I will have to take the lad to task." *That dimple nearly hidden within the wrinkles.* "Still a bit prickly about having relations who are peers." *Those leaf-green eyes.* "His American upbringing, I expect."

American. There could be no other. Unless God were playing a grand joke on her. Hell, God *was* playing a grand joke on her.

As apparently Farren Cavanaugh had.

The colonel had neglected to tell her, when he'd brought her to this very house, that the "friend" who was partial to Yanks was none other than his grandsire. Who, in turn, was no common farmer, as she had believed—as he had led her to believe—but a peer of the realm.

Likely the cottage where he had taken her was an outbuilding on a much larger estate. Now she thought on it, they had not strayed too far from the cottage, staying within the woods close by. A larger manse might be only a mile or so away.

Plain Mr. Farren Cavanaugh was none other than the grandson of a viscount.

She swallowed, and then half rose out of her seat, as if she could possibly pick up her skirts and run out of the room like a bedlamite. She made herself sit again.

Nora inclined her head politely. "Oh, I see."

The viscount smiled again. His eyes, the exact shade as his grandson's, seemed to see straight into her, just as Farren's did.

How could she have not seen from the outset? They looked so much alike. Her gaze strayed to the two miniatures still sitting on a table nearby. These boys must be relations. "You'll forgive me, Lord Clifford, I was not aware of the connection. Thank you for enlightening me. You are too kind."

"Kind?" The light dimmed in his eyes and his smile turned wistful. "No, I don't think so, just realistic. I am nothing if not realistic."

He looked at her as if he wanted to say more but thought better of it.

The door opened and Nora jolted forward.

Just the maid with their tea.

"Ah, here is tea." A maid deposited a tray and began to lay out the cups. "That will be all, Harper, the countess will pour." He inclined his head to Nora, who nodded.

Still Harper hesitated, "My lord, I would remind you—"

"Yes, yes, I know." He waved her off.

She finally curtsied and left.

"Harper is afraid I will use too much cream or dare to actually enjoy a sweet. These doctors have put the fear of God into my servants."

Nora smiled. Despite his making light of his health, the viscount had a gray pallor, and his hands trembled beneath his chin.

"It's my heart, you see. Not quite what it should be." He smiled. "Do help yourself, Countess. I will take a dish with just a splash of cream. I do not want them to accuse you of killing me."

Nora's gaze jerked from the teacup to his face. Did this man know of the rumors of her husband's death?

But no, the viscount's eyes crinkled with mirth, not malice.

"I think the doctors must have it wrong, Lord Clifford. You are the real danger. I shall have to guard my heart."

"Oh, if I were twenty—very well, thirty or so years younger, trust me, your heart would not stand a chance."

"I can well believe it, sir."

"Ah! There is the genuine article. A real smile."

She poured the tea and added a splash of cream and then handed him the dish. The fine sugar was tempting, but she did not partake.

"No doubt you are wondering why I have been so audacious as to poach on your valuable time with no formal introduction."

"Not at all, my lord," she lied.

He sat there smiling at her as if he had some delicious secret.

"Now, where is that list I made?" He batted at his pockets and then felt along the cushion of his seat.

"May I be of service?" Nora set her cup aside and started to rise.

"I am counting on it, dear lady. Ah, here it is, right under my nose." He pulled a sheet of paper from beneath a pillow.

Nora had the impression the lost list was a bit of a show. She resumed her seat.

"I have been rusticating for so long I know nothing

of society these days. I am hoping you can be of assistance."

"I am not sure I am the best choice. I have been rusticating myself to some degree, but I would be more than happy to help with anything, sir."

"Anything? Hmm, if only that could be true. However, I think you are just the person to advise me in this matter." He extended the paper "Would you be so kind as to look this over?"

She took it. A list of names. Young ladies who were to come out this season. Charlotte St. James's name at the very top.

"I do not understand, Lord Clifford."

"Of these young ladies, who do you think would suit my grandson best?"

Suit his grandson? "I beg your pardon?"

"Which of these ladies do you think he should choose as his bride?"

Again, Nora half rose from the chair. Tea sloshed and she immediately set her cup into its saucer.

The viscount smiled blithely, as if he had not set her world spinning. "What of your niece? Charlotte St. James? I believe you are sponsoring her this season?" The old man looked at her with an innocence she was sure was as false as his teeth. "We received an invitation to her come-out ball for next week. Sadly, I am not able to attend, but Farren would be delighted, I feel sure. An earl's daughter would match up quite well with the grandson of a viscount, don't you agree? Would Charlotte do for my Farren?"

For a man who claimed to be uninformed, he certainly seemed to have his ear to the ground now.

"Lord Clifford, I am—" The list fluttered to the

floor, and she bent to retrieve it. "That is, I do not think—"

The door opened once again. *Oh, dear God, Farren?*

No, thank the good Lord. Only a servant with another tea trolley.

Not a tea cart, a bath chair. The older servant swiveled the chair to face into the room. The paper she held slipped once again from her fingers.

"Ah, Geoff, just in time to lend your support."

It was the boy, the boy in the miniature. But instead of childish innocence, a man had taken his place. His open quality was still there in his beautiful almond-shaped, sea-green eyes, but the body below those eyes …

His jaw jutted out over his thin, corded neck. Claw-like hands hugged his twisted trunk, while the rug covering his lap lay askew, revealing his wasted legs.

"Here is my secret weapon, Lady Havermere. You may be able to resist my charms, but I challenge you to rebuff my Geoffrey. Geoff, come and meet Nora St. James, Countess of Havermere."

The manservant wheeled Geoff forward.

"Daaaaa! Farr looov!" He tried to clap his hands.

"Yes, this is the countess, Geoff."

Geoff nodded so vigorously the servant had to steady the chair. He reached out for her.

Nora knelt at his feet and took his hands in hers. Decorum seemed silly in the face of such goodwill. "Hello, Geoff. Your father is a wise fellow." His hands were butter soft but held hers with surprising strength. "And perhaps he plays just a bit unfairly?"

Geoff's mouth worked itself into a grin.

"Yes, I see you know what I mean." Nora gave the viscount a withering look.

He only smiled, very like his son and grandson.

The blasted door opened once again, and this time she knew she could not continue to be so lucky. It had to be him.

It was.

Surprise flooded his face. He had not been privy to this meeting. But in an instant, he gathered himself and entered the room as if her being there was of no consequence.

"Farr! Farr!"

Nora tore her gaze from Farren, wanting to sink into the floor she knelt upon.

Geoff's face lit up like a fully-opened globe lantern. He dropped one of her hands to grasp Farren's and grinned up at the two of them as he joined their hands palm to palm. Farren's bronze and square with a rasp of callus along his thumb, pressed against her smooth, pale flesh. Hands that had traced her body not so long ago. Did he feel the same heat? The same trembling?

Geoff bobbed his head and grinned, pressing harder, his hands surrounding theirs.

"Easy, Uncle, her ladyship may have to use that hand again." Farren extricated his and then pried his uncle's from Nora's. He took out a handkerchief and tenderly wiped the spittle from Geoff's mouth.

Three generations of charm, green eyes, and winking dimples. However, one set disappeared as Farren's mouth firmed, his gaze catching hers.

"Countess, I believe the carriage is waiting. I'll see you out if you've finished your—business?"

"Yes, thank you." She rose. "It has been a great pleasure meeting you, Geoff. I can see why your father and nephew are so smitten." She turned to his lordship. "Viscount Clifford, thank you for your kind invitation." She curtsied.

"Don't forget your list, Countess. Farren, would you be so good as to retrieve that paper from under the table? And, Lady Havermere, shall we meet again this time next week to discuss any progress?"

Not wanting to prolong this interview, Nora simply nodded.

"Good. Geoff and I will be expecting you, won't we, Geoff?" His son clapped his hands and then held them tightly together against his heart.

****

Farren herded her into the hall. He ached to take her in his arms and crush his mouth to hers. His fingers dug into the flesh of his palms.

"Did you receive another gift?"

She looked up, surprised and then shook her head. "No, nothing."

They both stood in silence, eyeing each other as if they were soldiers from opposing armies contemplating a temporary truce.

He'd been a damn fool with his impatience. Charging in with his proposal of marriage when he should have fallen back and regrouped—made her come to him. She was gun-shy after being shackled to that cruel old goat. And Farren had run roughshod over her newfound freedom in his haste to make her his.

What could he have been thinking? The problem was he hadn't been. And now his secret was out. She knew he was no poor farmer from the states. Call it pride, but he had wanted her to choose him simply for himself. Would she change her tune now that she knew he had some polished peers for family? Well, if she did, she would damn well have to broach the subject herself.

But she remained mute.

Her note, *no consequences*, lay in his coat pocket, the final period to their brief affair.

"Why are you here?" He winced at his aggressive tone, but he felt like a bull in the chute.

"Your 'friend' invited me."

He supposed she had a right to be miffed. But what could his grandpa want with Nora?

"He is a sly man, your grandsire. He does not play fair."

Farren's dreams had not done justice to her beauty. A man couldn't smell in dreams, couldn't feel heat.

"Why are you here?" he repeated, needing to know which way the wind blew.

"As I said, he invited me. Seems he had a desire to meet me. And to introduce me to his son. Lord Geoffrey is irresistible."

"Well, at least one of us is." Interfering old man. What did he hope to gain by shoving Nora under Farren's nose?

"I'll bid you good day, Countess."

She caught his arm. "Farren—"

The light touch of her fingers sent a shock from his toes to his crown.

He turned to her, searching for any sign of love in her eyes.

"I mean, Colonel—" she amended. "I have something for you. I've been carrying it around, thinking perhaps I might …" She shook her head and reached into her reticule and then passed him a silver object.

A snuff box in the shape of a four-leaf clover. "Dear God! How—?"

"I found it. It was buried in a tin Lily had stashed in the window box outside my bedroom window. Inside was a beautiful infant's gown and this silver box." She hesitated and then fished a paper out of her purse. "This note was inside." She handed him the square of paper.

The words swam as his eyes filled with tears.

... we will not be separated for long. This baby I am carrying will die and I with it. We will all be together again, my sweet Rose. And then, if the promise of Heaven is real, we will have no need to keep each other safe ever again.

He touched the signature. So carefully penned.

"She's dead, Farren. Rose is dead."

He looked into her beautiful eyes, wanting not to believe what seemed so definitive.

"They are all together now. That is what Lily longed for." Nora gently took the note from him, refolded it, and returned it to her bag.

He'd never known Lily, but hoped for the chance of knowing Rose. Now that possibility was gone, leaving him feeling hollow and yearning. Not to mention the woman he loved stood not two feet from him but might as well have been on the moon.

"I think they would want you to have it." She nodded to the silver box still in his hand. "So that you might give it to your brother, when you find him."

He nodded. And swallowed. "How are you?" He took a step toward her, wanting only to enfold her in his arms so that they might offer each other some comfort.

She stepped back and then seemed to be fascinated with the fringe on her reticule. "Fine." She nodded once. Then she looked up like a good soldier when called to attention. "Have you made any progress?"

"Progress?" *Right, Brendan.* She did not need his comfort. His love. Still, it took a moment to recalibrate. He stepped away from her heat. "A bit." He'd found out Iris Darvan had moved on to Gillingham after Brendan left England. A fact Gillingham hadn't seen fit to mention.

She hesitated by the door. "I—shall I see you at my niece Charlotte's ball?"

"As you say, my grandpa has a way of getting what he wants. I'll be there."

"Well, until then, Colonel."

Farren did not wait to see the carriage pull away. He toyed with bypassing his grandfather but reasoned he just as lief get it done with.

Geoff and Pratt had gone.

"Playing the matchmaker, sir?"

"It seems I must, since you will not tend to the business yourself."

He jerked open the drape, but of course she was gone.

"You've bedded her."

No sense in pretending coyness, the old man knew a hawk from a handsaw. "Yes."

"Now, you will wed her." There was no question in his voice.

"I would, in a heartbeat. But she won't."

"Won't? Does she understand you are my heir apparent?"

Ah, the English. A title should trump just about

anything. "I reckon she does now, but it makes no difference. She does not trust men—me."

The old man sat for a long time contemplating the fire. "Things have certainly changed. Time was a lady would count her blessings to be well provided for, and by such a handsome fellow. I assume there is no babe?"

Farren shook his head.

"Well, I am sorry for it. It is clear you love her. I cannot think she is so feather-headed as to not reciprocate."

Farren startled. Were his feelings so obvious? But his grandfather was wrong about Nora. She couldn't love him. Otherwise, she would trust him enough to commit herself to him in marriage.

"I was at school with the old earl, her husband. He was several years ahead of me, but the whole of Cambridge knew him for the rotter he was. A cheat and a blackguard."

Farren tipped a finger of brandy into a glass and tossed it down. He was getting right fond of the stuff.

"Apparently, old Havermere paraded his young wife around like some exotic pet. Perhaps one cannot blame the lady for steering clear of the bonds of matrimony. Still, a damned shame."

Yes, a damned shame. Nora St. James, for all her good works and willing body, was shut up tighter than a preacher in a brothel.

Another shot of brandy might dull the pain.

"Pour one for me too, lad."

Farren hesitated.

"Come on, I'm not dead yet."

Not dead yet.

The countess might not want to gamble on love,

but his grandpa deserved some happiness. Deserved to have an heir and a family in his last remaining years. Doctor McKay had come twice in the last week, each time shaking his head as he left.

His grandfather did not have long.

"Sir, I reckon Nora St. James isn't much interested in marriage. However, I am. I am sure some gal will take my fancy soon enough."

The old man looked so tired, yet he smiled and nodded. "Yes, we shall see my boy, we shall see."

Chapter Twenty-Four

Farren entered the Wellington Arms to check his mail and to clear out the last of his things.

Coming up the steps he nearly collided with a man who was not paying attention.

"Gillingham?" He righted the gent who had stumbled. "Are you looking for me?"

Oscar Gillingham jingled his watch fobs. "Ha! I forgot you ditched these digs and moved in with the old man."

"Where are you off to? Must be high stakes to have you in such a tear."

Gillingham pulled out a flask, took a long pull and then as an afterthought offered it to Farren, who shook his head. "Lady Hemphill's salon, old chap. Lots of dilettantes jockeying to be wittier than the next. I imagine you Americans are far too busy squabbling and conquering the frontier to pay attention to such frivolous endeavors." Gillingham slapped Farren on the back.

"I believe our Ben Franklin and Thomas Jefferson were right popular in the famous salons of London and the Continent, Gillingham."

"Touché, Colonel. A hit!" He staggered back, clutching his heart.

"Well, enjoy your poetry, Gillingham." Farren started toward the reception area.

"Thought you'd perhaps like to join me?" Gillingham fingered the chain where his watch would have hung. The many fobs attached created a jingle to his nervous habit. "There may be a few guests who would interest you."

"Oh, and who might they be?"

"The incomparable Countess of Havermere, for one."

A flare of heat licked up his body. "No, I don't reckon so," he said, hoping his pronouncement might extinguish this fire.

"Hmm, I thought you might have a *tendre* for the countess." Gillingham cocked his hip and pursed his lips. "Every other man does."

"Not this man."

"Ah, well, then you certainly have no need to meet Lord Finchley then."

"Why would I want to meet him?"

"Because rumor has it, our fair countess is set to marry the man."

Halfway up the steps, Farren froze. He turned to see the smirk on Gillingham's face.

"Yes, I thought that might get your attention."

****

A half hour later they arrived in the midst of a recitation. Farren scanned the room but did not see Nora.

"... Fair are your fowl's fine feathers ..."

Lordy, what a foul fowl. Farren thought. A plump poser stood framed by a bow window as he spouted atrocious poetry. Hell, it had to be truly foul if Farren knew it was dreck.

"Ha! Lady Hemphill has more money than taste,"

Gillingham whispered. "Her ladyship adores the arts and is always encouraging her friends to exhibit their— talents. But she keeps a French chef and has one of the best cellars in town. I can stomach a few fops and a bit of rhyme for a good claret. And perhaps, if I can persuade her, a few hands of faro. And this poor pigeon," he whispered, indicating the poet, "happens to be as atrocious at cards as he is at poetry. I feel lucky tonight."

"We flock to your nest yet you flee! Cocks crow, and chicks peck ... " the poet continued.

Farren scanned the room again. His gaze snagged on a tall, handsome man just entering the room. Lord Milton. The man looked back at Farren, his face a mask of disdain.

"I will surely preen and swell! As your bright plumage becomes me well!" The poet smiled and then bowed. The company took their cue to applaud.

"Well, what is certain, is his poem doth smell," Gillingham quipped. "Let me introduce you."

Where was she? Maybe Gillingham had it all wrong? The man was a born liar. But there was no opportunity to find out as he was pulling Farren directly toward the fop who was humbly receiving accolades.

"Colonel Cavanaugh, may I present Lord Finchley."

This man was Finchley?

Primed to go ten rounds, Farren almost laughed at this fussy, trumped-up fellow. *Hell, and damnation*, Gillingham had to have it wrong. How could she sell herself to such a buffoon?

"Ah, so *this* is your colonel." Finchley made a moue. "Well, I can certainly see the attraction. So, I suppose I must forgive you, Gilly, for shucking me off these last few weeks."

Gillingham only grinned.

"Do you write, Colonel?"

"Poetry? No, the best I can do is a bawdy limerick."

"Ha! Well, perhaps we shall have one from you as the evening progresses. I have no doubt you possess many talents." His lordship looked Farren up and down. "He certainly adds to Lady Hemphill's décor. Wouldn't you agree, Mr. Hatten?"

A slight, almost too beautiful, man stood beside Finchley, the antithesis of his companion's doughy excess. The man merely gave Farren a glance and then moved off.

"Ah, you see! You have frightened off the most gorgeous man in London. Bravo, Colonel! Bravo!" Lord Finchley clapped and seemed genuinely delighted with life.

How such a gaudy jumble of color and pattern could be thought stylish Farren would never know. But perhaps his lordship's clothing was worn to distract the viewer from his pasty plain face with its outrageous set of whiskers, likely cultivated to disguise a non-existent chin.

"Well, we will get better acquainted later in the evening, no doubt." He sucked in his gut, pulled out a jewel-encrusted snuff box and then flipped open the lid. "Ah! Milton is here. I thought he scoffed at these soirées."

Gillingham jerked toward the tall man in the corner then ducked his head like a boy on his way to the woodshed.

"Gilly, a private word, if you please?" Finchley snapped the jeweled box closed.

"Right," Gillingham said with a tight smile. "You'll find your way, Cavanaugh?"

Farren nodded.

Finchley hooked his arm through the younger man's and headed toward Milton.

Farren turned and scanned the room yet again.

A knot of guests surrounded one poor soul. Like a flock of gaudy parrots, they reared back cawing at some joke. Farren glimpsed a redhead. The group cackled again, and she disappeared among their bright plumes and pecking heads.

As he approached, the startled flock parted, scattering to reveal her.

This evening she wore deep red. The style and neckline modest compared to the other ladies. She had no need to display her bosom or swath herself in showy silks and flounces. Any fool with eyes would see Nora St. James was the most magnificent woman in the room. By God, how could she lay with him and then sell herself to Finchley in the next moment? Was she such a coward? Had he known her at all?

If she was surprised to see him here, she did not show it. A consummate actress.

He did not greet her beyond a brief bow. Why project a *savior faire* he did not feel? He could barely breathe, much less layer on a mask of civility. His arms itched to gather her to him, to press her lush breasts against his rioting heart, to feel those full lips tangle with his.

"This is becoming a habit, Colonel. First Lord Milton's musicale, then the auction, and now this salon.

Are Americans so lax in their manners that uninvited guests are free to push in at a moment's notice?"

Feelings spun inside him like a wheel of fortune—anger, lust, disdain, want. Why had he come? She had made it all too clear she did not want him—at least not in the way he wanted her. Some inane words rolled out. "Countess, I reckon you should be thanking me. From what I can tell, looks to me as if I may be the only person with a jot of sense at this shindig."

"So now you are my port in the storm? How dramatic." She took a sip of wine. "I am quite capable of steering my own ship, sir." Her words sounded sure enough, but her gaze strayed around the room like a lost sheep.

"I recall you relinquishing your rudder every now and again."

Her only answer was to take a deeper drink of her wine.

Men cast covetous looks their way, but that pair of silver eyes met his dead on and then settled on Nora as if he owned her. "I see Lord Milton is here. Doesn't seem like his sort of thing—this bunch."

The countess's gaze followed his. "No, but his attendance is certainly a feather in her ladyship's cap."

"Why?"

"Lord Milton is much sought after among intellectual circles." She raised her glass. "And very philanthropic. He sponsors several charity homes."

"So, is that why you are smiling at him as if he were the only man in the room? For his money?"

Never taking her eyes from Milton, the countess took a deep drink of wine. "You grow crass, Colonel Cavanaugh." Then she slayed Milton with another stunning smile. Farren suspected its brilliance might have something to do with putting a Yank in his place.

Finchley and Gillingham joined Lord Milton and Hatten. The younger man hung back as if he might not be welcome, while Finchley gesticulated like a bad actor in the throes of a love scene. Farren wouldn't be surprised if he sank to his knees to kiss Milton's pristinely shined shoes.

An enormous woman dressed in a costume that might have once belonged to an Egyptian queen coupled with that of a whirling dervish approached him and Nora.

"Who have we here, Lady Havermere?" The woman, who must be five and sixty, looked as if she had something in her eye. He nearly offered her his handkerchief, but then realized she was fluttering her eyelashes at him.

"Lady Hemphill, may I present Colonel Farren Cavanaugh from America. Colonel Cavanaugh, this is our hostess, Lady Hemphill."

"Oh, an American! How delightful. And where did you find him, my dear?"

"I didn't. That is to say, I did not invite him, your ladyship."

"Your pardon, Lady Hemphill, Mr. Gillingham said you would not mind my tagging along." Farren smiled and the woman batted her eyelashes again.

"Oh, jolly good! Mr. Gillingham is always so resourceful! You will sit beside me for the mesmerism, won't you, Colonel? I feel you have an intense aura." She reached out and squeezed his arm. "Heavens! First, Lord Milton arriving unexpectedly, and now you, sir. What a boon!"

Well, at least their hostess seemed delighted by Gillingham's offering of an American colonel fresh from war. Another amusement in her sideshow of posers.

"Excuse me, Colonel. I must steal Lady Havermere for a moment. Lord Milton is asking for her." She gave him one more lecherous look before leading Nora away.

"All right, old chap?" Gillingham was at his elbow, drinking deep.

Farren ignored the question. "This Lord Milton, who is he?" Lady Hemphill and Nora had now joined Milton and Finchley.

Gillingham tossed off the rest of his wine. "Didn't think he would be here tonight."

"I reckon there's no Lady Milton?"

Gillingham signaled a servant for more wine. He impatiently jingled the fobs on his watch chain while the servant finished pouring and then took a long pull as if he were parched.

Farren waited.

"No."

"Never?"

"Betrothed once, I believe. Before he came into his title. To a nobody, but supposedly a real beauty. No other woman has managed to snare him, though many have tried. Deep pockets and a title, along with very discerning tastes."

Milton and Nora stood out like classical pillars next to a jumble of baroque nonsense.

His lordship held out his arm to Nora. If he'd been a pissing dog, he couldn't have staked out his territory more clearly. Apparently, Milton wasn't privy to any rumor of an alliance between Finchley and Nora. Or if he was, he paid it no mind.

The sound of a bell had everyone turning to Lady Hemphill. "Thank you all for attending. We will have much more to see and hear this evening. And many toasts to come." She signaled to the footman to hand her a flute of wine. "But for now, I raise my glass to such superior company!"

The guests, flattered, raised their glasses. Finchley saluted Nora.

"Mr. Foxwood," her ladyship continued, singling out a little man wearing a *pince nez* and a flowing cravat. "If you would assemble your players, we will commence shortly with your offering of *The Recalcitrant Frog.*"

A large group of the guests moved to huddle in one corner of the room.

"Ah, Gillingham." Lady Hemphill said, approaching. "We have lost our chameleon. Mr. Trainer's gout is acting up again, poor man. You must step in for him. I will not take no for an answer." She shooed Gillingham off to join the rest of the players.

"Come, Colonel Cavanaugh, let me introduce you to the company."

He offered the lady his arm, and they crossed the room. The knot of guests peeled open to reveal Nora and Milton.

"Lord Milton, Lady Olivier, Mr. Winston, Mr. Hatten, may I present Colonel Cavanaugh, from the United States of America."

Farren nodded and exchanged pleasantries but found himself squared off with Milton.

"Well, you will excuse me. I must turn from

hostess into a butterfly, for I am set to play opposite Mr. Foxwood's frog." Her ladyship turned and trundled off.

"Lady Havermere, how goes your cause?" Mr. Hatten said with a perpetual sneer stamped on his handsome face.

Nora paused in taking a sip of her wine and looked slightly bewildered. "If you are referring to my charity home, we—have had a setback, but I am determined to move forward. I cannot rest while so many children are suffering." She smiled tightly.

"Hmmm … Do you wonder, dear lady," Hatten paused to look at Milton. "You aren't doing these unfortunates a disservice by prolonging their misery?"

"I beg your pardon?" Nora looked as if she had sat down to a game of whist and discovered it was Russian roulette.

"I presume you have heard of Herbert Spencer?" His gaze repeatedly flicked to Lord Milton as if he was some sort of barometer.

The countess raised her chin. "Survival of the fittest? Yes, Mr. Hatten, I have read his theories. But I hope we are above the beasts of the world."

He gestured for a nearby footman to fill his glass and hers. "We are animals at heart, Lady Havermere." His smile reminded Farren of a feral tomcat.

She covered her wine glass, and the footman stepped away. "But that is the point. At heart. What of God? What of charity? Do you utterly discount the teachings of Christ?" A rumble rolled through company.

"Come, you are too intelligent to be throwing the Bible at me. After all, it was written by men with agendas."

"Perhaps, but its teachings are universal."

"What say you, Lord Milton?" Hatten was clearly angling for an argument. "You are a forward thinker, yet you support your share of these degenerates. Is it wise? Or even charitable when all is said and done?"

Milton gave the man a freezing stare. He turned to the countess. "Spencer's theories have some merit. It is not charitable to prolong misery. And I believe that some souls are indeed superior. Just as some strains of cattle are more robust than others. It is nature. However, this topic is unsavory. It pollutes the company, sours our wine, and casts a shadow over the conversation."

Farren could not let Milton go unchallenged. "And I reckon, Lord Milton, if you had been born into a poor family and sent to the coal mines at age three, you would naturally rise like cream to the top? Because you are a 'superior being'?"

"Cream will always rise if left to itself. That is the nature of cream, Colonel." He lifted his glass and took a sip of wine.

"Enough of unfortunates," said the chinless wonder, Finchley. "Cavanaugh, you must tell us of your Civil War."

"Thus far, we in England have managed to avoid spilling the blood of our brothers," Hatten provided. "Along with abolishing slavery nearly a hundred years ago."

"What say you, Colonel? Let us hear from the American!" Finchley crowed, as if Farren hailed from the moon instead of merely across an ocean.

Farren's stomach roiled. *Here we go.* He took

another long drink of wine. "Correct me if I'm wrong, but didn't brother go against brother when the papists held fast against the emerging Church of England?" he said, directing his reply to Hatten. "And I believe you mean eighteen-thirty-three. Slavery in England was abolished on August twenty-eighth. But I reckon your colonies aren't so enlightened."

These pompous fops delighted in poking at the trials of his once beloved country. "If you'll pardon me, I'd rather not speak of war."

"Well, I suppose I can see why. His precious democracy nearly collapsed after less than one hundred years," Hatten said in a not so sotto voce whisper to his neighbor who seemed startled Hatten had deigned to speak with him.

Why did this man persist? What had Farren done to rile him? Farren took a last swig of wine and then carefully set the stemmed glass on a nearby table. Coming here was a bad idea.

"Yes, dear Colonel! Surely, a man such as yourself has numerous tales of bravery?" Lord Finchley clapped his pudgy hands together. "You saw some action, I'll warrant. I'm sure you were magnificent! Come, give us a flavor of one of your victorious battles."

"A flavor, you say? I am not sure my 'flavor' would complement our hostess's fine wine. Or be suitable for this company, sir." He nodded to Nora and Lady Olivier.

"Oh, come, don't be peevish. Lady Havermere, you are made of stern stuff, aren't you?" Hatten challenged.

Nora smiled thinly as the man once more motioned for the footman to fill his glass. "I think it best to leave this subject. The colonel has said he does not wish to speak of war."

"Nonsense, my dear, these sorts of conversations are just what these salons are for,"

Finchley said, oblivious to the mounting tension. "Besides, a soldier always delights in regaling us civilians with tales of derring-do. Don't you, Colonel?"

"Not especially."

"Ah, behind the scenes, were you? A desk man?" Hatten smirked.

Time to put this twit in his place. "All right, since you are so keen for a 'tale,' Mr. Hatten, I'll strive to *divert* you." He steeled his heart, the wine he had drunk roiling in his stomach. "Let's see. Where to begin? Would it interest you to know the last time I saw my cousin Freddie was at the battle of Gettysburg. Only he was no longer my cousin. He was my enemy. And then he was nothing."

His Aunt Elsie had begged Freddie, her only child, to stay at home. She would sell what little she had to pay for a replacement.

"Poor Freddie was not much of a soldier. He was a lover of music, never without his flute."

Farren had the bit in his mouth now. "You see ol' Freddie caught sight of me on the battlefield. He was still smiling his gummy grin when Billy Gorman, a raw recruit under my command and only fifteen years of age, shot Freddie straight through the head." Farren swallowed as bile rose in his throat.

Finchley's smile froze while Lady Olivier blanched and coughed into her lace handkerchief.

He'd had to live with Billy's night terrors for weeks afterwards. That is, until the boy caught a bullet in the gut at Stones River and died after five excruciating days.

"I paid a king's ransom to get Freddie's flute back. Why, you may ask? Why risk life and limb and pay out thrice what it was worth? Silver is one answer. The vulture dog robbers like to get in early and take anything off the corpses that might fetch a bit of coin. Teeth, loved ones' lockets, wedding rings. And flutes. The other reason is selfish. I could not stand to think of Freddie's flute in some stranger's hands to be melted down for a medal to decorate an officer's chest."

As if a sealed portal had been ripped open, Farren plunged on. "Or perhaps you are more interested in the prisons? I know I can't get enough of them. I think of them every day." He willed himself to breathe. "Both sides had their Hells where men begged to be killed. I was intimately acquainted with Libby Prison, in Richmond, where maggots were eaten right off festering wounds."

Madam Olivier nearly gagged.

"After the war, I traveled south to my Aunt Elsie's, who lived, ironically, not so far from where I had been imprisoned, to lay Freddie's flute in her hands. But Aunt Elsie's home had been burned to the ground. She was living with her old servant who had taken her in."

Hatten sneered while most of the other company looked at their shoes or the ceiling. All except Nora who gazed directly into his eyes.

"I saw Billy Gorman's mother too. Though I had nothing personal to bring her, as Billy didn't have much." He looked around the stunned group. "I reckon I've provided my entertainment for the evening. If you'll excuse me, gentlemen, Lady Olivier, Countess."

Cool air fanned his cheeks as he pushed out into a

back garden. Served those twits right to have their evening disturbed. Too fat anyway with their pale skin, padded suits, and corsets.

"You know how to break up a party, Colonel." Nora stood in the open doorway.

"Yes, I am not fit company. You'll pardon me." He bowed and turned to leave.

"Don't." Her voice stopped him. "Lord Finchley is harmless and only wanted to hear of your bravery, I suspect. Mr. Hatten deserved everything he got. These men know very little of the real world. They only care where their next amusement lies."

"Countess. I should—"

"I admire your devotion and your valor. I do."

He tried to laugh but it got caught somewhere between his belly and throat. "You admire me, Lady Havermere? I reckon you have an odd way of showing it."

"Yes, yes, I do," she said, almost to herself. "I apologize for—these men. I would ask your forgiveness." Her tone was too fervent, as if she were speaking of something entirely different. Something personal.

He stepped toward her, but she retreated, even holding her hands out as if to fend him off.

Who was this woman? She had lain within his arms, moaned as he had plunged into her sweet center, curled up against his body while she slept. And now, he was a pariah?

And to surround herself with such poor company. To marry that idiot for his money only to shield herself from the messiness of real love.

"My God, Nora, why do you put up with this

carrion? They pose and smirk, feeding on the misery of others."

She pokered up, her neck lengthening and breasts lifting like some exotically flustered bird. He'd gone too far but, damn it all, she made his blood rise with her cowardice.

"We are not all so fortunate as to be able to choose our friends as you do, sir. I must take the good with the bad and sometimes swallow my pride and my sensibilities for the sake of the larger scope of things. Diplomacy is a necessity for a woman if she is to have any success in this world." She pasted on a smile.

"Why him?"

"I beg your pardon?"

"Why Finchley?" *Why not me?*

"You have me at a loss, Colonel," she said, but could not meet his eyes.

"Marriage. Why would you agree to marry Lord Finchley and cast me aside?"

Her gaze snapped to his. "Who told you that?"

"Does it matter? Is it true?"

"That is none of your business." She didn't have the gumption to continue to look him in the eye.

"Because he has loads of money and won't ever come to your bed? Will never threaten your heart?"

She said nothing, her features rigid like some aloof Madonna.

"I am beginning to think you don't have a heart, Countess." He started to take his leave but turned back. "You are wise to reject me. For damned sure, I will never be one of your pet dogs who drool in your lap."

Her nose lifted as her eyes sparked. "Oh, I am relieved to hear it. We are of one accord, sir. The thought of you in my lap is the last thing I wish."

He smiled. One thing they both knew: her words were an utter falsehood.

"Brava!" A roar of laughter sounded from inside.

"I leave you to the dogs, then." He bowed. "Goodbye, Madam."

Chapter Twenty-Five

"First the cold pork with caper berries and next the other meats and then the salads, here." Nora indicated the end of the twenty-four-foot-long buffet table then skirted around Cynthia, Charlotte's next youngest sister, who had, along with Agnes, been Nora's shadow since early this morning. "The larger urns of roses and ivy will flank the table. Use the gold pedestals from the conservatory. There are two more in the attics, if needed."

"Yes, your ladyship." Mrs. Fullernoy waved to a nearby footman to dispatch the order. "Shall I put the orchestra in the library when they arrive, ma'am?"

"Yes, but see that they set up in the gallery first and then have their dinner in the servants' hall." Nora consulted her long list. So much still to do. Another list lay waiting for her on her dressing table upstairs. The list of prospective brides for Farren Cavanaugh. Charlotte's name at the very top.

"Cousin Nora!"

Nora squeezed her eyes shut. Not again. She had just sent Cousin Orville away not three minutes ago to inspect the wine.

"Mr. Pensgrave has brought out far too much wine. I cannot see how so much can be consumed in one evening. I told him it must go back to the cellars."

"Mum." Marigold tugged at Nora's skirt. "Me and Diana have been attending Charlotte's dance lessons. Look!" The two nodded to each other and then performed a pirouette simultaneously, nearly careening into a passing footman who held a tray of crystal flutes. How the footman managed to avoid disaster was a testament to his grace and training.

"Diana! Have a care, child." Havermere mopped his brow. "Can't you see we are in crisis?" He turned back to Nora. "And I have not told you the worst. I cannot find my Debrett's! How will I know who is who without my peerage guide?"

Nora had not entertained on such a large scale at Linden House when she was its mistress, but she had been raised to be a perfect hostess and to deal with all manner of debacles. "Cousin Orville, have no fear, I shall be by your side all evening long. I will introduce anyone whom you might not know. You will have no need of your Debrett's."

After a hasty bath, Nora stood in Charlotte's room in her wrapper, her little entourage sat in the middle of the bed amid a sea of jewels. They were not-so-patiently awaiting the donning of the gown and the coiffing of the hair. In short, the transformation of their elder sister and friend into a princess, or so said the youngest, Diana, who was quite a bit like Mari when it came to fairy princesses and knights in shining armor. Nora could remember that particular phase in her own childhood—waiting for her prince.

The Havermere emeralds encircled the neck of Gretchen, Charlotte's next eldest sister. Diana wore the tiara which listed over one ear. Cynthia, the practical one, with the help of Agnes, began sorting the gems back into their various cases.

Opal was conspicuously absent.

The jewels had all been cast aside, deemed too heavy for Charlotte's ephemeral dress of white voile. She declared she would wear her mother's simple strand of pearls and a wreath of lily of the valley in her hair.

The girl had sense as well as beauty. And her devotion to her deceased mamma made Nora's throat close quite painfully.

Besides, she hated those emeralds and the troves of Havermere jewels. Her husband had insisted she wear them. They had always felt like a chain around her neck, just one more thing to mark her as his property.

Gretchen, her fingers now full of glittering rings, bounced up from the bed. "Aunt Nora, could I watch from the gallery?"

"Me too!" echoed the younger chorus, as they bounded off the bed and fluttered around Nora.

"You must ask your governess, Miss Gowan," Nora said, catching Mari's clutching hands, hands that might be sticky with jam from her afternoon tea. "But I suspect, if you are quiet as mice, she will allow you to watch the opening set."

This sent the girls into their own dance, accompanied by giggles.

"What was your presentation ball like, Auntie?" Cynthia asked seriously.

"I did not have one. I married before I came out."

"But why?" asked Gretchen. "This is the jolly part."

Cynthia shook her head. "I am never going to marry. Men are silly." Perhaps she was thinking of her poor father?

"But princes are not. And I will only marry one of those," declared Diana, her hands on her hips.

There were no princes in America. They had just had a war to say that all men were created equal. But Colonel Farren Cavanaugh was above all men. Her prince …

Nora did not want any more probing questions. "I think we should do the final lacing now, Charlotte. It has gone half seven."

The ball gown had been fitted to a nineteen-inch waist. A hasty lacing could be disaster, leading to all sorts of unladylike sounds and sometimes even a swoon.

Hattie stepped forward, flexing her hands as if ready to do battle. Charlotte held onto the bedpost and took a deep breath. Hattie yanked and the little girls, like a chorus, sucked in their breath and stomachs. Nora threaded the tape measure around Charlotte's waist. "Just a tad more, Hattie." The maid nodded gamely and gave one last tug. "Perfect. You may tie the stays now."

The crinoline was next, and everyone was allowed to "help." Then came the gown.

Nora had guided Charlotte in its choosing, but the girl had a good sense of what flattered her figure and coloring.

"Ooooh!" The girls peeled back as if the gown had transformed Charlotte into a real-life fairy princess. Made of the sheerest silk voile, the dress looked as if it had been spun of silken cobwebs. Its softly pleated skirt edged with glistening pale-pink and silver ribbon. The modest neckline clung to her shoulders, where the tiny, capped sleeves were caught up with the same ribbon, ending in rosettes. A wider band of pink, shot with silver-embroidered lily of the valley, encircled her waist. Hattie tied it into a bow, the ends fluttering down the back of the gown.

Charlotte twirled and the gown's skirts lifted as the fabric caught air.

This action drew another chorus of *oohs* from the little girls and Hattie as well.

"Where is your dress, Auntie?" Diana asked, clearly wanting more of a show.

"I shall go put it on now while Hattie is doing your sister's hair." Hopefully, Opal would be waiting to assist her.

"And no, you all will stay here with me and leave Aunt Nora in peace, so do not ask." Charlotte pointed to the bed as she sat before her vanity table. "Sit." All five fluttered, finally hovering at the edge like butterflies, ready to alight if called upon to hold a pin or a flower.

"Now, watch Hattie work her magic."

And that she did.

When Nora saw the girl next, her hair was woven with a sprinkling of delicate lilies. Her mother's pearls circled her neck, pointing up the creaminess of her porcelain skin.

"You must wear these!" Cynthia said when Nora reappeared wearing her new jade gown. The girl held out the emeralds. "They match perfectly."

"I think I shall take a page from your wise sister, and wear something simple. We will save these gems for you and your sisters to wear when you come out."

"Gretchen, take everyone to the nursery. Miss Gowan must be anxious for you to get your dinner."

"But it is early—"

"Do you want to watch from the gallery or not?"

The girls made a beeline for the door.

"Ahem." Charlotte rose and the oldest girl stopped dead in her tracks whilst the others, not as quick, barreled into Gretchen's back. "You will make your curtsy to your Mum and Auntie."

A stair step of bodies bobbed one after the other, each jabbing an elbow into the next to perform their duty.

Nora could not help but experience a wistful moment seeing their obvious closeness. Charlotte, despite her censure, smiled fondly and waved them away.

"They are learning, Auntie."

"Yes, I suspect you will show the way admirably."

Charlotte's instincts as a mother were all that were loving yet firm. She would make some lucky lord a wonderful wife.

Nora touched the list of prospective brides which she had tucked inside her long white glove.

"Let us descend, my dear. Your father, I'm sure, will have worn a hole in the carpet by now."

****

Nora had deposited Cousin Orville with Lord Manderly. Apparently, both had a passion for fishing. Manderly had just lost his wife of twenty years, so they had that in common as well.

Nora filled a cup of punch for something to do, but realized she was, in fact, parched. When she turned back to face the ballroom, she nearly choked.

Farren Cavanaugh stood at the top of the wide stairway. She had never seen him in evening attire. The colonel looked as if he belonged among the *ton* this

283

evening. He had a smooth polish, from his slicked back hair to his mirror-shined pumps.

As he descended the stairs into the ballroom, matchmaking mamas, like the keenest hucksters, shifted their daughters, as if they were shiny baubles hoping to catch his eye. Gone was the wild American who might devour their poor innocents in one tidy bite. Forgotten were the rumors of a libertine who frequented brothels and gambling halls. No more ferociously hiding their precious chicks behind their backs as he passed by. Word must have got out he was the heir apparent, after his Uncle Geoff.

She did not want him here.

Did not want to see him again.

Yet seeing him was all she wanted.

She did not love him, she reminded herself. Could not. That ship had sailed, and she had set a new course, one whose future did not include an irreverent American who continually upended her ordered world.

Still, the image of them sitting by the fire at the cottage. Being held on his lap, him tracing the curl of her hair by firelight. Gathering her to him to carry her up to bed and cover her with his body. Sinking into her …

"He is an *American*, my dear." Lady Biggerly, a notorious gossip, had sidled up to the punch bowl and uttered the word as if it smelled of some foul cheese.

Nora snapped her gaze from the colonel to her ladyship.

"Has no wife. Rumored to have some bad habits, but don't all men?" Lady Biggerly tucked her double chin into her enormous breast, burying a fortune in diamonds within the folds. "I met him the other day when Patience and I attended the Edison rout. While Patience must look much higher, I thought he might do for Mrs. Jesson's youngest daughter. Lord Biggerly is forever saying I should stay out of these matters, but when I can do a good turn, I see it as my duty to do so. However, before I could even properly introduce him to her and my dear Patience, he informed me his life as a soldier these past four years had spoiled him for married life. No, he said, he would be well enough on his own with perhaps a dog or two for company. There, I think I have got it verbatim. I always try to do so, otherwise it might be construed as gossip, which, as you know, I abhor." She looked the man up and down. "Imagine preferring a dog to a wife."

"Really, Lady Biggerly? I wonder that any man would take a spouse over a good hound," Nora said. Though poor Patience Biggerly did resemble a French bulldog.

"I was told just the opposite." Ursula Cray, Lady Pomfry, poked her head between her ladyship and Nora. "That he is in Town expressly to *find* a wife. His father's dying wish, they say." She waved her lorgnette in the Colonel's direction. "The older brother is presumed dead. And his grandsire is none other than Viscount Clifford. And with his poor son an imbecile, I believe the colonel is set to inherit."

Nora opened her mouth to defend sweet Geoff but was cut off.

"A viscount?" Lady Biggerly snapped open her fan and applied it to her now heaving bosom. "Are you quite certain, Lady Pomfry? Old Colin Cavanaugh, of the Wiltshire Cavanaughs?"

"The very same."

"I thought he was quite dead. Haven't seen him in an age." Lady Biggerly dug beneath her chins to fondle her diamonds. "You'll excuse me, ladies. I must find Patience posthaste." The good woman trundled off in search of her daughter.

"Poor Patience. I fear all the funds in the world will not bring that dashing colonel to heel. He will have his pick of the season," Lady Pomfry said rather wistfully as she raised her quizzing glass once more to her longish nose. Nora was all but forgotten as her ladyship wandered off, most likely in search of a glass of ratafia.

Nora looked up to see the colonel making his way straight toward her.

Her heart ratcheted up in her breast. Closer and closer his gaze bore into hers. But at the last moment his eyes veered left and only then did he smile. The same smile he had bestowed on her not so long ago.

The recipient was Charlotte, who had appeared at her side, beaming her own inimitable smile right back at him.

"Good evening, Countess." Farren bowed to her, but his gaze remained focused on Charlotte. "Would you please do me the honor of introducing me to your lovely niece?"

"Oh." She felt like a veritable hag. "Yes, certainly. Charlotte, may I present Colonel Farren Cavanaugh? Colonel, this is Lady Charlotte St. James."

Charlotte bestowed upon him her most glorious smile to date and then dipped into a graceful curtsy.

Pride should have filled Nora's breast, but all she experienced was a bitter gall of jealousy.

"Colonel Cavanaugh, I have heard much of you." Charlotte did not simper or play coy but met his gaze with open frankness. "You are touted quite a hero in your country. I believe we read you were awarded the Medal of Honor? I hail from Canada, but my father kept up very closely with your Civil War. I must introduce you to him."

"I would be honored to meet the earl, Lady Charlotte, and give him my impressions, but I assure you, I am no hero."

Nora felt more and more *de trop*. Farren had never spoken to her of the war, beyond what he had shared at Lady Hemphill's salon. But she had never probed him, had she?

"What I am hankering for is a dance. Would you consent to take a turn with me?"

"Why, of course. I would be delighted to stand up with you, Colonel."

Nora was spared having to stand on the sidelines and watch his graceful figure—she already knew Charlotte had the grace of a gazelle as Nora had danced with her at least fifty times, playing the male partner in all manner of dances—when Lord Milton bowed over her hand.

"You are truly out of your mourning now, Lady Havermere. I am delighted to see you wearing color again. Though I'm sure you could make a sack look fetching."

"Thank you, my lord. I must own I am not sorry to put away all the black and gray," she said, smoothing the skirt of her leaf-green gown.

"Yes, it is high time to let your beauty shine." Milton seemed to want to say more but changed tack. "Will you honor me with a dance?"

Nora would just as soon not. His lordship made

little secret of his admiration for her. But she did not want to stand idle to watch Farren Cavanaugh and Charlotte light up the room.

"Yes, thank you, my lord."

"Wonderful. I think there is room for one more couple."

Too late she saw there was only one spot open to make up the fourth in the quadrille. The place next to Charlotte and the colonel. Nora nearly balked, but then she would appear ridiculous.

Never mind. The dance only required the touching of hands. She had, of course, done far more with the colonel. And they were wearing gloves.

She and Milton faced Charlotte and the colonel while two other couples made up the rest of the quadrille. The music started and she turned to Milton to curtsy. He, in turn, bowed to her. Charlotte and the colonel, being the head couple, took the floor in the first part of the dance, a waltz, while the other three couples looked on.

She had imagined him as not having many social graces. Ridiculous to assume simply because he was an American he would be backward and unrefined.

He danced beautifully. It was ungenerous of her, but she wished he didn't. Such a large man should not possess such grace and lithe synergy. But far worse was the way he gazed down at Charlotte, with such warmth. And she, in turn, looked up at him, a beaming smile on her face.

Nora nearly forgot her cue to *chasse* into the center, saluting Charlotte and then again as they then exchanged places. Now only a brush past Farren. His arm, three inches from hers. His heat and slightly spicy scent of clove and something earthy filled her nose. So close and yet so very far.

The side ladies performed their courtesies and then the gentlemen, thereby regaining their original partners.

"You seem distracted, my lady," Milton said as he swung her into the next steps of the dance, a waltz. Farren's shoulder passed hers as he and Charlotte sailed effortlessly past.

"I have not entertained in an age." She scrambled to defend her distraction. "And sponsoring a young girl is more involved than I'd imagined." Nora tried to smile into his silver eyes.

"It seems Lady Charlotte has benefited greatly from your tutelage."

Nora only smiled as it was now time for the "grand round." She proceeded to the left while Milton turned to the right. One gentleman to pass before she would come face to face with Farren. She steeled herself. But she need not have. He looked just above her head, his touch light and seemingly casual as he moved swiftly on to the next lady.

Now back at Milton's side, they formed two lines. Again, she faced Farren Cavanaugh. And again, he did not look at her. When the two lines passed through each other his coat brushed her arm, and she jerked away. Fool! Why could she not be as composed as he?

Milton took her in his arms to perform the last waltz.

Dear God, then they had to do it all again.

****

Apart from Nora's raging headache, the evening seemed to be going seamlessly. Charlotte had been claimed by one eligible hopeful after another. She had just finished dancing with Lord Sealing when Farren Cavanaugh approached the girl once again. Charlotte laughed at the two gentlemen as the younger Sealing sized up his rival.

They spoke for a few moments. Charlotte was so easy, so beguiling. So utterly young and beautiful—

Dear Lord, Charlotte couldn't be towing the colonel directly toward her? Wasn't it enough to endure watching them from across the room? Did the chit have to flaunt her conquest right in front of Nora's nose?

"Aunt Nora, I must ask you to take him from me." She smiled her bloody stunning smile just to add insult to injury. "I have explained that I dare not dance another with the Colonel. We have danced twice already. It is simply not done."

It was true; a third set and tongues would wag.

"Yet I cannot give him up to a rival." She laughed. Even now hopeful wallflowers were edging ever closer hoping to catch the colonel's eye. "Would you help us out and partner him for the next?" Charlotte nudged Farren.

"I told her I was sure you are too busy for the likes of me." He glanced to his left, and the young ladies on that side of the room stood just a hair straighter in their slippers. "I am sure I can find some other gal who could put up with me for the next half hour."

"No, I won't have it, Colonel. Besides, didn't you say you would only consent to dance with a woman as beautiful as me?" she asked, her mouth quirking.

"I suppose I did," he said, as if he were reluctantly saying a line from a play.

"You see? How can you resist such flattery?" Charlotte squeezed Nora's arm.

Not so flattering that her niece thought her Auntie so entirely safe.

"We cannot have such a fine specimen holding up the walls. You must dance." She turned to Farren. "And here I have provided the perfect partner. You would not deny me, would you, Colonel?"

"Lady Charlotte, I would risk the ballroom falling to rubble rather than disappoint you," he said with mock seriousness.

"The music is starting. Go!"

"Ma'am?" He held out his hand.

She looked at it as if she had never in her life been asked to dance. But he hadn't asked, she reminded herself. His rigid bearing spoke of duty, not choice.

If a lively country jig had sent her heart to fluttering every time their hands met, what would an honest-to-goodness waltz do? She set her hand in his, and somehow, they ended in the middle of the floor.

As he took her into his arms, Nora glanced about the room. Could these people guess what she and Farren Cavanaugh had done together?

But no, not one soul stepped forward to call her a Jezebel. And why should they? He certainly made no demonstration of ardor, holding himself stiffly, his gaze fixed somewhere above her head, as if he could not wait for this obligatory dance to end.

How utterly humiliating. It was as if those precious hours at the cottage had all been a fantastical dream.

She was merely the aunt of a girl he now fancied.

Still, her heart did not seem to comprehend this new state of affairs, continuing to hammer in her breast. Surely, he must feel it pulsing through her entire body—even through their gloved hands. She dared a look up at his face. His jawline stood out, his mouth a firm line, his eyes fixed above her head, but the pressure on her hand increased. He was not totally unmoved.

The music had begun. Chopin wept, sweet and painful, from the violins, while the bassoons provided a foundation of sonorous sympathy.

Couples began to eddy around them, and still, he did not move. Soon their hesitation would call unwanted attention.

"Colonel, perhaps we should—"

He cut her off by stepping out. The pressure on her back and extended hand firmed as he guided her backwards. They had done all manner of things at the cottage—made love on various pieces of furniture, pushed up against a tree—but they had never danced. Somehow, those private intimacies paled as he held her so lightly in his arms with the world looking on.

As Chopin played, their bodies loosened, melding into old patterns of being. As if they were dancing by their lake among the trees, the music providing descants and crescendos in which they rode. He, the captain, she like a sail lilting and turning as he guided her.

"Have you made much progress in your search?" she made herself ask. It was either let mundane reality in or run like a banshee. Anything to put the stamp of reality on this heady magic.

She did not think he would answer. "Yes, I reckon it's going pretty well. Seems the stench of the colonies has faded just a might now with the perfume of a title. The mammas are practically flinging their gals at me."

"Oh." How could she have forgotten? The list, like a brand within her glove. "Yes, certainly, your quest for a bride. But actually, I meant the search for your brother."

His gaze flicked to her and then away. "I am still hopeful." He clearly no longer thought such private matters were her business.

"I see you are quite taken with Charlotte. And she with you." He swept her into a wide turn. A breeze caressed her shoulders as they passed the open French doors. She had a terrible wish he might whisk her out into the night and never return. Instead, she tortured herself. "As her chaperone, I ask you to take care. I would not wish you to dally with her."

"Dally?" He raised an eyebrow. "Lady Charlotte is full of wit, poise, and beauty. But you already know that. And she is at the very top of my grandfather's list. I do not 'dally,' Countess. I reckon you are projecting your own behavior onto me."

Heat flushed through her already warm body. Yes, she supposed she deserved his censure. She had dallied with him. But seeing him so open to this new society—to Charlotte—Nora suspected she suffered far more than he.

He swung her into another languorous turn. She closed her eyes, wanting to simply feel him and surrender to the magic of this music, if only for the moment.

"I expect we would get on well together. She's a might young, but seems plainspoken and unaffected."

His words had the effect of throwing freezing water on her fantasy.

"You must have been a good soldier. And an even better grandson. You follow orders well." She smiled, but gall pressed at her heart.

"How do you mean?"

"Your grandfather's edict that you marry. And soon."

He said nothing.

"You have decided love is no longer important?" The question a torment, yet she could not help herself.

He finally looked her square in the eye. "I have not known them long, but I have come to love my grandfather and my uncle. I reckon I make up my mind right quick about who to love. That might be seen as a fault, but I would do just about anything to make them happy." He looked away then and continued. "Besides, I am learning a man can't have everything." Music filled the space between them as if it rose from the parquetry in the floor to separate them instead of bringing them together. "And who's to say Miss Charlotte and I won't fall in love?"

She smiled tightly into his suddenly hard eyes.

"Oh, I suspect she will, Colonel."

If God were benevolent, He would spare her and end the music. But the violins sawed on, and the other dancers whirled by.

"Please, Far—Colonel, after all we have been through, can't we be friends?"

"Friends?" His cold gaze flicked to her and then flicked away just as quickly. "I think not, Countess."

"Ah, so because I won't have you, you will cut me off? That hardly seems fair."

His hand surrounding hers tightened almost painfully and his step faltered for a moment. "Fair?' He snorted. "Why should I play fair?"

"But I have done nothing to you."

He laughed bitterly and shook his head. "Yes,

nothing."

They danced in silence for a few strains then he pulled her toward a niche at the corner of the ballroom. "By God, you hold out the moon to me and then take it away. You tease me with the possibility of happiness then you deny us both. Why shouldn't I punish you for standing in the way of my future? Of ruining me for any other woman?"

"Please don't—"

"Don't what? Don't wish to sit across the breakfast table from you while you sip your tea? Don't stand over your shoulder as you tend your dead plants? Don't ache for you? Don't ache to fill your body with our child?"

She blanched and covered her mouth.

"Have I shocked you, Countess? Well, I won't be sorry. I'm not yet so numb inside that I won't try for love. The war did not finish me off, but you just might."

She shook her head, unshed tears making the world a wash. He pulled her farther into the alcove and gripped her shoulders. His gaze burned into hers.

"By God, do you think I would ever hurt you?" He searched her eyes. "I am not your cruel husband who kept you only as some damn trophy. Or Lord Devlin, who used you in his own way. I am not one of your fops who could never give you any pleasure. I am a man. I want you in my bed. I want you as the mother of my children and any others you wish to bring home. I will never mistreat you. I will never keep you on a leash like some sort of pet to be coddled and indulged. If you can't see that, then I reckon I was wrong. We don't belong together. I can't keep fighting for us both. I am so danged tired of fighting."

Oh, to give in. To strip off her defenses—her past.

To wash it all away and be with this man.

"Lady Havermere, there you are!" Lord Finchley stood before them. "I had a devil of a time spotting you in among all these potted ferns." He turned and grinned at Farren. "Colonel, delighted to see you here. I hope my Nora has been treating you properly."

"*Your* Nora is all that is proper, Lord Finchley. Thank you, Countess." He bowed. "That was delightful," he said coldly.

"Colonel—I—"

"I believe Miss Bearden is next on my grandfather's list, am I correct?" He did not wait for a response. "Her father is a mere baron, but the family is old and has 'pots' of money, so I hear."

"Ha! You have done your research on the chit, Colonel. Good on you!" his lordship said as he took hold of Nora's arm.

"Not really, the gal's mamma practically handed me a ledger sheet." He bowed. "Good evening, Lord Finchley. Countess."

As Nora watched his bright head, ramrod back, and long stride make way across the ballroom she could not help but feel he took any hope for her personal happiness with him.

Chapter Twenty-Six

"Colonel Cavanaugh." Pensgrave, the butler at Linden House, stood aside and Farren stepped into a large drawing room.

The smile on his face withered away as he saw not Charlotte St. James but Nora.

She rose and scurried behind a settee. What, did she think he would assault her? Well, the notion was not farfetched. Like a pawn on a chessboard, he moved two paces sideways, putting another table betwixt them, just in case his heart overwhelmed his head, and he leapt over the furniture to crush her in his arms.

Her nose rose in the air and her eyes darted, wanting to turn tail and run. A trapped deer.

"Lady Charlotte will be down shortly." Pensgrave bowed and left.

Farren's head pounded in the silence. Too much drink last evening after leaving the ball.

The parlor looked like a dang florist's shop. Huge bouquets of every imaginable variety of flower were set in various vases and bowls. Their heavy perfume hung in the room, making it hard to draw breath and likely one of the reasons his head felt like a twenty pounder. His own modest posey of wildflowers, tied up with a bit of ribbon he'd found squirreled away in a drawer, drooped in his hand.

"I didn't reckon you'd be here." He pulled his shoulders back and stood in front of her as if he were before a superior officer.

"Oh?"

"Lady Charlotte said you had an appointment this afternoon."

Her only answer was to look away.

Was she thinking the same as he, that Charlotte had orchestrated this little meeting? Just as he was pretty sure she had maneuvered them into dancing last night.

"Sounds like Lady Charlotte has a tendency to get her own way."

Nora laughed. It sounded more like a bark. "You are coming to know her well already."

"My ma would say Miss Charlotte is 'a baker's dozen.'" And he realized it was true. Charlotte St. James was lovely and seemed to know what she wanted and what's more, how to get it. "A real breath of fresh air in this hothouse of English society."

"Yes, she is," Nora said with nary a whiff of pleasure. She looked at the door again and then turned to the window as if she might jump out. Instead, she skirted around the settee and sat.

Silence heavy as the cloying perfume filled the room.

"I think the ball was a success last evening." She smoothed her skirts.

He crossed to the window and stared out at the traffic.

"Even Amelia Gosforth, who is known for her lavish entertaining, said so. She cannot stand to be outdone. If the papers do not proclaim her ball "the gem of the season" her ladyship is apoplectic. To get the nod from her is truly a feather in our cap."

He looked back at her. The Nora St. James he knew would never utter such ninnyhammer inanities. Apparently, she thought so as well, for she covered her mouth, a horrified look on her face. He wanted to laugh. Instead, he turned back to the traffic.

A clock bonged somewhere in the depths of the house.

The sound pulled him back into the room. Time to get down to business. "I was going to speak to the earl, but since you are here ..."

She half stood and then sat again, like some restless robin.

"I wondered if I might take Lady Charlotte out driving?"

"Charlotte?" Nora frowned.

"Yes, I reckon since you are her chaperone and all. And her father seems a might distracted—"

"Oh, yes, I suppose that would be permissible. If she is amenable." She looked at the toes of her slippers. "Which I am sure she will be. Amenable, that is."

Again, silence stretched like the moment between sighting the target and taking a shot. The damned flowers seemed to have multiplied, their scent so thick he would swear he could carve the air with a Bowie knife.

"Well, perhaps I should check my calendar, I believe we are set to attend—"

The door opened, admitting a slight breeze and Lady Charlotte. "Colonel, I hope I have not kept you waiting too long, but I am sure my aunt entertained you in my absence."

Thank Job and his turkey. He crossed the room to

greet her. "Lady Charlotte." He realized he was still holding his pitiful posey. "These are for you. Small potatoes next to all of these."

She looked about the room. "Heavens, what is all of this?"

"You are apparently a diamond of the first water, my dear." Nora pulled off a less-than-perfect rose petal. "The cards are next to each offering." She smiled, crushing the petal tightly in her hand.

Charlotte had crossed to a console loaded with blooms and began examining each card, seemingly unmoved by the elaborate offerings until she came to one of butter-colored roses.

"Ah! Here is one for you, Auntie." She held up a gold-edged card.

"Oh." Nora looked shocked and then slightly frightened. She took the card Charlotte held out.

Farren stepped toward her. Was it another poem? "Well, open it."

Both ladies looked up at his harsh tone.

Nora touched the seal and seemed to relax. "Later." She turned to Charlotte. "The colonel is here to see you, my dear."

His hair bristled at the thought of some other man giving her flowers. "Oh, I reckon we are all curious," he said, trying to keep the edge out of his voice. "Open it."

Her raised eyebrows told him he hadn't succeeded. He made himself breathe and relax his stance all the while itching to rip the note out of her hands and tear it to pieces.

Her delicate finger slid under the wax and popped it open.

"Oh. How sweet," she said, reading the signature. "I think."

"Well, who is it from? Some heartsick swain, I'll warrant." Charlotte smiled.

Nora's gaze found his. "It is from Viscount Clifford."

Relief washed through Farren's body.

"Viscount Clifford?" Charlotte bounded over to the sofa and sat down next to her aunt to look over her shoulder. "Did I meet him last evening? Oh," she clapped her hands together. "Was he the handsome, though rather stern looking, fellow who danced the quadrille with you, Auntie?"

"No, my dear, that was Lord Milton."

"The viscount is my grandfather, Lady Charlotte," Farren said, finally able to smile.

"Oh, of course! How silly of me. What does he say?"

Nora touched the words but did not read. "It is a thank you of sorts."

"A thank you?" Charlotte took the card from Nora.

"Charlotte!"

"Oh, it is all right, Auntie. After all, it is from the colonel's grandpa." She scanned the note. "He compliments you on doing such a fine job in introducing his grandson to such lovely ladies." Charlotte looked questioningly at Nora. "'One young woman in particular has certainly captured my grandson's fancy.'"

Her frown released as sharp realization dawned on her. The beauty looked up at him and after hesitating a moment, bestowed upon him a smile that had him reaching for the nearest chair.

The countess jerked to her feet. "Pardon me, Charlotte, Colonel. The smell of all these flowers has given me a sick headache." And she hightailed it out of the room.

Chapter Twenty-Seven

More bouquets and callers came over the next several days.

Invitations rolled in. Thus far, they had attended seven balls, three musicals, nine teas, six Venetian breakfasts, and paid she knew not how many calls.

Tonight, the Harrington Ball—always a signal of the end of the season.

Nora moved her finger to the next slot on her calendar.

Charlotte was to have a final fitting for several gowns and then set to see Miss Adelaide Simpson in the afternoon ...

In the calendar's margin, a note for herself.

Lord Milton, charity home, Seven in the morning.

Drat. Why had she promised him? Yet another obligation and the very last thing she wanted to do.

Oh, to disappear back into the woods of their little cottage ...

Where the devil was Charlotte? Gone over ten minutes now simply to, 'See the colonel out'. Plenty of time to hold his beautifully strong hand, to brush her fingers down its callused thumb. Plenty of time to get lost in the green sea of his eyes. To tip her lips to his, to raise up on her toes just a fraction of an inch, to press her lips—

Oh, why had she not made her excuse and left

when Farren—the colonel—had first arrived? Damned job of chaperone. Nora found herself back at the window hoping to catch him leaving.

"He has asked if he might speak to Papa."

Heavens, she must have been so immersed she did not hear Charlotte enter. Nora yanked the drapery shut. "Pardon?"

Charlotte smiled a sweet secret smile. "The colonel, he wishes to have a private word with Papa."

The simple statement hit her like a blow. It should not have done. She should have been well prepared for this turn of events. Still, she found herself saying, "What?" and feeling for the wall behind her. "Now?"

If Charlotte noticed Nora's distress, she did not show it. Thank God for the self-absorption of youth. "He is anxious to begin a family. As you know his grandfather is ill." The girl plopped herself on the settee and reached for a biscuit and began munching away as if the world had not stopped spinning.

Nora made herself take a breath and sit when she only wanted to stop this madness. "And if the earl agrees to this courtship, you will say yes?"

The girl reached for another biscuit, but at Nora's glare her hand froze and wisely she blotted her lips and then folded her napkin into a neat square.

"Well, I am not sure."

"Not sure?" Hope bloomed.

"As you say, it is so soon. He is the first to seriously pursue me. And I am young." She smoothed the napkin in her lap. Nora wanted to fling the scrap of linen to the floor and trample it into the hideous cabbage rose carpet. Charlotte looked up, and with her sweetest smile said, "What do you think, Auntie?

Should I accept him?"

No! She wanted to scream. She rose and went to the window. If only she could heave herself out of it. "That is hardly something for me to decide."

"Oh, I know." Charlotte agreed as she joined her. She reached for Nora's hand and squeezed it. "But what do you think of him?" When Nora did not reply immediately, the girl continued. "He is very handsome."

"Has he kissed you?" The words came out before she could stop them.

Charlotte bit her lip and looked away.

Hell's hounds, he had. By God, she would flay the rotter. "I only ask because you must guard your reputation," she said in what she hoped was her best chaperone tone. "Once it is gone, you are damaged goods. There is no sense gilding the lily, Charlotte. You and your family are new to the ways of the *haute ton*. It is my duty to guide you."

"Do you think him dishonorable?"

Yes! Yes, he is dishonoring our time together. The tenderness and love he showed me was meaningless to him if he could move on so quickly. This is why I will never give my heart! Nora wanted to scream. But the damned pity of it was that horse had left the barn weeks ago.

"Ah, you are so silent." Charlotte took her other hand and held them to her breast. "Please, do not spare me if there is something you need to tell me about Farren."

Farren.

His Christian name on Charlotte's lips. A dagger in her heart.

Even when the viscount had given her that bloody list with Charlotte's name at the very top, even when Farren ignored her and dutifully ticked off each girl on that list, even when it was clear he preferred Charlotte to any other young hopeful, Nora held onto the fantasy that he still loved her. He would never actually offer for another woman.

Why *this* girl? Why would he hurt her so?

The answer was she had hurt him. She had rejected him. Why should he not find his happiness with someone else? And Charlotte was a delightful young woman. The painful truth of it was, he must be beginning to love her.

Nora looked down at the hideous floral carpet. A butter-cream petal from a bouquet had fallen, making the ruby-pink roses against the equally vibrant royal blue look all the more garish and overdone. She stooped to pick it up, feeling the plush of its velvet cup. But, on closer examination, the edge was already curled and browning.

"Charlotte, while I do think the colonel is a fine prospect, I want you to continue to look about. It is best to be utterly sure of the gentleman—well, as sure as possible—before settling on one in particular. A gentleman in the throes of courtship is often quite different than the husband who will own you, body and soul."

Charlotte began to say something and then must have thought better of it. "I thank you for your wise council, Auntie, but I believe I am quite certain of my choice. Though I am happy to look about, if only to enjoy myself first before committing to marriage."

Nora wanted to tear her hair out.

Charlotte smiled her most radiant smile, rose up on her toes and kissed Nora's cheek. "My mamma is looking down from heaven, and I know she thanks you. And my father, though he is often preoccupied and in over his head, would thank you for your wise counsel. Your friendship and guidance have made all the difference to my fitting in here in London." The girl looked deeply into Nora's eyes. "I would never want to hurt you. Ever."

"Hurt me?" Nora pulled back. "No, I don't believe you would, dear heart."

"So, Aunt Nora, I need to hear from you. What do you think?"

"Charlotte, I own I did not want to become involved in your come out, but you must know that I have come to love you. I want you to be happy. To have the man you love."

"Then you think I should take him?"

Did her smile seem a little sad, her gaze a bit too intense for a young girl in love?

Nora took a long, slow breath. "What I think … is Colonel Cavanaugh … is the very best of men. You could not do better, in my mind, Charlotte." And with that admonition, the flame of hope for her own happiness snuffed itself.

Chapter Twenty-Eight

Nora's brush clattered to her dressing table at the sound of the knock upon her bedchamber door.

"Lady Havermere?"

Only Pensgrave. Relief swamped her. Every moment she was sure Charlotte would burst in to exclaim her news.

"Pardon, your ladyship. I did not wish to disturb you as you will be dressing for the Harrington Ball soon, but there is a man here to see you. I told him you were not at home, but he was quite insistent, saying he must only speak with you, your ladyship. He would not come inside."

"Very well." Nora adjusted the comb in her hair, rose, and then followed the butler down to the front door.

A sober-looking man in a plain coat stood with a small notebook in his hand.

"You are Nora St. James, Countess of Havermere?"

"I am. And who are you?"

"Just the courier, ma'am. If you'll sign here, please."

Nora scanned the paper. A document saying she'd received a package.

"What is this?"

The man pulled a velvet box from inside his coat.

"If you'll just sign, I'll be on my way."

No mysterious gifts had come since moving to Linden House. Was the reason because the sender did not know she had moved? Or did it have more to do with Rose's being dead? Or could this person somehow know of her secret alliance with Lord Finchley, and that is why the gifts had stopped? Could this simply be a gift from his lordship?

"Who sent you? Who are you working for?"

"Don't know nothing, ma'am. I was just told to make sure you got this. I was to hand it directly to you."

Should she refuse it? No, better to know for certain. She scrawled her name and then took the box. The man tipped his hat and then scampered down the steps.

When Nora turned back, Opal was behind her. "Want me to follow him, Mum?"

"No." Nora blocked the way. "You will stay out of this, Opal. Do you hear me?"

The girl snorted and strode off.

Back in her room Nora closed the door and then set the sleek velvet box upon her bed, stepping back as if it was some evil reptile. She wiped her hands on her satin skirt.

Feeling ridiculous, she approached the bed and hastily tweaked the clasp, flipping open the lid.

"Oh!" She stumbled back.

Light caught dozens of sparkling white diamonds and rich rubies, making the piece seem alive within its nest of pale blue satin.

A brooch. And an expensive one. Unlike flowers and perfume, this gift would never fade away. Could never be worn out like lambskin gloves. These jewels would endure for decades to come.

Nora would have snapped the lid closed but there was a note wedged into the top of the box. She pried it out.

Same paper. Same writing. Same smell.

Dear God, could this mean Rose might still be alive? Why else would this man continue to taunt her? Someone who knew her desperation to find the girl? Who perhaps knew where Rose was?

Or was it sent simply to confound her, torture her? A bizarre coincidence?

She unfolded the note.

The blight that soils great beauty washed away
No more temptation leading you astray.
My thorns will tear vile errant vines to shreds
My strength alone shall bear your dainty head.
'Tis civil war to sport with slugs of earth
Blind belly dwellers must stay low for worth.
And so, take care how you your garden grow.
A rain of diamonds, sun of fairest gold
Is all one needs to make a Ruby glow.
The time grows ripe to pluck your glorious bloom!
With keen desire, I wait, your true bridegroom!

Bile burned the back of her throat.

How she wanted to crush these words. To set them aflame. As if the ashes could make her life new and clean from the taint of her past and of this madman who taunted her.

Oh, if she could do it all again, this life, these choices. But in reality, she'd had no choice. Her path had been mapped the moment her father had gambled away the little fortune he'd had. Gone the second her mother saw her only child as a commodity. Finished when the old man had looked at her with such greedy eyes and then cruelly pinched her nipple. Gone when she had inadvertently sent Devlin to a madhouse. And finally, when she had spurned the only man she truly loved.

Oh, this heavy burdensome life! She sank to the ugly carpet in her misery.

Laughter poured from her mouth. The same terrible sounds she'd emitted when her mother had informed her of her father's death. Uncontrollable laughter had torn through her nine-year-old body until she had clutched her belly rocking with it. Her mother, horrified, had slapped her so hard she had been thrown to the floor.

Nora touched the tiny scar on her left temple, a brand from that terrible day. But the wound inside—her loss—would never heal.

She was dying inside. Her fears, like worms infesting her core, leaving her just a shell. Soon she would have nothing left to give but bitterness.

She picked herself up off the floor, as she had at the tender age of nine. As a child she'd had no power, but now she had choices. Perhaps she could not have her every desire. But she could have enough. She could choose a kind man who would leave her be so she might live as she wanted. Sweet, Lord Finchley.

But she had work to do.

The note lay crumpled in her hand. She could not destroy it. Not yet.

There were clues here. Clues she must follow if she were ever to be free of the possibility of Rose. Free to move on to a life with girls who needed her. She made herself open the paper and smooth it.

The blight that soils great beauty washed away

Lord Finchley? She had received a note from him that he was poorly and had gone to the country seeking "fresh and healthful air," and would return to claim her before the season's end, if not before.

And *civil war?* Could the writer mean Farren? Surely, no one could know of their brief affair? She reread the note.

Very well. She would play this man's game. Array herself in his jewels and don his gloves, douse herself in his perfume. Become his "thing" on the chance of learning his identity and finding Rose.

And so, take care how you your garden grow.

She read the line over and over.

The time grows ripe ...

It *was* time. No more dithering about the best course of action or waiting for her prince to whisk her away to a fantasy cottage in the woods. Her prince had moved on, and so must she. But not before she exhausted all roads that might lead to Rose's recovery. Only then could she truly commit to Benton Finchley.

Farren. She should write him. She promised she would. Dear God, her heart leapt at having a reason to contact him, to see him.

She dashed off a note asking him to meet her at the Harrington Ball, that she had received another "gift".

Tonight, all might be revealed.

Chapter Twenty-Nine

Farren resisted the urge to yank at his neckcloth. This ball was a crush, and London's heavy fog seemed to hold in the heat. And smells. Even out here in the back garden he found no relief. He nearly had not come tonight but his grandpa had insisted Farren go out and stop hovering.

Dang it all. His grandpa was no better, he had made no new progress in finding Brendan, and the woman he loved did not love him,

"I heard they are secretly betrothed," the sibilant whisper hung in the stagnant air.

"Well, it's about time. It's common knowledge Finchley won't get a penny until he gets leg-shackled."

"And despite the old boy's tendencies, he appreciates a beauty. And she is unparalleled in that regard. Still, seems just as Finch is poised for the parson's trap, he starts feeling poorly."

"Yes, poor, ol' sot must be quite ill to have left London in the height of the season. What was the rumor? That the old earl met his end by being poisoned? The countess could be at it again. For my part, I'd rather take a plain girl and keep to this side of the ground."

The men guffawed. "Not likely. She has to bag him first to get the blunt, only then can she do him in." Cloying cigar smoke wafted Farren's way. No respite from the filthy air or filthy rumors.

Having no other amusement, this rabble would revisit this tale like an outhouse during a chili supper. Best to go and make his apologies to Charlotte. He'd likely missed their dance. But he really wanted to see Nora. A torture, but one he could not seem to escape.

"The Fallen Angel has some ripe ones just in." The man's voice wafted over the hedge. "Even a virgin or two, word has it."

Farren stopped.

"Virgins, you say? Not likely. I don't think there's a bloody virgin left in this filthy city."

"I have it on good authority, my dear. Alton told me just this evening."

"Alton? Really?" The man sounded right hopeful. "No matter, the price would be exorbitant. You know I am not made of that kind of blunt." Farren stepped closer. The voice sounded familiar.

"A small price for adventure. Think of the squeals." The man with the more petulant voice added. "Besides, I am flush. First part of the quarter, my darling. You know how I'm rewarded by Father when I behave." The man laughed.

"You tempt me."

Farren *knew* that voice. But who? He peered through the dense hedge of privet, but the men's backs were to him.

"I always hope to. Damned hard to get near you these days. That up-start poser has you under his thumb," the more nasal voice said.

"He's a man of conviction, very influential, not to mention, I owe him a small fortune. But I have a task to perform this evening, and once that is accomplished, I will be free of him. At least with regard to money."

"But I have told you time and again, I will pay your debts. Let me take care of you, my beautiful Mad Hatter."

Hatter? That's it! One of the men was Mr. Hatten, the extremely good-looking man who had needled Farren at that poetry reading.

"Do not confuse me with Gillingham. I don't blow with the wind, pandering to every Tom, Dick, and Harry."

"*Tush!* I know something I'd like to blow, my dear," the nasal man said in a theatrical whisper.

"Not now, lad. I have to be available. In fact, you are distracting me. I should go."

"To *him*?" The other man snorted. "Perhaps I can tag along?"

"You know he doesn't like hangers-on. You would be *de trop*."

"I could be part of the equation," he said in a suggestive tone. Farren could imagine the man's eyebrows waggling.

"It's not that kind of job. He is not even going to be involved. Has to get back to his daughter."

"Daughter? As I remember he's never been married. Who is this daughter?"

"He guards her very secretly even though she is not of his blood. Hypocrite." Hatten spat the word out as if it were poison.

"Ooh, a secret daughter. Likely a virgin. How old is she? Perhaps she might like a bit of sport?"

"That is not remotely funny. The girl is about fifteen now and from what I've heard a blonde beauty."

Farren dared not make a move, yet his heart

pounded in his chest. Could they be speaking of Rose? A blonde girl of the correct age hidden away?

"You've never seen her?"

"No, as I said he keeps his hothouse rose very private."

Rose. Hothouse rose. Blonde and fifteen. Could this be Bren's child? But she was dead, wasn't she?

"I begin to think you don't love me."

"I have to go. You are a needy brat."

"Yes, but so beautiful and with such a big cock that you cannot let me go despite how I try your patience."

All was quiet except for some rustling. Farren gritted his teeth and waited. Who? Who was the man who had Hatten so under his thumb?

"Come, not here, Maxwell. Make your excuses and then go on to The Angel. I will meet you there when my job is finished," Hatten said to his friend.

A branch snapped beneath his foot. He had to leave. Now. The men were turning toward the sound. He would shadow Hatten until he got some answers.

He'd nearly made it to the more formal gardens and parterre when he heard his name.

"Cavanaugh!" Gillingham was coming toward him.

Damn it all. The last thing he needed was Gillingham dogging him.

"Been looking for you all evening. Where the devil have you been?" Gillingham jangled his fobs while pulling a flask from his pocket. "Have a snort?"

"Another time. The ladies call." He brushed past Gillingham.

And if miracles could happen, maybe Hatten would lead him to Rose. And to Bren.

"Colonel." Farren turned. Hatten and his young

man stood still smoking their cheroots. "Just the man we've been looking for."

Blinding pain lanced through his head. He fumbled for the hedge, anything to break his fall. Too late. The world went black.

Chapter Thirty

The carriage lurched. Must have hit a hole deep as Dante's Inferno. Nora's head rang with pain, but Charlotte remained in a blissful world of her own.

What a dismal failure this evening had been.

The gifts, worn to lure the person who might have information on Rose or who might harm Farren, had failed. No one had remarked on them, save Sir Askew and Lady Higgins, who, gesturing to the diamond and ruby brooch, snidely opined they assumed all the Havermere jewels would have gone to the new earl. Intimating that she must have *earned* the bauble. And, Lord Milton, had made a brief comment, but only out of jealousy. Farren had never presented himself, missing his dance with Charlotte. Could he be in danger?

"Where was the colonel this evening?" The fact that Charlotte did not seem concerned irritated Nora all the more. "I thought he was to have the first waltz? I scoured the ballroom and terrace I know not how many times but could not find him."

"Yes, I shall have to take him to task. I do not know what held him up. As you know the viscount is ill, poor man. I'm sure I will have a note from him when we arrive home begging forgiveness for leaving me to the likes of Lord Sealing." She giggled.

Nora had the urge to bash the girl over the head.

"I dare say I will see him tomorrow, and he'll be

318

quite contrite." Charlotte smiled out into the darkness.

"Tomorrow? I thought you were set to see Miss Simpson. I have it noted on the calendar. I am not available tomorrow. Lord Milton is taking me out to see one of his properties." Heavens, she sounded like her mother just then, scolding and intractable.

"No matter, Auntie. I will send a note to Miss Simpson. After all, she will understand when I tell her how important it is that I be at home. And Papa has promised he will be there."

"Oh, I see. This is rather sudden, Charlotte."

"Is it, Auntie? I am quite sure of my choice. Quite sure. I love him."

"Love?" Her voice rang out in the confines of the dimly lit carriage. "My dear, there is no need for such haste." Then a terrible thought occurred to her. "Is there?" The thought of Farren and her beautiful niece lying together, Charlotte perhaps carrying his child …

"Heavens, no, Auntie! But why wait when I am sure? Oh, tomorrow can't come soon enough!"

And Nora wished tomorrow would never come.

The carriage had stopped—thank God. Thomas opened the door and set the steps. Nora had never wanted to see her bedchamber more. Oh, to finally be alone!

"I will bid you goodnight, Charlotte. Sleep in, you must be in your best looks tomorrow."

"Yes, goodnight, Auntie. I love you."

Nora looked back at her beautiful niece poised on the precipice of marriage. The girl beamed up at her from the foot of the staircase, so utterly in love. Yes, love was what mattered. "And I love you too, my dear. Goodnight."

****

Nora could not breathe. She thrust aside the stifling, black veil.

Farren!

But he was so far away. He stood, in a golden suit next to a woman dressed in radiant silver.

Huge decorative beams crisscrossed the ceiling far above. The heavy smell of incense and beeswax hung in the air. A cathedral.

If she could only get closer to see the woman's face, but a dense bramble of white and red rose bushes choked the aisle, seeming to spring from the wooden pews.

Still, she was impelled to move toward this couple. To see this woman.

Thorns tore at her black gown. The gashes revealed a red satin dress beneath. She clawed at the black covering, wanting to be free of its weight.

At last, she found herself at the altar. She called out to Farren, but she had no voice, and he only had eyes for his bride.

Turn, so that I may see your face! she willed.

The woman seemed to respond, and began to turn, the edge of her bridal bonnet now revealing a profile—

Lily! This girl was Lily. Instead of a bouquet, she carried a beautiful infant dressed in a christening gown.

Nora reached for the child, but Lily shook her head and pulled the babe away. Instead, she extended her hand, holding out a note.

Nora reached for it.

A dance card?

About to toss it away, a name leapt out at her—

Nora jerked awake. Sweat turned cold in the air. Dawn's light arrowed through the eastern window to fall on her dressing table.

Foggy from her dream, she crossed to the vanity, fumbling past her fan and gloves to find her dance card of the night before.

The name stood out boldly, especially the 'T.'

Milton.

She yanked open the drawer where she had stashed the note of yesterday afternoon.

By God, yes! The "T" was the same. The slant of the penmanship, the same.

Could it be Milton? One signature was hardly enough to compare, but the hand seemed to be his.

Her mind spun through their interaction of last night. He had remarked on the rose pin, and when he bid her adieu, the pad of his thumb had traced one of the embroidered roses on her glove. At the time, she had just put it down to his ardor, but maybe the gesture was something more. Something quite possessive.

The ruby and diamond brooch sparkled in the light of a single candle. She picked it up but it slipped from her trembling fingers. As it struck the floor, the bauble sprung open.

A pale pink ribbon, fine as gossamer, bound the contents. Her heart hammered in her breast as her longest finger brushed past the ribbon to what it held.

Also soft as silk. But not silk.

It could be any lock of hair, she told herself. Snipped off any girl with hair the color of moonbeams. Hell, it could be from the doxy she and Farren had found in Covent Garden, the one Nora had been so sure was Lily reincarnated. But somehow Nora knew it wasn't the girl's locks, or those of some other child. This token belonged to Rose. Her Rose.

A tiny slip of paper lay next to the locket.

The Lily is dead, but the White Rose is still Red

Chapter Thirty-One

Rope bit into the flesh on his wrists. His tongue felt thick and heavy against the rag filling his mouth. He'd give his right ball for some water. He sucked in air through his bloody nose. A bitter tang.

Now he remembered being cracked over the head. Gillingham had forced a flask between his lips. Nearly drowning him in the drink. Must have been tainted. No idea how long he'd been out.

The steady roll of carriage wheels—no cadence of cobblestones, so they were on a country road. He must have been out for a right long while. A booted toe prodded Farren's ribs. He fought to make no sound despite the pain.

"Damn it, how much did you put in that drink, Gillingham?" Hatten's voice sounded tinny and far away in Farren's ears.

"Why should you care? Don't tell me you fancy him?" Gillingham needled.

Hatten made no reply.

"I'll warrant he's a goliath in all aspects." A toe nudged his cock and Farren nearly betrayed himself. "Devil of a time hauling his ass into the carriage. Even with the three of us."

"That reminds me, I owe Max a night on the town for his assistance. And you, my fine foxed friend, will have to pay him back the blunt he shucked out."

"Why me?"

"Because you are the daft bugger that diverted from the plan and coshed the colonel in the middle of a blooming ball! All that blood. Good thing the groomsmen hanging about in the back mews were foxed and Max had enough blunt to pay them off, else we would be cooling our heels in Newgate."

"But I don't have any money!"

"Hell, it's a wonder Maxie didn't have to pay out more with you singing at the top of your lungs."

"I did it to distract them. We were supposed to be drunk."

"Don't ever think of treading the boards, old fellow. Your acting leaves much to be desired."

"Sod off, Hatten."

Someone rapped on the roof. The carriage slowed, then stopped.

"What the hell are you doing?" Gillingham spat out.

"Taking your advice and sodding off, old boy."

"What the dev—"

"I've done my bit. You handle him from here. Besides, I don't want to be involved should something go awry. We know how he gets when things don't go as planned. Besides, I happen to be square with him now, and I like it that way. You, however, are in but good." Hatten laughed. "And Max awaits me at the Angel!" The door slammed shut and then the carriage continued on.

Good, one down. There would be a driver, possibly two, but he doubted it. Only one horse by the hoof sounds. Farren felt along the floor for anything he might use as a weapon or something sharp to cut the hemp of the rope. With his eyes covered, his sense of touch would have to be more acute.

"Fucking arse," Gillingham muttered. He shifted on the seat, old springs creaking in protest. Farren heard the pop of a cork and then the *glunk* of drink.

Good, get good and foxed, Gilly.

"Damned poser. I'd kill the bastard myself, but I'd likely muck it up. Has had my ballocks in a vice ever since my run of bad luck."

The carriage hit a bump.

"Damn!"

Wet dripped onto Farren's forehead. He hissed as stinging spirits ran into the gash on the back of his head.

Gillingham suddenly stilled. The heel of a boot connected with his hip bone.

"Hey, you awake?" Gillingham said with what sounded like a bit of hope. Old Gilly seemed like he needed a friend.

Farren grunted against the foul rag in his mouth. When his effort was met with only silence, Farren grunted again with more insistence.

Instead of the rag being removed, the blindfold was lifted from his eyes.

Farren blinked. Even in the dim light of the interior of the carriage, his eyes burned as they adjusted.

Gillingham's face hung like a moon poised between his forearms. His hands dangled, one holding the neck of a bottle.

"You all right?"

Farren blinked and grunted again.

"Ah, hell, there's not a soul around to hear you." He jerked the rag from Farren's mouth.

Air rushed in and he closed his eyes, savoring the relatively clean air.

"Wa—a—a—" He couldn't make his tongue work.

"No water, chap, only this." He shoved the bottle between Farren's lips.

Liquor was the last thing he wanted, but it was wet, and he forced himself to take a painful swallow. Bile burned the back of his throat along with the spirits.

Gillingham shoved a hand through his hair and then swiped it along his mouth and shook his head. "Had to do it, old thing. Never could win against the blighter." He thumped the bottle against his thigh. "Drove me crazy. He knew it, of course, and egged me on. Where I lost even more." Gillingham was trembling now.

Who? Farren was desperate to ask. He did not think Gillingham was speaking of Hatten. Didn't Hatten imply he was only a toady himself?

"By God, I'm done with it. With him." Gillingham took another long pull from the bottle. "In my defense, I loved her, you know. Iris. But she took one look at your beautiful brother, and that was it. Dropped me like a hot poker. I even borrowed more money from that viper to lure her back, but she didn't care. Imagine The Butterfly clinging to a man without any blunt ..." He shook his head. "I hated your brother for taking her and then tossing her aside. He never loved her." He took another pull on his bottle. "But then she had the brats and thought he would surely come back to her. Stupid cow. By the time she figured out he wasn't, it was too late. Hell, it's all too fucking late." He stared off into the dark night.

"It's not." His voice sounded harsh and pained.

Gillingham jerked back to him.

"Not too late." His tongue, dry as toast. "Let me go. I'll get him. Who? Tell me who?"

The man's fingers twitched, and he shifted his feet. Suddenly, he stoppered the bottle and shoved it between the seat and the squabs.

But the carriage slowed and then stopped. The door was jerked open. "You're late. It's nearly five." Farren craned his neck. A huge man filled the doorway. "I'll help you get him in, but then I'm off."

Farren bit his split lip and sucked, hoping some blood might make his voice work but his croak was cut short as the rag was once again shoved into his mouth and the blindfold jerked into place over his eyes.

Chapter Thirty-Two

The carriage arrived promptly at seven.

Charlotte and Cousin Orville would still be asleep.
She had peeked in on the girls, and they were sleeping
as well.

Nora stood in the hall ready to meet whatever lay
ahead. She touched the note she had left for Farren
telling of her suspicions that Rose may well be alive,
and Milton may be involved, and finally, where she had
gone. She had no doubt he would be calling for
Charlotte today—soon-to-be betrothed. A similar note
lay on Nora's dressing table for Opal. Just in case.

"Ah, you look charming, my dear," Lord Milton
said, a picture of sartorial elegance himself in dove
gray. He did not so much as glance down at the rose pin
on her breast. "Shall we set off? I would like to make
the early train."

Pensgrave stood sentinel by the door ready to open
it. Catching sight of herself in one of the huge pier
mirrors that flanked the entryway, the diamond and
ruby brooch winked briefly as it caught a shard of light.
She longed to tear it from her breast.

Stop being so damned skittish.

Her few hours of planned strategy seemed like a
house of cards now in the full light of day as Lord
Milton handed her up into one of the train's first-class
compartments. He gave her the forward-facing seat and

settled across from her. Good. She could observe him better from this vantage point. His silver eyes, however benign-looking, seemed to want something of her, his gentle smile a bit too fixed.

Questions buzzed her brain, but she had resolved to give him no inkling she was anything other than a charming guest. Instead, she feigned sleep, pleading a late night.

"Nora."

Milton smiled indulgently as she opened her eyes. She shifted her sore bum while tentatively rolling her neck. The train whistle blew as the conductor called out "Chippingham."

In no time, she was whisked into a sumptuous carriage, and they started off at once. A short time later, the coachman called out *whoa* and the horses slowed and then stopped.

"Welcome to Seraphim House."

The place looked to be a large country manor. However, there were perhaps two dozen children playing in the gardens at the end of the east wing and scattered among the trees beyond. Could one of the girls be Rose?

Nora stopped herself from calling out the name.

Wait. Be patient.

A ball hit a tree, skittering straight toward them as they made their way from the carriage. The kicker, a boy about eight years of age, ran to retrieve it, but suddenly stopped as if an invisible fence ran down the lawn separating the two wings of the house. He stared open-mouthed at Lord Milton.

His lordship looked at the ball as if it were a vile pest. The boy looked quite terrified, shielding a withered and useless arm against his side. Again, Nora stopped herself from reacting. Milton finally kicked the ball with the side of his boot and then firmly took her elbow as they continued to the front door.

Upon entering a great hall, a servant bowed and took Lord Milton's hat and Nora's cloak.

"We will have tea in the drawing room after you have refreshed yourself. Powers, take the countess to her room."

Her room? She followed the butler.

Surely, Farren had got her note by now and was now on his way?

On the staircase, another manservant skittered by, head down, hands clasped behind his back. Something about him jogged a memory. There was no time to ponder. The butler gestured for her to enter an opulent bedchamber.

A maid bobbed into a curtsy.

"Welcome to Seraphim House, my lady. I hope you will find everything to your liking."

"Thank you. I only need to use the necessary and to wash my face."

"Of course. This way."

She was shown into a very modern bathroom with a shower-bath as well as a large step-in tub. A small separate room held a water closet.

This man was staging a proposal. Showing her his wealth, and how easily she could slip into this room, and his life.

"Oh, why did I come alone?" she said to the pale face in the mirror.

She scrubbed her hands hard. What if he had Rose? How would she convince him to give her up? Maybe best to gather information and then come back with reinforcements?

"Is everything all right, my lady?" It was the maid. How long had she been hiding in here?

Powers was waiting and led her through a warren of rooms and into a large library.

"His Lordship will be along directly," the butler said, before closing the door.

Nora ran to the desk. Neat as a pin with nary a sheet of paper in sight. She opened the drawer on the left-hand side. Paper, rich and creamy, lay in the bottom and something silver. The door opened and she turned, closing the drawer with her hip.

"I hope your room is to your liking?" If Lord Milton noted her proximity to his desk, he did not let on.

"Yes, I thank you. Though I am sure any chamber would have been sufficient to repair myself."

He crossed to her. "Nora, it cannot be a secret as to how much I admire you, my dear. I do not give my heart easily. Indeed, I have only felt this way once before, and I lost her." His gaze drifted to the fire, and his jawline tightened. After a long moment, he roused himself and turned to her. "But you are here at last, and my patience has paid off. At least I hope—" He paused and smiled— "It will be rewarded."

A shadow crept along the sunlit floor. Clouds moving in.

"I have waited so long for you. Ten years, six months and twenty-one days." He smiled again.

He was taking her hands. She should stop him. No words came.

"My dearest, Nora, will you do me the honor of

becoming my bride and fulfilling my dearest wish to be a family?"

That silver—in the drawer—it was in the shape of a four-leafed clover.

The snuff box.

Brendan's snuff box. The one he gave to Iris, who in turn had given it to her girls. The one Eunice Lockhart had said they had stolen. "I—I'm sorry, I must sit." *Could there have been two trinkets, one for each girl?*

"Of course, my dear. How thoughtless of me to plunge ahead. Forgive my impatience. Let us have some tea." He crossed to the silver urn that had been placed on a table next to the settee. "Cream, no sugar, correct?"

She nodded. Anything to prolong her answer.

Milton gestured for her to sit on the settee and then set a fine Limoges cup in her hands. The heady aroma of Darjeeling filled her nose.

"Thank you." She took a sip and closed her eyes. Be calm.

"Have you recovered, my dear?" His lordship had pulled a smaller chair next to hers, his face cast in an expression of concern. "I did not think my proposal would come as a shock. I know I am older than you by some margin. But I am steadfast and obviously well able to support you and a family."

"I—it is not—that is, I had never thought to remarry."

"Perhaps not just for a husband, but what of children? A child. A daughter?"

The tea sloshed over the rim of her cup. She set it down. "What are you saying?"

He made no answer, only smiled and then crossed to the bellpull. A moment later, a bald man entered through a hidden door. The same one she had passed on the stairway. Now, realization dawned. The same man who bought the painting at the auction.

"It is time, Fresley. Bring her to us."

Chapter Thirty-Three

Nora stood, her heart hammering in her breast. A million questions burned in her mind, but they all fell away when the door opened and time stopped.

The face was the same, but not the same. So alike, and yet so different.

"Rose." The name escaped in a breath.

The girl ran toward her. Nora held out her arms.

"Poppa! You have come!" Rose sailed by Nora to be embraced by Lord Milton.

"My dear, we have a guest. You must make your curtsy."

Rose turned to Nora, a smile lighting her face as Lily's never had, her plump cheeks swelling with glee.

"Good afternoon." She stepped forward and performed a sweet curtsy. "I am so very pleased to finally meet you, your ladyship." She turned to Milton and took his hand. "She is so beautiful, Poppa. Exactly like the queen you described in your stories. And even more beautiful than in the por—"

"Enough!" Milton held up his hand in a staying motion. Then he smiled. "My poppet, you must not spoil our surprise. After all, we have waited so very long for her to be free to come to us."

"Rose—" Nora reached out to touch the golden halo of hair that hung in artful curls about the girl's shoulders. Rose smiled again. Lily had never let Nora touch her hair. It had been a tangled mess when they had first met. Then Lily had kept its beauty hidden in two tightly bound braids.

"Rose, I cannot believe—"

Milton stepped forward. "My sweet girl, the countess and I must discuss a few things before we celebrate this evening. You must go with Fresley to get ready for the festivities."

"My new gown?" She clasped her hands to her breast.

"Of course, my pet. We will see you at dinner."

"We will have such a jolly time. I have planned so many things." Rose clapped and danced over to Milton. "Oh, Poppa, I knew it would happen. I prayed she would come to us."

"Go now with Fresley."

Nora longed for her to stay but questions needed answers first. "I look forward to seeing you later, Rose."

Nora found herself being embraced. Tears clouded her eyes. She shut them and swallowed. Rose perfume filled her nose.

So many questions. This madman had the answers.

Rose curtsied again and then left the room with Fresley.

"How? How did you come to have her?"

"I understand you have questions, my dear, but first things first." Milton moved to the huge desk and using a key unlocked and then opened a lower drawer. He removed a sheaf of official looking papers and handed them to her.

"What is this?"

He did not answer, only smiled.

It was a contract, her name clearly penned next to his.

Her gaze found his. "This is a special marriage license," she said, more to hear the words out loud than to state the obvious.

"Well, my dearest Nora, how else are we to be a family?"

"Lord Milton—I"

"Please, call me Rodger." He stepped closer.

"You sent those gifts. Those poems."

"I only wanted to keep you from further polluting yourself. The world has a way of corrupting even its most perfect specimens. I'm sure you understand now that all has been revealed."

This man was clearly deranged. She must be very careful. "Lord—Rodger, I am flattered you want me as your wife, but I—"

"Not only my wife, but Rose's mother." He was smiling, but the hard look in his eyes made her push back.

Dear God, Rose had been the bait. He'd brought her out to give Nora a taste and then sent her away. Marriage was clearly the only way she would get Rose.

The clock on the mantle showed nearly three in the afternoon. Farren had to have seen her note by now. He would be here soon.

"Come, my dear. I'd like to show you something, a sort of testament to my passion and confidence in this outcome." His lordship took her arm and brought her to an easel set up in the far corner of the room. "I was going to save this, but I cannot keep it to myself any longer." A covered painting stood on the easel. "Would you do the honors?"

Nora stifled the urge to run. Yet she could not resist seeing what this painting might reveal. She grasped the edge of the cover and lifted a corner.

"Oh, my God." She staggered backwards.

His fingers, still circling her arm, bit into her flesh as he moved in front of the painting as if to protect it from her oath. "You must not blaspheme, Nora. It is not seemly. After all, you have a daughter to think of now. We will be a family. The family Rose and I have dreamt of."

He released her arm and then turned and reverently, as if uncovering the holy host, he drew the drape from the painting. And then stepped aside.

Dear God. Yes, there it was staring her in the face, her family complete, even a beloved dog lying at her feet.

"I think the painter captured you quite well, my dear, don't you agree? He used the other portrait as a guide."

"The man who bought—"

"Yes, Fresley served as my agent to buy the portrait. I could not countenance some lout ogling such perfection."

"Oh." She could think of nothing else to say.

"You are shocked?" He clasped his hands behind his back. "Don't be. Do you remember the first time I met you? It was just after you were wed to the earl. At the Huxley Ball."

No, she did not remember meeting Lord Milton, but she did remember the ball with painful detail. The old earl had been preening like a peacock, displaying his trophy until a foreign count, who didn't know to steer clear, overstepped and flirted with her. She could not even recall his name now. Her husband nearly had an apoplexy jerking her out of the room so fast her pearl bracelet burst and scattered over the floor. The searing humiliation was more painful than the lashing she had gotten when they had returned to Linden House.

"I could not believe such beauty could be attached to an old reprobate who was not worthy to touch your feet, much less—well, never mind. I made it my business to flatter the old man, to seek his advice and council, but all I really wanted was you." He smiled. "And now here you are, at last."

He turned back to the painting. "Rose and I made a game of seeing your image take shape. She chose the color of your gown and the dog—she begged for the cur. I finally agreed, but only a noble and purebred animal. One must make some compromises in life." His gaze bore into hers. "You must see what a perfect family we make."

"But how? How did she come to you?"

"I plucked her from the dung heap. A true rose among so many thorns."

Nora shook her head and turned from the beautiful hideousness.

"Very well." His jawline twitched as his lips pulled tight. "I suppose you must have some answers. Let us sit."

Nora had not the slightest inclination to sit, but she must play his game at least for a while.

He gestured to the settee. She ignored him, taking a chair instead.

He frowned and seated himself across from her. "I have always been interested in breeding. My father was a mere tenant farmer. Though he was more interested in drinking and carousing than tending sheep. Anyway, I began to read Spencer and Darwin. Why spend so much time and energy perfecting a sheep or cow or horse when we allow mankind to spew and spawn inferior humans? Why not apply those breeding methods to humanity? Less suffering, less predilection for vice, fewer diseases and mental infirmity. Why not breed the more superior of our race?"

Nora's stomach heaved.

"Twins are a way to study some of these concepts. Oscar Gillingham owes me a great deal of money." He waved his hand. "Money does not interest me. I don't need it, but he had something I did want. Identical twins. So, he brought me to see Rose and the other one."

"Lily." Nora breathed.

"Yes, Lily." He grimaced. "Though she was the farthest thing from pure, the antithesis of my Rose, spiteful, devious—a devil. She ran away before I could begin to study her blotted character. Good riddance. I almost cast Rose away as well. She was useless to me without her twin. Or so I thought. But I did not know Rose then. She is sweet and bright, beautiful and talented. You will hear her play the pianoforte later this evening. And she sings beautifully. She has been cultivated by the best tutors."

He spoke of Rose as if she were a hothouse flower. "She never asked about her sister? About Lily?"

He shrugged. "I told her only the truth."

It took everything in her to sit there, in this insane man's mansion, and not want to claw his eyes out. She could not afford her anger. Later, she promised herself.

"And the other children here?"

"My hospitals are a sort of holding pen to keep the degenerates from polluting the rest of society. Better to have them all together. Here they are rendered impotent."

Her gut twisted. She forced the words out. "I don't understand."

"They can no longer breed."

Dear God. This man was a monster. "Sterilization?"

He frowned at her tone. "In the end it is kinder, and the world will be better for it. All great civilizations have a caste system. It is the natural order of things, survival of the fittest."

"Why me? I am certainly not perfect."

His jawline twitched again. "I decided to overlook your—friendship with Lord Devlin. Old Havermere was a monster. I finally had to put him down like the rabid dog he was."

"Are you saying … you poisoned him?"

"It was time you were free. I was tired of waiting and so was Rose. She needs a mother."

"There was an inquest. They thought I murdered my husband. You bastard," she whispered.

He *tsked*. "Strong words, my dear. I will not tolerate them when we are wed. You will honor and obey as the inferior sex is meant to do." He rose and then brought the contract to her. "Rose and I need you to complete our family." He put a pen in her hand.

Surely, Opal would be concerned when Nora did not return home this evening. She would see the note. She would go to Farren, or someone who would help.

"I took the liberty of sending a note to your home

saying you would be staying in the country for a few weeks."

By God, could he read her mind?

It was only a signature. A way forward to get Rose. She would play any game she must. She signed her name.

"Excellent, my pet." He bent and his lips brushed the top of her head. "Until dinner." He took the papers and put them into his waistcoat. He crossed to the bellpull. Fresley appeared.

"Her ladyship is ready to go to her room now." He turned to her. "You need not worry about your attire. Your maid has everything you need."

The bald man, Fresley, gestured for her to precede him. Oh, how she longed to run, but she could not leave Rose here with this monster. She would play her part and outwit this madman. "You must forgive my rude manners—Rodger, I am somewhat overwhelmed by all I've seen."

"Think nothing of it, my dear Nora." He smiled then.

And by God, she smiled back.

When Fresley ushered Nora back to her room, the lady's maid was again waiting.

The door closed. The click of the lock jerked her back toward the door. Spinning again, she caught the maid's look of contrition before the girl turned to fluff the skirts of the gown lying on the bed.

The only other door opened onto the bath and beyond, a dressing chamber.

She stepped into that room hoping for another connecting door. There was none. An entire wall, clad in etched Venetian mirror, reflected her image against five perfectly matched armoires.

Horridly fascinated, she opened one of the huge cupboards. "Oh!" It held a rainbow of day dresses. The next, tea gowns, the next, ball gowns. A chest held fans, parasols, handkerchiefs, and slippers. Sickeningly, she knew without trying on a stitch these clothes would fit her to perfection. She dropped the lid with a slam and ran past the maid.

At the window, she tested the lock. Open. The slight chill breeze fanned her heated cheeks. Escape.

But, no. At least thirty feet to cobble stones below. Besides, she could not leave without Rose.

The maid chirped like a frenetic bird as she flitted about the room, showing Nora all it offered. On the vanity lay a set of silver combs and brushes and a casket that must hold jewels. She couldn't look.

A perfume bottle, exactly like the one she had received as a gift, sat on a mirrored tray. The drawer beneath the vanity held expensive pens and neatly stacked paper. She picked up a sheet. The texture felt familiar in her hand. She knew even before sniffing what scent it would hold—yes, a faint whiff of rose.

"Excuse me, my lady, I believe we must get you dressed now." The maid picked up the ball gown on the bed. Silver silk as thin as tissue with pink seed pearls, one of the loveliest creations Nora had ever beheld. It turned her stomach.

"I will not wear it."

The maid started, her fixed smile dimming. "Oh, but you must, my lady. I—that is, I will be …"

She would be punished. Oh, what had this poor girl endured? "I'm sorry, how thoughtless of me to refuse such a beautiful offering. Please, help me."

The maid released her pent-up breath. "Yes, thank you, my lady. Thank you," she repeated almost to herself.

When Nora arrived in the drawing room, Rose was playing the pianoforte, wearing a dress of the same fabric only in pale pink with white seed pearls. The style far more suited to a girl of eight years rather than one almost twice that age.

"Ah, here you are, my dear," Milton said, rising as he slid his pocket watch back into his waistcoat.

"Oh! Poppa, she is so beautiful. I am so very lucky." Rose jumped up from the piano bench and then sank into a curtsy.

"Rise, pet. No need to curtsy to your mamma."

The girl's mouth opened in delight. "So, it is settled? She is to become my mother?"

"What was that you were playing, Rose?" Nora asked, diverting the conversation.

"Chopin's Sonata two in B flat minor, Op thirty-five," Rose answered, her smile a bit more fixed.

"Yes, the Chopin is coming along." Milton moved to join them. "Much improved over your last effort. I will tell Miss Norris you must devote more attention to the third movement. I believe there are still a few rough spots to be sorted out."

Rose's face fell and she dutifully nodded, biting her upper lip.

"I never even attempted Chopin." Nora whispered to Rose. "You did marvelously." She smoothed a curl from the girl's cheek and was rewarded with a shy smile.

"My lord." Fresley stood in the doorway. "Dinner is served."

Despite being only the three of them, dinner was an endless and stilted affair. The meal now lay heavy in Nora's belly, even though she'd only picked at the numerous courses. Lord Milton had seen fit to correct Rose constantly throughout the dinner. Nora had been ready to scream as the poor girl blushed in shame failing to please her "Poppa."

"Well, it is late." His lordship rang the bell. "We have a momentous day tomorrow. We shall all want to be in our best looks." He smiled at them.

Rose stood. "Oh, yes, the wedding!" She clasped her hands together.

There was something so young about Rose, a naiveté so unbelievable considering her early years growing up in the Seven Dials. It was as if her development had been arrested. Clearly, Lord Milton kept her very sheltered, but her delight, and conversely, her sadness, were so mercurial and childlike. If one did not know better, they would never guess she was fifteen years old.

"Tomorrow, I will wear a gown to match yours. It is very like the one pictured in our portrait." She spun, making her skirts lift, but then stopped and looked fearfully at Milton. When his lordship made no comment, Rose turned back to Nora. "You do like the color of violet, don't you?"

"It is one of my very favorites."

"Yes." She beamed. "I just knew you would like violet. Poppa described your eyes so perfectly. And a lady should always play up her eyes," she said, like some wise sage. "The wedding will be perfect. I only wish we could have it in the grand church."

"Oh, which church? If it is so important, maybe we

should postpone the ceremony?" Nora said, casually.

"Tell her, Poppa, your favorite, the one where all the great lords and ladies are wed."

"St. Paul's."

"Yes, that's it. The one with the massive dome." She turned to Nora. "Have you seen it?"

"Oh, yes, I always dreamed of marrying there just as you have. It would be perfection." She should turn and smile at Milton, but she could not.

"Well, my pet, we will have to forgo St. Paul's." He turned to Nora. "For I cannot delay making you my bride, sweeting. The wedding shall be tomorrow. We will make do with the small chapel here. Remember, Rose, a lady must be content with what she is given."

Rose started to twirl again but must have thought better of it. Instead, she pressed her hands against her voluminous skirts. "Yes, Poppa."

Milton stood. "Miss Rose and her ladyship shall retire now, Fresley." The servant must have slipped into the room.

Nora steeled herself. "Rodger," Her tongue curled over the "r" and thumped down on the "g." She turned to him, with what she prayed was a convincing smile. "Would you consent to my putting our Rose to bed? After all, I am to be her mother. I have long dreamt of tucking her in."

Milton hesitated. "Yes, I suppose that would be all right. Would you like that, Rose?"

"Oh, yes, indeed." Rose took Nora's hand. This girl's essence was so easy, so open and charming, so much the opposite of her poor sister.

Fresley followed them up. Rose's bedchamber was on the third floor to the left of the stairway. It must be nearly over the room Nora had been assigned.

As Rose readied herself for bed, she chattered on about how grand St. Paul's must be and how many hundreds of guests would fit inside such a splendid cathedral. All the while Nora's mind spun, trying to find a way out of this hellish place. Was Fresley waiting outside the door? Very likely.

She tucked the coverlet around the girl. "Rose," she whispered gently, "do you remember Lily?"

Rose frowned.

"Your sister, Lily?" Nora prompted.

"Lily is dead," Rose finally said. "She was wicked, and she died."

Oh, what had Milton done?

The girl rose up, leaning on her elbows. "She left me, you know. She said she'd come back but she didn't. Poppa said that is because she was selfish and bad."

"And your Poppa, is he good to you?"

"Oh, yes. But sometimes, of course, I must be punished." Nora flinched. "And sometimes I get lonely."

"Lonely? What about the other children I saw when I arrived?"

"Oh, that. They are the charity children." She said as if her statement explained everything. "Though, sometimes, on very special occasions, I get to play with some of the girls. But never the others."

"What others?"

She dropped down and burrowed deeper under the covers. Nora did not think the girl meant to answer. "I am not supposed to talk of them, or to even know that they are there," she whispered. "But since you will be my new mother, I can tell you. Can't I?"

"Of course." She smoothed a pale lock of hair from Rose's forehead.

"Well, those children are like Lily. They are the bad children. They look just like the good children, but they are dirty and bad. They live in a place deep in the forest."

Chapter Thirty-Four

Nora and Rose whispered their prayers together. Nora sending up a silent supplication for all those poor children. And another that Farren would arrive soon to save her and Rose before they were shackled to this madman.

She kissed Rose goodnight and then followed Fresley back to her own bedchamber.

Then she waited. A clock in the hall bonged once, signaling the half hour just after two.

Two hair pins slipped the lock. Opal had shown her the trick once when Nora had tired of losing at cards.

She dared not light her candle. Twelve steps to the stairway, then another fifteen stairs, and finally twenty more to reach Rose's room.

The doorknob turned easily. She released her pent-up breath.

Moonlight limned the furnishings. She crossed to the bed.

The girl's lips were slightly parted, her fist under her cheek, her hair, like spun silver, curtained her other cheek. So like Lily … and yet, nothing like Lily ….

"Rose." She gently smoothed the hair away from her face. The girl stirred but did not awaken.

"Rose." She shook her shoulder. "Wake up, my dear."

Butterfly lashes blinked and then her eyelids finally

opened.

"Momma?"

Momma. Dear God, Nora almost abandoned her plan. Tucked up in bed, Rose would be safe and sound. But, what then?

No, Milton was evil. She could never leave Rose with such a man. They must go, now.

"Sh-h-h, we must be very quiet." Nora pulled the bedclothes down. "We are going to surprise your Poppa."

Rose blinked and scrubbed her eyes with her fists. "Surprise him? How?"

"I did not want to say in front of him, but I happen to know the bishop at St. Paul's. We may not have hundreds of guests, but you and I can give him his dream of marrying in that great cathedral. I have left Poppa a note to meet us there tomorrow, but we must travel tonight so that we might prepare."

"But can't Poppa come with us?"

"No, that would spoil the surprise. Besides, it is tradition that the groom does not see the bride before he beholds her in all her wedding finery. It is bad luck."

"It is?"

Nora nodded. "I have packed our gowns already, and they are waiting in the carriage." She prayed the girl would not check her dressing room.

"But St. Paul's is in London, isn't it?" Rose frowned when Nora nodded. "London is dirty and full of bad people."

"Yes, some parts are, my dear. I am sorry you had to see that side. But there is great beauty as well. I would like to show you that side of London. Will you let me?"

Rose fiddled with the bow at the neckline of her night rail. Clearly, she was remembering some of the horrors of her childhood in the Seven Dials.

"Do you trust me, Rose?" Nora hated lying to the girl, and perhaps risking her trust for the future, but there was no avoiding falsehoods if they were to escape without Milton's knowledge. Rose was no small child; if she did not agree to Nora's plan, there would be no forcing the girl.

The clock bonged three times from below them. They needed to move.

"You knew Lily?" Doubt and hope danced across her face.

"Yes, I did." Nora sat on the edge of the bed and took the girl's hands in hers. "I loved Lily very much. You must believe me when I tell you she looked and looked for you, but then she got sick. You must know in your heart she would never have given up searching for you."

"She is dead, isn't she?"

There was no avoiding this terrible news. "Yes, Rose, she is. I believe her last thoughts were of you."

She nodded as if it was never a real question in her mind. "I loved Lily too," she whispered into her lap, as if just by saying the words, she might be struck down by some vengeful god.

Nora tipped the girl's chin up to meet her eyes. "And she loved you. Never doubt that, Rose." After wrapping a dark cape around Rose, she pulled her to her feet. "Now, we must hurry, for the carriage is waiting."

The hall was pitch black after the moonlight in Rose's room. Again, she dared not use her candle. "Do you know how to get to the east wing, Rose?"

The girl pulled away. "Why can't we go out the front door?"

"I told the coachman to wait by the charity wing. We might ruin the surprise if we leave from this side of the house."

"Oh, yes, I forgot." Nora felt a tug on her hand. "But are you sure Poppa will like us going? He doesn't normally like surprises."

Nora was glad she could not see Rose's face distinctly. Her voice sounded tight with fear.

"Sometimes, one must take a chance in life. You listen to your head or your heart. I have listened to my head far too often, and I have been unhappy. Let us follow our heart in this." She placed their clasped hands over her breast. "Will you trust me?"

Rose's gaze dipped and then met Nora's eyes. "Yes … Mamma," she said shyly. "I will trust you."

After descending several staircases, she pulled a stub of candle from her cloak pocket and struck her only match. It flared, throwing a long shadow on the wall. *Please light.* In her haste, the wick nearly extinguished the flame, but it caught.

"This way." *I think.*

They must head east, but the old house had so many twisting stairways and shadowed doors leading to more narrow hallways, they had no hope of determining east. With only candlelight and no knowledge of the house, they became hopelessly lost.

Rough stone walls now surrounded them. She and Rose must be in the very depths of the place. Despite being a warm day, the cold and damp pricked her skin, sending a chill to her very core. A trail of wax ran over her longest finger, burning. Only a few inches of candle left. The light caught the shimmering droplets of mist which coated the walls. A dank must of mold and rot filled her nose. The ceiling, low and heavy, pressed down on them as they edged further into this dungeon. A tomb.

"Come, we must go back." Nora took Rose's hand. But when they reached the door they had come through only moments before, it wouldn't budge. The long tunnel was the only way forward. Nora prayed it led somewhere out onto the grounds. But the tunnel split into several veins, each turning to a dead end.

"Who's there?" Chains rattled.

The candle's flame shuddered, and Nora had to drop Rose's hand to shield the fragile light. She quickly stepped in front of Rose. "Hold onto my cloak." Once she felt the girl's grasping tug, she tentatively held the flame out toward the darkest corner.

Nora's heart stopped in her breast. She took a step closer and raised the stub of candle high.

Farren stood chained to the wall.

"Rose?" Farren's voice was hoarse. He scrambled to his feet, blinking at the light. "My God, Rose, is that you?"

Again, she almost lost the light as she rushed to him. "Dear heaven, how did you get down here?" He looked as if he'd been beaten. "What happened?"

Farren's gaze raked over Nora. "Your brooch, give me the brooch." He gestured to her breast where the diamond and ruby rose was still pinned to her cloak.

She backed away. Something was wrong.

Farren lunged, the chain at his ankle snapped taut, but his fingers caught the bauble, ripping it from her cloak.

She gasped, shocked by Farren's feral demeanor. She pushed Rose behind her.

He dropped to the floor using the pin to pick the heavy lock. A second chain dangled from his wrist. "Where is he?"

Nora, now understanding, held the light closer for him to work by. Farren must have been a step ahead of her. Had he discovered something after the ball? "But how—?"

"Where is he?" Farren said sharply.

"He is sleeping, I believe. We got lost." His once bright hair was matted. With blood? His wide shoulders bunched and shifted beneath a thin shirt as he maneuvered the pin in the lock. "What happened? How did you come to be here?"

"There isn't time for that now." The lock clicked open. Nora wanted to throw herself into his arms, but he was right, there was no time.

He barely looked at her, instead he stepped toward Rose.

The girl backed away. "Mamma, I'm frightened."

Farren stopped. "Mamma?" He shot Nora a surprised look and then turned back to Rose. "Rose." He bent to fix his gaze intently on the girl's face. "I'm sorry if I scared you, gal, it is just I have been looking for you for so long. I know you don't know me, but I am—"

"Poppa!"

Even before Nora turned, she knew. He had found them.

A lamp threw Lord Milton's warped shadow over the walls and ceiling, making him appear huge. "What a nice little party. I am glad I could attend."

Nora and Farren jerked forward to protect Rose.

As icy and raw as the underbelly of this house felt, Milton's arrival ratcheted up the deep, settling cold. It crept over her skin like death.

"Ah, you have been naughty, Nora." He raised a revolver and pointed it at Rose. He gestured for the girl. "Come to me, my pet."

Rose had stopped halfway between Nora and Milton. She hesitated, looking from her Poppa to Nora. The girl's eyes told it all—horror, disbelief, betrayal.

Nora took another step toward her.

Rose shook her head, backing up closer to Milton. "You lied, Mamma. There is no surprise, is there?"

Nora weighed the success of weaving another lie. *Rodger, thank goodness you have come. Rose woke from a nightmare and, trying to find the kitchens for some warm milk, we got lost ...* No, it was too late. "You are right, Rose. I did lie, but I still ask you to trust me. Listen to your heart." She dared a step closer. "Listen to Lily."

"Poppa?" Milton still had the gun trained on Rose.

Rose pointed to Farren. "Poppa, who is this man, and why is he down here in the dark? He is too old to be one of the bad children."

"Do not regard him, my pet. He is an intruder who will be dealt with accordingly."

"He is the liar, Rose. They both are," Farren said, jerking his head at Nora. "This woman is not your mother and," he pointed at Milton, "he sure ain't your father."

Nora drew in a sharp breath. The days they had spent together—loved together—they had meant nothing to him. She had just been a means to an end. Yet, how could he be so cruel? Knowing how she had suffered at Lily's death, and when they thought Rose had followed her sister.

"And, by God, Rose is not your *pet*, you bastard. She is a Cavanaugh."

There was no time for the emptiness that filled her so utterly; getting Rose to safety was paramount.

"Rodger, he is right. Rose is not ours. I know you have taken good care of her these years, but this man is her blood family." This next part was harder. "Perhaps, when we marry, God will grant us a child of our own?" The words burned her throat, but she would ally herself with the devil if it meant Rose going free. "Let them go."

Milton's mouth worked almost convulsively, twisting his handsome face into something tortured. "No, I will have no child. Another lying whore saw to that with her filthy body." He turned to Farren. "And you Cavanaughs' will never take another thing from me. First Saraphina, then Nora, and now Rose."

"Saraphina? Who is Saraphina, Rodger?" If she kept him talking, perhaps she could distract him.

"Who *was* Saraphina. My betrothed, and the only other woman I have loved. But his father—" He jerked his chin toward Farren—"Duncan Cavanaugh, defiled her. Turned her from my perfect flower into a base weed, ugly and useless. It was best she was cut down rather than live to spread her bad seed. If one isn't vigilant, weeds will choke out the superior plants." He turned back to Farren. "It was your father I meant to kill. The bullet was for him." He shook his head. "But his fool of a brother, Geoffrey, charged in and the shot

355

went wide. The horses shied and Cavanaugh had his hands full with the runaway carriage. Your uncle went down. He called out to me to help him. His foot was hung up in the stirrup, his other twisted under his back like a broken doll, his wrists tangled in the bridle's reins. I could have calmed the horse and pulled him free, but that wouldn't have been fair. Someone had to pay. Another shot into the air and his daft horse danced a bloody jig on the beloved Clifford heir."

Like a rabid dog, Farren jerked forward, heedless of the danger. "You gutless bastard."

"You call me gutless? What of your father? He would not even meet my challenge of a duel. Wouldn't leave his brother's sick bed. Then the coward fled to America. What providence that his son is now at my disposal. And that whore, Sara, she would have had her titled, rich husband if she'd just bided her time. Plain Mr. Dashel soon became Lord Milton."

Milton seemed lost for a moment, but then straightened, re-leveling the pistol. "No more old history. The past is past." He gestured with the gun. "Come now, girl."

Nora's gaze found Rose's. They could not take a chance. One did not toy with a deranged man holding a gun. A rat scuttled somewhere in the depths of the tunnel. Nora tried to smile and nodded for Rose to go.

Rose walked slowly to Milton.

"That's it, come to Poppa."

"Let her go." A dark figure stood behind Milton.

Milton wheeled, one arm now around Rose, the gun now pressed to her chest. The lamp swung crazily, making the shadows jump.

Farren?

She jerked around. He could not have moved so quickly. No, the other man was still there just behind her, gaunt and filthy—

Brendan?

She turned back for further confirmation. The lantern's light caught the sheen of golden hair, and blood on his forehead, but if not for those distinctions the two men might have been one and the same.

Twins. My God. They were identical twins.

"Farr—"

Her cry was cut off as Brendan ran past her, diving for Milton. The lantern smashed against the stone floor. Rose shrieked as the cavern plunged into darkness.

Chapter Thirty-Five

My God, he had found them in time.

For the last two hundred or so steps in this dungeon he'd been without any light, his candle guttering. Nearly despairing he had pushed forward until he heard voices. Milton and his brother. Then he'd seen her. Nora. And Rose.

He was assessing the scene when all hell broke loose.

Damn it, Bren, always the hot head.

Farren instinctively stepped forward into the pitch black but stopped, the soldier in him taking over. Impossible to sort out the grunts and thuds and who they belonged to in this echoing hell hole.

"Nora? Rose? Are you all right? Bren?"

"Cavanaugh, I strongly urge you not to try any more heroics. Rose, tell these gentlemen where the gun is pointing, my pet." Milton's words freezing any notion of jumping into the fray.

Rose whimpered, confirming his decision.

"Tell them," Milton insisted.

"Poppa. Please—"

"Tell them!"

"My head," Rose whispered.

"That's correct. One move from any of you, and I pull the trigger. Don't think I won't do it."

Farren heard scrabbling in the dark from where

Milton's voice came from and then a match flared. He had found another lantern hanging against the wall. "Open it and light it, my poppet."

Rose bent to light the lantern. Milton wasn't lying, the bastard held the gun to the back of Rose's head. The weak flame flared briefly before the match sputtered and went out, plunging the room back into darkness.

"Stupid girl. Another!"

The rasp of a match and then another flare. This time she was successful. Rose closed the door of the lantern.

"Now hang it back on the wall here."

"Poppa? You're frightening me."

Nora stood near a pile of chains on the floor. Farren spared a brief look into her eyes. "You alright?" Simple words covering a heap of churning feeling.

"Yes, yes, I am well enough." Despite her answer, shock etched her reply.

"Bren?" His gaze flicked from Milton to his brother who was slowly rising from the stone floor. Sweet Jesus, to be calling out to his brother, his other half.

"Well, I reckon I'm a sorry sight, but I'm right glad to see your ugly mug."

Still focused on Milton, Farren could not help but reach out to clasp his twin's arm and squeeze. To feel his flesh and blood. Bren reached up to cover his hand and squeezed back. Tears pricked his eyes. Nothing need be said, they had always known each other's thoughts.

"Gillingham caved, didn't he?" Milton ground the words out. "Should have killed the cur eons ago. Never should have relied on him. Too much of a degenerate.

But he kept coming back to me, needing more money."

Gillingham had ended up giving Farren his pistol along with his blessing. Time to rid the world of the real vermin, he'd said. Farren reckoned old Gilly was on his way to the nearest port by now.

Milton gestured to Farren's pistol. "Throw your gun in that." He indicated a large trough situated next to the wall. "Now!" Milton pressed the barrel of his revolver into Rose's cheek, making her flinch.

Bren lurched forward. "By God, if you so much as harm a hair—"

In answer, Milton twisted his fist in Rose's hair and the girl hissed in pain.

Farren reluctantly tossed the gun. Their best hope ended with a splash.

He tried to make his voice casual. "Well, Gillingham isn't the sharpest knife in the drawer. Why don't you let the gal go and we can sort this out?"

"Sort it out? How quaintly American. There is no *sorting out*, my dear fellow. You've ruined it." Spittle flew from Milton's mouth. "Once again, Cavanaughs have spoiled my plans for happiness. My perfect family." He pulled, twisting Rose's neck, forcing her to look up at him. "I have learnt a valuable lesson, my sweet. You can pluck a rose from trash. The bloom may look like a beauty, but it is still a blighted weed. You are but a deceptive weed and must be cut down." He cocked the revolver. "All of you must go."

Farren held a staying hand out to Bren. Think. Make a plan of attack.

Looked to be a Root revolver. Six shots. Were all the chambers full? Likely. Milton seemed like the type to keep his gun primed and ready.

"I should have dispensed with you," he said, shifting the barrel to Brendan. "As soon as Gillingham reported you were back. Never thought you would be so persistent after Eunice Lockhart told you they were both dead. But, no, you wouldn't believe her. Kept trekking around the continent on a wild goose chase. Lockhart blew whichever way the blunt flowed. I paid her well to tell you Rose was dead, but when your brother came along with more money, she saw the opportunity to drag it out, hoping for more payoffs. Greedy cun—whore."

He held Rose's hair with one hand while the other with the gun shifted from Brendan to stroke her cheek with its barrel. "These children are a gift from nature. One we were meant to study. Else why would God duplicate one child? The other is expendable." His smile sent Farren's stomach into a twist. "I had a brother. Not a twin, mind you, but he was weak and useless. The inferior child." His jaw line twitched. "But in the case of the Cavanaugh brothers." He aimed the pistol directly at Farren's heart "Both are expendable."

"Nooooo!" Nora lunged toward Milton, but she was too late. Brendan had already thrown himself in front of his brother.

The gun went off, the sound booming in the cave-like room. Acrid smoke filled his nose and burned his eyes.

"Rose!"

Milton crashed to the floor. Brendan's blond head caught the meager light as he landed atop the older man.

The shot must have gone wide.

Nora rushed to Rose, whose hands were pressed

over her ears, her mouth set in a silent scream. She was shaking her head.

"Rose." Farren heard Nora say over the grunts of Milton and Bren.

Where was the gun?

"Rose." Nora repeated, more loudly. "Look at me!"

Farren ran toward the lantern on the wall. He lifted it high. Something sparkled on the stone floor. He picked it up. A brooch. He squeezed it in his fist. *Where was the dad burned gun?*

Brendan now straddled Milton. The chain, which still dangled from his wrist, was wrapped around Milton's neck. The man's eyes bulged as his fingers clawed at the chain.

"Brendan." Farren touched his brother's shoulder.

"Fucking monster!" Brendan roared into Milton's twisted face. "I have my sins, but they are ones of neglect and carelessness. You, you are a methodical, diabolical monster. By God, it's you who should be put down!"

"Bren, stop. He's not worth it. He will hang. Let him go."

Brendan looked up then into his brother's eyes as if he were seeing him for the first time. "Far—" A smile lit his face.

Years peeled away. That smile. His wayward older brother—by only three minutes—but Bren had lorded those few minutes over Farren on a daily basis. He answered his brother's smile.

"Oh God, he's been hit," Nora shouted.

Brendan looked down and touched his chest. His hand came back bloody. He looked back up in confusion and then toppled over.

The room spun. Farren covered his ears. His vision blurred and he shook his head trying to clear his mind. Not again. *No more blood and death. No more!*

"Medic!" Farren shouted. His voice echoed strangely. He shook his head again trying to orient himself. Where was the blasted enemy?

He held a man who was not in uniform. He had a manacle around his wrist. Fucking hell, not another deserter.

Had they both been hit? The man's chest was soaked in blood as was Farren's but the only pain he felt was from his pounding heart.

"Don't you worry, I'll get you safe," he whispered to the poor soul.

Shadows careened around them. Too damned dark to see the telltale gray or blue of a uniform. "I need light! This man is hurt. He needs immediate attention!"

"Farren."

A woman's voice.

"Nurse! If you bring me a light, some whisky, and a dressing, I can patch him up. We can move him then."

A man nearby shouted for help. Another down? But he had heard no gunfire. And the accent was wrong. Clipped tones, not the twang of a Southerner or the flatness of men from the north.

He swiped the sweat from his eyes.

The nurse brought a lantern. The light bathed the wounded man's face—

Brendan? Dear God, this man was Bren, his flesh and blood.

Blood.

Bile rose in his throat.

"Bren, it's me, Farren. Hang on, I've got you."

His brother's eyes fluttered open. "Dang it, I knew you'd turn up to play the hero." Brendan smiled though his eyes were filled with pain.

"Don't try to speak." Farren ripped the sleeve of his shirt off and then pressed it to his brother's breast.

"What, and miss my opportunity to have the final word?" Brendan tried to laugh, but it sounded more like he was choking.

"Not if I can help it. No final words for you, brother. After this damned war is over, we'll have plenty of squabbles."

But Brendan only shook his head. "I didn't deserve them. Should never have been a father. Hell, I wasn't, was I?" His eyes seemed to search for someone.

Bren was raving, talking of being a father.

"Take care of my little gal, Rosie, Farr. Will you?"

Rosie?

Farren looked around him. Nora. My God, it was Nora who knelt beside him. This was no battlefield. No war. Only the depths of an English country house run by a madman.

Milton lay passed out, Brendan's chain still around his neck.

And Rose … she was there just beyond Nora.

"We both will be here to take care of her." Farren took his brother's hand, so cold. He pressed the other against his wound.

"I reckon this beauty is somehow attached to you?" Brendan's gaze strayed to Nora, and he smiled.

Nora smiled back and leaned forward into the light. "Hello, Brendan. I have been waiting a long time to meet you."

"Ha!" The sound gurgled in his throat. "Let me

assure you, gal, if I'd met you first, my little brother wouldn't have stood a chance."

"I can well believe it."

"Can you bring her to me?" He could only mean Rose.

Nora's gaze caught his. They did not want to traumatize the girl further. But Rose stepped forward.

"Are you my real Poppa?" Rose knelt next to Nora, her face a mix of awe and concern.

"I am, Rosie gal." He smiled. "But you got a raw deal. I'm not such a good poppa. Trust me, you'll be much better off calling this man here your pa from here on out." His gaze went to Farren. "I reckon having a family is about the only thing this ol' boy has ever really wanted." A cough racked his body. Farren lifted his brother's head and shoulders. Nora gathered the hem of her skirt to gently wipe his damp forehead

"I'm so tired, Rosie. Wish me sweet dreams?"

Rose nodded sagely. "Shall I say the prayer I say every night when I go to bed?"

Brendan blinked his eyes in assent.

"Now I lay me down to sleep. I pray the Lord my soul to keep, thy love guard me through the night and wake me with the morning light." Rose touched his cheek. "Goodnight, Poppa. Sweet dreams."

A soft smile graced Brendan's lips and then his eyes closed.

****

Farren's eyes closed at that same moment.

He seemed frozen next to his brother. They all knelt around the body, Rose's gaze on her father, while Nora focused on Farren.

Brendan's arm jerked across his body. She gasped

and pulled Rose back and away.

Milton had regained consciousness.

His fingers clawed at his neck, trying to loosen the chain still attaching him to Brendan. But his efforts only pulled the chain tighter.

"Help me!" he rasped. "Rose, help me!"

Nora was ready to step forward, but Rose's softly whispered "no" stopped her.

Farren's eyes remained closed as if in fervent prayer. He seemed to be concentrating all his energy on breathing for Brendan.

"Do as I say, girl," Milton said, twisting to find Rose.

"No," Rose said again, this time more firmly.

"Help me, you insolent girl," Milton barked. One arm lay useless, twisted awkwardly at the side of his body.

Still, no one moved.

"Come Rose, my pet," Milton said between gritted teeth. "You will not be punished. Come and help your poppa."

Rose stepped forward. Nora reached out to pull her back, but Rose held out her hand to stay her.

"You made me believe Lily was bad. She ran away. She promised she would come back to get me. She promised. I waited, but she never came." A terrible sob broke from her as if her heart had cleft in two. Nora hated to hear that terrible sound, but the girl needed to purge some of the pain in her heart. To finally grieve.

"*I* was the bad one. The stupid one. You gave me a sweet and a red ribbon and I— But Lily, she *knew*. She was always the smart one. The one who took care of us. I was too gullible. Too slow. Oh, my brave Lily. I am so sorry. Why wasn't I the one to die?"

Nora shuddered at the girl's admission. Unable to remain aloof, she reached out needing to comfort Rose.

"Blasted bitch, I need a surgeon!"

Rose stiffened and then turned away. Nora opened her arms, but the girl only crossed to kneel once again at Brendan's side. She took his hand in hers.

"Ahhhh!" Milton writhed on the floor, then blessedly, passed out.

Shouts echoed from down the long hallway. Heavy feet slapping against the stone floor. The bang of a door against a wall.

"Here! They are here!"

Nora held the lantern high.

Opal? By God, it was Opal! She and some dozen men carrying pistols and lanterns.

Farren snapped out of his reverie as if, now that help was here, he could afford to loosen whatever tether bound the brothers.

"Over here. This man has been shot." The colonel he had been on the battlefield once more taking over. "Still breathing. Might have hit a lung." The men surrounded Brendan, but Rose refused to let go of his hand.

"Stay with me, Poppa. Stay with me."

A flurry of activity had Nora stepping back, unsure how to help. Milton, now awake and screaming he would have these men's heads, was loaded onto a stretcher. Farren directed several men as they eased his brother onto a second stretcher, and then, Rose holding one hand, and Farren the other, the group started down the long passageway.

"You all right?" Opal had come to her side. Nora

winced as the girl thrust her lantern in her face and then over her body. Nora nodded, and then said, "Yes. Thank you, my dearest."

Opal merely grunted and then firmly took her by the arm as if she might mysteriously disappear. They joined the procession, steadily wending their way upward, until finally the light of dawn spilled through an open doorway.

Chapter Thirty-Six

Five weeks later
Ryeland Park, Wiltshire

The open casket had been a mistake. Uncle Geoff, head shaking, a deep frown creasing his dear face, had circled the polished oak box, reaching out occasionally, to touch the body which lay in state in the ballroom of Ryeland. Finally, he sat sentinel next to the casket, Rose's hand clutched in his—Rose, now Geoff's constant companion. Kindred spirits. But whenever Farren strayed too far, Geoff would call out to him. And Farren would come to his side and get his hand mashed.

He kept looking for Nora to appear and take his hand, give him the comfort he craved. But she never did. She had stayed with the children after that dreadful morning in Milton's "charity" home. Knowing her as he did, she would be there for months doing everything in her power to give those damaged souls some hope.

Milton had been taken away to be treated for his injuries and then put under arrest. By God, Farren would see the man swing for his crimes.

He and Rose had sat on either side of Bren as they left Seraphim House. Rose's soft whispers of encouragement to her Poppa melding with the creak of the carriage and the clop of the horse's hooves on the flagstone as they headed toward Ryeland Park. But

369

Farren's gaze had remained fixed on Nora as the carriage pulled away. His brave Nora. Standing there, Bren's blood still on her hands. He kept hoping she might run after them to stop the carriage. To go with them. But she turned away. The children had begun streaming out of the west wing.

His grandpa and Uncle Geoff had left London immediately to join them at Ryeland. Three precious weeks together as a family …

The Cavanaugh graveyard lay just to the west of the small folly near the edge of the woods. The same woods that hid the cabin tucked next to the pond.

Every day since the funeral, Farren had ridden out to the grave.

He hunkered down next to the mound of newly-turned earth. "If you have any pull up there, could you put in a word for me? I know he can be a damn— darned fool, but I reckon he could use a second chance."

Farren swiped at the tears on his cheeks.

The carvers had worked overtime to finish the stone in time for the burial.

Colin Martin Cavanaugh, Viscount Clifford.
Beloved husband, father, and grandfather.
Rest in Peace.

Farren reached out to touch the rounded dome of the scarab beetle near the bottom of the marker. As a last-minute request, he'd asked the carvers to include the beetle, the Egyptian symbol of the sun, and one of his grandpa's favorites.

The old man had rallied every time his great granddaughter was brought to see him. But the effort to appear hearty left him weaker and weaker. He passed away quietly one morning, with the family gathered 'round, a soft smile on his face.

"Remember how you told me of my father sitting vigil by Geoff's bedside when he would not awaken? Well, sir, now Geoff is the one who won't be budged. Isn't that the dangest?"

He picked a weed from near the headstone. "And Rosie is right there next to him. Don't you worry too much about Geoff, Grandpa; with your great gran by his side, he will want for nothing. And that you can take to the bank."

A blue dragonfly dipped and hovered over the dark earth before whirring on to the clover beyond. "And call me daft but just like I told you I had a gut feeling Brendan was alive. I have to believe he will wake up if only to devil us once again."

He sat back on his heels, arms wrapped around his knees and looked up at the deepening sky. "I know. I've made a hash of things with Nora. I reckon you are up there shakin' your head at me for being such a blame fool. I expect for my penance I'll never be able to rid my heart of that gal. But please don't let me lose Bren too."

God could not be that cruel. Death had taken his sister, his mother, his Pa, Lily, and now his grandfather. Death could not have his brother.

During the war he had stood by, holding the hand of many a man as they waited for the sawbones to lop off a limb. He'd even assisted, readying the frying pan until it glowed red. And as soon as the arm or leg had been dumped into an ever-growing pile, he'd press the hot iron to the raw stump, screaming right along with the poor sod. The smell of blood and burning flesh filling his mouth and nose until he'd have to excuse himself to retch.

Months after, if the man lived, Farren would catch him scratching at the air, sure his missing arm or leg was still there.

Now Farren understood just a bit of how those men felt. Brendan was that limb.

The ground shook. Someone must be coming to fetch him. If only it were Brendan riding neck-or-nothing to have another race across the fields…

He did not even bother to turn around. They ought to know by now, he'd return only when he was good and ready. "I'll come in a bit. Go on back."

"I'm sorry to have missed the funeral."

He jerked around.

Nora.

Blazing fires of Hell, she looked like an angel. Hair loose and windswept from her ride, cheeks painted the prettiest blush, mouth parted from her exertion.

"It happened so fast." She shook her head. "I didn't know. Somehow, I thought he'd outlive us all."

He wanted to offer her words of comfort, but they wouldn't come. He swiped his hand over his eyes and stood, his legs stiff. "I reckon it's late," he said, looking up at the darkening sky.

"Yes, I am late. But not too late. I hope."

Lord, how could she be so beautiful? Three steps and he could touch her. Two arms reaching up and he could pull her from her mount and into his shaking arms. Bend his head and her lips would be one with his …

He ground his boot heel into the earth. "I'm sure my grandpa would appreciate a prayer or two, especially from you." He stepped back, away from the grave, putting yet more distance between them.

"Yes, I would like to pay my respects, but another time. What I have to say is to his grandson." She looked at him almost shyly. "Will you come with me?" She gestured to his horse which was nibbling at a tuft of grass near his grandma's headstone.

He looked back to his grandpa's grave hoping for a sign, but nary a blade of grass moved to tell him what to do. When would he learn no wisdom would come no matter how long he hunkered down over this grave?

He swung up onto Claudius, who was reluctant to give up his sweet grass, but as soon as Nora spurred her horse, his was suddenly game for a good run. Only instead of heading back toward the house, Nora turned toward the forest.

What could she want to discuss with him? Surely, she could not be here to claim Rose? Brendan was still alive and needed his daughter. And Uncle Geoff? Hell, losing Rose might just send his uncle to his death.

Now among the trees, gloom settled around them, the dappled path becoming all shadows.

They rode in silence, only the snap of a twig or a blow from a horse's nostrils punctuating the quiet.

His thighs tightened around Claudius. The cabin. She was heading toward their cabin.

She swung down before he could help her. Thank God for small blessings.

"If you've brought me here to ask for Rose, we should just turn back. I can't do it. We can't give her up."

"Come," she said, holding Claudius's bridle, her eyes glinting despite the deepening darkness. Still, he hesitated. What could be gained? Best to let her have her say and get it done with. Just another sort of death if she could not understand his family needing to heal together.

He dismounted and then followed her. He took her horse's reins from her and started to tie them both to a post by the front door.

"Best put them up. We'll be here a while."

A while? "What is this about, Nora? I am near scraped raw. I just can't take another loss."

She took a step toward him but then stopped as he drew back. If he could just keep his distance, he might be able to come away from this encounter with some of his pride still left, if not his heart.

"I wanted to come earlier. But the children—I…" She shook her head. "Helping them, well, it has consumed me. There is still so much to do."

Her words were brief, but Farren knew there was a heap that lay unsaid beneath her statements. Poor souls, who could say if they would ever be right again?

"You must go where you are needed."

"Yes, yes, I must …" She lifted her chin and stood straighter as if presenting herself for inspection. "That is why I am here."

"Now look here, we are taking good care of Rose—"

"Of course," she interrupted. "I know that. That is not what I meant." She looked down and traced a pleat in the fabric of her skirt. "Charlotte is engaged."

God, Charlotte … All the hoopla and pretense of the glittering ballrooms of the *ton* seemed like decades ago. "That Sealing fellow?"

Nora looked surprised. "Yes, how did you know?"

"Clear as a May morn they had a hankering for each other."

"Clear? Not from where I was standing." She narrowed her gaze. "Why? Why did you want me to believe you and she cared for each other?"

He shoved his hand through his hair. The whole game seemed so silly now. And all for naught. Nora still didn't want him. "Damned harebrained. We thought it would spur you on to a little jealousy. Maybe open your eyes to what I wanted you to see. It was foolhardy. And useless."

"Foolhardy, I will agree. Useless? Oh, I think not." She laughed ruefully. "I was as jealous as a spurned wallflower. I could not stand that you had shifted your affections so quickly. And I hated that Charlotte loved you. Or, I believed she loved you."

He knew his and Charlotte's plan had gotten under Nora's skin. But not enough. Seems Nora's pride was the only thing that got jostled, not any love for him.

"I believed you were falling in love with her. Certainly, that she was with you." She held her hands out as if she wanted to capture something but had no notion of what it was. "For, to my mind, who could resist you?"

A small ember of hope flared in his breast. "You did a right good job of it."

"Yes. Yes, I did. And even if I was not entirely certain you no longer held any regard for me, I could not be the cause of Charlotte's unhappiness. Besides, what had I done to deserve your love? I shared nothing of myself, other than my body. I was just too afraid. Afraid to truly live. To dare to have my dream—as you said so many weeks ago—the dream of a family, a loving husband whom I admire, one who makes my body sing."

"Nora—" He took a step toward her, wanted to touch her, but she held up her hand to stop him.

"Please, let me say this." She took a deep breath as she pressed her hands against her belly. "When Milton threatened you and Rose and nearly killed Brendan, something broke open inside me. As if this terrible fear that had gripped me all my life, was suddenly nothing. As if it was all made up in my head. A story—no, a lie—I had told myself over and over for years until I believed it wholeheartedly. But seeing the ones I loved in harm's way released me from that insidious tale. Life is too precious. I suddenly wanted to live. And why not? Why couldn't I have my share of happiness? Yes, I have sinned. I broke my marriage vows by lying with Devlin. But surely the sin of infidelity is not as egregious as taking one's life."

The horses tossed their heads and stamped their feet. He'd pulled too hard at the reins shocked to think of the world without Nora.

"Surprised? Well, I am not proud of it, but I had been ready to take that step. If Devlin had not come into my life, I believe I would have killed myself."

He shook his head, as if the action could negate her terrible words.

She touched his arm tentatively. "You say you are tired of death. I too am tired of this half-life. I want to live." She sank to her knees, her beautiful face shining up at him.

She caught his hand. Slightly cool and so white and elegant, her long fingers threading through his, capturing not just his hand but snagging his heart as well. *Damnit all.*

"Farren Cavanaugh, I want to live with you."

What?

She squeezed his hand. "I am asking you to be my husband. To live with me and all my brood of foundlings. And, if we are blessed, to have children of our own." She had both of her hands wrapped around his now. "Will you have me?"

His heart pounded within its cage of bone as if there was a stud bull in the shoot. He dropped the reins, wanting to crush her to him, to make this moment real. But a terrible thought wedged its way into his brain. "You're not just throwing your lot in with me to be near Rose, are you?"

She looked down and took a deep breath.

Dag nabbit. She was going to tell him the truth now, and his heart was going to break. He made himself stand tall as his teeth met and ground.

"You are correct. I do want Rose."

He blinked wanting the world to change, wanting her words to change, wanting time to go back or forward, just not to have this crushing pain.

She reached for his other hand. Like a dumb ox, he allowed it. God, would he settle for a half-life with her? Knowing she did not love him, yet willing to bind her to him anyway? He could not. Would not.

"Nora, I reckon we can work something out with Rose. I am not a monster to keep her from you entirely." His voice sounded far away as if it were some other fellow's.

"I do want Rose." She stood and stepped closer. "But I want you more."

His heart pounded in his breast, while his mind

calibrated this news.

She swallowed. "I love you, Farren Cavanaugh."

A rising swell rushed from deep within him, rolling over his thumping heart, down his arms, into the very tip of his fingers. My God, the three little words he had been waiting to hear from her lips.

As if she heard him, she said them again. "I love you so very much."

He flexed his hands, wanting to feel himself inside her. To feel her body against his, to look deep into her eyes as if he could pull her and those beautiful words into his very being so they would live tucked up next to his heart. "Tell me again."

She smiled and threaded her fingers through his hair, framing his face. "Farren Cavanaugh, I am by no means perfect. But you have taught me love is huge and overwhelming. Love does not need a reason to be, it just is. And, broken as I am, I am still going to have you. I am going to have my heart's desire. Not because I am stealing something I don't really deserve, but because, flawed as I am, I am still worthy of your love."

"Oh, woman, I love you so dang much." He pulled her hard up against him and kissed her, plunging his tongue deep. It had been so long. So very long. He fumbled with the fall of his breeches, while his other hand ruched her skirts up.

"No. Wait."

"Wait?" He shook his head. "Look, Nora, you either want me, or you don't."

"Oh, I do. I want you very much."

"I don't understand."

"I want to see you." She stepped away from him.

He felt the loss of her heat, ached to have her back.

But something in her eyes told him she needed to say whatever lay buried in her heart.

"And I need you to see me. All of me."

He said nothing, waiting for her to school him. She took his hands in hers and traced the lines and calluses there as if she might draw courage from them. He longed to pull her against him, but still, he waited.

"Do you remember the first time you undressed me? I was dressed as Norbert that night, and we made love?"

"Remember? I have replayed that evening in my mind so many times it is branded on my heart."

She smiled. "What you may not know is how very frightened I was. You see, I had the notion that you saw into my core, my very being. Oh, I know you might doubt me given that I allowed myself to be painted naked countless times. I believe Devlin saw me as well, but his seeing was different. His was an artist's eye. To him, I was an intriguing thing of beauty to be captured on canvas. There was a certain voyeuristic cast to our time together. It allowed me to still hide. Then you came along." She shook her head. "Oh, how I wanted to hide, and yet I longed to reveal myself to you. To trust you."

"Nora—"

"Please." She moved her finger over his lips. "Let me finish. I have been afraid all my life. Afraid to lose the adoration of my father, afraid of my beauty, afraid of my husband, afraid for my girls. Afraid to hope for the one man I wanted so very much. I am so very tired of being frightened."

"Nora, my love." The two words so novel, yet so right on his tongue. "I can't promise you will never be frightened again, but I vow, I will make danged sure to be by your side through thick and thin."

"Yes, that is one of the reasons I love you so. Your strength. But I needed to be strong all on my own. I am now. I do not need you to make myself feel whole, but I want you beside me. I am strong enough to risk losing you." She stepped toward him and took his hands in hers. "Will you have me?"

"Yes. Oh, yes." He bent to finally gather her to him.

She smiled and stepped back. "Now, put up the horses, Colonel Cavanaugh. We will be at this a good long while."

Sweet Jesus, he'd be danged if Norma Pledgeheart in her sugar-scoop bonnet and white bibbed collar suddenly embodied his Nora. He clicked his heels and gave her his best salute. "Yes, ma'am."

****

Unable to leave him, she followed as he strode down the path, leading the horses toward shelter. Love welled up, filling her eyes with tears. They ran down her cheeks and into her smiling mouth. She savored the taste of their salt.

Halfway to the barn, a bright leaf caught her eye. She bent to examine it. A volunteer seedling, barely three fingers tall, caught between two flagstones. Gently, she pried it out. As she cradled the tiny plant, the dry earth fell away, too brittle to sustain its fragile roots. She thought it might be Tansey—or perhaps mud root? Difficult to tell at this early stage. She would learn more about plants. She would become an expert.

Crossing to the kitchen garden, she crouched down and dug her fingers into the more fertile soil and then settled the plant. Her tears dropped on a leaf and into the ground. "May you thrive," she prayed as she pressed damp earth around it.

Farren's soft murmurs and the jangle of harnesses as he soothed the horses lent an everyday cadence to this extraordinary day. Oh, the wonder of such small seemingly insignificant tasks. She smiled again and more tears flowed.

She flexed her fingers. So white against the dark earth—crescent moons of black under her nails. She stood and carefully picked her way through rows of old pea shoots and faded marigolds toward the water pump. A feeling of lightness washed over her, as if she were suddenly filled with air, as though she might lift from the ground and float above the trees. She laughed at the thought, her spirit rising in a way that felt both freeing and impossibly full.

She remembered that same feeling nearly three years ago as she stood over the old earl's grave with dirt under her nails and such hope in her heart.

The old pump groaned in protest as she raised its handle. Was there still water?

A hiss, followed by a sputter. Then nothing. As she leaned in to get a better grip, a blasting belch of brown water shot out. She jumped back, laughing.

Strong arms slipped around her, pulling her close.

"Oh!"

Lost as she was in the splash of water and the flight of her thoughts, she hadn't heard him approach. His strength enveloped her, grounding her in this beautiful, fleeting moment.

Warm breath ruffled the hair by her ear as he took her hands within his. The water, now running free and clear, mixed with the earth and trickled down their wrists and up their forearms, Strong, capable limbs, glistening and beautiful as the water washed them clean.

She closed the pump with a soft click, then turned toward him, savoring the comfort of his embrace, this profound joy. A joy that felt as though it had always lived there, only waiting for this moment. For him.

He reached up, tenderly tracing the wetness on her cheeks with his fingertips, as if he might collect her tears like precious pearls.

"You are so very beautiful," he whispered, his voice thick with emotion. And in that instant, she knew he wasn't speaking only of her outward beauty. He saw her—the woman she was in the deepest corners of her soul, the woman he loved.

She clasped his damp hand in hers, her heart racing with a sense of belonging. "Come, my love," she whispered, pulling him toward the warmth of their cottage. "We will have an eternity to discover everything about each other. But for now… let us begin with this moment. Let me love you."

Epilogue

"Just put the north field in wheat. I think the soil is better there. Drainage is still a bear, but Kincaid and I have a few ideas." Farren mopped his brow with his handkerchief.

"I don't suppose you would like to continue digging?" Nora held up a small spade.

They stood in the middle of a new garden. Concentric circles radiated out from a central fountain, forming a sort of maze. Newly-turned earth covered the outermost circles, but the children had made much headway with those nearest to the fountain. They were filled with flowers—marigolds, sweet peas, peonies, dahlias, daisies, lilies, and roses. Most were not yet in bloom, but Opal had planned the garden so that something within a circle was always blooming. Even now, wide-brimmed hat jammed down on her head, map in hand, she marshaled her troops. "Not too close, Rose. The bush may seem small now, but that *Celsiana* will grow to four or even five feet."

Rose smiled and dutifully pushed Geoff's chair into the shade before digging her next hole.

"Mum, Aggy keeps smelling her lilies and not planting them," Mari said, her dirty fists perched on her

383

hips. "I am doing all the work."

"But they are so lovely." Agnes ran the long white flower over her lips.

"Angel-gal, they will be lovelier and a darn sight happier with their roots in the ground." Farren smoothed Agnes's dark curls and then guided her hands to find the hole just in front of her knees. A blue butterfly settled on the flower, a benediction on its planting. "Now, just give it a splash of water and that lily will be happier than a pig in—"

"A pig in what, Uncle Farr?" said Mari who was just a tad jealous of any attention Agnes got.

"Never mind, Mari, just tend to your own marigolds, if you please," Nora said, wiping a smudge from Mari's cheek.

"But I want to push Uncle Geoff now. You said I could after I finished this row."

"And so, I did." Poor Geoff had been wheeled around the garden by each child at least three to four times a day for the past week. But after Geoff almost landed in a particularly thorny rugosa rose bush, Rose always dropped what she was doing to accompany them.

"Hoy! It was my turn next," young Bobby Atwood said, a rather wilted forget-me-not clutched in his hand.

Nora had managed to place most of the abused children with loving families, but she and Farren always had a few here at Ryeland.

"No, I was next!" cried Cynthia, who then spilled her bucket of water on Gretchen, who yelped her outrage.

"Hallooo!" Charlotte's voice rang over the din. "If you'd stop your caterwauling, we might ask dear Uncle

Geoff if he would prefer a bumpy ride around the garden or to have his tea."

All eyes looked to Geoff, who was beaming, so happy to be amid all the brouhaha of the children.

"Teeee! Pleeee!" He clapped his hands.

Spades and shovels were dropped, watering cans hastily set aside, as the expectation of bread slathered in butter and jam supplanted any planting.

As the children settled at their own table under a large pergola, the adults gathered in a slightly more civilized manner at another table.

"Have you heard anything from Brendan?" Nora asked.

"Naw. Don't really expect to. He's not much of a writer. Rose might get a note or two if he writes at all. But as you know, he was pretty adamant we should have the rearing of his Rosie. I reckon he is busy grappling with the war office and will likely get himself clear of any wrongdoing. Wouldn't be surprised if they handed him a dad gum medal in the end. I expect he'll show up back in England when we least expect him just in time to stir up some trouble."

"Was he really a spy for the North?" Charlotte asked.

"I couldn't rightly say, but if it involved some danger and adventure, Bren'd be all in. The idea of doing it for his country is less certain."

Nora looked over at Rose, who had become the idol of all the little girls. If Nora had a penny for every time she heard, "Well, Rose said..." she would be a rich woman.

The girl hadn't said much when her father had left not long after he'd woken from his unconscious state.

Said he had things he needed to see to, and he would be back in a jiffy. That had been seven months ago. But Rose was a dear and gentle soul and never complained. She had her special friend in her Uncle Geoff, and a large and loving family. Still, Nora suspected Rose still felt the sting of his departure.

They had kept very quiet since the viscount's death. Nora had insisted on a reasonable period of mourning before she and Farren married. Just a small family affair. And she would not have changed a jot of it for the world. From her wildflower bouquet the children had gathered, to her simple gown made by Opal.

This mourning had given them all an opportunity to heal.

"Oh, now, where has Opal disappeared to?" Nora said, casting her gaze over the now empty garden. "Honestly, can she not sit for one moment?"

"Sit yourself down, woman." Farren caught her arm. "You're as fussy as a wet hen. Let the gal be."

Nora gave him a withering look. Only because he was right. She worried about all the children they had fostered, but Opal had a very special place in Nora's heart. In essence, the girl had lost her world with the various moves, the marriage, the final closing up of the Greene Street house. Agnes and Mari were younger, more adaptable, but Opal—well, Nora had secret dreams for the girl, but they would just have to wait and see.

Fortunately, the family still had another several months of mourning before the *ton* would infiltrate their snug world. And by then the social season would be over, and they might continue to rusticate.

She touched her belly and smiled. Still far too early, but hope had certainly taken root there.

"Here she is," Charlotte said as she passed Farren his coffee. "Opal, what are you hiding behind your back? You look like a cat who has got into the cream."

"It's a gift."

"A gift? From you?" Nora asked.

"Well, I'd like to say yes, but I'm workin'—working on not lying so much now that I'm settled here."

Settled.

Nora smiled. Silly girl, didn't she know a gift when she gave one? Farren reached for her hand under the table. Yes, they were all getting settled.

"I found it when I was organizing the library. It was folded in a book of botanical flowers. Must have come from the Greene Street house."

Nora took the folded paper tied with a ribbon.

"I knew you would want to have it."

Suddenly, Nora's hands were not quite steady. Opal sat and then slurped her tea, taking herself out of the limelight.

The faded ribbon released with one pull.

A drawing.

Delicate pencil marks, somewhat smudged and faded. Not Devlin's work. Unsophisticated, yet showing raw talent.

Three distinct figures, with a shadowy fourth in the back. A man. It could be any tall man, though the shading suggested blond hair and certainly dark brows.

But it was the foreground that drew Nora.

Rose, on the right—she knew it was Rose—her sweet profile turned expectantly toward the others.

Then Nora, her arms enfolding the two girls. And finally, the artist—

Nora caught her breath.

Lily. Her face looking fearlessly out at the viewer...

And she was smiling.

Next up is Brendan Cavanaugh's story, Vexed with the Viscount. It's a doozy—stay tuned!

Chapter One

The Scottish Highlands, late March 1863

Ballencrieff Hall crouched upon the crag like a wary giant, its arm-like towers thrust up as if to hold off the heavy clouds that threatened its battlements.

Anne Winton took in a draft of cold foggy air. Ignoring the sick feeling of dread lodged deep in her belly, she bent her head into the wind and made her way up the last of the stone stairs, stepping onto the castle's portico.

A huge brass phoenix hung fixed to the door, wings spread, talons at the ready, its red eyes daring her to enter.

She turned back toward Ballencrieff's massive gates, now far below. Like a broom, her too-long cloak marked her progress through the thin dusting of snow and up the steep drive.

A stiff wind blew, blurring her trail. Soon it would be swept away altogether.

She squeezed her eyes shut. There was no going back. Her fate lay within the walls of this madhouse.

Straightening her shoulders, she caught the stray hairs that lashed her cheeks and tucked them beneath her bonnet. She met the glare of blood-red eyes. "I want this." She reached up to lift the curved beak that served as the door's knocker.

"Ahhhhhhh!"

The scream from within sent her jumping back. Her foot caught the hem of her cloak, nearly sending her to her knees. Hesitating only a moment, she pressed the heavy iron latch expecting—hoping—it would not yield, yet the massive door swung open with nary a sound. She stepped inside.

The gloom of the outdoors was nothing compared to the cavernous dark of the great hall.

"Hallo?" Her greeting echoed as if the darkness was a living thing. She pulled her cloak more tightly about her.

Twin heavily-carved staircases hugged the stone walls like corded vines before meeting at the gallery above. Enormous pillars soared as if straining toward the light, whose pale beams washed the hall's timbered ceiling, but had no chance of penetrating to the dark below.

Hoping to find a living being, she headed to the back of the hall. Halfway across the room, a burst of color bloomed at her feet. Startled, she looked up.

Tiny panes of colored glass flashed and winked within a raised cupola. The sun, which she had not seen since crossing the Scottish border, must have momentarily breached its prison of clouds. She spread her arms, her drab woolen cloak transforming into a jeweled robe.

"You will not geld me!" A deep voice shattered the quiet. "I will not bow to your will to become some managed thing!"

The bright spangles of light jumped and shuddered as if the voice and light were one.

She leaped into the safety of shadows, searching

for the owner of that desperate voice.

Then she saw him.

He flew across the gallery. Head thrown back, arms spread wide, his shirt tails streaming like a shooting star. Taking three or more steps at a time, he fled down the farthest stairway.

A gaggle of women followed in his wake.

Unaware he stood only a few feet from her, he paused within the dappled circle of light, then, like a showman, he turned and made an elaborate bow to his audience.

Startled, the women stopped halfway down the staircase, seemingly uncertain how to proceed.

He laughed when they clucked in confusion.

Anne touched her fingers to her mouth, as if she might catch his joy.

The jeweled kaleidoscope melted away as more clouds must have moved in. His limelight lost, the man ran past her, his shirt a bright flash as he dashed up the opposite staircase.

Yes. Yes, get away. Damp wool filled her hands as she grasped the edges of her cloak.

Two large, dark shapes skidded to a halt at the top of the gallery. His keepers?

The beautiful man threw a long leg over the balustrade.

"No!"

Only when his gaze locked on her did she comprehend it was she who had cried out.

She should duck her head and retreat, leaving the keepers to do their job. But she found herself stepping toward him, caught in the warmth of his gaze.

"No sense runnin', ya devil!" One of the shadows

moved forward.

Her breath caught as both keepers moved in.

The man tossed his head, pitch-black hair whipping his pale face, and then slid down the banister, hopping off, light as an acrobat.

She backed under the stairway, praying he might somehow escape into the depths of the castle, or perhaps out the front door, which still stood open.

Only he didn't. He came straight to her.

Hot breath blew against her brow and eyelashes. A musky smell filled her nostrils—*a man's smell?* Utterly foreign. She should move away, but his gaze, so tender and alive, had her heart knocking at her breast and her tongue darting against her teeth.

Heavy boots slapped on the stairs above. The keepers. Closer now.

The man never flinched, seemingly oblivious to the oncoming threat.

Go! But the word froze in her mouth.

Dear God. What was happening to her? She must look away. She must at least step away.

She groped for the wall behind her. Cold rock pressed at her back, framing her in a curved niche. But he only stepped closer, his body radiating heat.

What did this beautiful madman seek? She closed her eyes to gather her own light, her powers of healing. Perhaps she might bring him comfort.

If only she could quiet her fluttering heart and chaotic breath. His scent filled her nose. A distraction. But soon familiar tingles coursed through her body. She took in more air and then raised her hands to touch him.

Rough fingers bracketed her cheeks, as heavy hips pinned her to the wall.

She flinched. Something hard pressed against her belly, but when she looked down, his fingers cradled her chin, asking her to meet his gaze. He frowned, cocking his head, his mouth now a soft smile, his eyes shimmering pools of silver. "You..." The feather of breath fanned over her lips.

He seemed at a loss to say more. Instead, his fingers wove into her hair, knocking her bonnet sideways. His breath came hot against her lips, his mouth so close.

Like a young child seeking to hide, she closed her eyes as if the darkness would be enough to conceal them. Bracing herself, she waited for the touch of his lips against hers—her first kiss.

Nothing.

Cold rushed in, and she blinked her eyes open. *Please...* Her hands pulsed with healing power, but now she wanted only the touch of his lips against hers. She reached to pull him back just as the keepers tore him away.

Her gaze snapped up to see the smirk on the larger jailor's face.

Oh, dear God. What had she done?

Her cheeks and neck flared hotly as horror and shame surged through her body. A hundred times since learning she was to be sent to Ballencrieff, she had imagined this first introduction. Always calm, assured, in control. What must they think? A silly, naïve girl, breathless over a madman. But just as she thought to drown in her disgrace, the beautiful man smiled.

Oh...Bless Bess. Perfect white teeth, one corner of his lips hitched up a fraction higher, his eyes crinkling to crescent moons. She could not look away. He seemed to pour himself into her, filling her with—

She had no inkling. But one word bobbed to the surface. *Yes.*

Her reply rose from her very center, over her belly, surrounding her heart, moving past her constricted throat to finally spill from her lips.

"Yes," she whispered. Whatever he wanted, her answer was yes.

He smiled wider.

Someone thrust a lantern between them, and her answering smile froze.

Held fast now, the keepers jerked his arms up. Light spilled onto his hands and wrists. They were smeared with something. His cuffs and shirt front were also soiled with red and black. Soot, she thought, and— *blood?*

"I say, miss, did he harm you?" A woman's profile appeared at the edge of light.

Harm? She touched her cheeks. His blood?

The man's smile hardened. And his beautiful eyes iced over.

No, this was wrong. "No—Wait—I—"

He jerked his head, snorting like a shying horse.

The woman touched her shoulder. "Truly, are you well?"

"Yes. Yes, I am…" But she shook her head despite her words and pulled her cloak about her. If only it were magical and she could disappear.

"Now you've had enough fun, your lordship. Sent us on a merry chase, you have." The older keeper's voice rang within the small niche.

"Do not harm him!" The words were not hers, though they echoed her prayer. A golden-haired man burst through the clump of bystanders and came to the bloody man's side. "Unhand him!"

"Nothing for it, Lord Austin." A nasty scar twisted the keeper's upper lip. "Your pardon sir, but Doctor Hives' orders. The marquess has to learn. Can't have them other unfortunates seeing this behavior and thinking to follow suit, now can we?"

"Mr. Macready, I do realize Lord Devlin is not the only patient here at Ballencrieff. However he is a marquess and our father the Duke of Malvern. You'd do well to remember that."

Lord Devlin? James Drake, The Mad Marquess? The girls at Ardsmoore had spoken of him in hushed tones calling him *Handsome as the Devil.* But in the same breath, *Butcher and Murderer.* She could not imagine this man willfully harming anyone. As to handsome, she had only seen a handful of men in her sheltered life, but even with his angelic-looking brother standing next to him, she could well believe Lord Devlin the handsomest man in all of England.

Lord Austin dropped his head and squeezed the bridge of his nose. "How did he get out this time?"

"Esther and I came with his porridge and—well…" Mr. Macready rose up on the balls of his feet, eager as a boy for his first taste of treacle. "Let's just say the marquess was very busy in the wee hours of the morning. While I was calming Esther." Lord Devlin snorted and Macready jerked his lordship's arm up sharply behind his back. "He slipped by us and threw the bolt."

Lord Austin turned to the woman. "Doctor Hives has not yet returned?"

"No, your lordship. He is still in Edinburgh. Then

with the upset over Major Cummings…"

The marquess' frozen smile cracked, his entire body seeming to draw in on itself. He wheeled on the keeper and spat.

"Why you damned—" Macready swiped at his face and then pulled back his fist.

"Enough!" Lord Austin stayed his hand. "Take him away. Do as Doctor Hives prescribes, but nothing outside the usual treatment. Do you understand me, Macready?"

"Aye. I understand *you* perfectly, my lord." He jerked his wrist from his lordship's grip.

Lord Devlin shifted his features from a grimace into one of boredom. But the pain in his eyes as he turned to her and performed a courtly bow made her want to weep.

Oh, why did you not run when you had the chance?

And what was this treatment that lay before him? Her hands still throbbed and burned, so ready to ease his pain.

"Enough gawking. You all have your duties. Get on with them." The woman made a shooing motion. The keepers jerked Lord Devlin away, and the group of servants began to disperse, further blocking him from sight.

"You must be Miss Winton, from Ardsmoore School." The woman offered her a handkerchief.

She took the linen napkin, taking care not to touch the woman's hand, as hers still burned hot. "Thank you. Yes, I am Anne Winton." She wiped her face and then folded away the blood and soot into a tidy square. Would that she could fold her emotions away as easily.

"Well, I am Mrs. Coates, matron at Ballencrieff.

Hobbs did not meet you?"

She shook her head. "Once I determined the direction, it was not far."

"In this weather? Useless boy. Couldn't find a rock in a quarry, that one. Or lock the door, apparently." Mrs. Coates sucked her teeth and signaled to one of the lingering women to go and secure the door. "I am sorry for your introduction to the place, but I'm afraid I cannot say this scene, or the weather for that matter, is all that out of the ordinary. Though, I am pleased to know you are not squeamish. The last girl from Ardsmoore was a hopeless ninny. Spouting Bible verses with her every breath, afraid of her shadow."

Mrs. Coates seemed more concerned with Anne's comfort than censuring her for unseemly behavior. But then, the matron had not been inside her body and could not know its turmoil.

Lord Austin coughed.

"Oh, excuse me, your lordship, I am forgetting my manners. May I present Miss Winton?" Mrs. Coates nodded to her. "She is come to be a general companion to Lady Tippit and Mrs. Nester."

"Miss Winton." He nodded. "I must apologize for my brother. Despite Mrs. Coates's assertions, he is not usually so…charged."

She curtsied. "Lord Austin."

"He did not hurt you, did he?"

"No, my lord—that is, I—no, he did not."

"If you will excuse us, sir." Mrs. Coates snapped closed the watch on her chatelaine. "I am short staffed what with poor Major Cummings"—she shook her head—"I must make sure every patient is accounted for and then deal with the marquess' room."

"Mrs. Coates." Lord Austin released a heavy sigh. "I would like to see my brother's room now."

The matron looked toward the gallery, then at the floor, and back to Lord Austin. "Your lordship, sir, there is a great deal of…damage. If you will give me an hour, I can get someone to clear up the worst of it."

Having no wish to sit about mulling her shame, or worse, imagining Lord Devlin's near-kiss, she ventured to speak. "Mrs. Coates." A long loop of hair grazed her cheek. It must have escaped when Lord Devlin's fingers wove their way into it. Ignoring another flush staining her already heated cheeks, she straightened her bonnet and pushed the lock behind her ear. "Perhaps, if you have no need of me, I might assist with the cleaning?" The older woman shook her head, but Anne pressed on. "I would like to be of service, ma'am. I know this kind of labor will not be part of my regular duties, but I assure you I am used to all manner of work and would be up for the task."

Once again the matron sucked her teeth. "Well, if Lord Austin is agreeable, then I suppose I will not look a gift horse in the mouth." The frazzled woman turned to his lordship.

His gaze raked over her, and she resisted the urge to stand taller than her scant five feet. "She will do very well, Mrs. Coates." He nodded. "Thank you, Miss Winton."

"I will have Esther bring water and such as soon as I can calm the girl." Mrs. Coates spied Anne's bags beside the now closed door. "Is that all you brought?"

Anne nodded and went to retrieve them.

"Do not bother yourself. I will see they get to your room. Eventually," she muttered.

"Thank you, ma'am." She slipped the soiled handkerchief into her pocket and turned to Lord Austin. "Then I am ready, sir."

His long strides had her picking her skirts up nearly to her knees to keep pace as he ascended the far staircase.

"Sir." He did not stop. "Lord Austin!"

He turned impatiently and she almost collided with him. "What is it?"

"I believe the marquess, your brother, might have a weapon." She swallowed. "Will he be punished for that?"

"A weapon?" He glowered. "Impossible." He started back up the stairs.

"I felt it."

He wheeled on her. "You felt it? Where?"

"I believe he had something hidden underneath his...fall."

Lord Austin frowned, shook his head, and then laughed. "Miss Winton, you are truly an innocent."

"I am not afraid. I am only concerned for others. And for him, the marquess."

The man swiped at his eyes as if trying to school his features. "You should be afraid, Miss Winton. What you perceived is a weapon—one Dev is all too adept at using—but it will not kill." He turned away, shaking his head. "Perhaps slay, *a la petit mort*, but not kill."

Little death? Her rudimentary French did not help. "I am not used to riddles, sir. I am afraid I do not understand."

"No. Better you don't, Miss Winton. Much better you don't."

He continued leading her through a warren of

passages, rooms, and staircases. She pressed a hand over the stitch in her side. They must be at the very top of the house. A massive door stood partially open at the end of a long hallway.

As they drew nearer, the beautifully carved wood shone with a patina honed over years of regular oiling. However, an incongruous, heavy-looking bolt bisected the door, an, just at eye level, a crude hatch had been cut into the wood. As Lord Austin pushed wide the larger door, the smaller hatch swung open revealing a grill of thick, black bars.

She released her aching side and took a deep breath. The room she was about to enter was no common chamber tucked away in an ancient Scottish castle. For all her fanciful, romantic flutterings, this was a cell for a madman.

His lordship stepped over the threshold, ignoring a huge rat that lapped at a bowl of spilled gruel. Anne covered her mouth, lunging back as the vermin scuttled down the hallway.

"Merciful God." Lord Austin had stopped just inside the room. "Perhaps you should leave, Miss Winton. I can manage well enough on my own."

His wide shoulders blocked her view, but she would not shirk her duty. "I am not afraid." Not precisely the truth, but she needed to get used to this new world. And quickly.

Her calm outward manner must have convinced him. He stepped aside and gestured her forward.

Oh, dear Lord.

"It is his blood," she whispered.

Author's Note

This book touches on the seeds of Eugenics, a pseudo-scientific movement that gained momentum in the late 19th and early 20th centuries, which sought to engineer 'racial purity' and justified forced sterilizations, segregation, and other inhumane practices. This misguided pursuit of "perfection," led, and continues to lead, to devastating consequences in history, serving as a stark reminder of humanity's capacity for both ignorance and cruelty.

Through this story, I hoped to shed some light on how easily fear and insecurity can drive us to judge others and perpetuate harm. But more than that, I wanted to remind readers of the power of empathy, compassion, and understanding. When we look beyond differences and recognize our shared humanity, we create space for connection and healing. We create a space for love.

Please let me hear from you!
jessrussellromance@gmail.com

A word about the author...

Jess Russell divides her time between New York City and the upper Catskill mountains.

She earned a BFA in Drama from the prestigious University of North Carolina School of the Arts. She is a sometime actress, batik artist (website coming), DYI renovator, seamstress, and a designer/builder--in other words, she loves to make things.

The Dressmaker's Duke, her first novel, was critically acclaimed, a double finalist in the Reader's Choice Award for Best First Book, and Best Historical, among others. Her second book (the first in her Reluctant Hearts Series) Mad for the Marquess, also won multi-awards and finaled in the RWA's RITA Awards.

Jess is currently working on two other stories in her series, Vexed with the Viscount, and Daft for the Duke.

She would love to hear from you: jessrussellromance@gmail.com